SIX METRES
OF PAVEMENT

– a novel –

SIX METRES OF PAVEMENT

FARZANA DOCTOR

Annemarie,
Enjoy!
Farzana Doctor

DUNDURN PRESS
TORONTO

Editor: Shannon Whibbs
Design: Jennifer Scott
Printer: Webcom

Library and Archives Canada Cataloguing in Publication

Doctor, Farzana
  Six metres of pavement / by Farzana Doctor.

Issued also in an electronic format.
ISBN 978-1-55488-767-5

  I. Title.

PS8607.O35S59 2011   C813'.6   C2010-902444-3

1   2   3   4   5   15   14   13   12   11

| Conseil des Arts du Canada | Canada Council for the Arts | Canadä | ONTARIO ARTS COUNCIL CONSEIL DES ARTS DE L'ONTARIO |

We acknowledge the support of the **Canada Council for the Arts** and the **Ontario Arts Council** for our publishing program. We also acknowledge the financial support of the **Government of Canada** through the **Canada Book Fund** and **Livres Canada Books**, and the **Government of Ontario** through the **Ontario Book Publishers Tax Credit** program, and the **Ontario Media Development Corporation**.

Care has been taken to trace the ownership of copyright material used in this book. The author and the publisher welcome any information enabling them to rectify any references or credits in subsequent editions.

J. Kirk Howard, President

Printed and bound in Canada.
www.dundurn.com

Dundurn Press
3 Church Street, Suite 500
Toronto, Ontario, Canada
M5E 1M2

Gazelle Book Services Limited
White Cross Mills
High Town, Lancaster, England
LA1 4XS

Dundurn Press
2250 Military Road
Tonawanda, NY
U.S.A. 14150

— ✳ —

To my families; born and chosen.

— I —

MOTION

YEARS AGO, LONG BEFORE Ismail Boxwala came to this country, a school friend told him that the only way to survive misfortune is to stay in motion. The friend was in a philosophical mood induced by too many beers and a recent heartbreak and imparted these words: if the body never moves, if the limbs are not exercised, sadness will turn the blood and lymph stagnant. Regret will cause the heart to grow weak, infection will creep in, and a person will die a slow, painful death.

Ismail Boxwala had no courage for this sort of dying.

After the tragedy that befell him, he remembered his friend's words. He went back to work, fraternizing only with colleagues who were better at forgetting than he was. On holidays, he visited his older brother, Nabil, and his family, people who showed him a measure of warmth and never pitied him too much. Ismail paid the mortgage, the hydro bills, his taxes. He borrowed library books and read the *Toronto Star* on weekends. He managed to get out of bed, shake out his arms and legs, moving through life purposeless, a man directionless; alive, but lifeless. His heart grew weak.

Ismail later supposed that his college chum would have said that he hadn't really stayed in motion, or not quite enough, anyway. He'd have to admit his friend would be right, for he was hesitant to draw attention to himself, maintaining the belief that he could be invisible if he just stayed still. For almost two decades, he kept his head down, became a watcher of sidewalk cracks, rarely noticed the sun.

He never imagined his life could change and so when it began to, he almost didn't notice the first tiny clues.

— 2 —

FALL 2008

Ismail was first introduced to Celia on a warm, late September evening. It was a brief encounter, casual, and easily forgettable. Despite this, each would remember it, even though they wouldn't see one other again for over a year.

At five-fifteen Ismail returned home, and prepared the same meal — an omelette and toast — that he ate every second day for almost twenty years. On alternate days, he opened cans of Patak's curries. That evening, like most others, he gulped beer while chopping a limp onion, a chunk of ham, and whisking the eggs. He drank more beer while waiting for the butter to warm and pool in the centre of the frying pan.

Routines comforted him, but not completely. Sometimes, in the middle of the night, he awoke from dreaming this supper ritual, only, in the dream he looked away for just a moment while the omelette was in mid-flip, and his dinner landed on the floor, where a carpet of cockroaches devoured it lustily while he watched in horror. His dreams were always like this — just a tad melodramatic. There were other dreams, with various insects and creepy crawlies, but the dreams' messages were always the same: *don't look away, don't let the mind stray, always be attentive.*

Luckily, that evening, his eggs landed safely on his plate and he ate them in the company of *Wheel of Fortune*. He mouthed vowels and consonants through two rounds, doing slightly better than the contestant from Idaho. He gulped back the rest of his beer, already itching for another. He grabbed his keys and headed out to the Merry Pint.

Scanning the sidewalk ahead, he cringed when he spied Rob Gallagher, rake in hand, tending his yard. Gallagher was the know-it-all of the block and one of Lochrie Street's few thirty-year veterans. Doesn't every neighbourhood have one of them? The person who could write a book about the area, knows everybody, and likes to be the local spokesperson whenever possible? Gallagher made a career of watching all of the neighbourhood comings and goings for decades, had written endless letters to successive city councillors, griping about potholes, burned-out street-light fixtures, and noise bylaws.

Ismail couldn't cross the street now; he'd already been spotted. He speculated on what flavour of animosity his neighbour would exhibit that evening. Would Gallagher stare coolly like he did three days previous, or turn up his nose like last month? He was sure that Gallagher had cast him in the role of villain, and Rehana, his ex-wife, as a tragic victim, ever since their daughter died eighteen years earlier. Fragments of previously rehearsed but never verbalized defences crowded Ismail's mind; he wished to say something to redeem himself, but never felt entitled enough to resist Gallagher's judgments, because he shared them, too.

His first and predictable line of defence in these situations was to perspire. Profusely. He cursed the early autumn sun pressing its way through the clouds and wiped his brow with his handkerchief. He felt a little faint, so he forced himself to do the breathing exercises a therapist once taught him: inhale one, exhale two, inhale two, exhale four, inhale three, exhale six. It didn't work at first, and he considered retreating to the house, and making his break to the bar later, after darkness had fallen.

On a breezy summer morning almost two decades earlier, Zubi squirmed in her stroller and pointed stubby fingers toward a small, white dog. It surged ahead of its owner, testing the leash. "Doggeeee!" she screamed, and Ismail thought, *When did she learn this new word? Why hadn't Rehana mentioned it?* Reflexively, protectively, he stopped, waited for the dog's owner to catch up to them, and to reel in his pet.

"Yes, that's a dog," he told Zubi. "Don't touch it."

"It's all right, he's friendly," the man said apologetically, pulling the dog just out of Zubi's reach. He stretched out his free hand, gave Ismail's a firm shake, and introduced himself as Rob Gallagher. Ismail, Rehana, and Zubi had lived in the neighbourhood since the previous winter, and although Rehana had met some of the neighbours, Ismail had not. He rarely accompanied Rehana and Zubi on their speed-walks, finding Rehana's baby-fat-burning pace and strapped-on ankle-weights both difficult and embarrassing. He wasn't sure why, but he hardly ever took Zubi out alone.

Perhaps being the one solely responsible for her well-being never sat comfortably with him, even then.

But that day, Rehana had an errand to run and had left Ismail with instructions to take Zubi out for some fresh air. He spent a good five minutes wrestling with the stroller before it popped open and he was ready to deposit Zubi into it. Then it was another three minutes of fiddling with the complicated straps, while Zubi squealed *Out! Out! Out!* before the pair finally left the house. So there he was, strolling to the park with Zubi, when he met Rob Gallagher for the first time.

"Well, isn't she growing fast these days!" Gallagher said, smiling exuberantly at Zubi. "I swear she's bigger than last week, even."

"Yes, she is," Ismail agreed, regarding his daughter proudly. And then he questioned how well acquainted the stranger was with his daughter and wife, a detail Rehana hadn't shared with him.

"How old are you now?" Gallagher leaned in, speaking in a high-pitched voice that made him sound like an old woman.

"Doggeee!" she replied.

"That's right, this is a doggy. His name's Jack. He's friendly, want to pet him?" Ismail watched as the dog jumped up, its front paws resting on Zubi's seat. Zubi recoiled, afraid.

"Er, she's probably too young for petting the dog. She's fifteen months old now ... actually almost sixteen months," Ismail said, pulling the stroller back until the dog's paws fell back to the ground.

The men talked about property values, the good weather and being amongst the few non-Portuguese people in the area. Ismail found it puzzling that Gallagher lumped himself and the Boxwalas, who hailed from India, in the same broad category of "non-Portuguese." Gallagher went on to detail the history of their neighbourhood, explaining that the original occupants were labourers at nearby turn-of-the-century rope factories. Ismail listened patiently, feigning interest, while Zubi babbled to the dog.

Their relations remained friendly for a couple of months after that. Then Zubi died, and Gallagher stopped talking to Ismail, as did many of the others on the street.

Ismail continued his debate about whether to continue walking to the Merry Pint. When he looked down the street again, he saw that Gallagher was busy chatting with two women. Gradually, his breathing slowed, and a fresh breeze blew through his open jacket.

He inhaled for a count of four, exhaled for eight, and prayed to nobody in particular to permit him to pass by Gallagher unnoticed. When he was just a few feet away from the group, Gallagher looked up, and Ismail thought he saw a look of hesitation cloud over his neighbour's green eyes. Gallagher frowned, cocked his head slightly to the right, and cleared his throat. Ismail stopped breathing, and felt heat rise through his collar and around his flushed face.

"Ismail, have you met Lydia?" Gallagher asked, with an oddly bewildered expression, gesturing to the younger woman, who was pushing a stroller with a young boy inside. "Um, well, she's your neighbour from across the street ... and this is her son, Marco. Meet Ismail Boxwala." Ismail flinched at the poor pronunciation: *Eyes-smile Boxwaala.*

Gallagher's face looked leathery and lined from the sun. Both men were in their early fifties, but Ismail thought Gallagher already resembled a retiree.

"And I'm sorry, I don't know your name?" Gallagher gaped at the older woman earnestly, who responded to his inquiry with a slight frown.

Finally she muttered, "Celia. Celia Sousa."

"My name is Marco!" the little boy screamed at Ismail. Then he giggled, witlessly. He shook his head from side to side, bouncing brown curls over his eyes.

"Uh, hello," Ismail replied, his voice squeaking. He gave each woman a tight smile and a loose handshake. He wasn't sure what to make of Gallagher's unexpected courtesy.

"This is my mother. She's just spending the day with us, helping me out," Lydia said, gesturing toward the older woman. "Three-year-olds can be so exhausting." The adults looked down at the boy, who was struggling to undo his stroller straps. "She lives nearby, close to College and Ossington," Lydia continued, pointing in a northeasterly direction. Celia's deep amber eyes locked on Ismail's, and he averted his gaze, realizing that he'd been caught staring at her. She wore an unbuttoned burgundy coat with feathery trim and with her tanned olive skin, small stature, and near-black hair, she looked almost Indian to him, perhaps a little like that eighties Bollywood actress, Rekha. The little boy laughed uproariously again and Ismail suppressed an urge to giggle along with him.

"Oh yes, you live in the *old* Little Portugal, the original one," Gallagher said. Ismail suspected his neighbour was trying to impress Celia with information that was more than likely made up. Still, she paid him no mind, focusing instead on Ismail. He noticed that her irises had an unusual shape, with rippling around their outside edges, resembling petals. They called to mind a girl from his college days who had the same uncommon eyes, who everyone called "Daisy" even though her real name was Sunita.

Surprisingly, the older woman's odd stare didn't make Ismail nervous. Rather, her attentions were a strange comfort; he felt the sweat on his neck and face drying in the cool breeze, and the sun's rays seemed to cast a golden glow over them all. Finally, she turned away from Ismail and looked to Gallagher. She shrugged in his direction, acknowledging him as though he were a bothersome child. He didn't seem to notice her indifference.

"Well, we should go, *Mãe*. We need to get Marco home and fed," Lydia announced. A rowdy flock of Canada geese flew over them in a crooked V formation, honking noisily, and Lydia had to raise her voice to be heard over them. They all watched the birds fly toward the lake.

"Nice meeting you," Ismail said, turning to walk away.

"Uh, yeah," Gallagher said, blinking and rubbing his eyes as though startling awake from a less-than-restful nap.

Ismail hurried off, surprised at the lack of enmity in Gallagher's voice. And the women didn't squint at him, like others had done in the past, their brains working to identify the troublesome details that accompanied the name "Ismail Boxwala." Rather, there was amiable conversation, sincere greetings, and of course, Gallagher's unexpected demeanour. Ismail had tried to follow along with this unfamiliar routine, hoping that he had responded in kind, appropriately shaking hands, talking to, and complimenting Lydia's three-year-old (*What a smart young man you are!*).

However, he was sure that once he was just out of earshot, Gallagher would lean toward the women, in that way that backstabbing neighbours do, and whisper, in not so hushed tones, the terrible history that kept him alone all those years. But when Ismail looked over his shoulder, he saw that they were not gossiping. Gallagher was back at work, raking leaves, and the women were pushing the stroller toward the house across from Ismail's. Was it possible that he was slowly being unwritten from the history books? Was he no longer worthy of gossip?

Ismail resolved to shrug off the encounter, not wanting to become too comfortable with its civility. But as he walked the rest of the way to the Merry Pint, he replayed the conversation in his mind, reviewing each and every word. Mostly, he evaluated his own participation, assessing whether he had said the correct, normal, expected things. He chided himself for one or two stupid-sounding errors. He also pondered the older woman's attentions, and the feeling of ease that came over him when she looked his way.

— ❋ —

As Celia and her daughter steered the stroller across the street, she regarded the honking geese above them. She disliked those birds for announcing the change of seasons, the arrival of cold.

She couldn't say why, but she liked the Indian man she had just met. He was tidy-looking; his thick salt-and-pepper hair combed into place, his jacket and pants crisp, even though it was the end of the day, and his face clean-shaven, without any hint of a scruffy beard-shadow. At the same time, his slight smile crinkled fine lines around his eyes, exposing something beyond his orderly exterior. She couldn't put her finger on it, but she felt its chaotic vibration. It made her wonder about him and where he was heading that evening.

What was his name again? Something starting with an "I"? She asked Lydia later, who shrugged and said she'd forgotten, too. But remembering his name didn't matter, anyway, because on that late September day, Celia had more pressing preoccupations.

She needed to get home and see how José was doing. Her husband had called that afternoon, complaining of feeling ill and saying he was coming home early. It was so unlike him; he'd never missed a day of work in his life. And then there was her seventy-four-year-old mother, who had moved in over a decade earlier, after Celia's father died. With advanced age, she was developing into a very fussy eater. Celia sorted through the cupboards and shelves of her mind; what could she cook for her mother today?

She would file away most of the small details of that day, the walk with her daughter and grandson, and meeting Lydia's neighbours, the stupid fellow and the polite Indian man. Instead, what remained were the irritations and worries; the sound of a flock of geese, her mother's refusal to eat, and her husband's chest pains would be the things indelibly etched in her memory.

— 3 —

INERT

ISMAIL WAS PACKING UP his things at work the next day, when Nabil, his older brother, called. A man in constant motion, Nabil had achieved many things that, depending on Ismail's mood, he either envied or mocked, sometimes at the same time: a five-bedroom, six-bathroom home in the suburbs; a beautiful wife who was a successful realtor and his business partner; and two handsome sons. Since the tragedy with Zubi, Nabil had been consistent in his attentions toward Ismail, his brotherliness regular, if a little too routine. His habit was to call once a week to check in, usually on a Thursday around Ismail's quitting time.

That afternoon, like all the others, Ismail knew Nabil was phoning from his Mercedes M-Class SUV while speeding along the Gardiner Expressway. He often wondered why his brother liked to call on the same day and time. Was it a scheduled task in his BlackBerry? Perhaps one of the highway exit signs along the way reminded him of his only sibling, or maybe his filial duty kicked in whenever he passed the Brother Cookie Company in Etobicoke.

Ismail envisioned him with his Trekkie-style headset hooked on his ear, as he simultaneously talked, drove, checked his text messages or whatever else needed doing, while traveling 120 kilometres an hour.

"Nabil*bhai*. I'm just leaving work and —"

"— Good, good. Life treating you well, then?"

"Yes, things are pretty much the same. I'm thinking about another renovation in the dining —"

"— One minute, another call is coming in."

And Ismail waited patiently, dutifully for his older brother to return.

"Sorry, sorry. What were you saying?"

"Oh, just that I was thinking about another renovation in the dining room, but will have to start getting estimates on —"

"— Yes, always get a minimum of three. Sometimes four, even. And check their references. So many of these contractors are such scoundrels, under-quoting on price and time just so you will say yes and then doing a lousy job. I'd refer you to one of the guys I know, but they don't tend to like small jobs in the downtown core."

"That's all right, Nabil*bhai*. I have worked with a few good ones already."

"But Ismail, how long can you keep upgrading the house? Haven't you done enough with that place? Seriously, how long can you stay in that house with its sloping floors and thin walls?" Ismail cringed while Nabil continued to insult his home. "Why not let me sell it for you? Then you can find a bigger place near us. Or if you want, we have so much space, you could even move in with us, take over the entire guest suite." Ismail had always felt a deep aversion for suburbia, but his brother's suggestions of family closeness, albeit geographical, felt like affection to him.

"I think I prefer the city, *Bhai*. But thanks for your offer."

"Alright. Just think about it. Have to go. When will we see you next? Maybe on the weekend?"

"Yes, maybe. I'll look at my schedule."

"Good. Call Nabila and schedule it. See you." Nabila was his brother's wife.

"Okay, I'll call Nabila. Bye." This was how the brothers ended most of their conversations, with promises to arrange to see one another soon. In truth, they tended to meet up every couple of months, Ismail's inertia and Nabil's momentum wearing at their filial bonds.

Ismail did consult his day planner, but instead of calling his sister-in-law, he reviewed the short to-do list he'd compiled earlier: compare prices on new windows, go to Ikea and look at drapes, research sofas at The Brick.

Ismail and Rehana bought the Lochrie Street house in Little Portugal as a starter home. It was a modest three-bedroom row house, bound to six others, all with the same postage-stamp backyards, flat roofs, and aging facades. The adjoining walls were thin, the joists of the entire row connected, so that when Mrs. Ferreira two houses down sneezed with vigour, her neighbours knew of her allergies.

A starter home is supposed to be temporary. Ismail was supposed to be the sort of husband who would ascend through the ranks of the public service, his income rising with each annual promotion. Their two children were supposed to be born while they lived there and then, before the first little one started kindergarten, they'd move to a detached four-bedroom with a big backyard and a two-car garage in an postal code where the property taxes were higher and the schools better. Such plans! Unimaginative, perhaps, but ambitious, at least. Ismail soon gave up on those dreams, but Rehana steadfastly maintained them, later finding those children, that husband, and the tawny house in the suburbs, without Ismail.

In their divorce settlement, Ismail bought out Rehana's share of the Lochrie house. Besides the customary division of other financial assets (which were fairly meagre at the time), she took little apart from her clothing and jewellery, perhaps wanting to leave behind anything imprinted with their life together.

Although he was an outsider, an immigrant among his immigrant neighbours, often without language in common, Ismail grew to see Lochrie as his home, became accustomed to its noise and bustle. It was the kind of place where people yelled across fences to greet their friends. During soccer season, revellers crammed the main roads and blocked streetcar tracks, waving flags and singing their allegiance to countries they hadn't visited for far too long. The old men there, the ones too old to work, spent their evenings watering cemented-over gardens. Somehow, Ismail felt he belonged there, too.

Over the following eighteen years, the neighbourhood shifted a little, taking on new tones and shades with each decade. Ismail watched the Portuguese kids grow up and move to the suburbs, leaving their parents to grow old alone. He witnessed the Chinese and Vietnamese immigrants move in, co-mingling with their Old World European neighbours in uneasy and unfamiliar ways. He observed the yuppies strip down houses, cultivate native plants, waiting for gentrification to move their way.

Meanwhile, Ismail stayed put, and altered little in his life. Even at work, except for one promotion caused by a co-worker's death, and a bureaucratic restructuring that had him changing cubicles, he never really changed jobs. He remained, as always, a Municipal Engineer with the Transportation Infrastructure Management Unit of the Transportation Services Division at the City of Toronto, a moderately interesting, low-to-medium stress position with civil co-workers, good benefits, and more vacation and sick days than he could tolerate to use.

He believed inertia would prevent him from being hurt by life. Mostly, he wanted to avoid making another mistake.

Ismail sighed, closed his daytimer, no longer interested in his renovations list. He drove home, all the while considering his brother's words and his empty house. He parked his car partway between his home and the bar, and half-walked, half-jogged into the Merry Pint, where he found his friend Daphne sitting alone at a table near the front of the bar. He allowed her to distract him with a drinking game. It was the one where its players watch *The Simpsons* and then take a drink each time one of the characters says something predictable, like when Homer says "D'oh!" or Flanders mentions God. The booze and Daphne obliterated the rest of the night.

— ❋ —

A few miles away, in a hospital room smelling of sour breath and floor cleaner, Celia sat beside José's bed, watching him sleep. She'd been there a full twenty-four hours already, and still wore her clothes from the previous day. She pulled her coat tight around her neck, and shivered; since arriving at the hospital, she hadn't been able to shake off a persistent chill. Although José looked warm enough, she tucked his sheet and blanket around him, which caused him to grunt and grimace in his sleep. The familiar sounds were a comfort, evidence of him still alive, still with her.

Someone in a neighbouring bed started to cough, first quietly and then erupting into a cacophony of hacking. She hoped the patient was covering his mouth. She'd seen all the new public health notices on the hospital walls telling people to sneeze into their sleeves and she wondered whether the cougher had seen those posters, too.

She stood up and closed the curtains around them, blocking out the three other patients' noise and germs.

— 4 —

ARRESTING

THE VESTIGES OF A bad hangover from the previous night's *Simpsons* game were still with Ismail the following evening. He'd had a terrible day at work, unable to concentrate during his unit's third-quarter budget meeting. His unsettled stomach had him tasting bile a few times that morning. By the time work ended and he was walking to the Merry Pint, he had determined to quit drinking, a resolution he'd made many times before. *Soon. I'll do it soon. Today will be my last for a little while. Then, tomorrow ...*

The cravings whispered their sweet nothings in his ear: *A cold beer would be perfect right now, what a terrible day! Cold on the tongue, warm in the gut ...*

He endeavoured to drive away those thoughts with a mental list of why he should stop:

1. Work performance suffering.
2. Stomach perpetually upset.
3. Spending too much money on drinks.

The quitting side prevailed for a minute or two, almost changing his mind about going to the bar. But then the drinking side, staggering and steadying itself, reasoned: *You really want to try quitting again? It won't work, you know. Besides, you can handle one.*

Ismail never related to the proverbial rock bottom that most alcoholics talk about, where people lose their lives to alcohol. He rationalized that his lowest low had already come and gone, a rocky bottom that still left him scraped and skinned at the knees. In his mind, drinking couldn't possibly take him lower than that. In fact, alcohol often rescued him from that barren place.

He knew it was ironic to be making plans to quit drinking while entering a bar (in fact it sounded like a bad joke: A man walks into a bar ...), but a compromise between the two sides had been reached: *Okay, tomorrow. Tomorrow I will stop. I'll just have one tonight and then go home. Hair of the dog ...* He saw Daphne at the bar in her usual seat, her hand clasped around a beer glass, and Ismail felt a rush of tenderness and camaraderie for her. At the same time, worry bubbled up. *Only one drink. Remember, no matter what Daphne says, just one drink!*

"Hey, Ismail. I saved you a seat," she said, smiling affably, sliding her jacket off the stool beside her.

"I'm just here for one tonight, Daphne. I overdid it last night. I have to go home to bed early." He climbed up onto the stool, balancing uncomfortably, his feet barely brushing the ground. He gestured to Suzanne, the regular bartender.

"No worries. I'm probably going to head home soon, too. I'm keeping it light tonight." Suzanne headed their way, carrying a fresh pint of beer, the froth sloshing a little over the glass's rim. Daphne gulped down the last of her beer, and exchanged her empty glass for the full one. Ismail had watched her do the same thing with cigarettes, too; lighting one with the smoking butt still in her mouth. He ordered a Blue for himself.

Within an hour, Ismail had abandoned his self-imposed limit and bought the next two rounds. He was on his third and Daphne on her fourth or fifth when the police arrived.

A pair of officers, one tall and white, and the other slightly shorter and South Asian, approached Suzanne, asking her something Ismail couldn't hear. Then they swaggered along the length of the bar, pausing just long enough to study his and Daphne's faces. Ismail reflexively averted his eyes, looking down into the depths of his beer glass. A warm breeze of manly smelling cologne wafted by as they passed.

"Fucking pigs," Daphne muttered. Ismail shushed her before she could say more. Alcohol usually made her prickly edges soften, but once in a while something could provoke her into an intoxicated belligerence. "Useless sons of bitches," she hissed once they were barely out of earshot, "coming in here to find someone to beat up, I bet." Daphne carried on with her venting while Ismail watched the police exit from the back-alley door. He didn't much like their presence either, but for his own reasons.

Ismail would never forget his arresting officer, Bill Todd, a man whose surname was also a first name. He was middle-aged, with an East Coast accent and a paunch that strained his shirt buttons. Puffy skin bags rested under his blue eyes. He surveyed Ismail's crowded cubicle, a nine-by-nine space large enough for a desk, filing cabinet, and a couple of chairs, and suggested that they speak somewhere more private. The office was quiet that afternoon, and so Ismail assured him it was fine to talk confidentially. He invited Bill Todd to sit down, and offered him a cup of coffee. Although he didn't often speak with police in his role at the City, their responsibilities sometimes overlapped and he assumed the matter had something to do with a tunnel or bridge, matters under his jurisdiction.

Bill Todd declined the coffee. He peered cautiously into the vacant neighbouring cubicles and then sat down only after Ismail did. His careful movements made Ismail grasp the seriousness of his visit and his body responded before his mind, sending perspiration to his palms and armpits.

"What can I help you with, Officer?" he asked, his voice cracking slightly, betraying the outwardly calm countenance he was trying to affect. "Is this about a municipal issue?"

"No. I need to ask you a few personal questions, Mr. Box —," he said, hesitating and reading the silver name plate at the front of his desk. Nabil had gifted him with it the previous year, on his thirty-fourth birthday. *Everyone needs a spiffy name plate, Ismail.*

"It's Boxwala. Personal questions? About what?"

"Yes, Mr. Boxwala —" he said, again consulting the name plate.

"— has something happened to my wife? Has there been an accident?" Ismail interrupted. He slipped a handkerchief out of his pocket and wiped his damp hands, but quickly stopped and put it away when he saw the officer observing him. His heart began to race and the air felt hot and stuffy.

"It's not your wife. Mr. Boxwala, do you own a Honda Civic, with the license plate number —" Ismail didn't hear the rest. He instantly understood what was wrong. Zubi. His eyes lost their focus, and everything seemed to vibrate. Ismail's mind dashed ahead of him: *I took Zubi to daycare this morning, didn't I?* He tried to picture the daycare's doors, its hallways, her teacher, but couldn't. He stood up to get more air, but no matter how much he inhaled, there still there wasn't enough. He understood that the reason for the officer's visit was in the backseat of his car, just as he'd left her, asleep, her soft black hair resting against her baby seat.

"Excuse me, I must go, I have to check on something —" Ismail said, rising from his chair, stepping around his desk. He wanted to go backwards in time, get Zubi from the car, parked just a few minutes away. And then he would take her to daycare as he should have. Bill Todd stood up and blocked his way.

"Please sit down, Mr. Boxwala. Sit down," he repeated sternly, his beefy hand gently guiding Ismail back around his desk and into his chair.

"You don't understand, you see I must go check ... I usually drop the baby off first ... my daughter, Zubi ... then my wife at her work, and then I come to work ... but the order got changed today ... I have to go get my daughter. Please, let me go to her!" Ismail sputtered, gasping for breath.

"It's too late, Mr. Boxwala. She was found about an hour ago." He barely heard the words; they were travelling away from him, faint, barely comprehensible syllables.

"What? What do you mean? Then she is ... okay?" Ismail grasped for any possibility, any hope that Zubi was all right. Bill Todd shook his head, bit his lip, grimaced. For the first time during his visit, he didn't make eye contact with Ismail.

"No, it can't be. Oh no ... oh no ... Zubi!" Ismail wailed, forcing himself up out of his chair again. "Please, I have to go see her." His mind refused to let go of the fantasy that Zubi was still alive: *Yes, of course her crying would have alerted a pedestrian, a Good Samaritan who would have called the police, freed her from the car ...*

"It's too late. She was found in your car, like I said, about an hour ago. Deceased. Most likely from the heat." This time he did make eye contact, icy blue ponds.

"Oh no." Ismail gasped, holding his chest.

Each time Ismail remembered this next part of the story, he viewed it in near-cinematic slow motion. A millisecond before he closed his eyes and fell to the ground, he saw Officer Todd's anxious expression as he lunged forward to steady him. A co-worker, young, pretty, recently hired Chitra Malik, peeked into the cubicle, alarmed by the commotion.

He had no fear as he lost his balance and the world spun away from him. Rather, he had an amazing and naive thought: he believed he was dying, his life being snatched up in a great dizzying whirl, and he was on his way to greet little Zubi so that he could hold her one last time. He might cuddle her on his lap, kiss her sweet-smelling head, and then, in the vast wisdom of all things celestial, switch places with her.

Daphne had finished ranting and was now watching him with curious eyes.

"What?" he asked nonchalantly.

"You've kinda been staring off into space for the last few seconds."

"Oh, sorry. Just tired I guess."

"It doesn't matter," she said and turned her gaze to the back doors, where the police had re-emerged. They travelled through the bar, the same way they'd entered, taking their time to scrutinize patrons. Before they could reach the front where he and Daphne sat, Ismail pulled some bills from his wallet, and muttered a quick goodbye to Daphne.

He walked the few blocks home, the glaze of intoxication making the sidewalk crooked beneath his feet. At his front door, he searched his coat and pants pockets for his keys, fumbling past loose change and bits of paper. Eventually he found them within his coat's inside breast pocket, an unlikely place, and he wondered how they'd gotten there. Dangling before his eyes, they seemed unfamiliar, like someone else's misplaced keys.

A silver key met its matching lock, a bit of grace on a graceless night. He crossed the threshold, and although he knew the house was empty, he sensed he wasn't completely alone.

— ❉ —

It was ten o'clock already and the nurse who came to check José urged Celia to go home for the night. "Have a rest, take a shower. He'll still be here in the morning," she said, clicking her pen open and scribbling something down in a chart. She efficiently moved around the bed, inspecting her husband's limp body and the beeping machines that sustained him.

Lydia had been by earlier, bringing food during her lunch hour and a change of clothes after work. Celia hadn't thought to ask for toiletries, and so she'd had to swish her mouth with water and wash her face and armpits with the harsh cleanser and brown paper towels in the public washroom down the hall. She guessed the nurse could tell she needed a bath. Later, she questioned why it hadn't occurred to her to just go down to Shoppers on the first floor for travel-sized containers of toothpaste and face cream.

She picked herself off the chair, glad for the nurse's permission to leave. By then, she'd spent two days at her husband's sleeping side while others in the family had come and gone. The doctor had checked in twice and reassured her that his condition was improving. He'd looked at her sternly, as though José's angina was her fault, and warned that there'd need to be lifestyle changes. She'd nodded dumbly and listened as he discussed recommendations for medication and future surgery.

She decided to walk home, even though Antonio, her son-in-law, had offered to come pick her up. She'd told him she'd take a cab, didn't want to make a fuss. Anyway, she was glad to walk after sitting for so long, and the crisp night air was fresh against her skin.

At home, she took a shower, and then listened to eight messages of concern on the answering machine, pressing the orange button that meant they'd be saved. She would ask Lydia to call everyone back from work the next day. Hopefully she'd remember the password she programmed in for them; Celia had forgotten it long ago.

She wandered the quiet house and peeked in on her sleeping mother. She watched as the bedclothes rose and fell, something she used to do when her children were small, checking to make sure they were still breathing. José used to tease her for it; he rarely feared for their safety the way she did. She wished now that her mother was awake to comfort her, to bring her a plateful of fish and potatoes, to tell her what to do next.

She looked at the wall clock, calculating that it was only nine-twenty in Vancouver, and dialed her brother, Manuel.

No one picked up. She rooted around the fridge for something to eat and found a bottle of wine José had opened a few days ago. She poured herself a tall glass, gulped it back, and then turned off the downstairs lights. By the time she landed in her bed, she could feel the cool wine heating her belly and carrying her off to unconsciousness.

— ❋ —

Ismail lay in his bed, his head still cottony from the booze. It was a good way to fall asleep; his muscles relaxed and thoughts slowed down until they almost stopped. But alcohol wasn't fail-safe. Its soporific effects only lasted so long before he'd dream his way into memories that would wake him in the middle of the night. That night, at 3:00 a.m., he saw Zubi's ghost at the foot of the bed, staring at him blankly. Then her pupils grew large, darkening her gaze, and he grew afraid. From somewhere outside the window, he heard Rehana's shrill voice yelling, "You forgot her! How could you have forgotten her?"

He backed up against the headboard with such force that he knocked himself fully awake. He switched on the bedside lamp, exorcizing Zubi and Rehana from the room. He left the light on a few more minutes before settling himself down to rest again. Before he fell asleep, he repeated the resolution he'd made earlier that evening: to stop drinking.

Right after the divorce, almost a year after Zubi's death, he saw a psychologist for forty-eight sessions. Almost a year, but not quite. He attended each appointment faithfully, following the mandate of a manager who felt he needed assistance with his "post-divorce job performance." It sounded like some kind of human resources category, but when Ismail looked it up in his employee handbook, he couldn't find it.

All of Ismail's colleagues signed a condolence card with platitudes to "take care" and "time heals all wounds," but none attended Zubi's funeral. A great cloud of silence crept over the cubicles of the Transportation Infrastructure Management Unit when anyone came close to mentioning the circumstances of his daughter's death, at least when he was present. Over the years, a new life story was created for Ismail at the office. He became a "bachelor," a "loner," "single without kids." He didn't tack any family photos onto his cubicle walls. No one expected him to attend the annual office holiday party.

Soon after therapy ended, Ismail found an almost perfect way to dampen down his memories. He'd been walking home from Dufferin Mall one Saturday when he saw a large yellow vinyl "grand opening" sign flapping in the wind above what used to be an empty storefront. For years, a dusty display of men's briefs occupied the front window, and he'd often wondered if anyone was going to come along and revitalize the old haberdashery. The new owners transformed the property into The Merry Pint, a typical-looking drinking hole, with a few tables spread along one side and a long bar down the other. The back had a refurbished pool table and a few booths where local drug dealers set up shop. The lighting was always on the dim side, although its south-facing windows drew sunshine on bright days. The bathrooms downstairs were kept fairly clean, but still managed to exude a faint smell of urine.

That day, the fluttering banner advertised, *"Come in for a $1 beer — this week only!!!"* and so Ismail followed its enthusiastic command, and went inside, intending to have a cheap drink and then go home to his leftover Patak's curry. It was during the frightful restructuring days at work, and perhaps he'd been a little more on edge than usual. That one beer turned into two more, drinks that provided him with a giddy, enlivened intoxication he eagerly welcomed. Until then, he rarely drank, except on special occasions: a sip of champagne at New Year's, a glass of wine at dinner with his brother's family.

And then there was the companionship; amiable chatter from a few patrons who, along with Ismail, would soon become Merry Pint regulars. By his third visit, he realized that none of the others recognized his name, were not interested in his history whatsoever. He was welcomed into their drunken tribe, and together, they enjoyed a perpetual present.

At first, a few drinks once or twice a week permitted him a respite from his life. Then, those drinks weren't enough, and he found himself there every night after work, drinking a few, talking nonsense with the regulars and eating lukewarm battered cheese until he was sleepy and nauseated. Not surprisingly, the tipsy fun was soon replaced by a dull, drunken routine:

Sleep. Work. Beer. Cheese. Sleep. Work. Beer. And so on.

This regimen had great staying power, but of course, it finally dawned on Ismail it wasn't sustainable. About a dozen years into his tenure at the Merry Pint, just after his forty-eighth birthday, he awoke with a strange radiating pain in his side, uncomfortable enough to force him to go to the local walk-in clinic. After an hour's wait, the young doctor took his history, twirling a strand of blond hair with her left hand, while she took notes, in green ballpoint, with her right. Her eyes widened when he calculated that he'd been drinking heavily for over a decade. Ismail attempted to avoid looking down her tight blouse or noticing her low-riding trousers while she strapped on a blood pressure cuff and listened to his quickened pulse.

In serious tones, she suggested residential alcohol treatment, and warned him about high cholesterol and liver disease. She sent him away with ultrasound and blood test requisition forms and called him in two weeks later to review the results. Despite the fact that she reminded Ismail of Britney Spears, he took her counsel seriously, shocked that he had let things advance to such a sordid place.

So, two years before his fiftieth birthday, he tried for the first time ever to quell his urge to drink. For about eight months, he managed to quit the fried cheese, switch to light beer, and not surprisingly, lost about twenty pounds, returning to his previous slender physique. He visited Dr. Britney at regular intervals, and since the mystery pain had disappeared, she seemed pleased with his progress. He never told her he hadn't quit drinking, that he'd only switched to light beer. Week after week, usually on a Sunday evening, he resolved to do so, making plans to take a few days off from the sauce. Some of the attempts lasted a day, maybe two. Most of the time, though, he spent his evenings hunkered down in his living room, sipping Blue Light and watching TV. Ismail's Sony Trinitron became a nonjudgmental, consistent companion and a somewhat adequate replacement for his old drinking friends.

But it wasn't as depressing as it sounds. Ismail discovered entertaining and productive shows on home décor, which reminded him a little of his old self, the person he'd been before Zubi died and Rehana left. Back then, he'd been a tidy sort, even slightly fastidious, according to Rehana, who hadn't been used to a man who knew how to use a vacuum. He'd lost some of that while his drinking was at its worst. Rings of grime coated his bathtub, empties piled up by the back door, and dust and cobwebs accumulated in every room's corners.

But from April to November of that year, Martha, Debbie Travis, and Mike Holmes motivated Ismail to bash down a living room wall, and install a skylight that let bright shafts of sunlight into his office. He painted the kitchen walls various hues of yellow and orange, back-splashed with new ceramic tiles, hung expensive-looking and pensive artwork in the dining room, and planted an attractive perennial garden out back.

With the encouragement of HGTV, he worked steadily, devoting himself to his projects each evening, weekend, and statutory holiday. He even used a few sick days for the really time-consuming and tricky jobs. As he destroyed places within the house that reminded him of the old days, he hoped to make homeless the memories that lingered long in that old row house.

Bad memories are like relatives who visit and overstay their welcome. Soon your irritation builds when night after night, you return home to find them lounging on your couch, or raiding the refrigerator. And bad memories can be a noisy lot, keeping you up late at night with their endless chatter. Sometimes, you rouse at night to find one of them standing next to your bed, pillow in hand, about to smother you to death.

Evicting them is futile, for memories are slippery and sly, able to find new hiding places and cubbyholes in which to live. They grudgingly vacated for a night or two, fooling him into thinking they were gone, only to make their appearance once again. When he repositioned his bedroom furniture to improve the feng shui, he found a pair of Rehana's socks trapped behind the dresser, coated in pinkish-grayish dust. He brushed them off, and, unsure of what to do with them, meekly folded them into a tight ball and tossed them to the back of the closet.

One day while digging a hole for a new Rose of Sharon bush, he spied something buried a foot down in the soil. He poked it with his trowel, yanked it free from the earth, and held it in his gloved hand. It was a bright yellow car, encrusted in grime, just the right size for a toddler's grip. Tiny cartoon faces peered out from its dirty windows: a father at the steering wheel, a mother in the passenger seat, and two children in the back. A gush of high-pitched babbling filled the air. Ismail looked around for children in neighbouring yards, but there weren't any. He closed his eyes and listened until the sounds stopped.

Sometimes, on rainy days, he'd enter Zubi's nursery, an abandoned, closed-up area of the house. He considered redoing the room, perhaps turning it into a mini-gym. He planned to donate the dusty pine crib, dresser, and change table to charity, but never managed the task. At least the closet was mostly empty; Rehana had packed up Zubi's clothing, photo albums, and toys long ago. She left behind three framed photographs of Zubi on the dresser. He hadn't moved them from where they'd been placed, and could hardly bear to look at them.

Over the years, the room turned musty and the wallpaper shabby, its edges peeling and curling up into itself. Rehana and Ismail had hung the wallpaper together, one of their first home decorating efforts. They had an argument about whether to go with a balloon or teddy bear motif, and as usual her choice prevailed. Rehana steadied a ladder for Ismail, and her seven-month tummy got in the way, rubbing up against the paste. After he'd hung the paper, Ismail painted the ceiling sky blue, with puffy white clouds, so that their baby would have something soothing to look at when she woke.

His renovations stopped there, at the threshold of Zubi's room. In the rest of the house, the lovely walls, new finishes, and garden left him feeling lonelier than ever. He returned to the Merry Pint for solace, and within days, was drinking to get drunk again.

For a spell he had cheerless sexual encounters with the not-so-merry, half-sauced women he met there. They seemed to efficiently manage their dance cards through some kind of unspoken agreement with one another, switching partners on alternate nights. Ismail was among the dozen or so men who frequently vied for their attentions, buying them drinks, going home with them on a weekday evening. The luckiest, the ones most in the women's favour on a particular week, got a Friday or Saturday night of inebriated tangoing.

They filled the vacant space in Ismail's cold bed, their panting or snoring distracting him a little from the ghosts who lurked at night. But like the rest of his survival tactics, the results were temporary. It took him a few months of drunken sex to stumble into the realization that middle-aged white women with smoke in their hair can't erase memories. He gave them up, and instead, found Daphne.

— 5 —

AFFAIRS

IT WAS SHORTLY AFTER Ismail's return to the Merry Pint that Daphne became his favourite drinking buddy. Almost every day, she'd arrive just after her shift at a nearby women's drop-in centre. She told Ismail once that she had a different personality during her workday, optimistic and helpful while she completed housing applications and distributed TTC tickets. By the time 5:00 p.m. rolled around, most of her cheer had run out.

Ismail found it surprising that Daphne had these two personas, on and off the job. But then, his work was in maintaining structures, not people. His almost singular focus was Toronto's bridges and tunnels; the city's great connectors. Ismail tested them for their soundness, inspected them to ensure they wouldn't fall down on people, applying himself to his job in the same tedious and consistent manner in which he approached the rest of his life.

It was obvious that Daphne was worn down by her work. She arrived at the bar in baggy sweatshirts and jeans, only in the most sombre of colours. Her attire cloaked her slender figure, hiding ribs and hipbones that jutted out against her skin. Her face rarely saw the sunshine and her fair complexion was the kind that blushed tomato red when she was livid or embarrassed. By the end of the night, her long hair, usually pulled back in a messy braid, would be in further disarray. Later, Ismail would learn that it always carried a faint, but heady scent of lavender.

She was caustically cynical, and could find a way to flood anyone at the bar, not already depressed, with her hopelessness and despair. Ismail thought she was just his type. Besides her ability to bring people down, Daphne held great powers of suggestion. Mostly, she was a bad influence on Ismail, peer-pressuring him into drinking one, two, five too many shots of whiskey with her. When she was beyond drunk, her mood lifted and she could entertain Ismail with jokes and tales he found hilarious in the moment, but could never recall the following morning. She introduced him to several drinking games involving cards, dice, and whatever TV show was playing on the bar's ceiling-mounted television. This held Ismail's attention, amusing him for almost three years.

Two weeks after *The Simpsons* game that left Ismail questioning the wisdom of his ways, Daphne shocked him by joining Alcoholics Anonymous. They were in their usual spot at the bar, but she seemed more alert than usual, while he was already feeling a buzz.

"Wait. Really? You always called them a cult."

"I was wrong," she said with a shrug. "But there *are* some weirdos there. But most of them, they're nice people." Although she'd been to the Merry Pint since joining up, Ismail could tell AA was helping her. That night, he saw her order a ginger ale between beers, a sobering soda pop intermission. Her previous negativity about the program even seemed to be replaced with some hopefulness and a tentative loyalty to its teachings. Without a hint of sarcasm in her voice, she told him about the previous night's meeting, using phrases like "one day at a time" and "higher power."

"Well, isn't it a contradiction to be here while joining AA?" he challenged.

"I'm going to go back tomorrow. I'm taking things slow. I've never been able to dive into things all at once." Then she smiled, "Plus, if they really are a cult, it's a good idea to do this gradually, right?"

"I guess it's better to go sometimes than not at all," he conceded.

"Come with me tomorrow, Ismail. It'll be fun." He raised a skeptical eyebrow, but she continued, her tone growing serious, "I don't know a lot of people there yet. It would be good to have a friend with me."

Ismail didn't answer just then, and she changed the subject. But while she talked about a new policy at work that was annoying her, he considered her invitation. The pains in his side had returned, and he was embarrassed to go back to see the doctor after his three-year relapse. Besides, Nabil was on a new campaign of nagging, scolding him for his excesses during his weekly fraternal phone calls. By the end of the night, he and Daphne had made a pact to leave the Merry Pint together.

— ❊ —

The day before José's funeral, the young teller closed her counter and guided Celia away, touching her gently on her elbow. They went to the manager's office, a glass box that faced out to the rest of the bank. She'd never been in an office like that; José had always been the one to do the banking. She was offered a cup of coffee and a seat in a plush leather chair. The teller spoke softly to her, in Portuguese.

Celia settled into the comfortable seat, approving of the special treatment she was being given as a widow. She looked out the glass walls of the office, sipped her coffee, and watched the tellers' line-up snaking along velveteen barrier ropes.

There were hushed voices in the corridor. She strained her neck to see the teller speaking to the manager just outside the door, their faces just a few inches apart. Although their blazered backs faced her, she could make out a few words that sounded like *overdraft, unaware, withdrawal*. Celia watched the teller return to her counter, and within a few moments the manager appeared, a short balding man with a grim expression. He sat down, cleared his throat, clutched at his desk with tight hands. He showed her all her banking records on the computer, pointing to rows and columns of light blue numbers that made no sense to her.

The manager looked away from her and back to his screen. She wished that his office hadn't been made of glass walls, an aquarium that barely contained her tears.

After the funeral, she hadn't much time for crying. She sold the house, José's old truck, most of the furniture, all the things that had marked them as successful people. Most of her possessions, anything of value, were signed away, auctioned off, bargained down. She kept for herself only a little furniture, her clothing, and a few keepsakes. All José left her was a small pension that she'd have to wait to collect on her

sixty-fifth birthday. At least the government was more generous than he, delivering her a small survivor's benefit once
a month.

Her children assured her she'd never want for anything,
but she knew Lydia and Filipe were just managing on what
they earned. She had food and shelter and family, and she
knew she should be grateful. But still, she longed for so
much more.

— ❊ —

Ismail and Daphne attended the Monday, Wednesday, and
Friday 6:30 p.m. Hope for Today meetings at the Centre for
Addiction and Mental Health on Queen Street West, becom-
ing regular, if somewhat ambivalent, converts. After meetings,
they went for coffee and shared a new, sober intimacy that
Ismail found almost as intoxicating as a shot of fine whisky.

He told her about Zubi's death and Rehana's rejection
and she didn't judge him for it. Soon, she started to share
her own terrible past: her abusive parents, feuds with four
siblings, and her early teenage troubles with cocaine. They
developed a closeness that had been impossible while they
were drinking buddies. To him, she was like a good therapist, inviting him to talk about Zubi, spurring on angry rants
about Rehana, and offering hugs. Ismail's memories became
less ubiquitous and more manageable now that he wasn't
alone with them.

It was no surprise that the pair soon began sleeping
together on Mondays, Wednesdays, and Fridays. Their
therapeutic routine was AA at 6:30, coffee and confession
at 8:00, and sex at 10:00, always at her place. Ismail never
slept over and was home by 11:30. They carried on like

this for many weeks, the AA and their deep talks a kind of heady, dry-drunk foreplay. He started to think they might make a go of a relationship until she finally worked up the nerve to tell him that they had to stop sleeping together because she was gay.

"No, you're pulling my leg!"

"It's true, Ismail. It's something I've known for a long time but never admitted to myself. I guess not drinking all this time has made me finally come to terms with it."

Ismail stared at her, dumbfounded.

She laughed and said, "Isn't it great? I'm not just a drunk, but I'm a gay drunk, too!" She beamed a self-mocking grin at him, showing off her coffee-stained incisors and the little gap between her two front teeth that Ismail loved.

"But ... it can't be!" What Ismail really wanted to say was: *But what about me?* In his mind, she couldn't be gay because they were dating. She was his first real relationship since Rehana. Visions of a future containing the two of them together, visions Ismail didn't even know he had, came apart like a poorly fitting puzzle. He realized he'd been fantasizing about Daphne eating dinner at his house, perhaps moving in, and meeting his family. The whole she-bang.

"I'm sorry if this is coming as a shock to you, Ismail. I've been thinking about it for a long time, but I wasn't ready to be open about it. And, well, now I think it's better if we went back to being friends. I mean, if I'm really going to come out as a lesbian, I shouldn't be having sex with men, right?"

Ismail was only half-listening, considering instead the Wednesday night they'd shared just two days earlier. Her fine hair had grazed his shoulder as she'd laid in his arms. He'd trailed his thumb up the length of her spine, tracing each bony bump. She'd stroked his chest, running her index finger over a small scar just above his sternum. The skin there had never healed properly, thickening and turning pink. She seemed to like that spot, returning to it often, rubbing it into smoothness. She asked him once how he'd gotten it, and he avoided telling her the truth, although he could have, in her dark bedroom.

"Really. I am sorry," she said, filling the silence, interrupting his reverie.

"But ... what about ... all the times we've been ... *together*?" Ismail sputtered. He knew he should have been scanning his brain for something appropriate to say, perhaps trying to remember the city-sponsored mandatory diversity trainings he'd attended, but all he could think of was how terrible he felt that she was breaking up with him.

"How can you be gay if you can have sex with men?" Ismail asked, his voice cracking. Thoughts of personal responsibility tripped through his confused head. *Did I drive her to this? Is this further evidence of my personal defects?*

"It's not rocket science, Ismail," Daphne sighed, sounding impatient. "I've been pretty much in denial my whole life about almost everything. Quitting drinking has helped me realize that. And, you know, it's not hard for women to have sex with men even if they are not *that* into it." Ismail fidgeted in his seat and thought back to their mediocre lovemaking. What had all that panting and moaning been about then? His ego bruised, he slumped back in his chair, crossed his arms over his chest. His armpits dampened through his poly-cotton shirt.

"Oh come on, Ismail. Don't feel bad. We had some fun together. And we've become good friends these past couple of months, haven't we? We'll still be friends, right?" she cajoled.

Ismail sighed. It wasn't the sex he was afraid of losing, but the evening chats, the pillow talk, the warmth of human skin. The possibility of something more. He closed his eyes, took in a couple of deep breaths, and tried to hide his hurt feelings.

"Yes, well, I suppose this is good news for you, Daphne. We are on the path to a more authentic life, aren't we?" He strained to remember an AA slogan that would fit the situation, but found none. They clinked coffee mugs, exchanged platonic hugs and parted for the evening.

Ismail resolved to be a friend and to support her new homosexual life. On the following Monday evening, at the café across from the mental hospital, he pulled from his briefcase a library book entitled, *When Someone You Love Comes Out of the Closet*, which he'd read cover to cover over the weekend. She picked it up, thumbed through its chapters, a blush reddening her pale complexion. She must have been very pleased with Ismail, because she invited him over that night. So relieved was he to be asked back to her apartment, that Ismail didn't raise the obvious contradiction of her being turned on by gay-positive self-help books. He worked extra hard to please her and perhaps he was successful, but he couldn't be sure. He wished her good night at elevenfifteen and prayed that things were back to normal.

When Daphne didn't invite him to her bed after coffee later on that week, or the week after, Ismail borrowed *Lesbian Lives, Lesbian Loves* from the Parkdale Library, avoiding eye contact with the librarian as he checked out. He sheepishly displayed it on the laminate table while he and Daphne chatted over coffee, hoping it would serve as a paperback aphrodisiac. Finally, after two hot chocolates and a lengthy

debriefing on Wednesday night's Hope for Today member-
ship, she acknowledged the book. She dispassionately read
its back cover and then thanked Ismail for being a good friend.

On his way home, he tossed it into the library's overnight drop-box, even though he'd only scanned its first
chapter. He turned away from the library and glumly stared
at a globelike metal sculpture that had been installed just
outside the library's doors. A fountain spurted up water
from its centre, splashing its rusted beams and leaking rivu-
lets onto the sidewalk. He fished in his pocket and threw a
linty nickel into the pool, not bothering to make a wish.

Ismail could tell that Daphne was growing less interested in his company. She had already substituted some of
their meetings for ones downtown where she was meeting
other gay women in recovery. He imagined her attending
gatherings with Birkenstock-shod women flirtatiously carrying on twelve-step banter.

Weeks later, Daphne admitted that she'd been dating
someone from one of those meetings. Ismail warned her
about starting a relationship with someone new in recovery, reminding her of the Program doctrine not to date during the first year. She didn't listen to his counsel, and soon
Ismail was twelve-stepping without her. He rarely saw her at
their Hope for Today meetings.

In total, Ismail stayed in AA for 197 sobering days. After
Daphne stopped being his comrade in abstinence, he got
down to business and earnestly worked through steps one
to eight, hoping to find the Cure for Bad Memories. He got
hopelessly stuck at Step Nine, Making Amends. He couldn't
fathom what sorts of amends were possible in a situation
like his; what could he offer his ex-wife, his baby child, or
God, to make up for his sins?

If Ismail was truly honest with himself, he might have admitted that by Step Four, when he compiled his moral inventory, he was missing Daphne, The Merry Pint, and growing cynical with the self-help doctrine. He never fully believed he qualified as a true alcoholic, anyway. At meetings, while others rolled their eyes, he used words like "coping tactic" or "survival strategy" instead of "addiction" or "disease." He supposed he was not a good follower.

He retreated to the bar, dejectedly dropping in for soda water and conversation, hoping that Daphne would show up. The old regulars welcomed him like a prodigal son returned, forgiving him his absence. Ismail was grateful to still belong. At first, he managed to pass his evenings there with soft drinks, but later, he'd have the odd beer. Once in a while a woman with smoke in her hair kept him company. But going to the Merry Pint never felt quite the same without Daphne.

How he longed for her! After Daphne abandoned him, the old memories rushed forward again. A new set of dreams plagued Ismail, always with him looking through the rearview mirror at Zubi in the back of the car. She'd sleep peacefully, her small body nestled in the baby seat. He'd look away for a moment, and when his eyes roved the mirror again, her seat would be empty.

He didn't know how to cope without his old friend. He considered becoming a drunk again, regrouting his bathtub, having more meaningless sex. But he knew none of that would work. And so he gave in, gave up. They lived on, the memories and Ismail, cohabitating sometimes fitfully, sometimes peacefully, at his little house on Lochrie Street. The irony was that his mistake, the biggest of his life, was one of forgetting.

— 6 —

FALL 2009

ON A SATURDAY IN November, Ismail was in his front garden doing a late season clean-up. He energetically pulled up limp marigolds and browned geraniums. He almost enjoyed wrestling with a particularly persistent morning glory vine that had colonized a good part of the yard, nearly strangling an adjacent rosebush. Ismail needed the work; he hadn't been back to AA for many months and was distracting himself from drinking too early in the day.

After all his exertion, he stood up, un-kinked his back, and rested a moment, gazing across the street. A curtain in the neighbours' front window fluttered, and Ismail realized that he was being watched. He continued with his work, bagging up dead plants, raking leaves, discarding garbage, but vigilance rippled through him, his mind troubling over the identity of his neighbour-spy; he guessed it could be the little boy playing at the front window, or his mother being nosy. Then he recalled a lady he'd seen going in and out of the house from time to time, a widow he mistakenly assumed to be Lydia's visiting grandmother.

— ❋ —

Over a year had passed since the day that Celia heard the migrating geese, forced her mother to eat, and rode in the screaming ambulance with her husband to Toronto Western Hospital. And in that year, the woman who had flowers in her eyes could only see sadness before her.

She had chores, and she babysat her grandson, but when she wasn't needed, she spent a good deal of time in her daughter's den, which had been converted into a bedroom for her. Her bed was inserted where the couch used to be, and an armoire replaced a bookshelf. A TV tray was her bedside table. The imprint of her son-in-law's computer desk still cut a rectangle in the carpet despite her efforts to smooth it down with the vacuum cleaner.

She pulled aside the drapes to stare out into the cloudy November day. *It's going to rain, look how dark it is out there.* She gazed up at the tall trees on Lochrie Street, their limbs almost naked now after shaking off their desiccated leaves. She sensed their devastation, felt their loss.

Something moved in her peripheral vision. Welcoming the diversion, she turned to watch a neighbour in his front yard. The man clawed at a dead vine with a fervour that suggested hatred. He wielded his rake as though it were a weapon, coming down hard against the defenceless grass. He formed leaf piles that were almost too tidy.

She shifted her gaze to the lawn just below her window, considering its carpet of leaves. Antonio kept saying, "Yeah, yeah! I'll get to the leaves soon!" and Lydia would retort,

"When? You keep saying you'll do it! But when?" Round and round they went in their carousel of nagging and ignoring one another. Celia thought she might rake them herself, just to break the tension. After all, she'd taken care of her own house, and garden and children for years.

She sighed and let go of the curtain. Darkness returned to her room.

Melancholy was something Celia couldn't see, but it touched her nonetheless. Years ago, she used to walk out into her garden first thing in the morning, perhaps to pluck a ripe tomato or to admire a newly opened trumpet blossom. Along her garden's path, she'd stumble into a freshly spun web, its silky strands coating her face, bare shoulders, elbows. She'd try to get the web off her, grasp it between her fingers, but the strands were elusive. All day, she'd feel its sly presence upon her. That's what melancholy felt like to her. She'd been ensnared by its invisible net for over a year now.

It disoriented her, snatching at her sureness of place, befuddling her while she rode home on the Dundas streetcar. Time after time, she'd gather up her plastic grocery bags in each hand, ring the bell, and get off at the wrong stop, seven blocks east of her new home. By the time she realized that her mind had turned trickster on her, fooling her into thinking she still lived in her old house, she would be on the sidewalk, watching the streetcar jerk forward, its dirty back windows moving out of sight. She'd mutter to herself, and have to wait for the next streetcar to take her the rest of the way home.

Sometimes, the confusion would offer her daydreams far more enticing than reality. While being carried westbound by the streetcar, she'd listen to her parents' voices swimming in her head. A young girl again, she'd hear their wistful conversations about São Miguel, the place her parents never stopped calling home, one she hardly remembered because she was still too young for nostalgia when they left.

Eventually she'd notice her streetcar approaching Roncesvalles, long past her stop. With a sense of resignation, she'd get off, cross the road and wait for a car going in the other direction. Sometimes, not wanting to use up another token, she'd trudge back along Dundas, over the bridge and railroad tracks, past auto-body garages and the burger place that was also a print shop. She'd arrive home worn down by the long walk and her confusion.

She did have her good days, times when she managed to ring the bell at Lansdowne and walk the one block to the semi-detached house on Lochrie Street without incident. She would retire to her bedroom-den, telling herself that she didn't mind her accommodations too much. She would reconcile the fact that Lydia and Antonio didn't want her in the upstairs guestroom, a proper bedroom, the one right next to their own.

On good days, she'd try not to long for the sounds of her old house, just a few city blocks away. She'd force herself to not listen for the drone of her mother's snoring, to stop waiting for José's heavy steps on creaky floorboards. On good days, she willed herself to avoid mourning a home of her own, a mother, a husband, her place in the world.

She made every effort to fit into her new home with Lydia's family, to accept her circumstances. She appreciated that at least Antonio was Italian, and understood she was family.

Although everyone knew José played cards — lots of men did — no one suspected it had become such a problem.

Now, it left everyone feeling culpable as they combed their memories for signs and symptoms they should have seen, mentioned, confronted. Celia especially fretted with: *Why didn't I know? Had his luck just run out towards the end?*

Lydia and Antonio assured her that she could stay as long as she wanted, and over the year, she realized they could afford to keep her; Lydia had just been promoted at the insurance company, and Antonio's hardware store, the one he ran with his father, was doing fairly well. Still, she knew that taking in her dependent mother wasn't something her young daughter had envisioned for herself.

She hadn't harboured such thoughts when it was time to look after her own mother years ago. Facts were facts; she was elderly, and didn't seem to be able to look after herself as well after *Pai* died, and Celia's brother Manuel lived too far away. Anyway, it's what daughters did. She moved her mother into Lydia's old room, next to her own. She left her son's bedroom mostly as it was, for the rare visits he made with his girlfriend. There was no question that her mother would join her household, no fanfare, no drama. But when her own husband died, Lydia and Filipe had hushed conversations, her children stage-whispering about "what to do with *Mãe*" when they thought she wasn't listening.

On her good days, she held her head high when Antonio mentioned finishing the basement to build a mother-in-law suite. He said she'd have more privacy. He loved that word: privacy. On good days, she wouldn't allow herself to dwell on the fact that she didn't want to live under the ground, in the half-dark, half-light rooms beside the washer and dryer. She wouldn't complain that basements were for kitchens, not bedrooms, and especially not for the bedrooms of middle-aged women who had cooked and cleaned and taken care of everyone their whole lives. On good days, she would resign herself to the fact that where she lived was no longer her decision.

That grey November day was not her best day. While she looked at the overcast sky, she was remembering José's first heart attack more than a year earlier. She arrived home from her visit with Lydia and Marco to find him sprawled out on the couch, a pained expression marking his face. She recalled the wailing of the ambulance's sirens, her frightening wait at the hospital. He was big and sturdy one day, a workhorse of a man, and the next, weak and embarrassed in a blue hospital gown, with rubber tubes sticking into him. She didn't like to dwell on that. She blinked her eyes hard, and the memory gradually receded.

Celia separated the curtains and once more trained her eyes on her neighbour's stooped back. A new recollection stepped forward. She saw herself on a warm autumn day, out for a walk with Marco and Lydia. They'd met an annoying neighbour, the know-it-all with the sunburn. And him — they'd also met him, that man across the street. She couldn't recall his name, but an image of his nervous smile flashed bright before her eyes.

— ❄ —

It started to rain. Ismail was determined to finish his work, long overdue already. He checked his watch, saw that it was only two-fifteen — much too early to go to the Merry Pint.

He picked up his pace, scooping up the last piles of moist leaves and dead plants into yard waste bags. He cinched the heavy paper bags closed, and lined them up on the grass, ready for the truck that would come for them in a few days. Ismail went inside, looking forward to warming up with a cup of hot tea. As he shut his door, he peered out its half-moon pane, focusing on the window from which he'd been watched earlier. The drapes were closed, and then suddenly, they opened again, and there she was, the older woman he'd seen around the neighbour's house the last few months. This time she stayed in the window, not hiding, allowing herself to be visible. Ismail's vigilance turned into a paranoid thread that wove itself through his addled brain.

— ❊ —

Celia saw the first fat raindrops marking the sidewalk. She watched her neighbour work faster, hurrying to clear the leaves. As he turned toward her to collect his tools, she narrowed the curtain, not wanting to be seen. She wasn't a nosy person and didn't want him to think she was peeping at him. Once he was indoors, she pulled aside the curtains again. But he was still there, looking back, through the little window in his front door. This time, she was the one being spied on. She froze.

After a shared moment of mutual gawking, he turned away first. Now that he was gone, she relaxed, and gazed at his house, the tidied garden, the small front porch. *Does he live with anyone? A wife? Does he go to sleep alone like I do?*

She watched the drizzle become a downpour.

—

José was sent home to recover with a rainbow of pills that Celia arranged for him in a clear plastic box, each compartment marked with a day of the week. He was more anxious that usual, but Celia expected that; he was still too weak to work. They were waiting for a surgery date that would come and go without him.

He was not the only one she worried about; Celia's mother was also unwell. While José rested, she took her mother out for one of a series of specialists' appointments, during which her mother was questioned about her mysterious lack of appetite. This time, it was a gastroenterologist named Dr. Chin who patiently waited for Celia to translate her mother's perfunctory responses. He frowned and listened while her mother made vague complaints about this-and-that ache, provided ambiguous answers about bowel movements, and offered fuzzy reports of fatigue. Like the other doctors, Dr. Chin poked at her intestines, inspected her chart, and requisitioned a new round of blood tests.

After the appointment, they stopped for coffee and cake at Nova Era: the sugar and icing a temptation for her fussy-eating mother. She ordered her a slice of lemon meringue pie, her mother's eyes lighting up at the sight of a white sugar cloud floating over glossy yellow filling. Celia wasn't going to have a dessert — it was only an hour until dinner — but the sweet smells of the bakery were intoxicating.

She estimated that it happened the very moment she took her first bite of chocolate cream cake. As her tongue tasted velvety pudding, the first pains pierced José's chest. While she scraped the last of the sweet icing from her plate he lost his balance and fell, his heavy body crashing down to the floor. His heart finally gave up as she gulped back strong, aromatic coffee.

They found him lying on the kitchen floor, his right hand over his heart, like a man pledging allegiance to some great cause. Only, there was no pride in his expression, his mouth shaped into an unfinished sentence, his wide-open eyes forgetting to shut. While she bent down and mimicked the CPR she'd seen on television, her hands pushing down against his unwilling chest, her mother pressed her fingers against José's eyelids, uttering a barely audible prayer.

— ❋ —

Ismail entertained the paranoia for few minutes:

Why's she watching me?

She must know about Zubi.

Maybe the neighbours have been talking again. I was a fool to think they'd stopped.

I am so stupid and naive.

But maybe I'm just being paranoid? Why would she watch me, then?

And on and on.

Eventually, he resolved to put the old woman out of mind. He made a cup of Orange Pekoe, and placed three chocolate chip cookies on a plate. While he enjoyed the sensation of mushy cookies mingling with hot tea against the roof of his mouth, it came to him. He realized he had met the old woman before. She wasn't Lydia's grandmother, she was her mother! And then he recalled that day, over a year ago, when he was on his way to the pub and Rob Gallagher had been oddly and unexpectedly cordial with him.

Only back then, the old lady had not looked so old. She hadn't been wearing head-to-toe black; rather, she had seemed sophisticated, even attractive. He considered that the stylish woman he'd met over a year ago had likely lost her husband, and entered widowhood.

He finished the three cookies and returned to the cupboard for more but they didn't satisfy. He grabbed a light beer from the fridge, and after a few sips, felt a little better. He looked out his back window at the rainy, November day. The clouds were darker now, casting a grey pall over the kitchen.

— 7 —

AGONIAS

Ismail was still contemplating the widow the next day, his mind troubling over the changes he'd seen in her. He wondered whether it really could be true that the woman sneaking looks out her window was the same one he'd met a year earlier. But then, he knew grief had a way of altering things, leaving indelible marks on people.

Many people — Ismail's brother, the therapist, Daphne — urged him to let go of the past, and move on with his life, as though letting go was some sort of simple procedure that would yield a positive outcome, if only he'd just applied himself more.

Just do A, B, and C thrice daily for result D. Hah!

On his last morning with Zubi, almost nineteen years ago, Ismail had risen early. It was August, and the wind wafting in through the bedroom window was already humid. He gingerly untangled himself from the sheets, trying to avoid waking Rehana. *My wife*, he sometimes said aloud to himself, for he liked the domesticity of the word.

He watched Rehana's rhythmic breathing and hoped she wouldn't stir; he didn't want to interrupt her last fifteen minutes before the alarm clock buzzed her awake. Since Zubi's birth, sleep deprivation had made her irritable, her frown lines deepening until she almost always looked cross.

Being a father was something he was still getting used to, although Zubi was already eighteen months old by then. He figured it was like that for most fathers, their children constantly changing and growing novelties. He tried to keep up with it all.

He looked in on Zubi before taking his shower. She was sleeping soundly on her stomach, her little face squished against the crib mattress, her blanket balled up around her right arm. He gushed inwardly at the beauty and serenity in her face. In moments like those, it was easy to for him to forget that she'd woken twice during the night, one of her crying spells lasting almost an hour. As Ismail gazed at her from the nursery's door, he foresaw that his lovely Zubeida would grow into a pretty girl, an attractive woman. He envisioned her having a wonderful life, a life full of every privilege and happiness she deserved.

He used the toilet, shaved, and while he was in the shower, Rehana awoke and stumbled, like a somnambulist, into the bathroom. She emptied her bladder and then brushed her teeth furiously with a firm-bristled toothbrush. While Ismail dried off, Rehana stepped past him, taking his place in the tub. She sang while she washed her hair, belting off a few off-key verses of Whitney Houston's *One Moment in Time*.

Ismail dressed, made tea for then both: strong and bitter

with just a drop of milk and no sugar for Rehana and three sugars and a long pour of condensed milk for him. While Ismail sipped tea, Rehana dressed herself, then Zubi, then shoved a bottle and Zubi into his arms.

He walked across the slanting living room floor, stepping carefully to balance Zubi, the warm bottle, and the municipal section of the *Toronto Star*. As he lowered himself to the couch, cradling Zubi in the crook of his arm, he tilted the bottle up for her to drink. He'd become quite expert at maneuvering her with his left arm so that he could hold up the newspaper with his right. Speed-reading as much of the paper as he could, he paid little attention to Zubi, who drank her milk with fervor. Like her mother in her youth, she had a strong appetite.

Rehana made toast, ate hers quickly, and came to get Zubi. He followed her into the kitchen to spread butter and jam on his bread. Rehana fed Zubi a bowl of instant baby cereal, while scanning the front-page headlines her husband held up like a shield.

Ismail finished his toast, gathered up his things for work, and impatiently called for Rehana to hurry up. *Chalo, Rehana, we are going to be late! I'll wait for you by the car!* He carried Zubi outside, strapped her into her car seat and heard Rehana open her door and settle herself in the passenger seat. While he buckled himself in, she reminded him that they would be changing their routine that morning, dropping her off first so she would get into work on time for a special mandatory meeting that she seemed nervous about.

He pulled in front of Rehana's building on Bloor Street, and she leaned over to offer him a dry cheek peck. As usual, Zubi had dropped off to sleep as soon as they'd left the house, the car engine and moving wheels her lullaby. Rehana blew sleeping Zubi a kiss and whispered. *Bye bye baby! See you later, Zubi!* Ismail asked Rehana to grab his briefcase from the back and place it on the front passenger seat so that it would be easier for him to reach later. She didn't question the request and complied. A car behind honked, protesting their pause in a no-stopping zone and Ismail grumbled another, *Chalo, let's go!*

Normally, they would have driven to the daycare first. Rehana would have unlatched Zubi's seatbelt and carried her inside and by the time they reached the daycare room, Zubi would have been awake enough for goodbyes. But that morning, Rehana could only wave to Zubi from the sidewalk, with Zubi still asleep, snoring quietly in the back seat.

Ismail regretted hurrying Rehana that morning.

And then he drove to work. He circled the already full municipal parking garage, cursing the city's lack of foresight that led to such insufficient staff parking. He found a free spot on a quiet side street two blocks south. *At least this is free*, he said to himself, looking on the bright side. He pulled up under a tree that would offer some afternoon shade, grabbed his briefcase, locked the car, and rushed into work.

— ❀ —

Celia washed the breakfast dishes, wiped the counter, and then retreated to her room. While she made her bed, she suppressed the urge to crawl inside the sheets she'd just tucked in. Her efforts were half-hearted, though, and in the end, she permitted herself to settle atop the cover, telling herself she'd only rest a few minutes.

She didn't hear her daughter pass her door, yelling, "We're going out now, *Mãe*. We'll be back soon." She didn't notice when an hour later the front door opened again, and her family returned. But she wasn't asleep — she was visiting another place, was caught in another time, back at her old house three weeks after José died.

The extended family had left and the other visitors had finally stopped dropping in with condolences. Although they were a comfort at first, she was glad to not have to receive any more pitying glances, or accept another homemade cake or Pyrex casserole dish full of bean stew. She had six different cakes in her fridge: lemon, chocolate, caramel, vanilla, raisin, and marble — her friends loved bringing her useless cakes! She would have liked to throw them all into the compost except that her mother said she liked them. Not that she had eaten any that morning, or the evening before. Celia wanted to take her to the doctor again, but her mother refused and in the end, Celia acquiesced. Grief had stolen away her own appetite, so who was she to argue?

Around six o'clock, Celia put leftover *leitão assado* in the oven and went to her mother's bedroom. She drew near to her mother's bed, softly calling to her, but still she didn't awaken. She was about to switch off the bedside lamp and leave her mother to her rest, but something stopped her: a woman frugal to her core, her mother wouldn't have left a light on, unnecessarily, while she napped. She shook her mother's limp body, checked futilely for a pulse, and felt her own body go numb.

The old woman succumbed to the infection that had been lurking, worming its way in and through her worn-out organs, stealing away her appetite, but greedily craving Nova Era's lemon meringue, *pastéis de nata*, and funeral cakes, their sickly sweetness the only thing able to satisfy its lustful and hasty growth.

Celia slumped down against the wall and stared list-lessly at her mother's body. She felt her eyes glaze over, and heard a whoosh of air pass through her skull. Where does the mind travel when there is nothing left to moor it? Celia's hovered just above her, and then floated up to the ceiling and surveyed the scene: a dresser, a bed, a cross on the wall. Two women wearing matching black outfits, one stock-still, the other barely moving. One with no breath left inside her, the other not seeming to need air. Her mind floated higher, pressed itself against the ceiling. It stayed there, high above the room's despair, thinking that soon, this house would need to be vacated and sold. From this angle, the idea of leaving was almost a comfort.

The smell of the burning pork roast was not enough to rouse Celia. When the smoke detector began its screaming, she wanted nothing more than to ignore it, to stay put, to allow herself and her mother to be cremated within her home's walls. She couldn't say what force made her stand up, stumble down the stairs and toss out the burned roast, Pyrex dish and all, into the backyard. She watched the black smoke billow up and into the sky, a distress signal. When the smoke dissipated, she went to the fridge and dumped each of the funeral cakes into the garbage bin, one at a time.

— ❄ —

Ismail wished there were a secret recipe for moving on. After so many years, he knew that finding one's way after a tragedy was like hiking an unmarked trail. He'd scramble down steep slopes, the path sometimes washed away by a recent storm. Familiar landmarks were often difficult to spot.

He considered his neighbour-widow's outward signs of mourning, her black sack-style dresses, which he guessed was very much in vogue with the widows of Little Portugal. He'd seen these dreary dresses on sidewalk racks outside local clothing stores. In a way, he admired the freedom widows had to be in the world without any pressure to look anything but miserable.

Ismail's remembering was relentless, his mind compelled to venture back, tragedy a kind of homing device for it. And remembering was rarely brief or casual; whenever Ismail travelled back to that terrible summer day when Zubi died, his mind was obsessive, grabbing on with rubber gloved fingers, poking and prodding at every memory fragment with vigour. His mind shone flood lights on these details, neurotically examining each and every minute of that day, searching for something to make sense of what happened.

Why didn't I look over my shoulder when I parked? Left my briefcase in the back seat? Why did Zubi have to be so quiet that morning? Why couldn't just one worrisome, sentimental, fatherly thought about my baby have entered my thick skull at some point during that day? Why didn't my wife call to inquire about the drop-off at daycare? She might have asked me if Zubi cried when I said goodbye. Rehana told me that Zubi often wailed when she walked out the daycare's doors.

Only when Ismail became utterly exhausted from this mental torture could his mind offer him rest and sweet affections. It led him by the hand to an imaginary world, fabricating a different day with a different outcome. It invented alternative plot twists and divine interventions.

As I left Rehana at work, I hardly thought about the tasks of the day ahead. Instead, I looked at Zubi in the rearview mirror. Something roused her from her sleep and then, suddenly awake, she cried in that way children do — as though shocked and appalled — when they wake up someplace different from where they fell asleep. I spoke to her in a soft voice, "Zubi, did you wake up? Were you sleeping?" When her whimpering started to slow, I sang to her, "I'm a little teapot, short and stout, here is my handle ..." With one arm, I did the accompanying arm movements, my hands dancing with the song. This soothed her until she laughed. At the next stoplight I unbuckled my seat belt, found her soother, and popped it into her waiting mouth. Her dark brown eyes looked at me with adoration. The light changed, I turned back to the driving, and pulled up at the daycare. She only cried a little when I said goodbye. Then I watched her for a few minutes from the hallway, peeking through the door's glass pane. The teacher placed her down on a spongy rubber carpet and gave her brightly coloured plastic rings to play with.

His mind's favourite time for these mental games was late at night, when all was quiet in the neighbourhood. It happened only after the children were called inside, the neighbours stopped yelling out to one another from their porches and locked their doors, and the murmurings through the shared walls went silent. That's when Ismail was left all alone with nothing but his remembering brain. Eventually, it would grow tired of the exercise, or alcohol would slow it down, and he could finally fall asleep.

— 8 —

NEARLY NAKED

ISMAIL SAW LYDIA'S MOTHER again, a week after he caught her looking at him from her window. He was on the front porch wearing only a bathrobe, the late autumn winds lapping at his bare legs. He was searching for his *Toronto Star*, which the delivery guy invariably tossed anywhere but within easy reach from his door. Finally, Ismail discovered it wedged precariously between two porch steps, threatening to fall beneath. He reached down with both hands and yanked the heavy roll out from between the steps.

Unfortunately, the effort left him unarmed against a sudden gust of wind that lifted his terry-cloth robe high above his skinny, goose-pimpled thighs. He pulled the thin fabric around himself with one hand, held onto his beloved paper with the other, and rushed back into the house like a self-conscious schoolgirl. Before closing the screen door, he scanned the street to check that no one had witnessed the spectacle. And there she was, peering at him through the clear glass of the living room window. After their encounter the previous week, Ismail wasn't terribly surprised to see her there. Their eyes met for a moment, and then his peep-show audience let the curtain fall from her fingers and she disappeared from sight.

Ismail mused about what the widow had seen in the immodest moment before he'd run back inside. Studying himself in the hallway mirror, he imagined himself a brown, male, middle-aged Marilyn Monroe caught over the gusts of a sewer grate. Did the lady notice his knocked knees, veiny legs?

Ismail patted down his wet-from-the-shower hair, straightened his robe, and looked in the mirror again. He'd never considered himself a handsome man, but didn't think he was all that bad, either. Crow's feet sprouted around his eyes, fine lines that implied he smiled more often than he did, but he was otherwise mostly unwrinkled. He proudly surveyed his full head of hair with its distinguished-looking grey flecks at the temples. Sucking in the slight paunch around his middle, he decided that he was still slim. And he only needed reading glasses when the light was poor.

Ismail locked the door, and soon forgot about his neighbour, allowing the fat Saturday paper to consume his thoughts.

— ❈ —

"Come on, *Mãe*! Do something! You'll feel better if you do something. You're making yourself into a depressed old woman!" Lydia chided. She did not like her mother's habit of sitting by the front window.

Celia did not have the energy to be offended by the comment, and anyway she *did* feel like a depressed old woman, even though she'd just turned fifty. She nodded as though she were listening, and promptly returned to her post by the window, which caused Lydia to sigh loudly.

Lydia never knew what her mother was looking at, and even if Celia told her, she likely wouldn't have approved, anyway. She nagged about her eating and sleeping habits, whether she had gone out that day, if she'd washed her hair that week. She constantly asked her when she was going to stop wearing black, had even brought up two boxes of her regular clothes from the basement. Celia understood this to be her daughter's way of caring for her, and not so different from the way she, herself, had raised Lydia or cared for her own mother. But now that she was on the receiving end of this treatment she found it disconcerting, their roles reversing in a clumsy dance; neither really knew the steps, and Celia wasn't sure she wanted Lydia taking the lead.

Celia disregarded her daughter's entreaties to join the family for breakfast. She smelled the scent of biscuits wafting warm and sweet, but didn't have much of an appetite those days, and besides, she was involved in something far more interesting.

She was watching the man across the street, who at that moment was standing in the cold, wearing a striped bathrobe. She stared at his chicken legs, uncombed hair, and smooth chest. Celia felt a twinkle in her eye, and mischievous thoughts crackled through her melancholy, surprising her. It had been some time since saucy ideas had come to mind, so at first she didn't know what to do with them.

Marco came and sat in her lap. He watched a tiny spider — barely the width of a fingernail — construct a web in the window pane: *Look, Vovó, a spider!* She smiled at his four-year-old sense of glee and then pursed her lips at the insect, blew into its web, frightening the spider and delighting her grandson. *You made it windy for the spider!*

While she listened to Marco's laughter, she looked up to see a sudden autumn wind blow under the neighbour's robe, its terry-cloth stripes transforming into exclamation marks. High into the air they went, revealing bits of man flesh that Celia hadn't seen in much too long. She giggled at the sight, stroked her grandson's hair, and recalled a walk on a cool autumn's day, and the warmth of her dressy burgundy coat. She peeked through the curtains again, watched the man's retreating back, and saw a flock of Canada geese cross the blue sky over his house.

Memories are like roving magnets that attract others along for the ride. As the Canada geese honked at her from the past, ambulance sirens pulsed fear through her body. The taste of too-sweet chocolate cake brought bile to her throat. She felt her palms pushing against a heart, willing it to beat again, and saw empty eyes, a spirit already displaced. She watched arthritic fingers make eyelids close.

Celia felt Marco scamper to the floor. She had a feeling that he'd been talking to her, but his words blurred in her mind. She wiped away wetness from her cheeks and then saw that his were wet, too. Lydia called him away and he ran into her waiting arms.

— 9 —

SWEEPING

ISMAIL'S NEXT WIDOW SIGHTING was from behind the cloak of his living-room drapes. It was a cool December day, and she wore only a long, dark cardigan over her dress. A plain black cotton kerchief covered her mostly grey hair. Ismail squinted through the streaked glass, trying to determine her age. She swept the sidewalk in front of her house, her stooped posture and slow movements making her seem much older than he guessed her to be.

At one point, she straightened up and peered in his direction, perhaps sensing his presence. Ismail stood back and after a moment, he parted the fabric again. He saw that she was no longer looking in his direction, her attention being diverted by someone calling out to her from the doorway. She replied in Portuguese and gesticulated crossly at her daughter, Lydia, who strode out of the house, carrying a black woollen coat in her arms. Ismail drew closer to the window again, and opened it a crack so he could hear better, too.

Ismail didn't know much about Lydia, except that she seemed a friendly enough woman. She, her husband, and young son had moved in a few years ago. He noticed they hung a Liberal candidate's sign on their fence during the previous federal election (Ismail also voted Liberal, but preferred not to advertise this), built a new porch, and planted flowers out front that bloomed well into the cold months. Earlier that year, Ismail had admired the size of Lydia's Black-eyed Susans.

Lydia's voice rose, penetrating through the crack of his window, distracting him from all matters botanical. "*Mãe*, it's cold out!" she yelled. In the same scolding tone, she said something in Portuguese and draped the coat over her mother, who tried, unsuccessfully, to wave her off. Lydia took hold of her mother's arms, struggling to coax them into the sleeves and after a bit of pushing and pulling, Lydia won the battle, and her mother admitted defeat, standing obediently, like a preschooler, while Lydia fastened each big button from her mother's knees to her chin. *How the young treat the old. What insolence! Let her be!* he protested silently from his post. There was something in how the widow allowed her daughter to dress her that told him her acquiescence had chilled her more than any late autumn winds could.

Lydia marched back into the house, blowing warm air into her bare hands. Only then did Ismail notice that she was dressed in a thin T-shirt, jeans, and bedroom slippers. The widow turned away from her daughter and looked across the street toward him. Beneath her tired expression, he saw that she had a pleasant face. He recalled that her irises were shaped like flowers.

She stared back at him blandly while he attempted to overcompensate for his presence at the window by grinning and waving gaily. She did not return the gesture, and so he quickly retreated behind the camouflage of his curtains, feeling foolish.

— ❋ —

The bustle of her daughter's household encircled Celia but couldn't break through her lethargy. The days became endless and the nights short. She wished they would reverse themselves so that she could sleep sixteen hours and be awake for only eight. Sometimes she'd lounge in bed as long as possible, squeezing her eyelids shut, willing herself back to unconsciousness, but her treacherous body rarely allowed her to sleep beyond sunrise.

She'd been busy all her life, and there had never seemed to be enough time in her day for all the many tasks she needed to do: the cleaning, cooking, caring for sick children, laundry, and gardening never seemed to end. When the kids were young, she'd even managed to take in a small brood of the neighbours' children to open a small at-home daycare. The days flew by. But on Lochrie Street, time slithered like a snail, dumb, slow, with nothing to direct it.

But that Sunday afternoon was different. As she sat at the front window, she looked out at the sidewalk and irritation crackled through her. The blustery winds of the night before had blown garbage onto the walk. And the dust! So much of it coated the normally white sidewalk. Usually, her lassitude allowed her to ignore such trifles, but on that day, dust and garbage were urgent matters. She rose from her perch at the window and went looking for a broom.

She stepped outside, and as she worked, she felt a little of her old strength returning, her muscles stretching and

straining with each movement. A steady energy spread
from her body up to her brain and she found herself humming a popular song she'd heard drifting from a neighbour's
window last week. She couldn't remember the words, but
the melody was familiar: *Da da dee. Dum dum da. Da da
dum. Dum dah!*

She lifted her face to the sunshine, sniffed the air, and
admired the blue sky above and sensed she wasn't alone. She
looked across to the Indian neighbour's house and glimpsed
him peeking through his curtains. She didn't mind. After
all, she'd been the one watching him these past few weeks.
Perhaps she liked the thought of a man, and that man in
particular, looking at her, reciprocating the watching. She
blushed as she recalled the day she'd seen his thin legs
and privates. He wasn't an unattractive man, certainly. She
hummed a little louder.

She didn't know why Lydia had to come out right then
and ruin her mood. It wasn't so cold out and for once, she'd
been enjoying herself. She didn't need a coat. And more
than that, she wished the man hadn't witnessed her daughter treat her so stupidly. After Lydia forced the coat onto her,
she felt all her energy drain right out of her, down her legs,
out her feet, and pool on the sidewalk. She left the broom
on the lawn and went inside to take a nap.

— IO —

KNEES

THE NEXT WEEK, ISMAIL finally saw Daphne at the Merry Pint. She moved through the bar, greeting the regulars with smiles, handshakes, and hugs. Although only a few months had passed since they'd last seen one another at an AA meeting, she seemed changed to him and at first Ismail didn't recognize her; her usual outfit of blue jeans, T-shirt, and sweatshirt had been exchanged for a red overcoat and a yellow dress that stopped just short of her knees. Thick white stockings came all the way up her calves, making her look like a teenager. She sat down beside him, he finally realized it was her, and Ismail instantly felt nostalgic for the good times they'd shared. She leaned over and embraced him from her bar stool.

"You look good, Daphne. New girl in your life?" Ismail probed, hoping for some ambivalence around her sexual orientation that would permit him a place in her bed once again.

"Not a new girl, Ismail! A new life! A new calling!" He watched her eyebrows bob up and down with each exclamation. "Instead of drinking, I write now. I am a writer!" She took a deep breath and then proceeded to talk non-stop about a class she'd taken at the university, the supportive students, her inspirational instructor. Ismail wasn't sure what to make of this new Daphne, this Daphne with a new calling, inspiration, and yellow dresses and so he ordered a beer and settled in to listen. He noticed that she looked at his drink longingly, sucking hard on her straw, emptying her glass of ginger ale in several long slurps. Ismail guessed she was back at the Merry Pint to reunite with old buddies and maybe test her fragile sobriety, something he understood. He'd attempted evenings of soda water after AA and at first he'd been successful.

"Well, enough about me. What's new with you these days?" Daphne queried.

"Me? Oh, nothing much. Same old, same old."

"So ... how are things? You still drinking?" She asked tentatively.

"Well, I drink a little here and there. It's not a big problem for me — I'm much better these days. More moderate," Ismail said, reaching for the pretzel bowl. It was somewhat true, and now that he was drinking less, he was already feeling the beer's liquid kiss. Nabil's voice rang through his head. *Moderation is the thing, Ismail.*

"I hope you aren't still spending time with the Mary Pinters here," she said, glancing at a pair of women sitting further down the bar. Although her expression seemed neutral — there was none of her tomato-red blushing — her voice carried a hint of jealousy, and Ismail felt himself brighten with hope. During their sober intimacies, he'd confided to Daphne about his encounters with a few of the lonely lady regulars at the Merry Pint. It was this gossip that inspired Daphne to coin the term "Mary Pinters."

As though sensing they were being talked about, one of the Mary Pinters swivelled her stool and smiled at Ismail. He knew her name was Sandra, because they had spent a couple of hazy nights together in the previous few months. He waved feebly at her, and her eyes narrowed into a suggestive "come hither" leer.

"I haven't slept with a Mary Pinter in a very long time, I'll have you know!" he lied, laughing nervously. "Not since you were one of them." Daphne smacked his arm in reply, sending a bawdy sting down its length, rousing his body awake.

"Hey, I've never been one of them! I don't have drunken sex." Daphne said, protesting, "At least not since I was in my twenties."

"Yes, me, too. Not for a long while. I think that one three stools over must be missing me," Ismail joked.

Daphne sized up Sandra.

"No really, I don't come here very often anymore, not since AA. I drop in maybe twice a week, and only have one or two," he explained, sipping his beer.

"Really? Just one or two, Ismail?"

"Yes, really. AA helped me cut down. It was good for me for a while, but I didn't really feel it was for me in the end," he said, looking guiltily into his glass.

"Well that's good. I'm still working at it. I almost had a full year and then I slipped, pretty bad. I'll have a month again next Monday ... I probably shouldn't have come. My sponsor would flip if she knew I was here — she told me to stop associating with people who drink. But maybe I'm like you, I like to test the rules sometimes," she said with a sad smile.

"I couldn't stand the meetings without you, Daphne. Those people were so serious, so earnest all the time ..."

Ismail trailed off, searching her face, fearing he had just offended her, after all she — and Ismail — had been "those people."

"Yeah, I know. Anyway, the class is a lot like an AA meeting without the AA. Has the same effect on me, maybe better, even. You might like it, too ... you should come. It'll be fun." Ismail raised his eyebrows, recalling that she used a similar argument to convince him to go to AA with her. She persisted, "Really, you should."

"I don't write, except for the very boring reports I do at work. Anyway, I don't think I'm very creative." Ismail knew he was being somewhat false. There had been a time, back in his youth, when he fancied himself a creative person. He wouldn't have ever gone so far as to consider himself a writer — after all he was an engineering student — but he did write the odd poem, and a couple of short stories. One of them, about the sectarian violence that was happening shortly before he left India, was published anonymously in a small journal edited by an acquaintance.

"Everyone's creative, Ismail. And you don't have to be good at it, you know. God knows I'm terrible at it. I know that it will never be anything but a hobby for me," she said, and Ismail heard the old cynicism in her voice.

"What are you writing about?" he asked, vainly hoping he might have inspired prose.

"It depends on what I feel like at the time. I've done some poetry — mostly sappy stuff when I was with Laura, you remember her, don't you? I wrote a lot of love poetry during that short time we were together," Daphne said, looking down into her plastic straw.

"Oh, so you're not still with her?" A tiny bubble of hope floated up.

"Nope. That turned out to be just a fling, and now I'm just a sad single girl again," she said, pushing out her lips into a mock pout. "I fell hard because she was my first — first girl, that is. She inspired a lot of bad lesbian poetry. Now I'm on to writing short stories. Maybe one day I'll write a novel." She paused, looked thoughtful, and pushed her glass away. "You know, I bet *you* could write a novel about your life. You've been through so much. And it's really therapeutic. It might help you."

"I can't imagine anyone being interested in my life story. Besides, I hardly ever read books anymore." As a youth, Ismail read all the classics: *The Great Gatsby, War and Peace, Ulysses, Heart of Darkness,* all of which had been assigned in school. But as an adult, he developed more of an appreciation for the inky reality of newspapers.

"What about all those self-help books from the library? You've read a ton of those." Ismail nodded, considering a few of the dozens of titles he'd borrowed: *Healing from Loss, Accepting Your Mistakes, Beyond Anxiety.*

"A lot of good they've done me," he quipped, but Daphne wasn't to be dissuaded.

"Maybe that's your genre."

"My what?"

"Genre. You know, category of writing. Genre."

"Oh, genre," Ismail repeated, pronouncing it *jan-rah.* He'd never heard anyone pronounce it her way.

"I think it's a French word, Ismail."

"Oh," he said, feeling foolish. He ordered another beer and sipped on it while she continued to talk about the short stories she was working on.

"I've done two stories loosely based on my family history. I feel like I am finally starting to get to some kind of resolution. I couldn't tell you why, but when I write down the stories, they don't take up so much room inside my head. And my teacher said they showed ... promise," she said shyly.

"I envy you, Daphne."

"Really? Why?" She looked at him quizzically, but seemed pleased all the same.

"I've done a year of therapy. A hundred AA meetings. Read a couple dozen self-help books. I'm still the same old miserable person after all of these years. I envy you for finding something that helps you. Good on you." Ismail lifted his glass to toast her. She bit her lip and reached for his arm, the soft padded tips of her fingers resting on his wrist. He put his glass down.

"So come with me to the writing class, then. It might help you with the drinking, too. They're registering people now for the February session." Ismail remained quiet, the beer and her touch creating a warm blush within him. "It'll be like old times," she purred. He met her eyes and she continued, "I've missed seeing you around." Ismail looked down at her hand in his and remembered their Mondays, Wednesdays, and Fridays. He told himself that perhaps they could rekindle their friendship, and things *would* be different this time.

"Maybe. Well, I don't have anything else on the go right now. And it looks good on you," Ismail said. She blushed, and he heard himself mumble, "Why not?" He wasn't really sure he meant it, but as he sipped his drink with his left hand, he allowed Daphne to scrawl the location and date of the class on his right. The press of ballpoint against his palm raised a field of goosebumps on his arm.

"Now, don't wash this off," she warned, smiling bright, sunny rays down on him. Ismail gazed into her eyes and promised he wouldn't.

— ❋ —

It was late, but Celia knew sleep wouldn't come for an hour or two yet. Still, falsely hopeful, she changed into a flannel nightie. As she passed a mirror, she glimpsed herself in the bright garment, her pale hands and neck reaching out and up from the aquamarine blue cuffs and collar. These colours were only for her underwear and nightclothes now.

She donned the mourning clothes for José, exchanging her stylish pants, blouses, and skirts for black dresses and loafers. She only intended to do so for a month or two, for she never saw herself as such a traditional person. Even for her father, her black attire was only for a week. But after her mother died, she just didn't feel like changing out of the widow's uniform. Besides, nearly all her other clothes were still in boxes in the basement, and she didn't have the energy to unpack them.

Old friends who knew the cheerful woman from before, and didn't follow the traditions of widows, questioned her about when she would come out of the mourning clothes.

"Come on, Celia, you grew up here, went to school here. This isn't like you," Adriana cajoled.

"Yeah, it's fine for a little while, but you can stop now," added Joana.

She would just shrug. *At least everything matches with black, yes?*

And the mourning clothes matched her mood, the sorrow and bitter resentments she exhaled with each breath. Her friends cautioned her about developing the *agonias*, the murky sadness for the self, but much more than that, too, a breathless sense of fear for the world. *It's our special kind of condition, eh?* She knew the *agonias* were the worst kind of ailment a woman could succumb to, for its quivering anxiety sapped the muscles of energy, the blood of vitality, and the mind of all hope. Mostly, it left Celia tired, more tired than she'd ever been in her life. She could curl up in ball, forget the past, and not have to worry about the future. *Perhaps*, Celia thought, *I am entitled to my* agonias. *After what I've been through.*

There were nights when she dreamt of José and mornings she awoke expecting to see him beside her. She would roll over in bed, cotton sheets wound tight around her legs. She'd reach for him, her eyes closed, her cheek searching for a place to nuzzle into his warm chest. There would be a moment, when in her half-sleep, she would feel his shadowy presence in the bed, and she would soak in his warmth. His curly chest hairs would be soft under her face and her breathing would regulate to his heartbeat. Usually, when daylight peeked past her curtains, she'd rouse from that dreamlike place, and the figment beside her would lift his head from the pillow, turn away, and leave the room. She would swear she could sense the mattress shift beneath her, the springs recoiling from José's departure.

A part of her, the one half-asleep and longing for him to return, wanted to call out to him, to wail, to pull out her hair in anguish each time he abandoned her. The other part of her, the one half awake, rebuked her husband, whispered curses at his spirit, forbade him to ever again return to her bed.

Half awake and half asleep. That was how her new life left her. In the mornings, bleary-eyed, she would reach for her water glass with her right arm, only to find that the TV tray was on her left. She'd open her top drawer for a pair of pantyhose and realize that they were stored in the second.

She would search her reflection in the mirror and not recognize the old widow looking back at her. *Whose sad eyes are those? Whose grey hair? Whose unrouged cheeks, unperfumed neck, barren lips?* She hadn't yet grown accustomed to it all, but didn't resist it, either. The other ladies on her block with dead husbands told her that she would get used to wearing black, to being a woman conspicuous in her grief, and invisible in every other way.

— II —

BIG *BHAI*

IT WAS ANOTHER THURSDAY afternoon, and Ismail was receiving Nabil's weekly phone call. He sat at his desk, coat on, the phone's receiver warming his ear. Looking for a suitable topic of conversation, he'd mentioned that he might take a winter trip to the Caribbean. Nabil liked to go on luxury all-inclusive vacations with his family.

"Yes, it would be good for you to have some new surroundings, get away from that bar you spend so much time in. And that bad-influence woman," Nabil said, finally taking a breath in the lecture he'd been delivering over the previous three minutes. He'd started by discussing the merits of travel agents and then somehow gotten diverted to Ismail's drinking. Ismail felt himself crumple into the small boy whose older brother protected him from the playground bullies but later scolded him for not standing up for himself.

"Oh, well, I don't drink much these days," Ismail said in self-defense, "and I rarely see Daphne much, either." He was almost about to explain that the reason for their lack of contact was Daphne's nascent homosexuality, but he stopped himself. He looked at his palm, seeing her faint, almost washed-off handwriting. He also chose not to tell Nabil about the writing class, which he'd signed up for the previous night before heading to bed. Half-drunk and sleepy, he'd managed to match the course numbers Daphne had scrawled on his hand to the ones on the University of Toronto's Continuing Education website.

"Glad to hear it. Moderation is the main thing."

"Yes, *Bhai*," Ismail sighed.

"Really, I'm not saying you should quit, but you should make sure you are moderate. That's the best thing. Even I enjoy a good wine with dinner from time to time. But be careful. Just take heed of what the doctor told you." Ismail often regretted telling Nabil about his health scare a few years back.

"Yes, *Bhai*, I haven't forgotten. I'm looking after my health," Ismail repeated. "So ... how are Altaf and Asghar?" he asked, wanting to change the subject. And he knew this topic would be a good one. When Nabil thought about his sons, some-thing unlocked within his brain, allowing him to exhale and slow his pace. Ismail pictured him easing up on the accelera-tor, guiding his car from the passing lane to the middle.

"Well," Nabil said, his tone brightening, "Altaf is about to begin his residency. And did I tell you he decided to meet that girl *Maasi* was talking about? You know, *Kakaji's* cous-in's daughter, Muriam? They've been on two dates already. She seems like a nice girl."

"Who? Which cousin?"

"Hatim *Kakaji's* cousin, Yusufali. His daughter."

"I didn't know Yusufali had a daughter named Muriam," Ismail admitted, as he mentally sifted through his aunts and uncles and cousins, reconstructing the complex family tree in his mind.

"He has three daughters. One of them is Altaf's age," Nabil explained impatiently.

"Oh, right, Yusufali. I was confusing him with Hassanali. So Altaf likes her? I didn't think he'd go for an arrangement."

"Yes, they have a lot in common. And it was more of an introduction, not an arrangement. I'm not that old-fashioned, you know." This was more or less true. Nabil kept up appearances by attending the mosque once or twice a year and avoided alcohol and pork when people from the community might see him. In the privacy of his own home, he did whatever he pleased.

"Glad he's met someone. And they're a good match?"

"Yes, I think they are compatible. She's studying medicine, too, and is also an accomplished tennis player."

"Good, good. And how is Asghar?" In every family, there is a child who doesn't behave as everyone expects, and for this reason, Asghar had always been Ismail's favourite.

"Yeah, he is fine." There was a cough, a honking horn, the end of Nabil's calm.

"You okay? Is traffic bad?"

"No, no, just changed lanes and the jackass behind me wasn't watching the road. What were we talking about?"

"I was asking about Asghar."

"Oh yeah, Asghar. He's had a little trouble at the university. Was involved in some stupid thing involving political protests or some such foolishness. Luckily at York they are a little lenient about these things, so he received a warning, but no suspension, thank God. And now he is talking about getting out of business and going into something else. And in his third year! And after taking a year off already," Nabil grumbled. He still was angry about Asghar's decision to travel and work for a year before entering university, believing it put his son "a year behind" everyone else.

"Yes, he told me he was involved in some anti-war protests when I was over last time. And that he was thinking about not staying in business."

"He told you that? You knew about that and didn't tell me?"

"I figured you knew already," Ismail lied.

"Well I didn't and he just went ahead and changed majors without discussing it with me first. I should cut off his tuition!"

"Come on, Nabil, he's a young man now. He has to follow his own direction in life. Think about how it was when we were young," Ismail said, hoping to appease his brother. When Ismail and Nabil were in college, their father expected them to come work as managers in his packaging plant. The business had been passed down for three generations and made plastic and cardboard boxes (explaining the origin of their surname), bubble wrap, and tiffins. Nabil endured the greatest pressure, when, after business school, he chose to immigrate to Canada.

"So, what does Asghar plan to study?" Ismail knew the answer already because he and Asghar had had a lengthy talk on the subject the last time they spoke.

"Oh, he wants to go into the Faculty of Art or Social Sciences, some such thing, Political Science or something."

"Political Science is not so bad, is it? If that is what he most wants to do, *Bhai*, you have to let him, don't you? Don't you think it's your duty to support his education?"

"What a sham, Political Science. Not even a real science! Let him follow his interests as a hobby. Can he feed himself on his interests?"

"Well, but that isn't the point —" Ismail stammered, trying to think of something to help Asghar's case, "Perhaps he'll go into politics one day."

"What's the point of that? Canada will never elect a South Asian Prime Minister ... look, I have to go. I've just pulled into a client's driveway. Let's plan a date for dinner, okay? You'll be coming over for the holidays, right?"

"Yes, sure. I'll call Nabila to arrange it."

"Great, got to go."

12

BLUE HAIR

IT WAS THE AFTERNOON of Christmas Eve and about two dozen people were in the house, mostly Antonio's family and her son, Filipe, in from Montreal. Celia tried to smile at the children, make small-talk with her in-laws, to match the gaiety in the room. When she could, she retreated to the kitchen, washed dishes, refreshed platters. It was her second Christmas without José and her mother, and it seemed she was the only one who noticed their absence. Last year the whole family mourned, the holiday low-key and half-hearted. Now, as she searched Filipe's eyes and watched Lydia greet her guests, there wasn't even a whisper of grief. From the kitchen, she heard the living room break into laughter over a shared joke she didn't hear.

— ❋ —

Ismail spent Christmas and Boxing Day with Nabil, Nabila, and their two boys, staying overnight in their newly redone guest suite. Furnished like a high-end hotel room, it had a sleigh bed with a mattress more comfortable than his own. The bathroom featured a soaker tub that Nabila said they'd never use, but would be a good investment if they ever sold the house. On his first evening there, he briefly contemplated his brother's offer to move in, thinking the suite might be a welcome alternative to his lonely row house. However, after two days of the family's minor squabbles, negotiations, and noise, he longed for his quiet downtown life again.

He phoned Daphne twice during the holidays, and even bought her a fancy notebook as a Christmas present. He hoped she'd like it — it had plenty of room for her to jot down her thoughts and was full of quotations from famous women, like Gloria Steinem and Jennifer Aniston. Daphne didn't return any of his calls, except once in mid-January to confirm that she was still planning to go to the creative writing class and would meet him there.

So, on February ninth, at 7:00 p.m., Ismail walked into University College 122, where twenty skittish-looking people of various ages sat around a large U-shaped table. He scanned the room anxiously for the absent Daphne, and then found a pair of vacant seats for them. As the minutes passed, his heart sped up and the sweats started. Luckily, Ismail was always prepared for his perspiration, and carried two white cotton handkerchiefs, one in his front pocket and one in his back.

While dabbing his forehead, he closed his eyes and tried to recall the mental "calm place" the therapist, from many years ago, had taught him to imagine. Away he went to a beach in Goa, sunning himself in the sand. For extra measure, he commenced his panic-attack breathing. This helped somewhat, so Ismail opened his eyes again and looked around. He saw that a woman with grey hair and a frilly blouse sat a few seats to his left, a notebook, a pencil, and a pen sitting neatly in front of her. Near the front of the room, a man and a woman, perhaps in their thirties, and presumably together, simultaneously opened up matching pea-green laptops. Ismail watched as the woman whispered something to the man, cupping her palm around his ear. He nodded and whispered something back.

The classroom itself was somewhat calming, reminding him of the courses he'd taken over thirty years ago at a campus across the world, in a similar Victorian building. He looked at the high windows, admired the arcs of the vaulted ceiling. He imagined that the long mahogany tables, slightly worn and scratched, had been witness to hundreds of courses and thousands of students.

Facing the front of the room was a tweed-coated teacher waiting fretfully for his room to fill. James Busbridge, Ismail had read online, was in his mid-forties, had written a novel, a book of short stories, and had been working on a third book, a memoir, for the past six years. James lived in Toronto with his wife and three children and had a column in *NOW Magazine*.

Ismail watched James glance at his watch and fidget with some papers in front of him, and then check his watch again. Ismail advised him, telepathically: *inhale three, exhale six. Here, follow me. Inhale four, exhale eight.* As though rejecting Ismail's self-help suggestion, James abruptly stood and turned away from the class. The room grew silent as he scrawled his name messily on the chalkboard, his sleeve's cuff attracting a smudge of pink chalk.

"Uh, hello everyone," he cleared his throat and continued, "let's get started. My name is James Busbridge. Let me tell you a little about where I come from and how I teach this class. I believe that we are all, in some way, writers. And we can learn to write well. But writing well takes work and practice and you will have to write something of your own if you want to get something from this course."

Just then, Daphne strode into the room, her heels click-clacking across the hardwood. James smiled her way, perhaps relieved another chair was being filled, and gestured to a seat near his. Ismail tried to wave her over, but she didn't seem to see him until she'd already sat down.

"Uh, before we do anything else, we'll start with some introductions. Turn to the person beside you and tell them your name and a little about why you decided to take this course."

Ismail groaned inwardly at the instructions. He'd been to too many government workshops that began with this introductory activity, which he judged to be inane and unoriginal. "This was supposed to be a *creative* writing class," he muttered to himself. With little choice but to acquiesce, he turned to the woman with the frilly blouse to his left, but she was already immersed in conversation with the man beside her. To Ismail's right was a vacant seat and next to that a girl who reached across the space to shake his hand. She appeared almost too young to be in a university-level course and had light brown skin, a shade similar to his own.

"Hey, I'm Fatima," she said, pronouncing her name in the Christian way: *Fa-tee-mah*. "I'm in my second year of pre-med, but I'm taking this class because I've always wanted to write and I'm kind of trying to figure out if I should stay in pre-med or switch over to Liberal Arts ... and you?" She'd spoken so quickly, Ismail had to pause a moment to absorb her words. He looked at her face, studying her large brown eyes lined with blue makeup that matched the electric blue streaks in her hair. Both her question and her appearance confused him. He did not have time to inhale or exhale.

"Um, well, I don't know why I'm here, really. I guess I'm just looking for a new pastime. And my friend suggested it, the lady who just arrived, over there." He turned in his seat, scanned the front of the classroom, and saw that Daphne was conversing with a woman sitting next to her. He swivelled around again, met Fatima's eyes and said, "Oh, er, sorry. My name is Ismail. I forgot to say that. Ismail Boxwala." He nervously patted his forehead with his handkerchief and then cursed himself for forgetting to withhold his surname. He watched for the familiar reaction that didn't come, and was reassured that this girl was too young to know his name. He inhaled for one count and exhaled for two and inspected her silver nose ring.

"Well, that's good," she said. "It's good to try new things." She played with a piece of her strange blue hair and Ismail wondered if she was being patronizing. "For me, though, I don't know if it's just a hobby or something I want to do, you know? Like for a living? Not that writers make much money from writing. But I've had a story idea for awhile and I hope this class will get me started." Ismail heard Nabil's voice in his head, his judgments about which interests should be hobbies instead of careers, but resisted sharing them with Fatima. Instead, he remained quiet, listening to the rhythm of Fatima's staccato speech. He considered that perhaps he was making her uncomfortable with all his breathing.

"So, yeah. My story is loosely based on my parents' immigration to Canada. All the things they faced? You know, like the hardships of coming to a new country?" For a moment, he thought he was supposed to answer her question, but then she continued talking. "The whole immigrant story? And you? What do you want to write about?"

"I think," Ismail said, "my daughter." The words popped out of his startled mouth as though he were just their obedient puppet. Sweat dripped between his shoulder blades. Accompanying his shock was a sliver of relief. Ismail looked over at Daphne and pondered whether writing about Zubi might offer a possibility of change, the kind that had obviously happened for her. She looked nice, just like at the bar weeks ago. This time, she wore an olive skirt that grazed her knees. She had dark brown tights and boots that came halfway up her calves. He thought that perhaps she'd gained some weight, and that the extra pounds made her seem even more pretty.

Ismail faced Fatima again, and once more felt frightened by his words, and especially to have said them aloud to a stranger. The fear caused a power surge through his body, adrenaline flowing through his veins in a prehistoric urge to flee the room. He forced his thighs to stay moored in his seat, but scanned the room for the least obstructed path to the door. *If only Daphne had sat beside me! We could have joked our way through this exercise!* Fatima seemed oblivious to his misery.

"That's kind of a coincidence, eh? Your story is about your daughter and mine's about my parents. And you're Indian too, eh?"

"Yes, and Muslim. Like you, guessing from your name?" Ismail asked, fanning his face with some handouts, the wind and the shift in conversation calming him.

"Yeah, my family is."

"You must be close to your parents if you want to write their story." He tried to imagine her as a good blue-haired daughter from a liberal family.

"Not really. There's a lot I don't know about them. Or they about me," she said with a grimace. "But back to your story, why do you want to write about your daughter? Does she know? How old is she?"

James yelled out to everyone to stop, directing them to introduce one another to the rest of the class. Ismail felt as though the merciful hand of God had come down and saved him from Fatima's queries.

Starting with the two thirty-year-olds with the matching laptops, and moving clockwise, the pairs shared their conversations with the rest of the group. Ismail had fully expected this kind of report-back, and planned to take notes about Fatima, but had become distracted and forgot. When it was his turn, he stumbled through Fatima's introduction while she nodded to him encouragingly. She went next and didn't seem to have any difficulty accurately regurgitating everything Ismail said. When she repeated that he planned to write about his daughter, Ismail noticed that Daphne's eyebrows went up in surprise. As his only true confidant, she knew how difficult it was for him to speak about Zubi. Ismail wasn't sure why, but he returned her glance, and simply shrugged his shoulders, wanting to appear casual about the matter.

Once the introductions were complete, James began a lecture on the arc of a story. At the break, Ismail watched Daphne exit the room quickly. He hoped there would be some time before the break ended to chat with her, but when the class resumed, her seat remained conspicuously empty. He watched the door for her return, troubling over what might have made her leave so suddenly. Was something wrong?

Later, James handed out a dated-looking photocopy of a short story. As she took a copy and passed the stack to Ismail, Fatima touched his elbow and said, "I'm really looking

forward to your story." Her dark brown eyes gleamed and he
averted his gaze. He kept his eyes trained on the instructor
for the rest of the class, except for when he futilely looked
over at the doorway, waiting for Daphne to return.

Later that evening, Ismail checked his voice mail and there
was a message from her:

"Hey Ismail. I changed my mind and decided not to take
Busbridge's class. I found it kind of boring, to tell you the
truth. I went to the office during the break and signed up
for the Wednesday Women's Literature class instead because
they just changed the teacher and it's this really cool woman
who writes short stories about lesbian utopias." There was
a pause that confirmed for Ismail that he was little more
than an afterthought to Daphne. "But, hey, you could join
that class too, Ismail. Why don't you sign up? Although, you
might be the only man there. Um ... here are the details."
He didn't listen to the rest, and hung up the phone on her
disembodied voice. A bitter anger rose up in him and he
vowed to quit both the writing class and his friendship with
Daphne. This time he felt deliberately scorned by her; she'd
discarded him as easily as she'd dropped James's class.

That night, Ismail slept fitfully, his mind swimming through
a wash of hectic dreams. In one, he was in James Busbridge's
class, standing at the front of the room, trying to read an
assignment. Sweat dripped off his forehead, onto the page,
first just small drops and then a rainfall that drenched the
paper. In vain, he squinted his eyes, tromboning the page in
and out, and still he couldn't make out the writing.

He looked up to see dream-companions, Rehana and Daphne, in the front row of the classroom, snickering. Behind them, a host of Mary Pinters elbowed one another and rolled their eyes. His dream self was wise enough to turn away, to seek refuge from their derisive looks. When he summoned the courage to peek over his shoulder, the classroom was empty except for Fatima and the widow from across the street, standing at the back. They smiled and beamed admiring looks. Fatima clapped her hands, while the widow yelled, "Bravo, bravo!" Strangely, their applause didn't comfort him, but alarmed him further, and so he ran from the classroom, his footfalls echoing down the long and empty hallways.

FAINT OF HEART

ON A FRIDAY IN mid-February, Toronto had its worst storm of the season. The meteorologists predicted its arrival, and the City had its plows lined up for the onslaught. By noon, City managers had sent emails instructing staff to head home before the roads became dangerous, and by twelve-thirty, everyone had vacated Ismail's floor. At home, he made himself a Patak's leftover lunch and watched the snow wrap itself around the houses on his block.

As he sat at the kitchen table, he recalled how his daughter had been born by Caesarian section after a thirty-two-hour labour during a blizzard in February. The difficulty was that Zubi's umbilical cord had wrapped itself around her little neck, simultaneously holding and choking her. While Rehana's uterus contracted to expel her, Zubi's noose clasped tighter. The young intern monitoring Rehana frowned at Zubeida's falling heart rate and then ordered the Caesarian, rushing her into an operation room. The staff offered Ismail a gown and mask so that he might accompany Rehana during the surgery, but he declined, aware that he'd be no help at all. Rehana still had a capacity to be generous with him, and she bravely waved him off to carry on. Ismail waited alone in the hallway, too scared and squeamish to join Rehana, and even more frightened to be on the outside, worried about the baby not being birthed safely.

Zubeida survived her first brush with death and emerged from her mother and the operating room looking beautiful, flawless, the way Caesarian newborns do. A nurse brought her out to Ismail and placed her into his arms. He held her timidly, both amazed and scared of her fragility, admiring the way her head made a perfect sphere, her eyes, nose, feet, hands, all tiny miracles. He sniffed her hair, gazed at her face, stroked her feet. He slipped his thumb into her hand, and with her eyes scrunched closed, her fingers gripped him, claiming him as her own.

The maternity nurse returned to take her for weighing, and relieved, Ismail passed the delicate bundle back. He'd held his breath the whole time she'd been in his arms. He'd always feared the possibility that he could hurt his little girl in some way.

After Bill Todd told Ismail the police had found Zubi, he crumpled forward, unable to breathe. When he regained consciousness, he felt a sharp pain searing through the middle of him. He clutched himself and gasped, "My chest! My chest!" Bill Todd shouted to a stunned-looking Chitra Malik to call 911, and instructed her to tell them that Ismail was likely having a heart attack. Ismail wanted to close his eyes again, to will his heart to stop beating.

The officer turned him over and exclaimed, "Geez, you're bleeding!" Ismail looked down at his good office shirt and saw a large tear in the middle of his chest. Around it was a spot of red, slowly spreading across the fabric. Bill Todd unfastened Ismail's tie, opened up his shirt and they both spied the source of the bleeding. On his way down to the floor, Ismail had collapsed against the side of his office chair, snagging himself on a sharp piece of metal that had sprung out of the upholstery years ago.

Bill Todd dispatched one of the secretaries from the recently formed throng of bystanders, to find a first aid kit. While they waited for the ambulance to arrive, he pressed some gauze against the small wound and Ismail slowly regained his composure. The bleeding quickly stopped and one of the onlookers was directed to cancel the ambulance call. Ismail felt stupid for all the excitement he caused in the office that day. Most of all, he wanted everyone to go away so that they wouldn't learn about the reason for Bill Todd's visit. He didn't think about Zubi in that moment, about her death; he only wanted to hide the terrible reality from his co-workers.

That was his first panic attack. A sufferer never forgets the first, for the first informs of all the rest that *could* come in the future. And that fear fuels the rest that *do* come. And so on.

And that is how anxiety would become a regular caller to Ismail's life. He thought it a truly perfidious and effective way for his own body to punish him for his sins. During a panic attack, his fear soaked through his shirt, squeezed his lungs of air, and flooded his brain with terrible thoughts. He believed he was going to die, and he welcomed death's sweet liberation. Then the attack would end, he would catch his breath, and realize that he was not dying after all, but that madness had overrun his life.

Once Ismail had recovered enough to get up off the floor, Bill Todd dispersed the crowd and continued with the rest of what he had come to tell him. He spoke softly, kindly, perhaps trying to prevent Ismail from having another fainting spell.

At the morgue, Ismail didn't quite believe Zubi was dead. She looked almost the same as when she was asleep; placid, content. He became consumed with the thought that if he just picked her up, she would startle from her slumber, her eyes rolling open like those plastic Sleepytime dolls.

Then, he would be able to pick her up and soothe her like a good father.

Inky pinky ponky, Zubi had a donkey, donkey died, Zubi cried, inky pinky ponky.

The silly song his mother had sung to him, a child's macabre limerick, was all that filled the vacant spaces of his mind while he stood over her small body.

He reached down for his darling, humming the song to himself and felt his arms being restrained. On one side, was the coroner, and the other was Bill Todd. "Please, Mr. Boxwala, it is time to go," he heard one of them say.

Ismail received a souvenir that day; the gash on his chest created a scar. The scar never healed properly, and became what's called a keloid. It's a shiny, pink overgrowth of skin, a dermatological overreaction. A complicated, incomplete healing.

—

Ismail didn't see the widow again until the morning after the storm. It had come down hard through the night, leaving behind three feet of snow. He'd always hated the season, even after thirty years of residing in Canada, but that day was different. As he shovelled the heavy snow from the sidewalk in front of his house, he watched the widow step out and begin to clear her own walkway. She was wearing her long woollen coat and hat, and he shook his head, wondering whether her bossy daughter had attempted to dress her again. He finished his own walk and crossed the street to help her.

"Thanks very much. It's a lot, isn't it?" She said, speaking with a faint Portuguese intonation and fluency that surprised Ismail. He'd expected her to be like the other Portuguese widows in the neighbourhood; ladies who knew little English and with whom he could only exchange a few words. He snuck a glance at the few inches of leg visible between the hem of her coat and the top of her boots. She smiled at him and he felt a soft flutter in his stomach.

"It's a pleasure. I think we met some time ago, maybe last year? I'm your neighbour from across the street." Ismail said formally, heat rising to his cold face.

"I'm Celia Sousa," she said pleasantly.

"Well, let me help you here."

"What's your name, again?"

"Oh, yes, I forgot to tell you my name!" he said, flustered, "It's Ismail, Ismail Boxwala," he said, and then, automatically held his breath.

Although he'd never been charged, his name remained in the papers for weeks, became emblematic of a tragedy, or homicide, depending on the particular opinion of the story. So often, upon introducing himself, he'd witness a familiar thought process unfurl before him: *Where did I hear that*

name before? a person might say silently or out loud to him.
And then Ismail would recognize an almost imperceptible
flicker in their eyes, the synapses in their brains flashing
double-quick, bringing forth a memory of the man who'd
let his daughter bake to death in the back seat of a car many
years ago. At some point he could expect smiles to turn
down, jaws to tighten.

"Nice to meet you," Celia said, looking up shyly at him,
her chapped lips once again turning up in a slight smile, her
eyes glowing with simple friendliness. And then he shook her
hand, which was already ungloved and extended out to him.

— ✾ —

The sound of metal scraping against pavement distracted
Celia from her reverie. That morning, she'd been crawling
back in time to the day she'd found her late husband dead in
the kitchen. Yes, she'd been doing that again, troubling herself in an endless loop of finding him, trying to revive him,
failing to save him. Her chest would grow heavy, a phantom,
sympathy pain. She'd have to catch her breath and then the
pain would recede, leaving behind a residue of resentment.
With a hand over her breast, she looked out her window to
distract herself. The snow made everything look clean and
tidy again.

Down the street, people were clearing their walks. Lydia
had been nagging Antonio about it all morning. *We could
get sued, you know!* He was busy ignoring her, focused
instead on the hockey game, just like José used to be. He
was a fan of all kinds of sports, spending a good deal of his
free time in front of the idiot box, a glass of Imperial in his
hand. And then in *futebol* season! He was crazed, like most

of the other men in the neighbourhood, drinking at the café, cheering like lunatics in the streets. Celia never could understand what all the fuss was about.

Outside, the Indian neighbour was making good progress with the snow. She doubted he watched sports. She pulled on her coat, grabbed a shovel, and went outside, her departure unnoticed by her family inside. She pushed the shovel along with a light touch, knowing that she would finish the short walk much too quickly if she worked too fast.

She waited for the Indian man to come over, be the gentleman she really didn't need him to be and offer to help her finish her work. She peered his way, watching him struggle to push a pile of snow over the bank that had formed by the side of the road. She decided to rest a moment, closed her eyes, and focused her thoughts. When she opened her eyes again, he was crossing the street, tromping her way.

Up close, his lips reminded her of José's. Her husband was almost as dark at this man, too, but stockier. A short man, he wore his bulk uncomfortably, his heart eventually caving in from its burden. Her body remembered his heaviness, too, his weight on her in the middle of the night, when she found herself awakened by her husband's needy body. Surprisingly, this thought warmed her, and she found herself looking down shyly at her feet. She focused on her neighbour's thick rubber winter boots, footwear that resembled little Marco's.

Her eyes travelled up the man's blue corduroyed legs to his brown jacket, and then back to his thin face. When they finally spoke to one another, she found herself listening to his foreign accent, noticing the flush on his cheeks, the sweat on his brow. He told her that they had met before, but she already knew this. She took his hand, and although the winter air was frosty, it felt warm in hers.

— 14 —

THERAPEUTIC

THE WEEKEND BROUGHT A thaw after Friday's freeze, dangerous conditions for roads, tunnels, and bridges. By Monday there were reports of crumbling infrastructure in neighbouring jurisdictions; a man in New Jersey almost died when a piece of asphalt and a guardrail came down on his windshield. The thought made Ismail somewhat anxious, but also smug. Under his purview, Toronto's bridges continued to be in good shape.

The local media loves the idea of falling-down city structures. His department had already received numerous calls from reporters scoping out information and in an attempt to pre-empt scrutiny, an emergency meeting was held to review their inspection plans. Ismail was charged with leading a team to look at one specific tunnel of concern. Luckily, the cracking at its centre turned out to be superficial, and it needed only minor repairs.

He was on his way to present a verbal report to his harried manager. It took him a few minutes to find the office, because his boss had recently moved to the new, previously abandoned and now refurbished managerial wing. He'd heard people on his floor grumbling that the higher-ups were going to be relocated to roomier offices with fresh paint and carpeting. He hadn't taken part in those water-cooler conversations but had to admit he felt envious of the generous suites he passed along the corridor to his manager's office.

A secretary sat at an ergonomic metal desk, eyeing him sullenly. Behind her, there was an enclosed glass structure that continuously trickled water across its panes. Ismail contemplated whether the waterfall was soothing or irritating, and he guessed from her demeanour that it was the latter. She directed him to wait in an alcove with red pleather chairs and art posters on the walls. She returned to her work and he watched her chew her gum, her jaw rotating clockwise.

As he sat in the slippery chair, a sudden nausea rose up and his sweat glands prickled. He soon realized that he'd sat in that alcove almost two decades ago, waiting for a previous manager, for another reason entirely.

Ismail's old boss, a grandfatherly man and efficient civil servant who later became a city councillor, pushed him to see Dr. Robarts, the city-funded psychotherapist. The less-than-subtle threat that Ismail's job was conditional on his therapy attendance insulted him, but what could he do? His work was all he had left. After Zubi's death, his marriage had lasted only a year, and he fell into what people now refer to, rather casually, as a depression. Back in the early nineties there were no Dr. Phils to expound on commonplace mental-health issues and Ismail had little self-awareness about his symptoms, which his boss listed as: lateness on more than three occasions, general lack of attention to detail, and two missed deadlines.

Of course, his boss was correct about Ismail's "Post Divorce Work Performance." For the first two months after Rehana left, Ismail had difficulty waking up, his sleep constantly interrupted by dreams and nightmares about Zubi. He often slept through his alarm, forty minutes of CBC's *Morningside* blaring from the clock radio beside him. He'd race to work, slipping into meetings mumbling apologetic excuses about bad traffic. Even when he set the clock radio for an hour earlier, he somehow still managed to snooze through Peter Gzowski's radio-host ramblings, which Ismail had to admit he found quite soothing.

At work it was hard to concentrate, his mind easily shifting away from his duties, meeting agendas and the reports he was supposed to write. Colleagues would sometimes find him staring off into space when they dropped by his cubicle.

Dr. Robarts was most interested in Ismail's unconscious mind, encouraging him to recount dreams in which he'd spot his daughter off in the distance, usually across a field, or a city block away. He'd run after her small form, trying to catch up, but she'd remain forever out of reach. All night long he chased after her. These dreams would make Dr. Robarts's brows furrow slightly. Sometimes, the corners of her mouth turned up or down. Once in while she would murmur, "hmmm."

Often, Dr. Robarts employed a technique she called Empathetic Logic, a term she'd coined and was having trademarked.

"It was a human mistake you made. You are human and any human could have made this mistake. Therefore, you should forgive yourself," she'd explain.

One plus two equals three. Ismail felt the logic was beautiful and he thanked her for trying, for assuming his humanity. But he questioned her assumptions: Could any human leave a baby alone in a car on a hot summer day? Leave her to die in the blistering summer heat of a closed-up car parked on a busy Toronto street in mid-August? No, only a terribly flawed human being could do such things, and flawed human beings did not deserve forgiveness, he argued.

At this predictable point in the sessions, Dr. Robarts would remove her glasses, their arms folding in neatly with quiet clicks. She's rub her forehead, stretching out the thin, pale skin between her eyebrows. She'd glance wearily at the clock. In the remaining few minutes, she'd tiredly reiterate her challenges to Ismail's self-blame, while he listened to her as though he were an obedient pupil. He figured that when she gazed at him across the glass-topped coffee table, her temporarily uncorrected myopia somehow made him appear more agreeable.

"Shall we review, Ismail?" She pronounced his name *Is-male*, and Ismail thought this was a Freudian slip for a Jungian. "You were exhausted after many months of interrupted sleep. You were off your usual routine because you usually dropped Zubeida at the daycare and then Rehana at work and then you'd head to work. These were the conditions that led up to your human mistake. You missed a step," she concluded.

He tried to see himself through his therapist's sympathetic lens, as the ordinary man who woke up, drank his Orange Pekoe, buckled his daughter into her car seat, dropped his wife at work, all while listening to CBC Radio. This man then parked on a side street, grabbed his briefcase from the passenger seat and rushed into work. He went about his normal routine that day, like any other day. Except that he missed a step.

After nearly a year in her office, Ismail was sure he'd worn the poor woman down with his constant self-flagellation. One day, during her bifocal-removing, temple-massaging routine, she gently suggested that he take a break, take stock, consider other ways to forgive himself.

"Ismail, I don't think this is the way you are going to reach a resolution. Perhaps you should consider your goals for therapy, take some time off, and see if there is another path for you."

She fired him, and he didn't blame her.

He later borrowed a book from the library called *The Self Forgiveness Journey*. It said that one could imagine the process as a long road ahead of oneself. At times the surface would be smooth, and at other moments, bumpy with reproach. He supposed his gravel-covered road of self-forgiveness was marred by potholes of his own making.

At least he had Rehana's forgiveness, more or less. As they left the cemetery, she dried her tears and said, "Ismail, I forgive you. You did not do this on purpose. You never would have hurt her." Her words were like pure oxygen and he breathed them in gratefully. Later, he wagered that for her to forgive him, she had to hold herself responsible. He thinks she cursed herself for marrying him, for giving him a daughter he would later kill. For asking that the routine be changed that day. For trusting him with the simple of task of driving their daughter to daycare and for not checking in with him later. In truth, Ismail didn't know if his perceptions were accurate, because the couple hadn't spoken about it since Zubi's funeral; she'd refused to speak of it again.

Silence began to pervade their Lochrie Street house like a toxic gas, making it difficult for them to breathe in one another's presence. They choked on their own unexpressed words.

— ❋ —

Celia stood outside Marco's preschool class with the other mothers and grandmothers, waiting for the bell to ring. A couple of the other Lochrie widows had taken her under their wing during these pickups, welcoming her and making introductions to the others. She was appreciative of their company, for she hadn't seen much of her old friends. After José and her mother died, they came to her with condolences and casseroles, but were less sympathetic about her husband's gambling. They told self-glorious fictions about how they kept their own husbands and children in line and offered her abundant advice on how to successfully maintain order once she reached her daughter's home. Celia thought that maybe this was easier for them than having to step into her shoes, having to imagine bearing such betrayal and loss themselves. Eventually, she stopped picking up the phone or answering the door, and now there were too many stale calls between she and her old friends. She attended church less often to avoid their sad glances and inquiries. It was only seven city blocks that separated Celia from her friends, but it felt like a hundred miles. With the Lochrie widows, she could almost start anew. With them, she didn't have to be the naive, misled wife. Instead, she could just be a loyal, grieving widow.

— ❊ —

It wasn't like Celia never suspected that José could be involved in dubious dealings — she wasn't a stupid woman. She knew to be concerned when he came home late from the café. She made tearful accusations of his infidelity and, once or twice, checked his pockets, and asked discreet questions of his buddies for clues of dishonesty. But his clothing and his reputation always remained clean.

Perhaps if she'd only asked the right questions, or looked at their chequing-account statements, things would have turned out differently. He might not have sunk them so deeply into debt. He wouldn't have been under so much stress. Perhaps a heart attack could have been averted. They could have kept the house. *If only.*

The school bell rang and she watched as one by one the children ran out to greet the women who would take them home. Marco came to the door and searched for her in the small gathering, his eyes scanning left to right, down the line of women in black. She waved to him, her fluttering hand distinguishing her from the rest. Their eyes met, and he flung himself at her.

THREE GOOD DAYS

ISMAIL WAS ON HIS lunch break, buying a hot dog from a street vendor. Behind him in line, were two sets of mothers with young children strapped into their strollers. The mothers talked to one another about a movie they'd recently watched, one that starred Angelina Jolie. One of children, a boy perhaps, was fast asleep, while the other one kicked her pink Wellington boots up in the air, her heels slamming up against the stroller's footrest. With the next jerk of her leg, she punted Ismail in his calf. He inched forward in the line.

Toddlers are a whole species unto their own. They are adorable and loud, drawing attention to themselves, celebrating their recent emancipation from the confines of babyhood. They run with nearly coordinated limbs, finding ample opportunities to raise sharp-shrill voices with just-acquired words.

Ismail began noticing them after Zubi was born, but felt bombarded by them after her death. It seemed as though they'd call out to him in the mall food court, in the lobby at work, from strollers at the park; a perpetual reminder of what was lost. Usually, he kept his gaze averted when they passed by, his eyes studying shop windows, or salt stains on his winter boots.

In moments when Ismail was less guarded, when he didn't manage to look away, he found himself staring too long, lid-locked. Faces would shift before him, blue eyes turning brown, white skin darkening, boy children morphing into girls.

He quickly paid for his hot dog, kept his head down, and didn't bother to squeeze out a red line of ketchup for fear it would take too long. He rushed back to his office.

Bill Todd allowed Ismail to call Rehana from the station. He was led to an old metal desk which held nothing but a phone, the Yellow Pages, and a blunt pencil. Ismail thought it appropriate that there were no scissors, or staplers, or mail openers available to criminals and madmen. He got Rehana's voice mail. He gasped into the receiver, unable to find words for what he had to say. Bill Todd leaned over and coached, "Tell her to meet you at fifty-two division." He passed Ismail a card so that he could give her the address. Ismail didn't know why Bill Todd would treat a killer so nicely. It made his eyes well up, and as soon as he hung up the phone, he turned away from the officer to hide his tears.

Ismail watched the clock, waiting for Rehana to arrive. It was the same type of bulk-order, institutional clock they used at City offices, with a stern face and silver rim. Twenty-five minutes passed, the second hand moving slower than his heartbeats. She entered the police station, her hair loose around her shoulders, bobby pins having long lost their grasp. Ismail tapped on the glass wall that separated the offices from the waiting area and her eyes travelled to where he was. Relief replaced the apprehension marking her face. For a brief moment that would never again be repeated, his presence provided reassurance.

He stood up to meet her, but Bill Todd restrained him, guided him back to his seat.

"Please wait here. Is that your wife? I'll go out to see her." Ismail helplessly watched as the officer strode out to meet Rehana, his thick body forming a barrier between the couple.

"Toddler Dies in Heat of Car, Charges Being Considered."

"Expert Says: Sleep Deprivation Caused Parental Neglect."

"Investigation Reveals that Father Left Baby in Car for over 3 hours."

"Horrible Tragedy Should Not Be Viewed a Homicide."

Ismail read the headlines, watched the news, listened to every radio report he could find in the days following his daughter's death.

"Turn it off! I can't take it anymore," Rehana screamed, shortly after the funeral. Ismail complied, switched off the television and crossed the living room to hold his wife. She stood rigidly in his arms, her hands at her sides.

"I'm going to bed," she said and he felt her arms finally reaching up, but only to break from his hold. She hurried up the stairs, her back curled into a stoop. There was the sound of a toilet flushing, water running, a door opening, and another closing.

—

Three months later, Rehana declared that she wanted another baby. Ismail was uncertain about the timing, but acquiesced, as he knew he must; he was aware that he was not entitled to an opinion on the matter.

And so the couple set out to *work* at having another baby. He learned that most women have just three good days in which to be impregnated, a piece of women's fertility information he never needed to know before then. Rehana bought a special thermometer, and they opted to strengthen Ismail's sperm count by abstaining on all other days except when Rehana was ovulating. Not that abstinence was difficult; after Zubi's death, they were both too physically drained and emotionally distant from one another to be interested in each other that way.

On those few precious nights of fertility, Rehana waited for Ismail in the bedroom while he nervously stalled in the bathroom, examining his face in the mirror, searching his conscience for an answer to his endless moral questions on the matter of having another child. He secretly hoped that Rehana would fall asleep waiting for him.

She'd called out, "*Chalo*, Ismail, what are you doing in there? You know I'm ovulating!" He cringed at the thought that the quarrelsome couple next door might be listening through the thin, shared walls. Since they had heard about Zubi, those neighbours seemed to bicker less, and Ismail believed their quiet life could only mean that they were united in spying on the Boxwalas.

Again a loud yell from the bedroom: "Are you coming?"

Ismail yelled back, "Just be a few minutes." Sweat, a constant in his life at that time, seeped through his pajamas. He took a shower, hoping to buy himself a little more time. He prayed the sound of trickling water would lull his wife to sleep.

—

Of course, Ismail understood why Rehana wanted to try for another baby so soon. They both harboured the hope that a new child would ease the pain of Zubi's absence, a new life distracting them from her death. A baby would facilitate their moving on, placing the tragedy firmly behind them, downwind, allowing them to breathe fresh air again.

Support for this project came from all sides; both sets of parents sent air-mailed letters, chock-full of advice informed by previous generations who'd lost children within their first year. One embarrassing blue envelope from Ismail's mother contained drink recipes to increase a man's potency.

"Juice for your juice!" Rehana guffawed, while Ismail winced in embarrassment. Of course, the advice was far less amusing to her when her mother visited that year and began to focus her energies on her daughter's ovaries. She chided Rehana for being "as thin as a servant" and tried to fatten her up with *badam halwa* and bowls of creamy *shrikhand* to fortify her womb.

Even more intolerable to Ismail and Rehana were the dinners with Rehana's sister, Zahra, and brother-in-law, Hussain, who were intent on helping the pair recover.

"So are the two of you doing okay these days?" Hussain would ask, eyebrows raised.

"Yes, we're fine," would be Rehana's answer.

"Good, but you know, it is all right to talk about it," Zahra would broach.

"We're fine," Ismail repeated. There would be another full round of this before both couples could sit back, break into gendered pairs, and discuss more inane subjects.

Once, Zahra and Hussein invited dinner guests that Ismail and Rehana hadn't met before: a couple whose six-year-old had died of leukemia earlier that year. Although never explicitly stated, all parties involved understood that Zahra and Hussein were playing matchmaker for bereaved parents. The Boxwalas and the other couple carefully avoided any conversations about children, or death or disease, in an unspoken pact against Zahra and Hussein's scheming.

With their tendency to shy away from contentious or emotionally uncomfortable topics, Nabil and Nabila were far easier company. They wanted to be helpful and so they simply behaved as though everything were normal. And since normal was still a long shot for Ismail and Rehana, they found the pretense calming.

Back home, alone in their bed, Ismail grew terrified of the possibility of making another fatal mistake with a second child, and this fear brought with it a powerful impotence. Under the sheets in their dark bedroom, the couple bumped up against one another like uncoordinated teenagers, knocking elbows against hips and shoulders against chests, the new awkwardness like a foreign invader annexing their bed. Rehana toiled to arouse Ismail while he struggled to maintain interest.

Ismail never could tell if Rehana was aroused herself, but it didn't seem to matter to her. He, or rather his limp, uncooperative penis, was the sole focus on those embarrassing nights. Eventually, sleepy and frustrated, she would give up, smile wanly and say it was all right, while Ismail apologized and silently pleaded with God to either let him die or permit Rehana to give up and leave him.

But Rehana persevered against Ismail's problem, battling against his impotence as though it were her worst enemy.

She pressured him to see his family doctor and then made appointments with two different, but well-recommended, specialists in the field of male problems. The first, a popular older doctor, had a waiting room full of shame-faced men like Ismail, who hid behind withered copies of *Time* and *National Geographic*. After an hour's wait, the physician ordered a set of tests that duplicated those done by the family doctor, and then upon follow-up, scratched his head and apologetically told the Boxwalas that he couldn't find anything wrong with Ismail's health.

The second doctor, who was punctual and had an empty waiting area, also reassured Ismail that he was fine, slapped him on the back, and counselled the couple to keep trying. On the way out of the office, he offhandedly shared with them the bit of wisdom everyone had offered, "You know Mr. and Mrs. Boxwala, the best thing you can do to recover from a child's death is to have another one." Ismail and Rehana smiled tensely as they hurried out of the office; they hadn't mentioned Zubi to that doctor, and realized that her death had been recorded somewhere in Ismail's medical file. They worried about how this information had been written up and in what level of detail. By that point, they had learned it was best to remain vague, allowing people who hadn't already heard about them, to make assumptions about Sudden Infant Death Syndrome, and other childhood illnesses.

When they got into the car, Rehana scrounged around in her purse and placed a glossy brochure in Ismail's hand. He'd seen it in the racks of both specialists' waiting rooms, but had been much too self-conscious to pick one up. He shoved it deep into his coat pocket and started the car. They drove home, both of them in a hopeless funk.

Later, Ismail locked himself in the bathroom to study the brochure in private. On the front cover, large yellow letters flashed:

ERECTILE DYSFUNCTION (ED)
AND IMPOTENCE

He sat down heavily on the edge of the tub, then got up, checked the lock on the door, and sat again. He looked at the image on the brochure's front, a photo of a blissful-looking white couple walking hand in hand on a beach. He closed his eyes, imagining Rehana and he on that beach, their fingers interlaced, the two of them happy again.

Zubi squealed as Ismail held her forearms, letting her bare feet dip into the surf. It was a trip they'd all taken together: four adults, three children, and an overstuffed cooler, packed into Nabil's station wagon. Ismail felt close to Nabil that day; they were two proud brothers with their young families on a day trip to Wasaga Beach. Altaf was almost five and had just started swimming lessons while Asghar was turning three. They both stayed in the shallow water, testing out the lake with orange water wings strapped to skinny arms.

Zubi wasn't yet old enough for swimming, but Rehana had dressed her in a green polka-dot bathing suit that the women oohed and aahed over. She tottered around in the sand, picking up tiny fistfuls and then flinging the grains back into the water. It was a month before she died.

—

Ismail opened his eyes, Wasaga Beach disappearing. He spread open the pamphlet and read:

> Erectile dysfunction (ED), or "impotence," is the ongoing lack of ability to attain or maintain an erection that is stiff enough to engage in sexual intercourse. Impotence may also refer to difficulties such as severely reduced or limited libido, ejaculation or orgasm.

Ismail's buttocks were numb from sitting on the hard porcelain. He readjusted, crossed his left leg over his right, noticing his reflection in the full-length mirror that hung on the bathroom door. He uncrossed his legs, and sat more like a man.

He skimmed the section on "Causes of Erectile Dysfunction," long paragraphs about ED and vascular disease, diabetes, and aging. Finally, at the very bottom of the last page was a single line that seemed to apply to him:

> Although little is known about psychological causes of ED, it is believed that stress and other psychological causes may play a part in some cases of impotence.

He concluded that he was among the stressed, nervous, or crazy men who could not get it up. He turned over the brochure, seeking more information about psychological issues and treatment, but no relief was to be found there. He reread the material twice more. Then, he tossed the brochure into the dustbin.

—

Since the problem was only in Ismail's head, the couple redoubled their efforts. He came to dread those "three good days" each month, and a once-pleasurable activity turned into a gruelling and humiliating chore. Rarely could he achieve an erection, and if he did, it didn't last long enough to matter. After nine months of this tiresome routine, Rehana finally gave up.

She was generally a patient woman who took her time to arrive at important decisions. The couple had a two-year engagement so that she could be sure about marrying him. She considered emigration from India for many months, doing research and speaking to countless relatives about the matter. It somehow made perfect sense to Ismail that she conceived, gestated, and birthed the idea of a divorce in about the same amount of time it would have taken to have another baby.

Psychology is a mysterious thing. Once the divorce was finalized, Ismail's ED problem cured itself, in an ironic sort of way; suddenly, erections appeared spontaneously, and were terribly timed. They were also freakishly frequent, as though his penis had to make up for all that "dead" time. He'd have to excuse himself from meetings, a file folder or binder his camouflage as he found the nearest exit.

It seemed almost anything could trigger the condition. The outline of a colleague's bottom through a tight skirt, a momentary glance at cleavage while on the bus, a kissing scene on television. Ismail was thoroughly embarrassed when once he didn't change channels quickly enough while watching a documentary about male bodybuilders. At times, the cues were more innocuous and he couldn't understand how a city development meeting or a chore like laundry could have a similar libidinous impact on him.

The staff bathroom became an oasis in which he found limited succor and privacy. He'd try to calm himself in the stall farthest from the door, willing away the throbbing stiffness by visualizing the most unstimulating things; he took his mind on excursions into his project files, traveling through tedious details about curb heights and traffic volume on residential boulevards. He wouldn't have wanted to admit it, but sometimes images of his mother in Mumbai, or her frumpy sisters in Ahmedabad, sprung to mind. Imagining the taste and smell of North American food, which at the time he was still unaccustomed to, was also a useful strategy.

Most of the time these tactics worked, but unfortunately there were moments when Ismail's mind turned traitor, finding reckless enticement in negative fantasizing; lewd acts inserted themselves into highway diagrams or plates of open-faced hot turkey sandwiches. Once or twice, an old aunty's saggy breasts revealed themselves when he least wanted them to.

Every now and then, there wasn't enough time for lengthy de-arousing meditations. In those moments, he would have to listen for the bathroom to empty, and then, as quietly as possible, he'd shamefully permit his gluttonous body to be satiated. He didn't even consider looking for a lover. There was something about the entire experience that gave it the feeling of a penance to be suffered alone.

He pondered the larger meanings behind the problem. Had he let Rehana go too easily? He considered calling her to tell her that his problem was resolved, thinking she might return if she knew. Ismail sat by the telephone, Rehana's new number memorized, dialing the first three digits, then the fourth, and hanging up. Once he completed the entire seven and was relieved when she wasn't home. Ismail knew he wasn't in control of his spontaneous erections any more than he was in control of the impotence. He predicted it would only be another disgrace he wouldn't be able to hide from her.

Anyway, he couldn't allow Rehana to be dragged back into his life — setting her free was something he owed her. Besides, he didn't want to face a second scrape of rejection; he'd heard from Nabil, who heard through Nabila's grapevine, that Rehana was heading to India for an arranged marriage. Despite her age and divorceé status, she was marriageable enough with her Canadian citizenship and lack of children.

In the end, Ismail shook off his desire to telephone her, eventually forgot her number, and allowed her to go on without him. Over the years he heard snippets of gossip about her and learned that she did quite well for herself. She married an entrepreneur who grew wealthy in the auto parts business. Within a few years of their marriage, he gave her two more children (a boy and a girl), and a sprawling home in the suburbs of Windsor. They'd never have the occasion to see one another again, Rehana and Ismail.

— ❈ —

Celia and Marco stepped into the warm house, snow puddling onto the foyer's tile floor. She began the process of freeing him from his outer layers. First, she unwound the long scarf, turning him round and round until his flushed face emerged and he was giggling with dizziness. His hood slipped off sweaty hair and wet mitts were laid over the heating vent. She bent down, unzipped his blue snowsuit,

and he leaned on her shoulders to step out. Like a prisoner liberated from restraints, he did a jig around the foyer,
shaking his arms and legs, singing an ode to his next meal,
"Lunchtime, lunchtime, yaaaay lunch!"

"Okay, okay," she muttered, irritability meeting his joy.

She prepared them each a sandwich and nibbled at hers
while he chomped ravenously through his. He was having
a growth spurt, filling out around his middle and stretching up an inch in the last month, while she was gradually
shrinking. Her housedresses were looking baggier than
usual and last week she'd had to safety-pin the waist of her
Sunday skirt so it wouldn't slip off in church. This morning
after her shower, she glimpsed the changes in the bathroom
mirror: narrowing hips, flattening stomach, new lines etch-
ing themselves beneath skin. It was like she had a teenager's
body, only without the energy of youth. Surprisingly, her
breasts were as ample as they'd always been. As she cupped
one in her palm while putting on her bra, it felt like a useless
appendage she no longer wanted to carry.

Marco rose from the table and ran to the living room.
She called after him to wash his hands, and, like a wind-up
toy in reverse, he zipped into the powder room. She heard
the water go on. "Use soap! *Sabão!*" She had a habit of speaking to him in a Portuguese-English blend and sometimes
feared it might be confusing for the boy to hear English and
Italian and Portuguese all in the same house. But she supposed it was alright; she managed Portuguese at home with
her family and English in school. She even picked up some
French along the way. Her brain figured it all out.

The water stopped and Marco raced back into the living
room and switched on the television. She sat down on the
couch beside him, heavy in her vanishing body.

— 16 —

HOMEWORK

ISMAIL CLEARED OFF HIS desk at home, and piled under a stack of newspapers, were the notes and handouts collected during that first writing class almost two weeks earlier. He scanned the sheets, admiring the level of detail in his note-taking. There were three pages of description about the arc of a story, reminders of important dates and scratched in the left-hand margin was a little box with the words: *Fatima. Writing about her family's immigration.* He wasn't sure why he'd written that down, but perhaps he'd felt at the time that it was something to remember.

On the next page was a detailed description of the week's writing homework, which was to describe his story's main character. PROTAGONIST, he'd inscribed in his notebook, all in capital letters as James had done on the board. The assignment was to create a physical and psychological depiction that would guide them in their story's development. The following words were circled in red pen: GESTURES, INTERNAL STRUGGLE, CONFLICT TO BE RESOLVED, AND HABITS. At the bottom of the second page, was a reiteration of the word PROTAGONIST, and three consecutive question marks. Although he'd blurted "my daughter" when Fatima asked him what he wanted to write about, he wasn't completely sure at the time whether she should be the main character of his story.

He gathered up the papers into one meagre handful and took them downstairs to deposit in the recycling bin — he had already missed the second class, and had no intention of returning. But before he could get to the blue bin on the porch, something stopped him. Perhaps it was a sense of challenge, boredom, or curiosity, but instead of throwing the sheets away, he left them on the kitchen table.

An hour later, he brought his laptop down to the kitchen, untangled its cord, and plugged it in. He ignored the one hundred and seventeen emails waiting for him — he was not much of a computer person at home. He opened up a blank document. The black cursor blinked expectantly against a white background. He stared at it for awhile, waiting for something to happen.

He opened *Creative Writing for Idiots*, which he'd recently borrowed from the library. A skim of its first chapter provided some reassurance. He recalled how much he'd enjoyed writing as a young person, and how he thought it would be worth a try to re-establish the hobby. He considered how he'd already paid the creative writing class's non-refundable fee.

He typed: Protagonist. He centred the word, bolded, and underlined it. He changed the font from the default eleven point Times to a more forgiving Arial twelve. He widened the margins, inserted a page number in the footer, and, as an afterthought, included the date in the header.

Then he decided it was time to turn on the kettle. He ogled the tea bag as it soaked languorously in the hot water, its leaves leaking brown into the clear. While adding heaping spoons of sugar and condensed milk, he glanced over at the blank screen as though half-expecting it to have magically populated itself with words while he wasn't looking. He burned his tongue taking a first sip of the tea. And then the shortbread biscuits, so provocative in their red box, lured him with buttery charms. The computer waited like a wallflower.

While he munched the cookies, he chided himself for his misguided desire to spend more time with Daphne, via the writing class. He took another gulp of tea, this time burning the roof of his mouth and a momentary fit of vengeance overcame him. Perhaps he'd send Daphne a bill for the course registration, or maybe a bitter-sounding letter. How would he word it, though? He put fingers to keys, but his mind remained blank. He ate another cookie.

Then his real desire for signing up for the course — the true motivation — came to mind. He'd been envious of Daphne's positive changes, her sober and positive thinking. She'd seemed to procure for herself a sort of fresh start, complete with pastel yellow dresses that exposed bare knees in the grey of winter. The promise of getting over his terrible past, just as she'd been able to do, was what Ismail coveted. He abandoned the tea and biscuits and returned to the computer.

Ismail closed his eyes, breathed deeply, and willed the memories forward. He listened to his restless breathing for over a minute and waited. Then, they stepped forward slowly at first, tottering forward with reluctance, like a child just learning to walk.

—

On the morning of her death, Ismail put Zubi in her car seat, strapping her into the complicated array of belts that always confused him. He shut the door and watched Zubi reach for the "Baby on Board" sign hanging on the window to her right. She grabbed the bright yellow diamond, testing the suction cup that held it in place.

Rehana had dressed Zubi in a light pink summer dress and tiny red sandals. She snapped two yellow butterfly-shaped barrettes in her hair. The daycare's air conditioning had been malfunctioning that week, so Rehana made sure to dress Zubi in clothes that would keep her cool.

Ismail's next memory was at the morgue. She was still clothed in the cotton dress and sandals, but one of her barrettes was missing. He found it later on the back seat of the car, a single hair stuck into its clasp. He imagined her yanking at it while she cried out in distress for her mother to come and take her home. Eventually, as the car grew hotter than any kind of hell Ismail could imagine, the barrette fell to the floor.

He only had a minute or two with her at the morgue. After that, his memories of her came to a full stop.

For some time, Ismail kept that barrette with him, in his pocket, or briefcase, like a kind of talisman. He'd take it out sometimes to look at, imagining he could still smell the scent of her baby shampoo. Later, when he bought a new car, he placed it in the glove compartment, a keepsake and a reminder of an old love and an enduring mistake.

While Ismail slumped at the kitchen table, the barrette left his mind and other memories took their place in the queue, jostling noisily to be seen and heard: the police investigation, the funeral, the marriage breakdown. They rushed forward in quick staccato flashes; Bill Todd's blue eyes, the *imam* saying a few prayers on a sweltering August day, Rehana's brother-in-law loading her suitcases into the boot of his Ford. These were all things Ismail knew well and were not what he wanted to write. These things had nothing to do with Zubi.

What was evading him was Zubi's *life*, the time before. He rubbed his closed eyes, trying to massage out a mental picture of something earlier, something of her playing, or eating, or her living. What were her favourite songs? Her best-loved toy? Ismail couldn't come up with any GESTURES, INTERNAL STRUGGLES, CONFLICTS TO BE RESOLVED, AND HABITS. After so many years, it was hopelessly difficult to remember her brief eighteen months of life. He focused on physical description. What shade of brown were her eyes? He became paralyzed with the unbearable thought that he could — and had already started — to forget her.

And so he began to type, hesitantly at first, his fingers tapping out a few letters at a time, followed by an insistent reach for the backspace key. Then, gaining momentum, words skittered over the screen, paragraphs colonizing blank spaces. He furtively wrote a fiction of a baby who became a toddler, who grew to be a preschooler, a young child, an adolescent, and then a young adult. Ismail wasn't able to parent the real child, but he could grow another, make-believe, child in his head. She was beautiful, and made friends easily, like Rehana. Although she had many male admirers, she was wise enough to hold off until she was older for a serious relationship. She studied engineering in university. He filled five pages of fantasy and then, disgusted, closed the document without saving it. He had an urge to throw the laptop across the room, smash it with bare hands. Instead, he forced himself into stillness, holding his head, breathing fast. He lamented that Zubi, his dear Zubeida, would forever be missing from his story just as she had been missing from her own.

And this is what finally allowed Ismail to cry. It wasn't his usual regret and crusted-over self-loathing. It was sadness, for Zubi, for Rehana, for himself. True sorrow, for what hadn't been and what wasn't going to be. Before this, there hadn't before been any room for Ismail and sadness to cohabitate, for he'd always believed it was a luxury, a privilege he didn't deserve. Since he built the oven in which she burned, and sent her to her death, he felt everyone else could be sad. But not him.

But there it was. And he took it, accepted it for himself, for the first time. Finally.

There was nothing else to do but to weep and there was no stopping it even if Ismail had wanted to. The tears took him over, forcing their way forward and he bobbed in their waves, holding onto the edge of the table so he wouldn't be pulled under. He sobbed tears that had waited patiently, almost two decades, to arrive. He crumpled over the computer and cried until his chest hurt and his throat was sore.

Eventually, Ismail raised his head to see that afternoon's light had softened into evening's dusk. He listened to the quiet around him. It might have been a relief to hear the ladies on his street yelling across their gardens to one another, or calming to listen to the drone of his neighbour's television through the thin walls. But all was silent that day, and Ismail was left there in the hush, all alone. The noisy memories had left the building for the moment, too, and without them careening and screeching through empty rooms, his home was a vacant frame.

And then the doorbell rang.

— ❊ —

From the living room, Celia could hear them bickering. She strained her neck to peer over the top of the couch and saw Lydia and Antonio sitting at the dining room table. Lydia held a calculator and sifted through a mess of receipts while Antonio glanced at a magazine. Celia listened awhile and although the couple's quarrel was fairly circular, she was able to ascertain the crux of the matter: money.

Lydia wanted more money to go to Marco's education fund, while Antonio was resolute about the need for a new car. Celia judged them for their lack of compromise. *Buy a cheaper car and put a little more in the fund. What's the problem?*

She and José used to have money arguments in the early days of their marriage, each digging heels into the shag carpet of their bedroom. She could barely remember what they fought about now. As time passed, they argued less, their wisdom leading them away from the need to be right or to have their own way. *But was that it, really?* The convenient explanation made the skin on her lower back itch. She scratched and reconsidered things; in time, she and her husband learned to avoid the issues that made them tense, she distracting herself with one chore or another while José went out to God-knows-where. Now she knew where he disappeared to. Now she wished they argued more about money. *Boy, could I ever use a good argument with you now, you lying bastard.*

The sound of Lydia's chair chafing against linoleum shook Celia from her thoughts. She watched her daughter cross the living room to the foyer and deposit an envelope on the front hall table. She muttered, loud enough for Celia to hear, "This is for number 82, not us. The mailman needs to pay better attention to his sorting."

"Babe, just look at this model," Antonio said, pointing to a glossy photo in his magazine, "If we go cheaper on the car, we'll just end up regretting it later. We won't find this deal again." Lydia glanced over at her mother, who was pretending to mind her own business, and released a dramatic-sounding sigh, before returning to her argument with her husband.

Like a thief, Celia crept to the foyer. She picked up the envelope, carried it with her to her bedroom-den, holding it tightly to her chest. She shut the door and fingered its sharp edges. She read his name and address: Mr. I. Boxwala, 82 Lochrie Street, Toronto, Ontario, M6K 2B1. She balanced the weight of it in her palm, sniffed the address label's dried ink. While holding it up to the light, she saw it was a credit card bill or donation solicitation, nothing so interesting. She allowed it to rest on her lap.

Her eyelids grew heavy. Her lungs flooded with something dark and burdensome and her eyes welled with tears. She sighed, put the envelope on her bed and reached for the tissue box. By now, a widow for over a year, she was used to this force rising up in her, was well acquainted with its spontaneous and pushy nature. She expected her tears to flow without any prodding at all, and, knowing there was nothing she could do to stop them, she waited for the storm to pass.

She wiped her eyes with a tissue, took a deep breath, recovered a little. She picked up the envelope again. Once more, her eyes became wet, and her breath caught in her chest. She dropped the letter and the sadness released her from its hold. She picked it up again, dropped it, picked it up. The tears started and stopped twice more, like a faucet turning itself on and off. She frowned at the letter, pushing it farther away from her on the bed.

No, it couldn't be. Really, it was just a plain white envelope, a stamp, an address! She reviewed all the things that usually made her sad: *Mãe? Could it be José? Was she missing her old house?* None of these called out to her.

She looked out her bedroom window, scanned the empty street, and saw a light on at Ismail's house. She hastily found a sweater and, not wanting to go back to the front door and be questioned by her daughter, she snatched up the first pair of boots she found in her armoire. They were from her pre-widow days, an impulse-buy from a spring sale a few years ago. She fingered the soft leather as she pulled them on, admiring their contrast against her black tights.

She crept out the side door, closing it quietly behind her, and, in long, determined strides, she crossed the street to number 82. She marched up the steps, and rang the doorbell. Then, she stood on his porch, and waited.

— ❋ —

Often, Ismail didn't answer his phone and sometimes ignored the doorbell. Those who interrupted his privacy were likely to be telemarketers, Greenpeace canvassers, or door-to-door evangelists, anyway. On Hallowe'en, he turned out the lights and went upstairs before the children could come begging for candy. And so, at first, he remained in his chair, expecting whoever-it-was to go away. But the doorbell didn't stop, its melody playing over and over, like a manic organ grinder.

Ding-dong-ding-ding, ding-dong-ding-ding, ding-dong-ding-ding, ding-dong-ding-ding.

He assumed his caller was leaning on the button, and he grew irritated, and then infuriated with their gall. He rushed to the door, wiping his damp face and runny nose with his sleeve. After some fumbling with the lock, it swung open, and there stood the widow, smiling up at him. The doorbell played on. She clutched a white envelope with both hands.

"Sorry to bother you ... I think this is your mail," she said. *Ding-dong-ding-ding*, the bell continued.

"Wait a minute. It's stuck," Ismail said, leaning out and poking the doorbell button with his thumb. Mercifully, its noise stopped. "Excuse me, what were you saying?"

"Um ... the postman, he delivered it to number 81, my daughter's house, but it should have some to you, 82 ... this is you, yes?" She said tentatively, holding up the letter for him to see. Her soft voice seemed to echo in his silent foyer, and her face was like a bright beacon against his dark mood. He studied her features, her olive skin, the crows' feet around her dark eyes. It was a strange thought to have then, but he imagined what she might look like in Indian clothing instead of her widow's frock. Mentally redressing her, he pulled a green *kameez* over her head, the colour bringing out the luminescence in her amber eyes. He looped a yellow *dupatta* around her shoulders and head, a golden halo that covered her greying hair.

Ismail smiled stupidly at her. She thrust the letter into his hands. The *kameez* and *dupatta* fell away, leaving only her dull widow's garb. He took the envelope and they both stood there a moment, two awkward strangers.

"Well, thank you for this — Celia, right?" He stumbled, not knowing why he asked. He already knew her name, and without knowing why, had repeated it to himself many times since they'd last met. He liked the double "s" sounds her given name and surname made when spoken together.

"Yes, that's it. Celia Sousa."

"Yes, I remember your last name, too," Ismail said, almost defensively. She shivered in the night air. He hadn't noticed the cold until then.

"OK ... good night then," she said, her halting rhythm betraying her words. With a warming around his collar, Ismail realized that perhaps she didn't want to leave so soon.

"I do appreciate you bringing this over," he attempted, knowing his words were not quite right. His mouth gaped open, wishing for more syllables, but his brain was too sluggish to respond in time. Celia turned slowly and crestfallen, Ismail watched the black angel cross the street to her house. She looked back at him just before she closed her door behind her, and he managed a wave. She waved back, and that's when he noticed them. Her boots were purplish red, the colour of a fine shiraz. He cursed himself for not asking her in.

— ❋ —

Celia glanced over her shoulder, and saw his hand raised in a wave. His cheerless expression strained towards friendliness. Having noticed his grayish pallor and soggy collar, she wondered what the matter was with him.

When she entered the house, she found Lydia sitting on the bottom two steps of the staircase, resembling a mother awaiting her tardy teenage daughter's return.

"*Mãe*, you went out? Where'd you go?" she asked.

"Just across the street to give Ismail his letter," she said casually, bending over, unzipping her boots.

"His letter?" Maria asked, observing her mother's dressy boots.

"Yes, the one the mailman delivered here by accident. I heard you tell Antonio about it. I thought I'd be helpful and take it over. You two seemed busy." Celia shrugged off her sweater.

"Oh right. Thanks. So ... you know his name?"

"Yes, I know his name," she answered, guardedly.

"I always forget it when I see him. What's it again?"

"Ismail. Ismail Boxwala." Celia locked and chained the door behind her.

"Funny surname. How'd you find out his last name, too?"

"We've said hello once or twice on the street. Besides," she sniffed, now defensive, "it was on the envelope."

"Huh." Lydia exhaled, looking intently at her mother.

"What? What's that look mean?" Celia asked, her face growing red.

"Oh nothing. I'm not giving you a look ... I was just thinking that I like those boots," she said, with a faint smile.

"Yes, they are nice," Celia said, relaxing a little. "Nice, soft leather. I found them on sale years ago, at Dufferin Mall."

"You haven't worn them for while. Not since ..."

"No, not since ..."

Each completed the sentence in her own mind, grief clouding over the foyer and settling on their soft shoulders. Lydia almost said good night then, almost went upstairs to watch *Law and Order SVU*. Celia almost walked past her daughter to return to her bedroom-den where she might have crawled under her covers for the rest of the night.

"So you've chatted with him, on the street," Lydia ventured.

"Hmm?" Celia asked, her husband still on her mind.

"Ismail. The neighbour-guy across the street," Lydia tried again. Celia shrugged at her. "Well, he seems nice enough."

"Yes, a nice man," Celia agreed, noncommittally, and picked up her boots, intending to return them to the armoire in her bedroom-den.

"But strange, too. Lonely. Always by himself. I think it's just him over there. No wife or kids."

"Maybe. Maybe lonely," Celia said quietly. She distractedly put the boots down again. Lydia watched her mother's eyes well up. Celia had come in the door smiling, and now looked as though she might weep.

"You should wear them more often," Lydia said, wishing to steer her mother out of any murky feelings.

"Huh?" The subject once again had changed more quickly than Celia's emotions could accommodate. Lydia pressed on.

"And you have that nice lavender-coloured blouse that goes well with it. I brought it upstairs from the basement. Is it still in the box? You should unpack those things."

"I don't know ... not yet."

"Come on *Mãe*, it's been a year now. No, more than that," she said, counting on her fingers. "It's been sixteen months. You can do that now. A little bit at a time. It's the twenty-first century — you don't have to wear black your whole life." Lydia cajoled.

"Maybe. Maybe in a couple of months. Not yet. I'm not ready yet," she said, walking away, and back to her room. Lydia sighed, turned off the front lights and stomped up the stairs.

Celia's pretty boots remained in the front hallway of 81 Lochrie Street, temporarily forgotten.

POINT OF VIEW

ISMAIL REALLY HADN'T PLANNED to return to Busbridge's writing class, feeling like there was no point without Daphne being there. Besides, he'd missed the second session and hadn't even completed the homework from the first. He didn't like falling behind.

But on the following Tuesday, the course was on his mind all day, distracting him from his work. So was drinking. He'd visited the Merry Pint four times the previous week and was troubled about returning to his pre-AA excesses. He needed a plan, a way to kill some time so he wouldn't spend his entire evening at the bar. He bargained that he could reward himself with a light beer at home if he forced himself to go to the class.

King's College Circle was quiet that evening, newly fallen snow dampening the sounds of student footfalls and the nearby street traffic. Ismail neared University College and saw Fatima standing by the heavy wooden doors, blue-haired and shivering. She waved her cigarette hand in greeting.

"Hi there. You came back," she said, her brow furrowing in concentration. "It's Ismail, right?"

"Yes, I had to miss last week's class because of work," he said, dismissively.

"You didn't miss much," she said, blowing smoke into the cold air.

"How are you tonight, Fatima?" He praised himself for remembering her name.

"Good," she said, pulling on her cigarette. She sputtered into a coughing fit.

"Hey, you know, that's going to stunt your growth." Ismail chuckled, and immediately regretted the old fogey words. She scowled at him and regained her composure.

"No problem there. My genes have taken care of that already. Just like yours, I'm guessing," she said, sizing him up. Ismail pushed out his chest and stretched his five-foot-seven frame half an inch taller. "I haven't grown since I was eleven. I'm not about to start at this age."

"Which is?" Ismail asked, still feeling like an old man in her presence.

"Well, as a matter of fact, I am nineteen and eleven-twelfths. Here take this." She handed him a piece of paper from her coat pocket. "I'm having a big party for my twentieth in three weeks. You're invited." He took the photocopied handbill from her. There was a black-and-white caricature of the birthday girl holding a balloon and a glass of wine. It was almost a good likeness to her: long dark hair, big friendly eyes, toothy grin. Inside the balloon were typed details of the party: March 14th, 9:00 p.m., Polish Recreation Centre Hall, 97 Wallace Street.

"Thanks."

"Really, you should come. It's going to be totally cool. There's going to be tons of people," she said, her eyes widening, "and I've ordered lots and lots of platters of maki, and DJ Billyboi is doing the last set."

"Oh, that's nice," Ismail said blandly, still looking at the drawing. He noticed the artist had even drawn in deep dimples.

"You know, you'd probably have a good time. And bring a date if you want."

"Sounds fun. I'll check my calendar," he said politely. A ridiculous image of him boogying at a party for twenty-year-olds flashed across Ismail's mind. *Boogying? Do they still say that?* He looked at his watch. "Hey, we should go in. It's getting late."

"Oh, right." She dropped her cigarette. Ismail stomped it out, and they went inside.

When they entered, the class was already in progress. A woman with a sequined blouse was directing her comments to James Busbridge, who was nodding his head emphatically at her. Behind him on the blackboard were the words: point of view, narrator, first-person, second-person, third-person.

"... So I like multiple points of view," the woman said, her blouse glittering at James.

"Thank you. It really is a balance between our creativity and following the 'rules,'" he replied, glancing up at Fatima and Ismail as they paused to search for vacant seats. She found a spot in the centre of the U-shaped table arrangement and Ismail took the only other available seat, next to James. He wondered if more students had turned up since last class or if someone had removed some of the chairs, like they do during stressful children's party games. Embarrassed, he mouthed, "Sorry I'm late," to the teacher and nervously scanned the room to see if others were

bothered by his late arrival. It seemed that all eyes were on
him as James nodded in his direction before continuing to
talk about the complexities of voice in writing. Ismail took
out a notebook and busied himself, copying down all the
words on the blackboard.

After a few more minutes of lecturing, James asked for
volunteers to read aloud completed homework from the previous class. A hush fell over the room as James scanned the
'U' clockwise. Ismail followed his gaze, watching students
develop intense interest in things on the floor, on the pages
of their notebooks or inside their bags. James's roving eyes
eventually landed on Ismail, and, like a schoolboy caught
without his homework, he gave the teacher an embarrassed
grin, and explained, "Sorry, I wasn't here last week to get the
homework." Ismail's cheeks grew hot and his armpits damp.

"Well, I can go," called Fatima from across the room. The
classroom breathed again, twenty pairs of grateful eyes
focusing on her.

"Great, come on up here. Thanks, Fatima." Ismail studied
her as she stepped to the front of the class and took a deep
breath, as though inhaling courage. Her nervous fingers made
her typed sheets shake slightly. She had less than a month
to go before she left behind her adolescence, yet she seemed
strangely mature to him. At twenty, he was still in Mumbai,
being coddled by a houseful of women. He didn't know what
sushi was, and wouldn't taste it until his forties, just a decade
ago. He'd never had a party with a DJ, not even at his wedding.

As Fatima read, her grip on the sheets grew more relaxed
and her voice more even. Ismail felt for the birthday invitation he had earlier slipped into his trouser pocket, the
paper crisp against his damp fingers. And then it dawned
on him: Zubi would have been twenty, had she lived, and

her twenty-first birthday would be on February twenty-sixth, just two days away. He grew warm and lightheaded as he stared at Fatima, a girl who could have been one of his daughter's contemporaries, perhaps even one of her friends.

For some years, Zubi's birthdays and death anniversaries played on his mind weeks before their arrival. Other years, they seemed to fade into the background, arriving like a surprise when he consulted his day planner or woke up and realized what day it was. Try as he might to ignore these dates, he knew he'd never forget them.

He struggled to bring his attention back to Fatima and their eyes met, just as she was reading out her last sentence. There was a short silence, then, overcompensating for his lack of attention, he clapped heartily for her, and others followed his lead.

"Thanks, Fatima, well done. Does anyone have feedback?" James asked. Fatima leaned towards Ismail and whispered, "God, I hope they won't be too brutal." He smiled at her encouragingly, almost paternally, as she made her way back to her seat.

Ismail managed to get home from the university without a detour to the Merry Pint. He threw his car keys into the fruit bowl on the kitchen table, turned up the heat, and opened the fridge. Five light beers lined up like sentries on the fridge door shelf. He grabbed one, twisted off the cap, and took a long swig, welcoming the icy beer's warmth.

Upstairs, he drew the bedroom drapes, looking out at the neighbouring homes. The snow was still coming down, blanketing the roofs in white. Across the way at Celia's house, the porch light switched on. He turned off his bedroom lamp and stood near the window. Finally, Celia stepped out wearing her long coat, the same one she had donned while out shovelling a few weeks back. He remembered its smell of damp wool mixed with a fruity perfume. Her black scarf flapped in the wind, and she grabbed it in mid-air, taming it into a loose knot.

He stepped away from the window long enough to run downstairs to grab another beer from the fridge. When he returned, Celia was still on the porch. Who was she waiting for? She looked up at the sky in his direction, sniffing the air like a feral cat, and then, as though giving up the scent, looked away. Feeling silly to be watching her again, Ismail backed away from the window, but not for long. Like a bird impervious to the dangers of a glass pane, he once again moved closer to it.

The street was deserted. She stood alone on the porch, a solitary figure out in the snow. Sensing her loneliness, Ismail wanted to cross the street, unwind her thick scarf from her neck, unbutton her long black coat. See what she was wearing underneath. A dress? Blouse and skirt? All in black as usual? She turned, opened the front door and went in halfway, perhaps calling to someone. With her back turned, he took another good look at her, frowning to see that her lively burgundy boots had been replaced by grim, sensible black ones. She was the picture of full-blown grief, a suitably dressed woman in mourning. Even her black leather purse complied with what Ismail assumed to be her spousal duty. Yet something about her was different.

Lydia emerged from the house, and, in tandem, she and Celia stepped off the porch and headed down the street, leaving behind their footsteps in the fresh snow. He leaned forward to get a look at her disappearing back, thinking something had changed about her since the last time he'd seen her. A gust of wind fluttered her scarf, billowing it from her head, and there it was, poking out flirtatiously from under it. Ismail laughed out loud. What had been grey the day before had turned scarlet. Her hair was like a red flag, waving to him in gloom of the winter night.

— ❋ —

Upon awaking earlier that day, Celia knew she'd been visited by her dead husband's ghost. She scanned her bedroom-den for him, but of course, he'd left by then. She shuttered her eyes closed and other sensations intensified; his smell coated her skin, a musky combination of sweat, drywall dust, and figs. She billowed the sheets, and his scent dispersed across her room.

But he'd left behind more than that. Pulling her knees up to her chest, her body told her that it had been man-handled while she slept. Imprints of thick hands lingered on her breasts, stomach, and hips. She licked her warm lips and tasted his brand of cigarettes. Rolling over to his side of the bed, she held his pillow tight, grasping for his fleeting heat. Her body soon grew cold.

She wrenched off the covers, and pushed herself out of bed. Within moments she was dressed and stomping toward the foyer. She'd already pulled her coat on when Lydia called out to her from the kitchen, "*Mãe*, where're you going?"

"Out," Celia fumed, unsure why she was directing her anger at her daughter.

"How long you going to be? We're leaving for work in half an hour. Will you be back before then?" Lydia's startled voice wafted down the hallway, her words gathering around

Celia's feet. She dodged them, hastily shoving her feet into her boots.

"I'll be back when I am back," she snarled, turning the doorknob and swinging open the front door.

"But what about Marco? Can you take him with you?"

"No, not today," she said petulantly, enjoying her rebellion. Hadn't she dropped off Marco at preschool almost every day since she'd arrived on Lochrie? And then picked him up every day, too? At noon the schoolyard was always full of grandmothers, waiting in the cold for grandchildren. Had anyone ever asked them if they had other plans, if they wanted to look after yet another generation of children?

Celia bristled with indignation and outrage. She stamped out the door, and for good measure, she slammed it soundly behind her. She ignored Lydia's protests and marched east on Lochrie, and then north to Dundas, passing empty cafés and darkened dollar stores. Her pace was brisk and she was winded by the time she reached Dufferin.

She paused at the intersection to rest a moment. Her anger no longer fuelling her, she grew limp with shame. Why had she made such a production about nothing and left Lydia in the lurch? She almost turned around right there, but the traffic light changed from red to green, and, taking this as a sign, she continued on with her trek. She crossed the street, gulping in February air that barely warmed before reaching her lungs.

And she just kept walking, passing the XXX video store with its embarrassing posters of scantily clad women, and past the bakery with its yeasty aromas sneaking under the door. And then a neon light in a storefront ahead caught her eye. She read the bright pink sign: *New Life Hair and Nails*. She hummed the words, smiled, and entered the salon.

— ❊ —

Ismail watched Celia and Lydia walk away. Finally, when they were out of sight, he pulled himself away from the window. A restive energy followed him through the dark of his home, to the kitchen. He gulped back the rest of the beer he'd been nursing and then opened another. He sifted through the mail, finding nothing of interest: a gas bill, a credit card statement, a newsletter from the Liberal MP. The furnace switched itself on, its rumble startling him. A few minutes later it turned off, sighing itself back to sleep.

It was almost ten o'clock, just an hour before bedtime, but Ismail deliberated about heading to the bar. The edginess that had been gnawing at him morphed into a craving for whiskey, a drink he no longer kept at home. The urge itched at him until its taste and smell were almost palpable. *Maybe just one.* Ismail grabbed his keys from the fruit bowl, and put on his jacket, looking forward to the familiarity of place, the easy company of the regulars. He envisioned being greeted by Suzanne, the weekday bartender, and perhaps pulling up a stool at the bar and making conversation with a Mary Pinter. And then he thought of Daphne. Might she be there tonight? He'd heard from the other regulars that she'd been in earlier in the week, and he was glad he'd missed her. He shrugged off his coat.

He slumped down at the kitchen table again, and replaced the keys in the fruit bowl. He held tight to his light beer, gulping fast, sucking down its last drops. While he contemplated getting another, a hazy intoxication crept up on him; he hadn't eaten for hours. He cracked open a fourth beer. *It's only light beer. Not even light, but Lite.*

After a few more gulps, the filaments of his back muscles loosened and extended, and his posture slackened. The minutiae of his day circled his mind once, twice, and then drained away. The mail scattered upon the kitchen table felt far away and soon he was very much alone in his drowsy head. It was the same wobbly relief he used to experience back in the day when he drank with Daphne. He wanted to join in her merriment once more, to delight in her jokes and her open-mouthed, gap-toothed laugh.

Ismail gulped back more beer. *We had a good friendship, didn't we, Daphne?* Another swig of beer and his eyes moistened, rendering his vision fuzzy. *What? Is that Rehana and Zubi? Yes! Over there, by the sink.* Mirage-Rehana pointed to the fruit bowl in front of him and he gazed into its delicate design, noticing for the first time the way the colours swirled up and lashed the sides of the bowl, a rainbow hurricane. His vision softened and his eyes grew wetter.

Ismail was perusing the Saturday newspaper when he heard Rehana's key turn in the lock. Soon she was in the kitchen, Zubi bobbing against her chest in a carrier. They had just returned from a yard sale down the street and Rehana proudly set a painted ceramic bowl down on the kitchen table.

"Look, Ismail, this was only a dollar! The neighbours are selling off half their house for almost nothing," she announced with amazement in her voice. Before Lochrie, the Boxwalas had never before had a yard, much less a yard sale, and the concept was still an amusing novelty to Rehana.

"We have so many bowls, don't we? Why buy another one?" Ismail muttered, in his characteristically killjoy way.

This was before Zubi died, but even so, he was no less irritating a companion back then.

"It's for fruit, Ismail," she said, sighing. "We don't have a nice fruit bowl. We should eat more fruit. I'm going on a diet, so I'll eat more fruit and put it in the bowl." She pronounced each word slowly and deliberately, as though explaining the simplest of concepts to a child. She placed the bowl in the sink to wash later, and then turned away from her husband, unclasping Zubi from the carrier. He stared at her back while she worked the buckles.

Rehana hadn't always been like this with Ismail. At first, when he lobbed his naysaying at her, she would cajole, sweet-talk; it had almost been a sort of game between them. But after years of marriage, Rehana lost her patience and grew easily annoyed with him. Ismail guessed that was how it was in most marriages; in time every couple learned how to cut to the chase, reduce effort, be economical with energy.

"Another diet? Come on Rehana, you are fine. Why are you always dieting? It's not healthy." Although unsuccessful, the comment was meant to be conciliatory, a clumsy compliment.

"Ismail, never mind. This one is a healthy regimen." That was another thing that had changed during the Boxwala marriage. At first, Rehana had a voracious appetite that Ismail found both surprising and arousing. He'd watch her sometimes, as she spooned large helpings of rice and curry onto her plate, using her fingers to clean away every last grain, each drop of daal, licking and sucking her way up to her first knuckle. But by the time Zubi was born, she had tried the Scarsdale, Weight Watchers, and Jane Fonda. Despite her weight loss, she remained obsessed with shrinking her small body.

"But you are already slim enough," Ismail continued his weak protest.

"I still have some baby fat. See?" she pointed at her flat stomach. "It's a five-day fruit-only fast a co-worker of mine has been using. She lost ten pounds with it."

"Well I don't see any fat on you, but whatever makes you happy."

"It would make me happy if you took Zubi now. I need to start cooking dinner," she said, handing him the baby.

Zubi had been about six months old then. Ismail held her close, sniffing her sweet scalp. She smelled of talcum powder, baby shampoo, and bliss.

"Okay, okay. Sorry, a fruit bowl is a good idea. It's very nice, very colourful," Ismail said, feeling silly for arguing about a one-dollar bowl. He kissed Zubi on her cheeks, making loud smooching noises that caused Zubi to giggle and the corners of Rehana's mouth to lift into a reluctant smile. Then he kissed Rehana's cheeks in the same way until she laughed and shoved him aside.

Ismail took Zubi into the living room and settled her onto the thick carpet. She was still learning to crawl, but managed to pull and creep her way toward a collection of her toys stacked in a cardboard box. Ismail sat on the floor with her, looking at the rag doll she held close to her face, trying to see what she was seeing. He laid down on his back beside her, cupping his hands behind his head. From this vantage point, the room was imposing, the spackled ceiling faraway. Zubi and he, so tiny by comparison, seemed lost in the room. The sensation was unsettling to Ismail, but when he looked over at Zubi, she didn't seem bothered in the least.

He opened his eyes and looked up at the living-room ceiling, which was now smooth, its spackles scraped away the previous year. He reached for the carpeting that had been there just a moment ago and instead felt hard laminate beneath his head. Zubi, and the almost twenty years between them, had disappeared.

He stumbled back to the kitchen, and finished the last of the beer. Then, he groped his way up the darkened staircase and fell into bed.

After the divorce, Rehana cleared out most of the kitchen crockery, but she left behind the fruit bowl for Ismail. He never knew why. Perhaps the bowl held memories that she didn't want to keep. Or, perhaps, it held nothing at all.

— 18 —

STREETCAR

ISMAIL SAW CELIA AGAIN the next Saturday, this time through the streaky window of the Dundas streetcar. He was on his way to the Eaton Centre to buy reduced-price winter boots during the end of February sales. He looked up from his *Toronto Star* and saw her standing at the corner of Dundas and Ossington, waiting at the streetcar stop. He thought: *She's getting on!* His belly lurched and, mistaking this unfamiliar sensation for indigestion, he fumbled in his pocket for an antacid.

Ismail craned his neck to get a better view of her. She stepped around a slushy puddle and waited for the driver to open the doors wide. She wore her scarf loosely tied, like an ambivalent *hijabi*, and so he could still see much of her new red hair. He sat up tall in his seat to watch her climb the steps, which were a little too high for her small frame. While she dug into her leather handbag to extract a token, the driver leaned down from his high-seated perch. Did she smile shyly at him just then? The driver said something to her, which made her laugh long enough for Ismail to notice her slight overbite and bright-red lipsticked mouth. Before Ismail could look away, he realized that she was gazing back at him with a look of friendly acknowledgement.

Self-conscious, he sucked in his gut, and straightened his slumped posture. She approached slowly, cautiously holding onto the handrails as she made her way toward him. Her smile and nod made Ismail's armpits bristle awake. With no vacant seats nearby, she headed to the back of the bus, leaving him alone, an island, in the centre of the crowded streetcar. Ismail silently cursed the passengers around him, especially the lady in the seat next to his, whose shopping bags were bumping against his knee.

Ismail turned around, perhaps a little too desperately, to follow Celia's small figure as she stopped at a window seat about fifteen feet away. No longer seeming to notice his gawking, she pulled a newspaper from her purse, one of those free dailies found in boxes near bus stops. Ismail faced forward again, and patted his damp forehead with his handkerchief. He attempted to slow his racing pulse, chastising himself for behaving like a hormonal teenager. Still, he wished the woman next to him would get off the streetcar, and leave the seat beside his vacant, imagining this would be an invitation to Celia to come to him. He unbuttoned his jacket, slid open the window a centimetre and inhaled cool air. The lady with the shopping bags stood up at Bay Street, just one stop before his and Ismail opened the window wider.

When Ismail gathered up his things and stood to leave, Celia looked his way. He nodded to her and she casually returned the gesture. He stood stock-still at the bustling corner of Yonge and Dundas, his jacket open to the wind, his eyes fixed on her while she thumbed through her newspaper. The light changed, the streetcar jolted forward and he started to walk away. But then her gaze tapped him on his shoulder, forced him to turn around. Their eyes met and Ismail grinned long after the streetcar crossed the intersection and continued its eastbound journey.

— ❊ —

Earlier that day, Celia stood in front of 68 Shannon Street, the house that had been hers for more than a quarter century. She'd raised her two children there, planted gardens (flowers out front and vegetables in the back), made countless meals in the kitchen, and scrubbed every corner. They'd moved into the small three-bedroom semi-detached a young family; a husband and wife in their twenties, Lydia in kindergarten and Filipe in grade two. When her son moved out, she left his things there, but moved in a rarely used Singer machine and an even more rarely used exercise bike. It only made sense to her that her daughter's room would become her mother's after her father died. The three of them, José, Celia, and her mother, made agreeable housemates for almost ten years.

Sixty-eight Shannon was the house where Celia was widowed and orphaned within the same month. It was a house that grew silent, all at once.

José had been a good provider. She didn't have to work two jobs like some of her friends. She had it easy; she babysat children while her own were growing up, which paid for their groceries. The rest she left to José and he seemed to manage well: he'd paid off the house, and even saved a little to help the children with college.

Once a month or so, he came home with a roll of bills and told her it was a "bonus" he'd earned for staying late or getting a contracting job done early. She never questioned him, using the extra money for small luxuries like new outfits or furniture. They were a respectable family.

Celia sighed and inspected the front window of 68 Shannon. In her mind's eye, she expected to see the old lace curtains fluttering in the front window, the ones she'd stitched herself and later packed away in a cardboard box. She looked for the hand-painted sign above the mailbox, the one that said *Família Sousa*, even though she knew it had cracked into three pieces when Lydia unscrewed it from the aluminum siding. Lydia tried to convince her that a little glue could save the sign, but Celia wasn't interested in a keepsake of her husband's handiwork. It was just another example of the how the world in which she lived had turned out to be only a facade with a rotted-out foundation. She threw José's broken sign into the trash.

Anger left an acrid taste in her mouth that was like hours-old coffee on the tongue. She spat it on the street. A cold wind blew and she pulled her black scarf around her hair. But it wasn't only the cold she was protecting herself from; she hoped to keep herself hidden from the neighbours' glances. She was in no mood to be greeted by their pity today; most had heard that she had been forced to leave her home because of her husband's shameful debts.

Yes, José had been keeping many secrets from her — that he was out of work, playing too much poker, had taken out loans. He'd even re-mortgaged the house — her house — to pay for his debts. Celia hadn't known about all that, didn't pay much attention to the finances; she had her own house-hold responsibilities and José had his. In her mind, it was such an old, familiar story. And she hated that, was angry to have become the stereotype she had never imagined herself to be. A woman first dependent on her parents, then her husband, and later, her children.

She wiped a tear with the edge of her scarf and then wound it more snugly around her head, making sure to tuck in stray locks of her new red hair. She glanced quickly down Shannon Street, glad that it was deserted at this hour. What would her old friends and neighbours think if they could see it? A widow with crimson hair! She felt a little silly for the impulsive choice she'd made a few days earlier. Of course, the enthusiastic young Vietnamese hair dresser had spurred her on, tut-tutting at her dull, grey-brown hair and presenting her with a stiff cardboard display of dyed hair samples. Celia was about to choose a dark mahogany when the hairdresser pointed out the "Cinnamon" fringe.

"Look, this is a nice one. It will look good against your complexion. It's good for older women to brighten up their look." Celia bristled at the word "older" yet knew the label fit. Widowhood had catapulted her to a more mature age, drew lines around her eyes and sprouted white hair that hadn't been there a year ago.

"Well," she demurred, fingering the silky crimson fringe between her fingers, "I don't know if this colour would be appropriate for a widow. Maybe too flashy?"

"Really? I don't think so ... are you not allowed to have nice hair if you're a widow?"

"Well there's no rule, really. It's just that you're supposed to downplay the colour, come out of mourning slowly, grad-ually. And some widows never wear colour again after their husbands die," Celia said. "I guess it is a personal choice, but still, there are conventions."

"We don't do that in my culture. We mourn for a little while, get it over with. At least that's how it is in Canada. How long have you been a widow?"

"Since last fall. Over a year now."

"Over a year! And really, you're not that old. What are you — late fifties? Early sixties?"

Celia told her she was fifty.

"Oh! Well! You know fifty is the new thirty!" the hairdresser said, stumbling out of her faux pas. Celia thought about that. The new thirty. She inspected the samples again, holding each up against her skin and studying herself in the mirror. The hairdresser raised an eyebrow at Celia's reflection, and said, "Well it's up to you. You tell me. You want to be Mahogany or Cinnamon?"

Celia pointed to the one on the right.

That same evening, when Lydia saw her new hair, she forgave her mother for walking out on her in the morning.

"*Mãe!* It's great! A little bright maybe, but it'll fade. This is just the right thing for picking up your mood."

Celia muttered to herself and strode to her bedroom-den, pushing the door shut behind her. She didn't want a hairdo to fix her mood.

She continued to stand on the sidewalk and stare at her old house, troubling over its appearance. Nothing looked the same. When the buyers arrived for the final inspection with measuring tapes and a digital camera, she'd overheard them using words like "gut," "tear down," and "strip." And that's what they'd done to her home — they'd renovated, upgraded, changed everything, as though the home she'd made over the last twenty-five years was rubbish to be thrown away.

She guessed the ground floor no longer had any dividing walls and all her carpet was ripped away. Where once there was aluminum siding now was coral stucco. *Who likes coral stucco?* But she had to admit that she liked the brand-new porch and freshly painted green door. The front window, from where she had supervised her children playing on the lawn, had been made into a larger, grander, bay window. José had once promised to install a window seat for her, but never got around to that project.

A car approached, and drove into what used to be her driveway. She avoided the driver's curious eyes, and turned away, trudging through the slush, south on Dovercourt to Dundas Street. Snow soaked right through her boots, into her socks, making her pinky toe go numb. Still, she continued east, only pausing to look into the steamed-up windows of Nova Era. She appraised the trays of *pastéis de nata*, fruit tarts, and cookies. Her eyes dwelled on the chocolate éclairs lined up on a cooling rack. The taste of chocolate icing, mixed with her bile, burned upwards through her esophagus and into her mouth; reflux from another time.

Now, she walked on without a destination. Ahead of her sat the white bearded man who kept vigil on a piece of cardboard on the sidewalk, just outside St. Christopher House. The old panhandler reminded her of a picture she once saw of St. Christopher, the patron saint of travellers, and she found it fitting that he would take up his station right there, as though he were the community centre's ambassador. She dug into her coat pocket and handed him two quarters, their mittened hands touching. She didn't feel so different from him, understood that she was just a bedroom-den luckier than he. He nodded to her, as though agreeing with her unspoken thoughts.

She stood at the corner, intending to cross Ossington and catch the westbound Dundas streetcar home. But when the light changed to green, she stayed put. The other pedestrians stepped around her, her body a minor inconvenience. The light turned red again. She turned and crossed Dundas, changing direction, changing her mind. The eastbound streetcar pulled up just as she reached the curb, an answer to a question she didn't know she had. As she climbed the steps, she gave the driver a knowing look, as though he was a co-conspirator in her spontaneous journey.

"Looks like I came at just the right time," the driver said, grinning down at Celia. His words weren't all that funny, but they made her giggle and pinked her face.

When she made her way through the half-empty streetcar, she glimpsed her neighbour Ismail sitting by the window, looking in her direction. Expectant. She averted her eyes in shyness. When she got closer, she noticed a woman sitting beside him — *was that his friend? His girlfriend?* She quickly found an empty seat near the back and pulled out a newspaper from her bag to distract herself. She peered in his direction from time to time and then the woman next to Ismail vacated the seat. *Good, she was a stranger.* The streetcar lumbered up to Yonge Street and Ismail stood, along with most of the riders, to get off. He descended the steps, crossed to the sidewalk and tromped toward the mall. The he turned, met her gaze, and she waved at him. The streetcar continued eastbound, and she settled herself back into her seat, looking out at the sky-high billboards and television screens of Yonge-Dundas

Square. She passed Victoria and then Church, not caring where the streetcar took her.

— ❋ —

That day Ismail bought two pairs of boots; one he needed and one he liked.

That evening he scrawled in his writing-class notebook, "I was not aware that Portuguese widows were allowed to wear red lipstick." After so many brief encounters, Ismail knew that it was time for him to find a way to have a real visit with his grieving lady neighbour.

He slept well that night, dreaming he was riding on the back of a black raven, flying over the neighbourhood, surveying the small houses and shops of Little Portugal. He took in the frozen, waiting rose gardens and the large, stately churches whose bells called out each Sunday. He watched men, shivering and smoking outside sports bars, slapping each other on the back in tipsy camaraderie. He looked over at grandmothers pushing toddlers in strollers as they lugged their groceries home. He glimpsed the young non-Portuguese couples moving into starter homes, making broken-English conversation with elderly neighbours who, thirty years ago, were the new kids on the block. He noticed his neighbourhood's quaint beauty from way up high, a beauty, that despite his twenty-five years living there, he'd never before allowed himself to see.

SIX METRES OF PAVEMENT

THE FURNACE WAS MALFUNCTIONING that day, and the classroom overheating. Joseph, a tall, young nursing student, had managed to climb up on a desk and pull open windows, offering some relief to the stifling air. Ismail removed his jacket and tie and was still too warm, but perhaps that was due to Fatima's pestering.

"Oh *come on*, Ismail, you just *have* to pick something that interests you. There's *gotta* be *something*," Fatima insisted, her long, silver-ringed fingers stroking the air, punctuating her words. She had pulled off her wool sweater and wore only a thin T-shirt with the confusing slogan "what part of *no* don't you understand?" Even though she was small-chested, he could tell she wasn't wearing a bra and this knowledge unsettled him. He was regretting the decision to reclaim the chair he'd chosen at the very first class, the one next to hers.

"I don't know. Maybe that's the problem. Nothing much of interest comes to mind."

"But you said you wanted to write about your daughter. What about that? Tell me about her."

Ismail looked away, his pulse quickening. He checked the clock, hoping that the "in-class exercise" time was almost over. Unfortunately, James Busbridge had only left the room a few minutes ago, giving his class a full half-hour to discuss story ideas with a classmate.

"I've decided against that topic," Ismail said quietly. "I can't write about her after all." He sniffed, rifled through the pages of his notebook and looked away. Fatima stared at him pensively, her lips pursed, unspoken words forming on their edges. He filled the brief silence before she could. "It's for personal reasons. And since I can't find a new topic, I might as well quit this class," he said resolutely, unbuttoning his shirt down to the middle of his chest and fanning himself with his papers. He had an undershirt on underneath, but its neckline plunged low and he felt self-conscious exposing himself. "My goodness it's warm ... perhaps I should just leave now. James was clear that we each had to write something and I clearly cannot do that."

"Hey! Hold up! You can't quit. Of course you can write. Everyone can write. Come on," she said, lowering her voice to a near-whisper, "we're the only people of colour in this class. I need you here," she said, her thick eyebrows raised as high as she could push them. Ismail looked around the room, scanning the faces of the other students, registering their skin colour for the first time. He nodded to her, acknowledged the class demographics, but was noncommittal about her need for him to stay.

"Hey," she said, before Ismail could question her sentiments, "here's an idea. Start with something you know, like James said. Or create a character based on someone you know or have been curious about," she said earnestly, stroking her chin. Ismail studied the column of piercings that traced their way up her left ear. She frowned, and he tried to refocus.

He looked blankly at the white page of his notebook while Fatima continued her stare-down. He shifted his gaze out the window at the grey March sky. Soon, his mind travelled through its thin panes and traversed the neglected campus soccer fields. It passed Chinatown, then Little Italy and Little Portugal, and finally settled in his neighbourhood, on his street. His mind hovered there, and waited until Celia stepped out from her front door. She wiped her hands on her black apron, scanned the skies, and waved up to him.

"There! You're thinking about someone. I can see it in your face!" Fatima said, interrupting his reverie.

"No, no, it's nothing. I wasn't thinking about anyone in particular. I was just letting my mind wander," he said, waving his hands in the air in protest.

"You're lying, dude. I can tell. I saw it. All of a sudden your face softened, you smiled ..."

Ismail couldn't help but grin at her wide-eyed expression.

"Fine. There is someone I'm a little bit curious about. Someone I've been thinking about, but I don't know if I want to write about them. And maybe it wouldn't be appropriate. I barely know this person."

"Ah, I get it. You're *interested* in this person," Fatima smirked, leaning forward in her chair. Ismail felt himself tense; there was nothing smirkable happening between Celia and himself and he didn't like Fatima's insinuation. He crossed his arms over his chest, but his thoughts returned to Celia.

"Oh, come on. Tell me about this mystery person. Please? Is it a man or woman?"

"Er, a woman," he admitted. An almost imperceptible look of confusion crossed Fatima's face. "What? Why are you looking at me like that?"

"No, no. It's nothing.... Tell me about her."

And then, although he never expected to talk this way to a teenager, he recounted their brief encounters, sightings, small talk, and what seemed to him like mutual curiosity. Speaking it all aloud, he realized he did have much to say. He and the widow already had a kind of story together.

"Huh. I'd say you have someone to write about. I'll be very curious to know how this all turns out. So, is she cute?"

"Fatima, come on, it not like that. Besides, I'm an old guy. I can't talk about this with you," he said, growing uncomfortable again. "How about we talk about your writing? We only have a few minutes left, so let's get to what you're writing about."

"Okay ... well, I continued from where I left off, you know, the thing I read last week?" Ismail barely remembered her piece, but nodded, anyway. "So the class told me to do more research and get more information, right? And so I called up my parents to get some more details, but, well, that didn't work out so well."

"Why, what happened?"

"It's a long story, Ismail....We don't get along very well. Never have. But it's been worse recently ... I wish I could just afford to move out," she said, examining a lock of her hair and squirming in her seat. Fatima suddenly resembled the teenager she truly was.

"Did ... something happen?" he asked, tentatively.

"It's just that my parents are, well, kind of traditional, old-school. You know they're older ... like your age." She looked up at him, raised her eyebrows. "No offence."

"Have you had a disagreement with them?" Ismail asked, his *uncleji* voice slipping out, the one he reserved for Nabil's boys.

"That's an understatement. But look, I can't get into it now," she said firmly.

"Well, all right," Ismail replied, surprised to be feeling cheated by her guardedness. An awkward pause floated in the air between them. After a moment, Ismail recovered, "Well, have you thought about another way to do some research on their experiences? I mean, your piece is going to be fictional. And like you just said to me, maybe you don't need to know everything about your parents to write characters based on them. You can weave in some typical immigrant experiences into your story."

"Yeah, you're right," she said, sighing. "Looks like I'll need to do that. But I'm disappointed. I sort of wanted to know more about them. Not just for the story, you know? I really wanted to know more about their lives." She fluttered her eyelashes down and stared at her lap.

"Maybe things will change? The tensions will clear and then you can talk to them."

"Doubt it." She slouched deeper into her chair, and pouted in that bored way that only young women can pull off. "Anyway, I don't want to talk about this anymore."

Ismail watched her for a minute, unsure of what to say. She picked up her pen, and doodled in her notebook. He pretended to make notes until James interrupted them again.

"All right everyone. Now work for ten minutes on your own. Take what you discussed and write a character sketch based on your character's motivations, desires, deepest wants." He held up his watch. "Ten minutes ... and start ... now!" Ismail gazed tiredly at his teacher's keen expression. James's roving eyes locked on his, and so he turned back to his notebook.

He pondered Celia, the widow he barely knew anything about. What were her motivations, her desires, her deepest wants? To live peacefully with her daughter, to buy a new polyester dress next week? To see her grandson grow up?

He glanced at Fatima, who frowned at him, and then resumed her fast scribbling, her pen making furious scratching sounds against the page. All those around him seemed to be engaged in industrious writing: James Busbridge chalked something on the board; the older woman with the flowered dress to his left printed slowly and methodically in pencil, stopping periodically to erase something and then blowing away the eraser bits; the two thirty-somethings tapped away on their matching green laptops. Everyone, busy writing. Except him. Finally, he picked up his ball point and in one long rush of ink he wrote:

The widow across the street is an enigma to me. And yet, she is so very familiar, in a way. We co-exist, almost co-habitating, a six metre stretch of pavement the dividing line between us. We're waiting for the other to cross the road.

All too soon, James yelled, "Time's up!" and then pointed his students to some keywords he'd written on the board about character development. Ismail turned a brand new page, abandoning the paragraph he'd just written. He took copious notes on James's lecture, finding a certain satisfaction in filling his white notebook page with more than empty thoughts. He caught Fatima watching him when he looked her way once or twice, but didn't pay much attention. Then, class ended, and the other students packed up their books and laptops and shrugged on winter coats. Fatima remained in her seat, rereading her writing. After a moment, she ripped a page out of her book and carefully folded it into quarters. She clasped it in her hand a moment, her eyes dancing between it and Ismail, back and forth, in a way at made Ismail tense without knowing why. Finally, she stuffed the folded paper into her bag, grabbed her coat, pushed past him, and mumbled a goodbye.

Ismail shuffled two pages back through his notebook and found the paragraph he'd written about Celia. He reread it, lingering on the words once, twice, thrice. Like Fatima, he, too, had an urge to rip out his page, and fold it into neat quarters.

— 20 —

LAUNDRY

THE BEGINNING OF MARCH was strangely warm that year, with temperatures reaching the low 'teens for two lucky days. It was all anyone talked about and weathermen became minor celebrities as Torontonians tuned in just to watch them announce the good news. Global warming was suspected to be the cause of the weather anomaly, and every reactive journalist was suddenly interested in stories about "going green."

Celia's *agonias* weren't allowing her to appreciate the good weather. After dropping Marco off at preschool, she sat alone at her window, alternating between listlessness and restlessness. It was quiet already by nine in the morning; all of the productive people had driven away in their cars or caught buses to reach important destinations. What would she do today to be a useful human being? She considered starting dinner, perhaps chopping the vegetables, making some rice, marinating beef. A man pedalled past on a bicycle. A delivery van drove by, going the wrong way down the one-way street.

Drowsy, she allowed her eyes to close, felt wetness against her lashes. Then, she felt nothing.

She was dreaming of José again. He was there with her, standing at the opposite end of the living room. She sized him up warily, taking in his familiar salt-and-pepper hair, beard shadow, and pot belly, but he came and sat down beside her, anyway. He rested his strong hand on her thigh, and she grimaced. Ignoring her, he leaned over and kissed her. She resisted him at first, pleading, "No José, you're making this too hard for me. You aren't supposed to be here. You have to let me go." He shrugged and flashed her a toothy grin that deepened the laugh lines around his eyes, reminding her of the cocky young man he once was.

She gave in to her loneliness and longing, and kissed him back, feeling first his soft top lip, and then his rougher, chapped bottom one. She got a taste of his tongue, and wanted more.

Twenty-two minutes later, she awoke with a start. He was gone again. She sniffed the air and the couch: drywall dust and sweat and figs. A contamination of drywall dust and sweat and figs.

She hurried to the kitchen sink and scrubbed her face clean. And then her arms and forearms. But it wasn't enough. She stripped off her dress, put on a clean one. She tossed the dress into her hamper, and still his scent lingered. She hefted the hamper to the basement, emptied the whole lot into the washer without separating the darks from lights, added too much detergent, turned the dial, exhaled. Finally, he seemed to be gone. She climbed the stairs, and noticed, for the first time that day, or maybe even that week, the sun shining brightly through the kitchen window. She gazed into it, allowing herself to be impressed by the simple, heady stream of light. She stood in its rays and let its heat burn off the last of the fog left by her dream.

She dampened a cloth, feeling cool water trickle between her fingers and went outside to clean the winter's grime from the laundry line. With one hand, she held her wash-cloth over the cord and then pulled it through with the other. The line danced and shook under her touch. Later, when the wash was done, she hung it up, the first air-dried load of the year. Then, she waited for the wind to do its work.

— ❀ —

The big thaw meant that Ismail's department would likely come in below their snow-clearing budget, the weather doing the work of dozens of staff and machines. His boss, a man who enjoyed being in the black, had come to Ismail in a celebratory mood that Friday afternoon, congratulating Ismail for the favourable budget lines he'd submitted earlier that day, as if Ismail were somehow personally responsible for the warm temperatures. In a rare show of generosity, he announced that anyone without a pending deadline could start the weekend early. A few grumbles emerged from cubicles near Ismail's, colleagues still working on year-end reports. Ismail checked his watch and saw that it was already two-thirty. He accepted the two-hour gift and left for home along with a few co-workers pleased to not have any pressing work to do.

He found a choice parking spot on Lochrie, just across from his house. He stood in the middle of the road, unbut-toned his jacket, and enjoyed the fourteen degrees of warmth the winter sun offered. He admired a few green stalks peeking out of the thawing soil in his next door neighbour's yard and estimated that they would soon push up bright purple flowers if the weather kept up. If not, they would likely suffer for their premature awakenings, wilting before having the chance to bloom. Ismail plucked up a sodden plastic bag that had blown into his rose bushes, envisioning the flowers that would soon emerge from their desolate, woody branches.

Across the street, a clothesline squeaked. A sack dress, two black sweaters, and three pairs of tights fluttered in the breeze, beckoning from around the side of Celia's place. Breaking up the dark laundry were a few pairs of white underwear, hung by their droopy waistbands. Ismail leaned to his right to look further around the side of the house and smiled at the scandal of an orange bra nestled amongst the mourning clothes.

There was another squeak and the line jerked to the left. Although he couldn't see Celia from where he stood, the twitching line told him of her presence. He envisioned her reaching up and tugging pieces of clothing off. In the pauses between the squeaks, he guessed she was folding, her hands caressing the fabric, and piling each dress, sweater, and undergarment into a basket. While he pondered whether he should walk between the houses and speak to Celia, a dark cloud obscured the sun's rays and the sky darkened. Eventually, the last pair of black tights vanished, and he heard a door slam as the widow went indoors. A slow rain shower began, dripping down his forehead and onto his cheeks.

21

CONSOLATION

PREDICTABLY, ISMAIL FOUND FATIMA smoking on the steps outside University College the next Tuesday before class.

"Hi, Fatima." He fumbled with the change in his pocket, remembering her upset the week before. He considered asking her how things were going with her parents, but thought better of the idea. "So, how's your story coming along?" he asked instead.

"Fine, I guess." She frowned, and flicked ash off her cigarette. Ismail saw a raw vulnerability just beneath her tough-smoking-girl posture, and this prodded him to linger at the steps awhile longer.

"So ..." he exhaled, "were you finally able to interview your parents?"

"Nope." He let the matter drop. Janice, the older pencil-toting student, passed by. Ismail nodded to her as she headed up the steps.

"That's too bad. I'm sorry to hear it. Hopefully they will

come around." He held onto the handrail and climbed a couple of steps.

"Doubt it." She took a final drag of her cigarette and then stubbed it out angrily. "Our communication has pretty much broken down. They kicked me out of the house." She looked away, in the direction of the soccer fields.

"What? Oh. That ... must be difficult." He looked at Fatima more closely, noticing the dark wells beneath her eyes. Beside her sat a large backpack, stuffed to its bulging seams.

"You want to know why?" She stood up, hands on her waist, as though issuing some kind of challenge.

"Um ... all right."

"Well, I might as well say it. I don't care what they or anyone thinks, anyway." Ismail gathered that "anyone" included him. He held his breath in the silence that followed. Then, she looked down at her hands and her tone softened. "Well, it's complicated, really. It's for a bunch of reasons. It's not like I've done anything really terrible ... it's because of the article I wrote for *The Varsity*. I never thought they'd see it.... Did you see it?"

He shook his head and she dug into her pack and handed Ismail the newspaper.

The headline read: *Beyond Bisexual: a Queer Girl's Take on LGBT*. He scanned the first three paragraphs, in which Fatima discussed the "fluidity of sexuality" and "the limitations of the gender binary on notions of sexual orientation." Ismail understood little of it, and tried to recall what's he'd learned about bisexuals from the first of the library books he'd borrowed to impress Daphne. He felt Fatima's gaze upon him and so he searched his mind for an appropriate response.

"Oh. I see." He'd discussed a variety of intimacies with Daphne after their Hope for Today meetings, but he'd never talked about such matters with a young person before. His sweating commenced.

"Yup, it isn't what they expected of me, you know? They were shocked that I was even having sex with guys, never mind anyone else."

"Well," Ismail mumbled, clearing his throat, "this is a ... difficult situation ... I'm sorry." He looked around to see if anyone had heard her say "sex."

"We'd better go inside. We're going to be late," she said, and he breathed a sigh of relief when she brushed past him and up the stairs.

Fatima was silent and aloof for most of the class, avoiding Ismail's glances. He was glad James didn't assign an in-class pairs exercise that week; most weeks, the students claimed the same seats and paired-up with the same students, and Fatima had become Ismail's de facto writing partner. During the lesson, he snuck glimpses of her brooding figure; she'd pulled off her boots and was hugging her knees to her chest, scratching away in her notebook. He mentally reviewed their brief conversation multiple times and assessed his clumsy responses. He hoped she wouldn't want to resume the discussion over the break or at the end of the class. To avoid such a situation, Ismail vacated the classroom during break-time, spending its duration in the men's washroom. When class ended, he packed up his things and left quickly, pausing only briefly to wave goodbye to her.

Ismail headed south on King's College Circle toward College Street. The dim, turn-of-the-century lampposts cast a yellow glow on the narrow road. Up ahead, in contrast, a restaurant sign on the main street shone neon bright. A streetcar trundled past. A moment later, Fatima caught up with him.

"Ismail! Hey, wait up!" He winced at the sound of her voice. Looking back, he saw that she had traversed the thawing soccer field as a shortcut. Thick brown mud coated her boots.

"Oh. Hello, Fatima." He slowed until she was walking beside him.

"Ismail, sorry for laying all that on you before class. I guess all this stuff is weighing me down and I just blurted it all out. I didn't really plan to tell you all that," she said apologetically. He thought he also heard a tinge of embarrassment in her voice. Maybe she did care what "anyone" thought of her after all.

"It's okay, Fatima. You didn't make me feel uncomfortable," he said, contorting his face into neutrality. For good measure he added, "and I want you to know that I don't ... er ... judge you ... for your ... preferences." *Was that the right word? Preference?* Ismail scanned his memory of the glossary he'd read in *When Someone You Love Comes Out of the Closet.*

"Well that's ... cool," she said, her eyes narrowing slightly. "I really wish my parents would try to be as open-minded as you." *Open-minded.* Ismail found her evaluation gratifying. With Nabil's boys, he had always tried to be the understanding uncle they could approach when they couldn't talk to their parents. Altaf never seemed to need him in this way, but Asghar confided in him periodically.

"So they kicked you out because they found out about ... it?" Ismail broached.

"I think so. But more than that they kicked me out for being public about 'it.' But you know, I never thought they'd see the article. It's just a campus newspaper, not *The Globe and Mail* or something."

"So how did they see the article, then?"

"Through the *desi* grapevine. A U of T student — I still don't know who — brought the paper home, one of his parents read it, and then called a family friend, who called my uncle, who called my mother."

Ismail smiled wanly. He understood too well how bad news travelled.

Fatima paused as the couple from class approached them at the intersection. Ismail and Fatima acknowledged them with nods and they did the same. The light turned green, and they strode ahead, falling into a rhythmic march, their matching carry-alls bobbing up and down on their backs. Ismail and Fatima followed a few steps behind them.

"Anyway, we had a huge fight. I won't bore you with all the details. They accused me of publicly shaming them. Then they told me to pack my things." Fatima lit a cigarette and a puff of smoke blew into his face. She apologized and then waved the smoke away.

"That's terrible."

"You know, I always thought they knew something, but we never talked about it. I planned to come out to them when I finally left home. Though I never really knew how that conversation would go," she scoffed. "Queerness is a little difficult to explain." She must have noticed his look of confusion then, and continued, "I mean, maybe my parents would understand gay or lesbian, it's slightly more clear-cut. Not that they approve of that, either."

"Oh. Yes, I see," Ismail said, pretending to understand. They stopped at a bus shelter and she looked down the road for a streetcar.

"I think that if I had just done what I wanted, but not been so open and honest about it, things would have been fine with them."

"I suppose they're concerned about how the community will see them," he ventured. "Not everyone has been exposed to these things."

"You obviously have. I could tell you were different from the moment I met you in class. Until you mentioned the widow lady I assumed you were gay ... you aren't are you?"

"No, of course not!" Ismail retorted, unable to hide his shock.

"It's just that you don't wear a wedding ring," she explained. "And you are non-judgmental about this. And well, not that many South Asian men go to writing classes, from my experience."

"Well, yes, I'm not married. I'm divorced ... and I know a little about this because I have a very good friend who is gay ... I mean, she's a lesbian."

"Oh, okay. Well, that's good, I guess." She hefted her heavy pack from one hip to the other.

"So, Fatima ... how are you managing? Where are you staying?"

"With a friend, for now. I'll figure it out. And at least there's one good thing in all of this ... my parents already paid for the party as my birthday present. My mom sent off the cheque last week. At least they can't pull out of that," she said, with a cheeky grin. Ismail couldn't help but return her smile. Despite the huge problems Fatima was facing, she still somehow managed to make her birthday bash the centre of her world. Beneath all her bravado and sophistication, she was still a teenager, at least for another week.

"A small consolation."

SIX METRES OF PAVEMENT   177

"You know, I only meant to find you and apologize. I really didn't mean to lay all this on you. I mean, I don't even really know you," she said, adjusting her scarf and fiddling with her mittens. He, too, wondered why she was oversharing. Did she sense that he wouldn't criticize her? Could she discern that he was a man who'd been judged most of his life and knew well enough to not judge her? Ismail felt a rush of warmth for the girl, a sudden protectiveness.

"Listen, it sounds like you are up against a lot of pressure. If there is something I can do for you, let me know," he said, pulling a business card from his wallet. "Here, I mean it. Feel free to call me."

"Thanks, that's nice of you," she said, stuffing the card into her coat pocket. "But I'm sure I'll be fine. I think that I'll be able to go home again once they cool off. Especially my father." She stepped out into the street to meet the lumbering streetcar.

They parted there, with her climbing on the eastbound car, and Ismail walking to his parking spot on Beverley. As he replayed the conversation, he felt some trepidation about his impulsive offer and hoped she wouldn't take him up on it.

On the way home, he drove along College and passed the Merry Pint. He slowed to look through its front windows, and thought he saw a woman about Daphne's height. He put his foot on the accelerator, and drove down Brock Avenue to the liquor store just before its weary employees locked its doors for the night.

22

INTERVENTIONS

"HEY, IT'S ME, FATIMA." Ismail had to press the telephone to his ear to hear her better; his coworker in the next cubicle over seemed to be waging war on her filing cabinet, noisily opening and banging its drawers shut.

"Er, hello? Oh, yes ... Fatima, from class, right?"

Although they had just seen one another two days earlier, they made awkward small talk for a few moments; out of their usual context, Ismail wasn't sure what to chat about. Finally, Fatima asked him to meet her after work to talk about "something important." When he hesitated and then asked for details, she told him she preferred not to elaborate over the phone and would only need a half hour of his time. He remembered his offer of support, bargained that he could spare thirty minutes, and agreed.

Ismail pushed Fatima and her troubles out of his mind for the rest of the afternoon, returning to a report he was writing on the refurbishment of an east-end bridge. The recent thaw had caused it to shed a few kilos of cement onto a service road below. The whole situation made him nervous, but he was glad that the newly implemented inspection plan had at least caught the problem before the media had. Luckily, the bridge was above a rarely used thoroughfare, and the damage was not serious.

At three-thirty, Ismail dropped off the report in his manager's mailbox and then checked his email. Half of it was junk, and he accidentally opened a message titled "Fw: meeting today" that opened up to a display of pastel-coloured pills promising to cure erectile dysfunction. He scanned the round and diamond shaped tablets, a ball of acid churning in his stomach. Heat prickled over his body and he removed his sweater. Before long, he was sweating through his shirt.

After Rehana remarried, Ismail fell into a long period of lonely bachelorhood. His solitude was only punctuated by work meetings, sessions with the therapist, and infrequent trips to Nabil's place. Those family visits were difficult while Nabil's boys were still young; Altaf was almost five and Asghar nearly three when she died. Watching them grow up was a painful reminder of what he'd lost.

"Ismail *Kakaji*, where is Zubi?" Asghar would ask his uncle, at three-and-a half, or four, or four-and-a-half years old, his brow furrowed, as though trying to remember some fact he'd lost track of. An uncomfortable silence would follow, Nabil perhaps switching on the television, and Ismail, turning to stone, still and silent on the couch.

"Asghar, don't ask *Kakaji* so many questions. We'll talk about it later," Nabila would reply, shushing her son.

"I told you already, stupid," Altaf would say earnestly at

age five-and-a-half, or six or six-and-a-half years old, "She
went to heaven. She's dead, right, Mummy?"

"Yes, that's correct, boys," Nabila would mumble, ush-
ering them out of the room, looking apologetically in her
brother-in-law's direction. Nabil would clear his throat, and
talk about the stock market, or the Blue Jays while Ismail
regained his composure.

Eventually, mercifully, around the time Asghar turned
five and Altaf was seven, they seemed to forget about their
little cousin and their inquiries stopped.

Fearing that Ismail's lack of social contact was making
things worse for him, Nabil and Nabila repeatedly offered to
set him up on dates, and insisted that he should get remarried.
Get your life back on track, they'd insist, ignoring the fact that
his life's derailment was unlikely to be remedied in this way.

Ismail relented, and met two women, both of whom
refused him a second date, perhaps because he seemed so
miserable or because they knew of his past. He never asked
how many women never agreed to a first date. He wasn't terribly upset by the rejections, for he still couldn't trust his body,
which had swung from sexless with Rehana, to oversexed after
the separation. Although the spontaneous erections eventually ceased about a year after Rehana left, he wasn't eager to
test things out with someone new. He was sure the tragedy
had damaged him irreversibly in that department and that it
was probably a punishment he would have to accept.

It wasn't until Ismail became a regular at the Merry Pint
that he felt himself growing social again. His bar buddies
cracked open his isolation, offering him companionship
and a fresh start. To them, he was just a friendly stranger
with whom they could talk nonsense, have a laugh or two
and be memorable, yet relatively anonymous.

A few years into his tenure at the Merry Pint, Ismail gathered up the courage (or perhaps it was the alcohol that did the gathering) to go home with a Mary Pinter for the first time. Her real name was Chantal, or so she told him; Ismail was never sure about this detail. Their relations were graceless, lasted just a few minutes, and were potentially dangerous (she told him he didn't need to wear protection because she was on the Pill, and Ismail wasn't savvy enough at the time to question her). However, and much to his relief, things were relatively normal between the two of them. There was no erectile dysfunction, and afterwards, no spontaneous erections, either. How grateful Ismail was to Chantal that night! He credited her with his sexual healing, and, in his gratitude, pursued her with flowers and chocolates and phone calls until she managed to brush him off a few weeks later. The experience left him hopeful that his punishment had abated.

Ismail closed and deleted the email, banishing Viagra, Cialis, and Levitra from his desktop. He dried his forehead and set his hankie to dry on the edge of a desk drawer. It was almost four o'clock and he remembered that he would be meeting Fatima shortly. He fretted about the "something important" she wanted to discuss and what help he could possibly offer a bisexual nineteen-year-old girl. He shook off his worries and resolved to be a good listening ear for her. He reasoned that she just needed an older person's good judgment. He spent the last half hour at work Googling articles on coming out to parents, and looking up "queer" on Wikipedia, a term he'd previously presumed to be an terrible insult. He considered calling Daphne for some advice, but by the time he'd worked up the nerve, it was time to go.

At five, Ismail waited at a drab café just across from the university gates. It was filled with young people hunched over laptops or talking loudly in small groups. Many of the girls wore blouses that looked embarrassingly like lingerie to him and he puzzled over how they managed to stay warm in winter. Ismail realized for the first time that Fatima was different from these other girls, tending to dress in baggy jeans and tops with various political slogans on them.

He ordered a cup of expensive *chai* and watched five, ten, and then fifteen minutes pass on the large wall clock above the door. Just as he was beginning to think he'd been stood up, Fatima arrived, out of breath, her coat open to reveal a T-shirt with the cryptic words "No One Is Illegal" emblazoned across her chest. There was a look of near panic in her eyes, and so when she apologized for being tardy, Ismail forgave her easily and bought her a four-dollar latté.

She did most of the talking at first, telling him she'd had another argument with her parents the previous day. She'd gone home, hoping for a partial reconciliation, but ended up packing up more of her things. They informed her that they were withdrawing all financial support, and she'd have to find a way to sustain herself.

"You really sure it's not temporary? You don't think that another week or two will make a difference?" Ismail asked, knowing that youth could be a time of extremes. When Asghar first talked about changing his major, he was sure his father would "never forgive" him and Ismail had to persuade him otherwise.

"No, this is serious. I know my parents. They won't reverse this decision," Fatima said dolefully, spooning up froth from her latté.

"This is bad news," he said, not really believing her, but because he could tell she was upset. He did feel bad for the girl; no matter how long this standoff was going to last, it was a current stressful ripple in her life. "And such a bad way to celebrate your twentieth birthday," he added.

"Well, at least that's not ruined, at least not completely, anyway," she said, taking a sip of coffee. "They've already paid the non-refundable fees for both the hall and the sound system. One of the DJs has promised to play all night for free now."

"Well, that's a relief, isn't it? You'll still have your party, then," Ismail mused, trying to not sound patronizing.

"I've cancelled the maki order, though," she bit her bottom lip and looked like she was about to cry. "Now that I'm homeless, jobless, and broke, my friends have turned it into a fundraiser for me. They got a liquor license and think they can raise a couple of thousand, maybe."

"Well, you have some good friends looking after you. And a place to stay. That's good, right?"

"Yeah. I can probably couch-surf for a little while, but not too long. Most of my friends have tiny places and room-mates who won't like a guest beyond a few days. And the fundraiser will help, but I'm not naive enough to think this is a long-term solution. I'll need tuition next September. I'm looking for work and I'll save what I can over the spring and summer, but I don't know how I'll be able to go to school full-time and afford to live in the fall. I don't even think I'm eligible for student loans," her voice rose in pitch with each sentence jangling Ismail's nerves.

"Hmm," was all he could manage in reply. He reached for his handkerchief, his mind racing with a jumble of thoughts. It dawned on him that Fatima might ask him for financial assistance, a possibility that made him uncomfortable. He reminded himself that he was going to be a good listener, a reasonable adult. "This *is* tough," he said. *Did that sound understanding enough?*

"I've still been thinking about an MFA if I don't do medicine. My parents were going to take care of all of this. They've got the money, you know.... That's why —" She looked up at Ismail, and then back down into her bowl. "That's why I need your help." He raised his eyebrows and readied himself to politely refuse the request for money he assumed was coming.

As though sensing his alarm, she said, "Don't worry, I'm not asking you for *money*. I wouldn't do that. I just need someone — someone like you — to speak to my parents for me. To convince them to support me again."

"Me?" Ismail asked incredulously.

"Yeah, I know it sounds strange, but I've given this some thought. I need an advocate. You're someone of their age and culture and they —"

"Wait, you have to be kidding," he interrupted, "I can't possibly be the right person to help you. Surely, you must have someone else?" He felt his pulse quicken and he took a deep breath, and involuntarily, simultaneously, so did she.

"Listen for just a minute. I really think this could work. My friends and I have gone over every possibility we could think of and we all agreed that this was the only way —"

"— but what about your family? You must have a family member who could talk to your parents for you? Uncles? Aunts? Cousins? Family friends? A teacher?" At each suggestion, she shook her head.

"Here's the thing. We don't have a big family, and most of them are in India, and I barely know them. And the few who are here — they are pretty conservative people, even more so than my parents. A lot of them are really devout, too. I swear, Ismail, most of the extended family would be scandalized if they found out. No one in my family has ever come out. No one's gotten knocked up outside of marriage, or been divorced, even. They say really bad things about people who do."

"But I'm divorced." She didn't seem to hear him.

"If I took this to the extended family or the community, they'd judge my parents, too. That would make things worse." She was now sitting at the edge of her seat, leaning far across the table. He inched himself as far back in his chair as he could.

"Are you sure? There must be people who would be more understanding than you think. I mean, just because they are conservative or religious doesn't mean they won't understand. Perhaps some of them will show you some compassion?" Ismail considered the ways in which community members had responded to his own scandal. Although the overwhelming reaction was avoidance, there had been some surprises from kind-hearted acquaintances who offered condolences and sympathy. Just after Rehana left, he received one unexpected dinner invitation from a colleague of Nabil's, a very devout man who attended the *masjid* regularly with his family. In hindsight, Ismail wished he'd accepted.

"Oh jeez, did I offend you? I mean, I have no idea if you are religious. I mean, I just made an assumption about you."

"I'm only saying you shouldn't make assumptions about whether people will understand or not ..."

"I'm sorry."

"Look, you didn't offend me. I suppose I am a bit of an outsider when it comes to my own community."

"Really? Me, too. I've always felt different," she said, her expression brightening for a moment. Then she turned despondent again. "If I just hadn't written that article. I think my parents could tolerate a lot of the things they couldn't understand about me. I mean, they only complained a little bit about my hair," she said, holding up a blue strand.

"That would seem like a promising indicator to me," he said. She ignored him.

"I wish I hadn't put it all out there, in black and white ... although in a way I'm glad it's out in the open now. Oh, I don't know!" She held her head in her hands.

"Keeping up appearances is very important to some people," Ismail ventured, feeling fatigued now. "It can mean losing your place in the community if you don't." He took a sip of his chai, which had already grown cold.

"See, I knew it. I knew you'd understand." Fatima repeated her entreaties, while he tried to figure out how to let her down easy. He heard only fragments of what she said. At one point, she took out his business card from her pocket and waved it at him, as though it were a winning lottery ticket. "See! My father's an engineer, too!" He pressed his temples — a headache was started to form behind them.

"Listen, Fatima, what you need is a counsellor or mediator. A professional." Dr. Robarts had once suggested that he use therapy in this way, advising him that a session or two with Rehana might help him to find self-forgiveness. Ismail considered her counsel, but just couldn't see his ex-wife coming to Dr. Robart's twenty-third story office to talk about something so private. Besides, therapy was something only he and his boss knew about, a weekly, secret exercise.

"No. They think counselling is for crazy people. But you — a guy their age, from the same culture, religion, even the same profession as my dad."

Ismail gulped back the rest of his tasteless chai and looked at the large wall clock, waiting for their coffee date to be over. Sensing his unwillingness, she said, "Will you at least think about it? It couldn't hurt for you to just talk to them, right?"

"Fatima, I don't think I should get involved. This is a matter between you and your parents." She looked crest-fallen. Despite her sharp features, he saw a softness, a child-like quality in her expression, which made him soften a little in return. "Okay, I'll think about it," Ismail offered, wanting to be kind.

"Thanks," she said. Her eyes moistened and she dabbed at them with a paper napkin.

"I haven't said yes, Fatima."

"I know. I know. But come to my fundraiser, okay? And maybe bring some friends? I need all the support I can get."

23

PWYC

AT EIGHT-THIRTY, MARCO was finally asleep. It had taken two storybooks, a glass of water, and all Celia's patience to get him to go down for the night. She switched off the upstairs hallway light, but lingered there, amongst the upstairs bedrooms. Like a burglar in the darkness of an empty house, she had an urge to stray where she didn't belong. First she crept into the master bedroom. Two party dresses lay over the bed, Lydia's rejects. The top of the dresser was littered with jars and bottles toppled by the rush of the evening's preparations. A single stocking lay on the floor by the bathroom. She almost picked it up, but didn't want to leave behind any evidence of her snooping.

She looked in on Marco again, saw that he hadn't changed position since she last tucked him in. She listened awhile to the soft whistling that came with each of his exhalations and then tiptoed over to the guest bedroom down the hall. It was suitably furnished with a double bed and small dresser. The closet was filled with Lydia's overflow

work outfits. The Shannon Street house had a similar lay-
out, with three bedrooms and a bathroom upstairs. When
Celia's mother became a widow and needed to move in, she
was given the third bedroom. But in this house, it remained
empty, while she lived downstairs. She lingered in the guest
room, bounced on the bed, opened and closed the dresser's drawers. What if she exchanged her bedroom-den for
this room while her daughter and son-in-law were out? She
imagined switching closets, emptying dressers, changing
bed sheets, all under the cover of night — she guessed it
could be done in less than twenty minutes, hours before her
daughter and son-in-law returned home. They might not
notice until morning.

They were out celebrating their sixth wedding anniversary at a fancy restaurant downtown. They planned to go out
dancing later, and wouldn't return, slipping into bed, boozy
and happy until one or two in the morning. It had been ages
since Celia and José went out, just the two of them, and she
couldn't recall what it was like to be someone's date, to be
flirted with, wined and dined. *Why can't I remember?*

She might have known that questions like these would
invite memories of José, ones that felt almost like ghostly
presences. Before she could scamper down the staircase and
distract herself from him, there he was, the smell of figs and
sawdust trailing behind him. She turned on every light in
the living room, the side table lamps and even the chande-
lier, yelling adamantly: "No! No! No!" Her volume caused
him to back away a few steps and regard her warily. Then,
perhaps not believing her, perhaps thinking a maybe might
follow her no, he advanced again. She snarled another "No!"
at him, backing into the foyer and then onto the porch. She
slammed the door shut behind her and held it tight, fearing

he might slither through the quarter-inch gap above the threshold that let in cold air on windy days. But the clarity of her gesture seemed to be enough, and he left her out there alone, shivering in the cold.

She blew into her hands, feeling silly for allowing her imagination to get the better of her. A car engine started up and she startled. Looking down the street, she saw Ismail's car pulling out from its parking spot and speeding away. She checked her watch; it was 9:05 p.m.

— ✳ —

Ismail found the Polish Social and Recreation Centre after circling its industrial neighbourhood three times. His plan was to make an appearance at the party, offer Fatima some kind words, and make it back in time to watch the eleven o'clock news. He hefted open the steel door, and made his way over to a card table. A hand-written sign hung from it reading: *Fatima's birthday fundraiser, PWYC, suggested donation $5.* A boy, a little younger-looking than Fatima, peered over the sign at Ismail and smiled when he dug a ten-dollar bill out of his wallet.

"Do you need change?" An alto voice came from the boy's mouth. Ismail squinted at him in the darkness, but besides his short blond hair and metal-rimmed spectacles, he couldn't make out the boy's features.

"No, that's all right," he said, "it's for a good cause, right?"

"Definitely. Thanks. Here, let me stamp you." Ismail held out his left wrist and was branded with a red happy face. "In case you want to go out and come back in."

"I don't plan to stay too long. I just came to support Fatima."

"I'm guessing that you're Ismail, her friend from Creative Writing?"

"Yes." He felt an unexpected gush of gratification at being known as Fatima's friend. What else had she mentioned about him?

"Hi, I'm Ashton. Fatima told me about how you're helping her out. It's great that you're going to speak to her parents for her. Maybe you can convince them to stop being such jerks."

"Well, I —" Ismail began to protest, to tell Ashton that he hadn't agreed to be Fatima's advocate. Before he could explain, they were interrupted by two girls coming to the door. They flirted with Ashton, ignored Ismail, and unloaded pockets full of change on the table.

"Have a good time," Ashton said, waving Ismail in the door. "And thanks again." Ashton turned his attention to the girls and their quarters and loonies.

Ismail walked into the cavernous space, searching through the darkness to find Fatima. A sparkly disco ball, hung slightly askew on the ceiling, speckled his dark pullover. Only a couple dozen guests milled around, mostly young people who stood against the crepe-paper decorated walls. A few gyrated on the dance floor to a song with a thumping beat and lyrics Ismail couldn't make out. He didn't see Fatima anywhere, and was glad to spot a makeshift bar in the far corner, really just a set of three card tables that looked like they were normally used for the Polish seniors' bridge games. He ordered a beer from a girl slouching behind one of the tables. She narrowed her eyes, scrutinizing his face in a way he'd seen many people look at him in the past. He pulled off his coat, suddenly too warm.

"Hey, are you Ismail?" she asked, a wide smile spreading over her face, surprising him. She extended her hand, introducing herself as Sonia, Fatima's best friend.

Ismail couldn't hear her at first over the music, but since she was smiling, he leaned in. "Sorry, what?"

She made her introduction again, this time touching his shoulder and shouting hot breath into his ear. "It's so great that you're going to talk to her parents. When we had the brainstorming session, and your name came up, I knew she was in good hands."

Ismail had no idea what she was talking about. Brainstorming session? He scrounged in his pocket for a five-dollar bill for the beer. "Here, take this," he said, handing her the money. "But listen, I haven't decided yet about that." She nodded and smiled, and swayed with the music.

"Don't worry about it, it's on the house," she yelled, and turned her attention to the next person in line.

He walked farther into the hall, wondering who else at the party knew his name and would offer premature appreciation for the help he hadn't promised and didn't plan to give. How had Fatima described him to her friends that made him so recognizable to them? Of course, he was the only fifty-four-year-old in the house, the lone old codger among all the youngsters.

He found a wall to lean against and scanned the room. More people had arrived in the previous minutes. He tried to look casual, stuffing one hand in his pocket while he drank his warming cup of beer. A couple of women in tight dresses walked in his direction, and he assumed they were more of Fatima's friends, coming to thank him. He smiled at them, but they didn't seem to notice him. One of the girls shoved the other against the wall, and kissed her, hot and heavy, as though he wasn't there. He looked away, wanting to be invisible, but then remembered that, to them, he was. Feeling perspiration beading his forehead, he moved a few feet away from them, put his drink down on the sticky floor, and transferred his jacket to one arm so he could take off his pullover. His white shirt glowed bright in the black lights of the makeshift dancehall.

Ismail rescued his drink just before a boy with multiple eyebrow piercings almost kicked it over. He touched the plastic cup to his forehead, hoping it would cool him a little. There didn't seem to be a cloakroom anywhere, and so he held his coat and sweater to his chest like woollen armour. Still too warm, with heat rising to his flushed face, he decided it was time to exit the party. He took a few steps toward the entrance, and just then Fatima appeared wearing an electric-blue bow tie that matched her hair, a white shirt, and jeans. She grabbed his arm, jostling his beer, splashing a sip or two onto his white shirt.

"You came," she trilled, "I'm so glad you made it! Come meet some of my friends." Ismail followed her, relieved to be in the company of someone he knew. He held the beer above his head as they snaked across the dance floor, bumping into Fatima's guests, weaving deeper into the party hall. He felt cool beer trickle down his wrist and past his shirt cuff.

By the time Ismail got home, it was 4:00 a.m. By then, he'd provided a ride to the DJ, including transporting all of his equipment in the trunk of his car. Along for the ride were Ashton, the doorman, Fatima, and her best friend and bartender, Sonia. Sometime just before midnight, Ismail succumbed to Fatima's friends' cajoling and agreed to ask Fatima's parents to reinstate their financial support of her.

This was all because he'd had another beer, danced lewdly with girls less than half his age, and then had two more beers after that. The surge of attention from Fatima's friends played on his sense of vanity, and days later, he suspected that it was part of Fatima's grand plan, a subversive plot to recruit his support.

He'd managed to stop drinking around 1:00 a.m., realizing that he was far too intoxicated to drive. He switched to cola and waited to sober up for the ride home. Much to his surprise, it wasn't difficult to stay after his personal last call. Girls and boys, all part of Fatima's inner circle, continued to pull him onto the dance floor, including him in their fun. The DJ even played some bangra/hip-hop combination that Ismail quite enjoyed. The beer had loosened his joints and he danced like he'd never danced in his life, his body awakening as he swayed and swooshed to the music. He thought he must have looked absurd, but he couldn't care less.

The party began to empty out by 2:30 a.m., which was when Ismail first noticed that things were going awry. The DJ was going to be stranded because his ride hadn't shown up. The classmate who had offered Fatima his couch for the week got very drunk, tried to grope her on the dance floor, and was bounced out of the venue by Ashton at 2:40. And five minutes later, Sonia realized that she had lost her house keys.

The final catastrophe happened when the Polish Social and Recreation Centre manager appeared at 3:00 a.m. to lock up and collect his money. He informed Fatima that her parents had put a stop on their five-hundred-dollar cheque, and that she was financially responsible for the venue and sound system payment. Ashton and Sonia handed her the evening's take, a thick wad of bills and a tin pail overflowing with change. Fatima tearfully counted out the money she owed into the manager's beefy hand while Ismail bargained, unsuccessfully, with him for a discount. She tallied the rest to find that what remained was just over four hundred dollars. Four hundred and seventeen dollars to be precise.

"We didn't make as much as we hoped we would," said Ashton apologetically. "I was sure we'd end up with way more. It's probably because there were other competing events happening tonight."

"Yeah, the *Rock Your Tits Off* party was tonight," mumbled Sonia, distractedly, while she rifled through her coat pockets, for the third time.

"And so was the benefit for *Homes Not Bombs*. But we still did pretty well, Fatima," Ashton consoled. "If your parents hadn't been such bastards, you would have had close to a thousand."

"At least you didn't lose any money. That's pretty good, isn't it?" Ismail offered weakly.

"Yeah, but what am I going to do?" she sniffed. "Where am I going to stay? How long can I survive on four hundred and seventeen dollars?"

Sonia, fatigued from searching for her keys for the past half-hour, said, "Well maybe my roommate will be home by now and we can get her to let us in. But I don't know. What if she isn't home or asleep already? And she's already mad at me because I didn't 'consult' with her when you stayed over last week. God, I need a new roommate. I'm so tired of her drama."

"You should move out of there. You and Fatima could move in together," Ashton suggested.

"Sounds like a good solution," Ismail added optimistically, looking at his watch and considering how to make his exit.

"She's hardly there and the place is really nice and the rent is totally cheap. Plus," Sonia said, looking directly at

Fatima, "we tried that already. We don't make good room-mates. Remember? We didn't talk to each other for almost three months after our trip to Europe."

"You guys, help me think. Where should I go tonight?" Fatima whined.

"Sorry, Fatima," Ashton said, "Helena has already made it clear that you can't stay at our place. She's still feeling jealous of *us*. She's never maintained a friendship with any of her exes, so she doesn't get that *we* can be platonic now."

"Argh. Ashton, how is it that you always manage to find these transpositive, yet such heteronormative girls to date?" Sonia quipped, eliciting a slight smile from Fatima.

"She's not heteronormative, just easily jealous," Ashton rebutted.

Ismail listened to their exchange. *Trans-what? Hetero-what?* He found all of their relationships rather tender, but the complexity of their lives quite unruly.

"Hey Fatima, can I have some of that door money for a cab home?" the DJ yelled from across the room. "Twenty bucks should cover it." Fatima's eyes welled up.

As the only, mostly sober, adult in the room, Ismail felt he had to help out. Plus, his was the lone car left in the parking lot. Perhaps, he considered later, they all would have gotten along fine, would have found their way safely home. Perhaps no one would have been left out in the cold, homeless, hungry, desperate, and without keys. But at that moment, it felt to Ismail that the forces of chaos had collided to ruin Fatima's night, forcing him to rein in the mayhem.

24

PRETTY GIRLS

THE NEXT MORNING, ISMAIL groggily rose at 8:00 a.m., dressed, and shuffled to the front door to extract the weekend paper from between his front steps. He looked across the street at the widow's house. How had she spent her night? Would she have watched a little television? Babysat her grandson? What would she think if she knew he had danced the night away with twenty-year-olds? Ismail went back inside and made a full pot of tea for himself. He didn't expect Sonia and Fatima to be up for hours.

Halfway through his first cup, Sonia bounded down the stairs.

"Oh, hello. You're up early," he said.

"Yeah, I thought I'd better get up. I've got to call my roommate, see if she's home and get the extra set of keys. Then I have to change before work." She gestured at the short, red dress that clung to her plump body. She crossed her arms over her chest, modestly covering the deep cleavage bursting from her low neckline. Ismail remembered meditating on that cleavage while dancing with her the previous night. He forced himself to gaze down at the swirly patterns of sediment at the bottom of his teacup.

"Want some tea? Coffee? Uh, I think I have some instant in the cupboard. Are you hungry?" he asked, feeling ill at ease with this young woman in his kitchen, the situation uncomfortably reminiscent of a Mary Pinter morning with its awkward conversation after a night of sloppy sex. Sometimes those women would leave at first light, embarrassed for their drunken promiscuity, worried about details they'd blacked out. Others happily stayed for a hot breakfast, making friendly chatter over an omelette if their stomachs weren't too queasy.

He guessed that Sonia, too, was self-conscious about being alone with him in the glow of his yellow kitchen.

"No, that's okay. I work at a coffee shop. I can get something there. But thanks. And thanks for letting us stay over, too. And ... driving Ashton and DJ Billyboi home," she added, smiling sweetly and clasping her hands together in front of her chest. "I don't know what we would have done without you."

"That's all right." Ismail blushed and poured himself more tea.

"No, really, you were a big help. You were really nice to do all of that for Fatima, for all of us."

Ismail blurted, "Has anyone ever told you that you're the spitting image of Sonia Gandhi? Did your parents name you after her?"

"Sonia Gandhi? Who's she?" she asked, with slowly rising eyebrows. Ismail did his best to give her a summary of the Italian-born Indian politician's biography without sounding like a boring historian. *Of course she wouldn't know who Sonia Gandhi was, you idiot!*

"Oh. Interesting," she said unconvincingly, "I'm named after my Salvadoran grandmother." He walked Sonia to the front door, and, feeling fatigued by the interaction, sat down at the kitchen table to finish his pot of tea.

Half an hour later, Ismail heard stirring upstairs, and he started breakfast preparations. He took out a carton of eggs, an onion, bread, and some ham. Then he put the ham away, just in case Fatima followed Islamic prohibitions against eating pork. He replaced it with cheddar cheese and rooted around in the crisper, finding a slightly puckered red pepper. He chopped everything up, whisked the eggs, and poured the mixture into the hot pan. As he was flipping the omelette, Fatima appeared in the kitchen, looking tired in her crumpled birthday party clothes. She sat down at the table and watched him cook.

"Hungry? Want some breakfast?" he asked.

"Sure, that would be great. I'm starved," she said. And then, with a nervous laugh, she added, "I eat all the time. My friends make fun of how much I can eat."

"And yet you remain so slim. That's how it was for Rehana, my ex-wife, when she was younger. Loved to eat, but always thin as a stick," he said, holding up his index finger to demonstrate. He reflected on how easy it was to speak so casually about Rehana.

"I suppose it's a lucky metabolism to have ... so, when'd you get divorced?"

"A long time ago ... in a year or two it will be about two decades already."

"Huh ... and what's your daughter's name? I don't think you ever told me in class."

"Zubeida. Do you like eggs?"

"Yeah, that smells good ... Zubeida. I have an aunt

named Zubeida," she said, getting up and looking in the pan. There was a long silence, and Ismail braced himself. She retreated to the table again, but he sensed her silence would be brief.

"You never got married again?" He shook his head, turned away from her. What should he tell her? Whenever faced with benign inquiry about his personal life, he could never fabricate something appropriately clichéd and chipper, like "I guess I'm meant to be bachelor" or "I'm still waiting for the right woman to come along." No, these things never came to mind. Instead, the truth played itself like a movie in his head, images of Zubi flickering across his mental screen, or sometimes, it would pause in a freeze frame of Rehana's disappointed expression. He pushed the images away and concentrated on the eggs.

"Hmm," she replied to his silence.

Ismail flipped the omelette again, let it sizzle a few moments, and then cut it in half. He served portions onto each of their plates. The toaster popped and Fatima jumped up to bring the slices to the table.

"What about the widow across the street you told me about? Have you talked to her yet?"

"Briefly, but I'm not really very good at that sort of thing."

"Oh, come on. I don't believe that. Look what a good time you had with my friends last night. Dude ... I mean, Ismail, you're totally outgoing."

"That's different."

"Why?" She buttered her toast with even strokes, colouring within the lines.

"I don't know, Fatima." He stood up, took some juice out of the fridge, and shook it too vigorously. Changing the subject he said, "Sonia left about an hour ago."

"Yeah, she woke me to say she was going to work. She said she thought you were cool to let us stay over." While Ismail lay in bed the night before, he'd strained to listen to the whispering from across the wall, catching slim fragments of words and laughter. He yearned for Daphne and their pillow talk right then, to be able to debrief the party with her, to share how free he was on the dance floor with all those youngsters, and how strange, yet wonderful it was to be inside the kids' inner circle.

"They're nice, your friends. They really seem to care about you," Ismail said.

"Yeah, I don't know what I'd do without Ashton and Sonia."

"It's too bad you can't stay with either of them. It would be much easier for you."

"Uh-huh. But even if things weren't so stressy with Sonia's roommate or Ashton's girlfriend, I couldn't live with either of them long-term, anyway. I love Sonia, but she's kind of a slob. She's always losing her stuff. I don't know how many times she's lost her keys. She needs a twelve-step group for disorganized people," she laughed, and Ismail laughed along, too, but not as heartily — those sorts of jokes were never the same for him after Alcoholics Anonymous.

"And Ashton's girlfriend is super jealous of me," she continued. "And, anyway, I wouldn't want to live with an ex."

"So Ashton, um, is he, uh, he's a guy, right? Er ... sorry, that's none of my business, I just wondered?"

"He's transgendered. Born female, but doesn't really fit into the gender binary. He's transitioning. So, he prefers a male pronoun," she said earnestly, in a tone that reminded him of the educational diversity videos the City forced his department to watch each year.

"I see," Ismail said, although he didn't. They ate their breakfasts in silence. Fatima stood up and cleared the dishes. Ismail watched as she filled one side of the sink with hot water, and squirted in some detergent. She popped a couple of bubbles with her finger and then turned off the water. She looked comfortable in his kitchen.

"Leave the dishes. Why don't you sit? I think we need to discuss the issue of me talking to your parents. I want to get a little more information before I decide." She swivelled around, alarmed.

"Oh, but I thought you'd already decided last night. You said you'd do it," she said, the pitch of her voice rising like a little girl's.

"Fatima, if I'm going to get involved I need to know more about them, about your situation, about you," he said firmly. She nodded, dried her hands, and slumped down in a kitchen chair.

"What do you need to know?"

"Well, I don't know. Just tell me about this problem with your parents. What they said, how you responded. I want to know how they see things."

Fatima rested her face in her hands to collect her thoughts and then began to tell him a longer history than he thought he needed to know. During the half hour, she matter-of-factly reviewed all of her relationships, starting at age thirteen. Shamila was her first girlfriend who her parents assumed was her best friend, and after her there was one girlfriend a year until she was sixteen. With the help of a fake ID, she went to gay bars and even worked in one as a go-go dancer the summer of her seventeenth birthday, while her parents thought she was working in a restaurant or spending time with her "study partner," Monique. She dated two boys that summer. Ismail had an urge to get a pen and paper to keep the details clear in his mind.

By her last year of high school, she'd been in love four times, joined gay youth groups, marched in parades. She used words Ismail had never heard of and that she had to define for him, like "polyamorous" and "kiss-in." He did write those words down, for by then, he was feeling rather out of his depth.

He struggled to push aside his judgments, his Bombay Catholic school attitudes, and Islamic teachings. Not that he was a strong believer in any of that early religious dogma, but still, her ideas unnerved him. He assessed that Fatima, a girl less than half his age, had vastly more romantic experience than he ever would in his entire life. Not only that, she was so casual about it all. He understood why her parents were scandalized.

Once she had sufficiently exposed all the baudy details of her love life, she described her relationship with her parents. Ismail listened, amazed, at the multitude of secrets she'd been keeping from them. He recognized that, like many daughters, she fibbed, omitted, and told outright lies to gain the freedoms she enjoyed. And her parents naively accepted them. He questioned what he would have done, in their position. Didn't all parents want to believe the tales their children spun, the ones that fit best with their misguided notions of who they wanted their offspring to be?

And then she recounted her parents' discovery of her *Varsity* article. They were shocked to read that she was not as innocent as she seemed, and wanted to believe that she had been coerced, fooled, taken advantage of by "bad people."

"I could have let them think that, you know, but I didn't. I was sick of lying to them all the time."

"What did you tell them?" Ismail asked. She scrunched up her face and formed an uneasy smile.

"Everything."

"Everything? The go-go dancing? The political involvements? Your girlfriends?" Ismail drew his facial muscles into a poker face. She nodded.

"I told them everything. I just wanted to be finally free from all of their old-fashioned beliefs and attitudes. I guess I got my wish, in a way."

"Oh my! Fatima, you really must have really thrown them."

"They said they'd take me back in if I would stop being queer. I'd have to have a ten o'clock curfew, drop my friends, and meet 'good boys,'" she listed, numbering off their conditions on her fingers.

Ismail knew it was foolish for her parents to try to control her in this way. Though, he did understand their motivation to restart her in the life they'd once planned for her: medical school; a marriage to a nice boy; and a couple of children when she was ready. A good life. They could set aside their public shame, paint it as a brief, youthful deviation caused by "bad influences." Again, he put himself in their shoes and couldn't blame them.

"I know it isn't ideal, Fatima, but what option do you have? Perhaps you should do what they ask, at least in the short term," Ismail reasoned.

"What are you saying? Live like a prisoner? Date people I don't want to date?"

"Surely that's better than being without a home? And maybe after some time they will loosen their restrictions, and you will be able to do what you want again."

"I can't do it," she pouted. "Why can't they just accept me

for who I am?" she asked, her defiant tone wavering as she struggled to hold back tears.

"Maybe they will, one day. But right now, you've just given them quite a shock. Give them time," Ismail counselled.

"I sometimes wish I could just go back in time. Why couldn't I have used a pseudonym? I was so stupid. It was such a dumb mistake," she said, covering her eyes with her hands. Just around the edges of her fingers, a couple of tears escaped, and trickled down her cheeks.

"Maybe, but it's impossible to go back in time. What's done is done. Regrets will only eat at you," he said, his own eyes moistening, his mind drifting.

Why hadn't I looked over my shoulder when I parked?... Why didn't just one worrisome, sentimental, fatherly thought about my baby enter my thick skull at some point during that day?

"I guess you're right. No point wishing for something that's impossible," Fatima said quietly, drying her face. She pulled her feet up on her chair, and pressed her knees against her chest, resembling a turtle retreated into its shell. Ismail studied her posture, understanding that her story was one of an inadvertent mistake, a public one with big consequences. He understood that kind of mistake.

"Fatima, what's your last name?"

"Geez, I never told you? You know a lot about me. I guess you need to know my surname."

"No it's not that, it only just dawned on me that your parents and I might know one another."

"Really?" Her dark eyes brightened. "That would be even better, right? It's Khan." Ismail knew many Khans.

"And your parents' first names?" She told him, but he didn't think he knew them. Might it be possible that they wouldn't recognize his name? Beyond some small, infrequent gatherings at his brother's house, he hadn't mixed with other Muslims for a long time. And Fatima's family and his were from different communities, which had each swelled over the years with new members from India, Pakistan, and elsewhere. With this growth, each community had become more insular and less likely to socialize outside of itself. Ismail told himself that Zubi had died a long time ago, and hardly anyone would remember anymore.

Fatima called her parents from a phone in the living room while Ismail washed the dishes. After a few minutes she was back, grabbed a dish towel, and stood beside him at the sink. Her good manners impressed him. After dinner, Nabil's boys usually left their plates on the table, took off to their rooms, or out with friends, not giving a second glance to the sink full of dirty plates and pans that awaited their mother.

"So?"

"My dad was out, thankfully. I spoke to my mother and she agreed to tomorrow. She tends to be more reasonable than my father ... I guess she misses me."

"Of course she does. How could she not miss her only daughter? It must be terrible for her," he said. She shrugged.

"Do you miss your daughter?"

"Yes," he answered, avoiding her eyes. "Do you miss your parents?" he held his breath, hoping he'd effectively diverted her attention back to herself.

"Yes and no. Sometimes." She wiped a plate in slow circles, from the outside in. "I would miss them more if we got along better. Like we used to when I lied to them all the time." She became quiet then, only breaking the silence to ask where to put the frying pan and glasses.

She gathered her things and left a half hour later, with plans to spend the day with Ashton. She told Ismail that she hoped to crash at Sonia's despite her roommate's discontent. He walked her to the door and they stood on the porch, confirming the details for the trip to Mississauga the next afternoon. The widow stepped out her door at the same time, smiled their way, and dropped a plastic bag into her garbage bin.

"Ismail, is that her?" Fatima asked, too loudly. "Is that the widow you told me about?"

"Shhh. She'll hear you."

"It is her! Wow, look at her! How old is she? I never thought she'd be all in black," she whispered.

"Well, she is a widow."

"It's just that her clothes seem to weigh her down. I think traditions like that are shackles for women. I read about that in one of my Women's Studies classes last year. It forces women into an oppressed role of being married to God or something like that. It makes them asexual," Fatima frowned, trying to remember the words from her textbook.

"Maybe it's comforting to conform to traditions. I mean, it allows everyone to know that she is grieving her husband, right?" Ismail ventured, feeling unsure of his words. Was it true that Celia was now married to God? He watched as she re-entered her house, leaving the door ajar.

"Well, go talk to her. Looks like she's coming back out. Here's your chance. Ask her out," she advised, nudging him with a sharp elbow. *Pest*, he thought. It had already been a long morning, followed by a short night, and Ismail was glad Fatima would soon be leaving. He looked forward to a quiet house and an unread newspaper.

"Fatima, it's not like I want to date the woman. I'm just, sort of, interested in her, you know, curious about who she is, that's all. And she is in mourning, anyhow."

"Yeah, right. So why are you so nervous, then?" She picked up her backpack, walked a few steps and then turned to wave. She smirked at him in a way Ismail judged unattractive on young people. "See you tomorrow. And thanks for helping me with my family." Ismail didn't answer her, but lifted his arm in a wave. A knot of dread troubled his stomach.

She ambled along like a girl without a care, pausing to pull an MP3 player out of her pocket. Ismail watched her for a few moments and then turned back to look at the widow, who had come outside with another bag. She waved from across the street and called out, "Not too cold today, eh?" She unwound a bungee cord from around her compost bin's latch, a defence against the raccoons. She deposited the bag and reattached the cord.

"Yes, not as bad as yesterday. At least it hasn't snowed this week."

"We haven't seen the end of it yet." She pushed a strand of hair off her face and Ismail imagined what her red hair might feel like between his fingers. Was it coarse like Rehana's or silky like Daphne's? He allowed her voice to pull him down from his porch and to the sidewalk. She, in turn, stepped onto her lawn.

"It's true, maybe another month to go." The widow glanced down the street and Ismail followed her gaze. Fatima was nearly at the end of the block, waiting at the crosswalk.

"Is that your daughter? Pretty girl." She brushed a stray red lock from her eyes.

"No, she's not my daughter." Celia's eyes narrowed. Ismail wobbled on the edge of the curb, and said, "Uh, well, we're in a writing class together." That didn't seem to alter the widow's disapproving expression, and he fretted that Celia might have seen Sonia wander out of his house earlier that morning, in her high heels, skimpy outfit, and short winter jacket. "She's a young person who I am helping out. I'm sort of a family friend." This explanation seemed closer to the truth, but still inaccurate. "She's a nice girl, in university, but having some problems with her parents."

"Oh, that's good of you. I hope things aren't too bad for her," she said, looking genuinely concerned. She now stood at the dividing line between her lawn and the sidewalk.

"Well, we'll see. I think she may be overreacting in some ways, being extreme about things. You know how young people are these days ..."

"Yes, sometimes things can seem more dramatic, so urgent when we are younger. And then we figure out that life is long and we can take our time to do things." Celia grinned at Ismail in middle-aged commiseration, her eyes twinkling. He beamed back at her, almost sure she was referring to their slow-rising friendship. Suddenly Fatima's troubles and his decision to lend a hand seemed a mere trifle. Celia and he made more small talk, each mundane sentence a subtext in possibility. The olive skin on her exposed collarbones shone golden under the soft sunshine. The soil smelled of the earth thawing, the promise of the spring to come.

25

COMPROMISE

"EXACTLY WHAT IS YOUR interest in my daughter?" Hassan's voice was a muted growl, his anger barely hiding below its surface. He and his wife sat directly opposite Ismail and Fatima in the Khan family's formal living room, which reminded Ismail of Nabil's "company-only" parlour, with its cream-coloured sofas, teak side tables, Indian artwork, and delicate statuettes behind glass cabinets.

"We've always been protective of our Fatima, so naturally, we'd want to know," Shelina said evenly, diplomatically. She pronounced her daughter's name in the traditional way, the "I" bouncing lightly off her tongue. Ismail noted this and followed suit.

"Just as Fatima has said. I am a friend, and she hopes that I can act as an intermediary to help resolve the disagreement between you," he said, repeating the words Fatima and he had rehearsed in the car. Hassan regarded him skeptically, and Ismail felt himself flush under the scrutiny. "I assure you, Hassan, I am only here to help."

"How did you two meet? I find it very strange that a man your age — our age — should be making the acquaintance of my daughter." Hassan glared at him from under impressively bushy eyebrows.

"Dad! We're both in the same class," Fatima said, coming to Ismail's defense. "He's been really kind to me. You should be thanking him, not giving him such a hard time! He even let Sonia and I stay over the night before last, after the party." Ismail saw Hassan's jaw tighten and heard Shelina's sharp inhalation.

"Perhaps you should clarify, Fatima," Ismail suggested, and then turning to her parents, he said, "Er ... it's not what it sounds like."

"We were stranded because Sonia lost her keys again," Fatima added. Shelina looked at her daughter and sighed, while Hassan continued to direct his unwavering stare at Ismail. Fatima regarded her parents and then turned to Ismail, "You tell them. They don't believe anything I say anymore."

"Yes, the girls didn't have anywhere else to go. I put them up in my guest room, and they both left in the morning. That's all," Ismail said tensely. "I'm afraid we aren't getting off to a good start here." There was a long pause, followed by another sigh from Shelina.

"I think he comes with good intentions, Hassan," she said, looking to her husband. "Let's talk a little at least and see what they have to say." Ismail found himself shrinking in Hassan's alpha-male shadow. He was built large, like a shot-putter, and struck an imposing figure with his severe expression and compact, muscular body. Ismail averted his eyes from Hassan's steady gaze, focusing instead on the hem of Shelina's lavender *shalvaar kameez*. She passed a cup of tea to him. He reached for it, telling his hand to remain steady.

"Mom, Dad. Listen, both of you, I understand that you are upset with me." Fatima bit her bottom lip.

"Yes, I'm sure there is a solution that will ensure that Fatima's well-being is taken care of while respecting your concerns," Ismail said, returning to their script. He held tight to his tea cup.

"Oh, Fatima, why did you have to do this? Are you trying to punish us?" Shelina pulled an embroidered hankie from out of her sleeve and wiped her nose.

"It is just more of her senseless, shameless behaviour," Hassan said. "This is not the daughter we raised. *She* would have listened to us, been obedient."

"I'm the same person I always was. I'm not trying to punish anyone. I'm just living my life in the way I have to —"

"— in the way you have to? Going to all-night parties, lying to your parents, doing perverted things —"

"Please, Hassan, this is not constructive. We —" Shelina interrupted her husband.

"— perverted! That's not fair, Dad! That's homophobic!" The volume in the room rose as all three Khans talked over one another, Shelina in a wail, Hassan in a roar, and Fatima in high-pitched yell. They went on like this for what felt to Ismail like many minutes.

"Please," Ismail finally broke in, his voice rising above their cacophony. He put down his teacup. "Please!" He repeated, more loudly. The Khans turned to look at him. "Let's be reasonable. You obviously don't agree about Fatima's lifestyle, er ... choices, but perhaps you can find a way to accept her, nonetheless," he attempted, regurgitating advice from a website he'd consulted the previous week.

"We can't accept this. It's just not possible," Shelina dabbed her eyes.

"She must change herself, live with our conditions, if she is going to live under our roof, eat our food, and receive our money," Hassan said, his index finger pointing at Ismail, emphasizing each point.

"It's not possible to change, Dad. This is who I am." She held her head and stared at the floor.

"She is probably correct, I think. From my reading on the subject, this is not something a person can change. It seems that this might be hard-wired and —"

"What makes you such an expert on the topic, huh? What, are you a homosexual, too?" Hassan spat at Ismail.

"No!" Ismail exclaimed, suddenly more flustered than before. It struck him that this was the second time in one week that he'd been asked the question.

"Fatima, you told us you like boys and girls. What I can't understand is why you can't just choose boys if you like them, too," Shelina whispered, in a side conversation with Fatima. Ismail couldn't hear what Fatima whispered back.

"What? What are you two talking about? Stop whispering," Hassan ordered.

"Listen, I think I have a compromise, maybe," Fatima said. Her legs shook slightly, in betrayal of her calm-sounding voice. She laid out a plan in which she would find her own housing and requested their help with tuition and living expenses. She suggested to them that living away from home might be a way to reduce the family's conflicts and rebuild trust over time. She sounded articulate and mature and Ismail was impressed with her.

"This is not right. Fatima, you don't know it yet, but you are too young to know what you want. You come home, start living properly, stop spending time with bad people, and everything will go back to normal," Shelina pleaded.

"That's right. Why should we support you living that way? It's impossible." Hassan crossed his beefy arms across his chest. "And what's more, it will cost us more money than if you lived at home. You have no sense!"

"Perhaps there is a middle ground here? Um, what I mean is, perhaps you could offer her support for the things you do approve of, like her education, books ... meals? And perhaps she could find a way to pay for some of her other expenses on her own?" Ismail was beginning to feel like it was time to negotiate with lower demands. Fatima nodded and looked to her parents hopefully.

Shelina and Hassan each regarded the other, engaged in silent negotiation while Fatima watched with a worried expression. Finally, Hassan shook his head obstinately. Shelina turned to Fatima and pleaded, "Just come home, just try to change, find some new friends. We'll be a family again." Her appeal seemed sincere to Ismail, who felt a measure of sympathy for her. He looked to Fatima, judging that it might be better for her to meet their conditions, if only temporarily.

"For a little while, could you?" Ismail whispered to Fatima. She didn't respond, and stared off into space. He looked up to see Hassan's unblinking gaze upon him.

Finally, Fatima spoke. "Mom ... maybe Ismail has a good idea. If you could pay for my tuition, and books at least?" she implored.

"It's our conditions or nothing," Hassan pronounced, his words like a magistrate's final judgment. "We don't know Fatima anymore. We thought she was a good girl. And then we find all this out. Lying to us for years. And she won't even let us help her fix it and return to normal."

"I am a good girl. I mean," Fatima searched for words, "I

am a good person ... I don't know what I can say to make you happy," she said, her eyelashes wet with tears.

"Just do what we are asking. It's for the best," Shelina said, leaning across the table and touching her daughter's arm.

"It's not rocket science. You go to school, you get yourself a good career. You get married, et cetera, et cetera. It's not rocket science," Hassan said, chopping at the air with his hand.

Fatima sat back, pulling away from her mother. "I can do the first two things. That's why I need your help with tuition," she pouted. "But the rest ... I don't even believe in state-sanctioned marriage, gay or straight."

"Stupid girl, what are you talking about?" Hassan shot back and Ismail cringed at his insult. At the same time, he did feel that Fatima was unnecessarily provoking her parents. *Why question the institution of marriage at this juncture!*

"My God, how have things turned out this way?" Shelina asked, looking off into the distance.

"Listen, everyone, perhaps we should return to the main issue," Ismail said in a pacifying tone. "Although she is not doing things in a way that you approve, she is still your daughter. She wants to go to medical school." Fatima looked his way, was about to speak, but Ismail silenced her with a stern look of warning. *Don't talk about the Masters of Fine Arts!* he told her telepathically. She remained silent.

"Ismail, we have given this a great deal of thought. We have always been generous and trusting with Fatima. Perhaps we have been too indulgent with her. Anything she has asked for, we have given to her. Maybe it is time for her to live with her own consequences," Shelina said quietly.

"Yes, she made her own bed. Now sleep in it!" Hassan glowered at his daughter.

"Maybe you will have to learn the hard way," Shelina whispered. Ismail couldn't believe what he was hearing.

"And we have to live with the consequences, too. So many people know because of that bloody article you wrote. Soon everyone will hear. They will find out that she no longer lives with us. That is our cross to carry," huffed Hassan.

"Bear. Cross to bear," Fatima muttered under her breath.

"What!" barked Hassan.

"It's all about appearances for you," Fatima pronounced. Ismail glanced at Hassan's and Shelina's souring expressions.

"We are not stupid people, Fatima. We are people who have worked hard in this country to make a good life for you and we have worked hard to gain the respect of our friends and community. Our whole life we worked to create a good life for you, and then you had to go and ruin it. Well, you can just live with that." Hassan stood up and walked out of the room and into the foyer. He gestured to the door and said, "You both can leave now."

"Wait, Hassan, let's talk a little longer," Shelina said in an alarmed voice, following him to the door. She addressed him quietly, her back to Ismail and Fatima.

"Yes, please, she didn't mean to offend. Let's try to reason this out," Ismail stammered.

Fatima crossed her arms over her chest, mimicking her father's posture.

"Go." Hassan opened the door wide.

Shelina gave her daughter a perfunctory hug and shook Ismail's hand. He didn't know what to make of her mixed signals.

"When you are really ready to talk to us with respect, then come back, but only then. And don't bring this fool with you." As Ismail walked through the door, Hassan hissed,

"And don't think I don't know who you are, Ismail. We've all heard about you. My wife told me to give you a chance, but I knew there would be no point."

Ismail drove south to the QEW highway and then snaked along the Gardiner Expressway. Fatima sat with her head in her hands, sobbing. Intermittently, she sputtered angry words that bounced around the car's interior.

"Fuck, shit, damn."

"Hypocritical jerks. Fuck."

"Can't believe them."

Ismail kept quiet, allowing her to vent. And, anyway, his mind was on Hassan's hostile words: *We've all heard about you.* Of course they knew who he was. How could he have been so stupid to assume that he was safe? Why didn't he warn Fatima to avoid using his surname? He realized that the whole time they'd sat in the Khan living room, Fatima's parents had viewed him as the monster who killed his own daughter. His presence had only been a liability.

After some time, Fatima's crying stopped and she watched the road silently for a while. When they passed the Humber River, she turned to him. "What did my father mean when he said that they'd all heard of you?"

"I'm guessing that you gave your mother my last name when you called her?"

"Yeah. I had your business card, and I told her your name and what kind of work you do, that you're an engineer, too."

"They recognized my name."

"So?"

"I can't talk about this right now, Fatima. I'm sorry. Where should I drop you?" Ismail pressed down hard on the accelerator.

"Um, well, maybe Sonia's place." She gave him the directions, regarding his face warily. They didn't talk for the rest of the trip and Ismail was relieved for the silence. He kept his eyes forward as they wound their way across the west end. They drove past the arching gates of the CNE, beyond the old lakeshore factories destined to become expensive lofts, and through Queen's Quay with its boats on grey water. Ismail turned left on Jarvis and right on Dundas Street, across Regent Park where the city had destroyed its own impoverished buildings and was rebuilding itself again. They traversed the Don Valley, and he dropped her off in front of a shabby-looking triplex on Broadview.

"This is it," Fatima said, gathering up her bag and unlatching her seat belt.

"This place?" Ismail peered at the building's unwelcoming facade. A toppled garbage bin lay in the middle of a brown lawn. The front door was unlatched, swinging open and shut with the wind.

Fatima stepped out of the car and mumbled, "Well, thanks for everything, Ismail." They exchanged matching gloomy looks.

"No problem," he said. "See you." His words felt false for he wished to never again see the troublesome girl. At the same time, he worried that she would never again want to see him.

An hour later, he was numbed by his second double whiskey. The Merry Pint was about one-third full; it was still too early for the drug crowd who would later fill the back booths. Most of the customers sat near to the windows, bathed in the gauzy, late winter sunlight spreading across the front of the bar. Nearly all sat alone, in the company of favourite drinks. Just a few were paired up, speaking quietly, faces close together, as though sharing long-held confessions. Some stared up at the muted TV, tuned to a local news channel. The Merry Pint was one of those places where city-folk arrive on Sunday afternoons when there is no church that can house them, no mosque that can bear their suffering, no family in which to nestle. Ismail's head grew heavy, clouding over with spirits.

He looked toward the ceiling and asked no one in particular why he had been led to hope that people might have long forgotten his crimes. Why had he foolishly believed he could play the role of knight in shining armour to a hapless girl?

He emptied the glass, whiskey washing down sultry and warm. Hassan, Shelina, and Fatima slowly drifted to the margins of his consciousness. A soft melancholy came to take its place. He ordered a third drink.

— 26 —

BAD APPLE

"ISMAIL," NABIL'S VOICE WAS stern. It was Monday morning, not the usual time for him to be calling. Ismail's stomach tightened.

"Hi. Is everything okay?"

"Yes, yes, listen," Nabil said impatiently, "I'm calling because I heard from a friend that you went to see Shelina and Hassan Khan yesterday."

"How in the world do you know about that?" Of course, Ismail didn't really have to ask. He guessed there was a complex and many-branched phone tree that connected Fatima's parents to his brother.

"I do some work with Shelina's cousin's husband sometimes."

So, Ismail surmised: Shelina had probably cried to her cousin, who pillow-talked the news to her husband, who then gossiped with Nabil. There were just three degrees of separation between the Khans and his brother, a proximity that, in hindsight, was not surprising.

"He was vague about why you were there, but I gathered that you were trying to interfere with a conflict they are having with their daughter. Is that true? How do you know her, anyway?" Nabil's tone reminded Ismail of Hassan's accusations, and had nearly the same effect.

"Well, I met her at a class I'm taking. A writing class, at the university. She and I often sit beside one another. Anyway, she told me that she needed my help," Ismail explained, preparing to defend himself. What had Shelina confessed to her cousin? He assumed she'd want to keep the matter private.

"I don't think you should get involved."

"Nabil, you don't even know the situation —"

"Listen, I know enough. I know that the girl is trouble."

"Did Shelina tell her cousin that?"

"Of course not. She probably only mentioned you to her cousin so that she could find out more about you. But there have been rumours about the daughter for a long time."

"Rumours?"

"She is a bad apple."

Ismail felt his face growing hot. Although he didn't know her well, he certainly didn't think that Fatima deserved such a label. How often had he heard people describe him in similar terms?

"She's not a bad apple. She's a girl who has being thrown out of the house by her parents because she's gay. I think what her parents are doing is shameful," Ismail blurted at his brother.

"So the rumours are true, then? She's a homosexual?"

"Yes. But please don't share that with anyone. I think I've said too much already."

"But what are you doing associating yourself with the girl? I've heard she was using drugs, and being promiscuous, and consorting with the wrong types of people. I suppose it shouldn't surprise me that she is *that way*, too. I heard the *National Post* even published an article about her." It was like a game of "broken telephone," which his staff group played as a team-building exercise the week before. The sentence, "Our mayor is terribly competent at budget projections and almost ridiculously bad at forgetting figures" was whispered from ear to ear around the civil servant circle. The last person announced the statement as "The mayor is terrible at budgets and has a ridiculously bad figure."

"Nabil, don't fall for the rumour mill. What you heard is very much inaccurate, and exaggerated. Don't believe it. There is another side to the story. She is young, in some difficulty, and her parents have rejected her."

"I don't know why you need to get yourself mixed up with this business. Do you know that it has only been the past few years that people have stopped gossiping about you? You want to have the whole community start talking about you again? How do you think this looks that you are vouching for a girl like her?"

"Nabil, do they treat you any differently based on what I do? Did they after Zubi died?"

"In what sense?"

"Did anyone shun you? Did they stop working with you? Did they gossip about *you*?"

"No, well, maybe behind my back. But —"

"Right, so you don't know the first thing about this. I'm sorry, *Bhai*. I'm sorry that you don't approve. But I have to do what is right. I am assisting a girl who needs some help. I am doing a good thing for her." And then a sense of clarity accompanied his next statement: "And I will continue to do what I can for her. Perhaps people should be gossiping about her parents, and how heartless they are to kick out their own daughter." It was as though he was standing up to his older brother for the very first time in his life, and the effort left him feeling strong, but winded. He was surprised that his shirt was not soaked with sweat.

"Well ... you and I have a difference of opinion on this matter," Nabil said, backing down more easily than Ismail would have imagined. "But please tread carefully with this girl."

Ismail didn't respond and a moment of silence crackled across the line before Nabil said, "So, I was also calling because we are hoping you can come over on Saturday for dinner. For Easter. Nabila is making *biryani.*"

"Next weekend?" Ismail asked, thumbing through his agenda book, knowing already that he would find a blank page. "Let me see. Um, I'll have to let you know."

"Okay, call Nabila."

"Fine," he said, hanging up before his brother could utter the final word.

27

GOOGLE

"I GOOGLED YOU."

Ismail had just returned from another bridge inspection, one with some worrisome structural cracking all along its centre, when the phone rang. It was Tuesday afternoon, just two days since their doomed trip to Mississauga, and Fatima had caught up with him already. Ismail needn't have worried that she would stay away. He pulled off his jacket and set his briefcase on the floor.

"Hi, Fatima," he said, bracing himself.

"Hi. So, nothing really came up when I entered your name, except some stuff about your job. And other people with the same surname. There are actually a lot of people named Boxwala." Where was she going with this? "Anyway, I was going to turn off the computer at that point and then I had a thought. I don't know why I thought of it, but I did." His heart began to race. *Inhale one, exhale two,* he instructed his lungs. He booted up his own computer.

"So then I remembered your daughter's name. Zubeida,

right? So I Googled 'Zubeida Boxwala.'" Ismail inhaled two, exhaled four, and waited for the computer to load his settings. *Come on! Hurry up, computer!* He startled when the Microsoft chime bleated out its welcome and he rushed to turn down the speaker's volume.

"At first, I thought the reason why you couldn't write about her, why you didn't want to talk about her, was because the two of you had some kind of falling out. I started to think that maybe you're so nice to me was because you understood what it's like for parents and kids to not get along. But then, I read through the hits." Ismail gasped for three, his chest heaving for six, his eyes welling up. He guided his mouse to the Internet thumbnail on his desktop, double clicked.

"So ... is it true? That she died when she was a baby?"

"Fatima, hold on a minute." By then, his heart was racing. He managed to put down the receiver and blinking back tears, typed Zubeida's name into the Google home page. Two hits. He picked up the phone again. "Listen, Fatima, I have to go."

"Wait, are you coming to class tonight? Maybe we can talk —" Ismail hung up before she could finish her sentence.

He went back to his desktop and read each of the references, ignoring the phone when it rang again. He skipped over the first search item, a story about a Pakistani marathon runner. The second was an article about babies who had died after being left in hot cars. There were a list of names, and Ismail read through them one by one until he reached Zubi's. He read that there were twelve reported cases of this kind in Canada in the past twenty-five years and dozens more in the United States, where summer temperatures were hotter.

He pressed print and hurried to the common office printer to collect the story. His colleague, David, was there, stapling stacks of paper together, when his pages pushed themselves into the printer tray. Closer to the printer, David reached for them and passed them to Ismail with a congenial smile. Ismail nodded to David, clasped the pages in his shaking hands, and practically jogged back to his cubicle.

He read quickly, searching out the parts with Zubi's name. The story detailed the justice system's response to the deaths, and the journalist leaned toward a lenient approach in cases where parents appeared to be innocent. Zubi was listed as an example of such a situation. No foul play.

Ismail re-read the writer's name and guessed she might have been the same reporter who called years ago to request his input on a story about infant deaths. Her tone had been formal and businesslike and at first Ismail assumed she was a telemarketer; by then, over ten years had passed since Zubi's death and the reporters had long ago stopped phoning him. When she told him who she was and what she wanted, Ismail hung up in a panic, just like he'd done to Fatima minutes earlier.

He sent an email to his supervisor that he was going home sick, and hurriedly left the office. The drive home was a blur, his foot pressing down on the brake and accelerator, his hands turning the steering wheel, his mind elsewhere.

He raced upstairs to his spare bedroom and fumbled in a desk drawer, searching for his filing cabinet keys, jabbing and poking at the lock with a half dozen of them before he found the correct one. At the very back of the cabinet, almost hidden but never forgotten, was a worn manila folder. He lifted it from its place, held its weight in his hands, and in a moment of hesitation, almost put it back. He clasped the thin cardboard against his chest, guarding its contents, and made his way down to the kitchen.

He fingered the cardboard folder tentatively and then opened it, placing the newest article on top of the dozens he'd collected since Zubi's death. It shone white against the older, yellowing newsprint, reports and obituaries of other infants who had died in hot cars, freezing vans, forgotten and abandoned by some terrible mistake or parental oversight. Arranged chronologically, the stories about Zubi were at the bottom of the pile.

Ismail never bothered to archive cases ruled as homicides, just those where negligence was the cause of death. He also didn't clip articles about the lucky kids found by kind strangers, the children who were plucked from death-trap vehicles, saved from freezing stairwells and whisked to the hospital in time. Those media "miracles" were reunited with grateful mothers or remorseful fathers. Sometimes, they inspired long adoption wait-lists with the Children's Aid Society. Those children were lost and found, while the ones Ismail archived were not. It became a kind of obsession, saving them, remembering them.

He told Daphne about the folder one night after an AA meeting, a secret never before revealed, not even to Rehana. Daphne appraised him sympathetically, her eyes moistening and the loose skin under them crinkling. She offered to have a look at his collection, be a witness, if Ismail wanted one. He never took her up on the offer. Then, one day, shortly after his confession to her, something changed for him. He didn't know why, but he stopped. He began to press mute when newscasters highlighted the newest abandoned toddler, turned the page when a journalist detailed another neglected baby. He shoved the manila folder as far back into the file cabinet as it could go and never looked back.

Now, with the addition of the online article, Ismail faced his grim archive once again. He spread the musty news-print across the kitchen table's surface, re-reading each of the clippings. He started with the children he never knew, strangers whose stories had grown familiar to him. When he finally got to Zubi's stories, he barely scanned the typeset headlines for he knew all the words by heart already:

"Baby's body temperature was 106.3 degrees when she was found."

"It would appear that the father went to work and forgot his child in the back seat of the car."

"Charges not filed. Prosecution unlikely unless there is evidence of intention to harm the child."

"Car was in full sun most of day, and likely reached a temperature of 125 degrees."

For Ismail, heat was an abyss of desolation. Zubi, at eighty-three degrees Fahrenheit, awoke, shocked to be alone in the stillness of the closed-up car. She shaded her eyes because the Baby on Board sign was useless against the rays streaming in against her face. At eighty-nine degrees, the heat prickled her skin, and she waited for a draft to cool her. But mostly, she waited for her mother, the one she falsely believed to have abandoned her. Ninety-four degrees, and the tears flowing down her cheeks and neck became indistinguishable from the sweat soaking her dress. Finally, at one hundred and two degrees, there was respite and she stopped flailing her arms to escape the straitjacket of her car seat. She slipped into a comforting unconscious-ness. By one hundred and ten degrees, there was deliver-ance from her terror and her organs slowed, and they finally surrendered to the scorching temperature.

Ismail closed his eyes, blocking out the headlines, his own body replaying her story at his kitchen table. His already warm body grew hotter, humid skin drenched itself, and his overwhelmed head spun. He remembered, just before fainting, that he wished to die, to be delivered from the heat.

— ❋ —

Celia was bent over barren flower beds in a fit of premature excavation. Lydia had suggested that she take over the garden that year, told her it might be therapeutic for her, and would help with her depression. Celia snorted at the rankling words: *therapeutic, depression*. What did her daughter know about the *agonias*? What right did she have to dispense any kind of advice?

It hadn't been Lydia's intention to enrage her mother out of her inertia.

Celia's irritation with her daughter grew the way a minor rash turns into a skin-crawling hive. Eventually, she had no choice but to scratch. She replayed the conversation with Lydia in an endless loop, then inventoried each slight and insult her daughter had reaped upon her over the previous year. Finally, she reviewed every unacknowledged kindness she'd offered Lydia since her birth.

Fine, Celia fumed silently. *No problem*, she'd take over the garden. *One less thing for you to bother yourself with, heh?* And she'd cook dinner and take care of Marco, as usual. *Shall I do the laundry and scrub your dirty floors, too?*

What does one do with a surplus of energy that hasn't been experienced in a very long time? Celia had no idea. By the time she picked up Marco and then dropped him off at the neighbours for a play date, she'd scrubbed the house from top to bottom, done three loads of laundry, and put a roast in the oven. She had no choice but to head out to the yard and do the gardening, too.

She wrenched out last year's stalks and stems from the earth, clearing away the old growth, all the way down to the dead roots. Long-browned vines and shrivelled flower heads went to compost to make room for new plantings. Densely packed thawing soil got turned over in fist-sized clumps. It was still March, and the soil probably wasn't ready for all this activity, but she hacked away at it, nonetheless, swinging the hoe high above her head.

She rested a moment, fantasizing about warmer weather, a delusional pastime for northerners suffering through March's tail end. *Ah, spring! Ah, summer!* she said to herself, filling her lungs with air. The weak sunshine brightened her face, and she visualized the beautiful annuals she'd plant in May. *Ah, May, I'd skip right past April for you.*

She wanted only the gaudiest combinations of purples, yellows, reds, and oranges for the garden that year; she admired their brashness. Her daughter preferred a selection of one or two colours, perhaps lavender and yellow, what she called a more sophisticated look. Lydia had shown her photos from *Better Homes and Gardens*, and Celia had smiled and nodded, complimenting the magazine's spread. It was pretty, but she knew she would end up buying marigolds, a rainbow of pansies, the loudest begonias she could find. She scanned the yard, considering where she might dig up grass for a new bed. She envisioned a narrow strip near the sidewalk, just deep enough for a few rows of snapdragons.

Although she'd never been one to wait until Victoria Day, when the weathermen said it was safe, she reckoned she'd have to put off the planting until at least mid-May. But perhaps she'd go earlier, and plant on May 2, her fifty-first birthday. It would be a small gamble, and more than that, a gift to herself for surviving the *agonias*.

So consumed in her mourning, she didn't celebrate her fiftieth last year. Lydia made a nice dinner, complete with streamers and balloons, and baked a sponge cake, but she refused to come out of her room. Celia knew she couldn't face any false cheer that day. Not even little Marco scratching at her door like a kitten could make a difference. She put a pillow over her head, laid flat on her aching back, and considered what it would be like to not be able to breathe through down filling.

Maybe this year would be different and she'd partake in a little cake and celebration. Why not? She looked at the dark, naked earth, and then, scanning the clear sky above, she wished for it — one full happy day. But only that. She didn't want to hope for much more.

She looked over Ismail's way, a stray, cheeky notion entering her mind: *would he like to eat a slice of my birthday cake?* She surveyed his abandoned-looking house and then shook the thought away. *Silly. Why think about that?* He likely had enough friends of his own, and many birthdays to attend. She recalled seeing him speaking with the young woman two days ago. Their body language conveyed an intimacy she couldn't identify.

She worked a while longer, until the cold reached under her sweater, brushed past her thermal undershirt, and settled against her chest. She pulled off her muddy gloves, dusted her skirt, and gathered together her tools. Just as she was retrieving her hoe, a squirrel scampered close, chirping frenetically. She guessed she was being scolded for disturbing his winter hiding places. She smiled as he danced in a chaotic circle, twittering away, looking like madness broken loose. Then, he ran down the sidewalk, disappearing behind some bushes.

She followed the noisy rodent's movements down Lochrie and noticed that the street's composition had shifted while she had been working. Ismail's small blue car had appeared, filling a previously vacant space a few metres away. Celia checked her watch and wondered why he was home so early; she'd been at her window perch enough to know that he always left and returned at about the same time each day and Lydia had told her that he had some kind of employment with the government. A good position, with office hours that seemed to bring him home on time for dinner each day, not like her own late husband's job.

She squinted at his red front door. It was ajar, and the screen door was wide open, too, letting in the cold breeze. She watched his house a minute or two, waiting for him to come and shut it — perhaps he'd just had his hands full and would be back soon. She watched and waited, and still Ismail's entrance remained open, unprotected. She left her tools and gloves on her front step, and crossed the street. She pressed the doorbell and heard its *ding-dong-ding-ding*. Then she knocked on the door frame, her knuckles all urgency and hardness. She called out his name, her voice box tight, her tone too shrill. Then, she rushed in.

She found him on the floor, sprawled out, a tangle of limbs. His skin was pale, his body still. She froze, mistaking unconsciousness for death. A widow's wail rose within her, but caught in her throat so that all that came out was a faint whimper. She held on to a nearby chair, felt herself pulled into a dizzy stupor. Within an instant, Ismail and Lochrie Street dropped away from her, and she was once again in her

own kitchen on Shannon Street, standing over her motion-
less husband, again, too late. She should have hurried, come
sooner, not dallied. The past swirled before her, obscuring
her vision. José, on the floor, his heart stopped, the breath
no longer in him, was all she could see.

She clasped the chair's back, her fingers somehow
knowing to hold on. Her lungs willed her to breathe. After
a moment, her husband receded enough for her to see an
unfamiliar kitchen: yellow walls, stainless-steel appliances,
bamboo floors. Like a latch coming undone, the past released
itself, freeing her. José stepped away and she saw Ismail.
Relief, but panic too: *Wait! José, are you still there?*

She kneeled down and gingerly felt Ismail's moist forehead, leaving behind traces of garden soil above his brow.
Heat radiated from him, the fire in his body fuelled by
something she couldn't recognize and knew better than to
touch too long with bare hands. At the sink, she rinsed a
towel with water, wrung it out, fashioned a cold compress.
She wiped his forehead, sensing his fever's reprieve, and
repeated the process twice more. His eyes fluttered, but his
body remained limp.

She pressed the towel against his cheeks, down his
neck, and then unbuttoned his shirt to place the towel on
his chest, over his lungs. She left her hand there too long
and she thought she could feel his sorrow burning inside
him. Then, a panic rose within her. She said aloud, "Ismail,
where's your phone. I'm calling 911."

She rose, and Ismail's eyes fluttered again. "Don't call an
ambulance. I'm okay," he moaned.

"Are you sure?" she asked, but he went silent again,
brewing in his pain. Finally, there was a slight nod, no more
than a tremor, and she understood. She let the phone drop

beside her and sat with him on the floor holding his hand, waiting for his fever to stop its burn behind his eyes and within his heart. Her mind wandered. *José, did you suffer like this? What memories fluttered about while you lay alone on the floor?*

Tears streamed past Ismail's dark lashes. They washed over his cheeks, dripped off his chin, slid down his neck, and were absorbed by the collar of his shirt. Eventually, his tears became indistinguishable from the sweat that had already poured over him and soaked him through.

— ❋ —

Celia floated above Ismail, a frown pinching the skin between her eyes. He felt her hand against his palm, cool skin against hot. His hair and face were drenched. Salt stung his eyes.

"You sure I shouldn't call an ambulance?" She gazed at something behind him and at first Ismail thought she was talking to someone else. He craned his neck and saw they were alone.

"No, don't do that," he whispered and groggily wondered how she had gotten into his house. Had he left the front door unlocked?

"Are you having any pains? In your chest? Down your arms?" she asked, tapping lightly on his bare breastbone. He noticed that his shirt had been unbuttoned, and her cool breath raised goosebumps on his skin. He watched as she looked down at her fingers on his chest, and brushed over his scar. It seemed to thicken and pulsate under her touch. Ismail pushed himself up and onto his elbows.

"No, I just feel a little nauseated ... and dizzy. I think I passed out," he ventured, feeling suddenly silly for all the fuss. He fumbled with his shirt buttons, but couldn't make them work.

"Good, no pain. Wait. Don't get up yet. You just came to. You might faint again," she said, the pads of her fingers strong now, pressing him to the floor.

"Really, I think I'm all right. I'll just sit up a little." He waited for her to ponder his proposal, lest she push him down again. After a moment, she held out her hand and hauled him up to sitting, one of her hands in his, the other firm against his back. "How long have I been out?"

"I don't know. I've only been here maybe five minutes or so," she guessed, frowning, looking again at the wall behind him. "I don't quite know. Not long ... how do you feel sitting up?"

"Fine," he said, although really he was a quite light-headed, the blood thundering down too fast. His head sounded like old plumbing, pipes ready to burst.

She remained pensive, her gaze unfocused. She sighed and with their faces only a few inches apart, he felt her exhalations on his face. Finally, inexplicably, she smiled, the gap between her front teeth gleaming. She stroked his forehead with her fingers, tenderly, not like a stranger would, and Ismail hesitated to say anything more for fear of interrupting her.

"Oh, you *are* going to be just fine," she sighed again, her tone almost wistful, childlike. Ismail nodded, cleared his throat, ruined the moment. Celia blinked hard, backed up, and scanned the room, as though looking for something, someone. She shook her head, then turned her gaze back to Ismail.

"Yes, really I think I'm fine. I'm not dizzy anymore. I think I can get up now," he replied. He waited for her permission

once more. She nodded her assent, stood, and then helped
him to his feet. Ismail felt her arm encircling his waist, and
noticed that her touch had turned stiffer, more formal. He
swayed, lost his balance, and she clutched him more tightly.
He steadied himself and she released him and looked away.

"Are you okay? You seem ..." Ismail couldn't name what
seemed to be ailing her.

"Oh, it's nothing ... I'm ... fine. What were you doing that
made you faint?" she asked, turning her head to the kitchen
table, looking at the jumble of newspaper articles spread
upon it.

"Just ... just reading." He wanted to sweep the articles
off the table, to make them disappear, but her eyes were
already locked upon them. Helpless, he watched her read
the headlines.

"Oh! This is terrible. These are *terrible* things ... some
of these look like they're from a long time ago." She rifled
through the articles, her hand coming up to her mouth in
dismay. Ismail could tell the moment she saw his daughter's name, recognized the surname that linked them, for
this was when her eyes stopped roaming the page and her
breathing became more shallow. "Boxwala," she murmured
quietly, pointed to the letters in courier font in the centre of
the table. "Zubeida Boxwala. Ismail, is this about someone
you know, a relative of yours?"

His eyes blurred with tears and he slumped into a
kitchen chair. She watched as he slowly gathered the articles together into a messy pile and shoved them back into
the manila folder. "Did I leave my front door unlocked?" he
asked, evading her question.

"Not just the lock. The door was wide open. Even the
screen door, letting in all the cold air. That's why I came

over. Something looked wrong." She sat down in a chair beside him.

"I'm sorry for frightening you like that. I guess I was a little distracted when I got home."

"Distracted by this, yes?" she asked, pointing to the closed folder. "May I ... look at it again?" Her eyes were gentle, kind. Ismail looked long at the flowers in her eyes and surrendered to them.

She pulled her chair closer to the table and read the article that bore Ismail's daughter's name, continuing where she had left off. Her eyes widened with each scanned line, her skin holding taut her pained expression. Ismail submitted to the reality that she now knew his secret. And so did Fatima. But how could this be happening? He'd guarded his privacy for so long, allowing the tragedy to almost slip away. Strangers could imagine him without that ugly past, and in their company, he could almost pretend it away. Almost, but not quite.

Ismail waited for Celia to finish. He closed his eyes and sat up straight, bracing for the inevitable verdict: bad father, baby killer, murderer. A vision danced underneath his eyelids, memory coming alive.

After a terrible week of staying at home avoiding the telephone, Rehana and Ismail had cabin fever. The media had finally stopped calling, the newspapers slowly, mercifully, losing interest in their lives. Rehana begged Ismail to go out for a walk with her, to escape the heat and the claustrophobia of their house. They stepped onto Lochrie, vigilant for the neighbours they didn't want to see. They'd already had their fill of explaining the accident to everyone in their circles: supervisors who had approved time off, their families, the police. The story had been repeated, the facts laid bare. Now that Zubi had been buried, Ismail and Rehana didn't want to talk about it anymore.

They walked down Brock, and under the bridge, just as a train came rumbling over them. They climbed some steps onto a dead-end street with a ghostly grey cement parking structure they'd never before noticed. The found their way to Lansdowne, then back up to Dundas. The evening air was like a humid blanket, but still they enjoyed the liberation of being outside. They admired gardens, watched teenagers playing ball in a park, window-shopped, as though their lives were normal again. Then, as they sauntered along St. Clarens to the alleyway behind their house, they saw him: Rob Gallagher. Their chatty neighbour would have normally stopped them, drawn them into conversation. But that day, he met their eyes, turned and walked away, his back gate clattering shut. Rehana dissolved into tears, leaning heavily against Ismail. *Look how people are treating us, Ismail!* He held her in the alleyway, his anger toward Gallagher a boomerang that returned as self-hatred.

A week later, when she was alone, Gallagher stopped Rehana on the sidewalk and offered her sympathy, telling her he blamed her husband for everything. Ismail didn't know why she chose to repeat his words. She never mentioned if she challenged Gallagher's viewpoint or agreed with him.

— ❈ —

While she read, Celia glimpsed him out of the corner of her eye. *José.* He paced the kitchen, back and forth, watching her, trying to get her attention. She chided herself: *Come on, Celia, you know he's not there. Stop being crazy; it's just the déjà vu of the situation.* Meanwhile, Ismail stared into his lap, his lids heavy and his expression blank. When she glanced up again, her imagination took hold of her once more. In her mind's eye, José had stopped his pacing, and was studying Ismail.

What are you doing here, José?

I could ask you the same thing. She recognized his tone, the accusatory look she'd seen on his face before.

What? What are you saying? He's just my neighbour.

Yeah, right. I've seen how you look at him. How you're always watching him.

It's nothing, José. And what's it matter to you, anyway? You're not here. You left me a long time ago, remember? You left me alone with your debts. Remember?

And then he was gone, her shrill thoughts chasing him away. She turned back to the newspaper article, and read about a sweltering car, the suffering of a child, the shock of a mother, a father's regret.

— ✿ —

Finally, Celia raised her head, and pushed the manila folder back toward him. He saw her look of compassion, her eyes brimming with tears not yet released. Still, he judged this to be an initial reaction and waited for it to shift, for her to speak sharply, to walk out of his house.

"She was yours, wasn't she? This was your daughter?" Her voice was soft. She remained planted in her chair. She blinked, and a tear escaped her left eye, and travelled down her cheek to her chin. Overwhelmed by her kindness, Ismail's throat went dry, and he couldn't speak. She waited.

"Yes," he finally managed to say, his voice barely audible.

"These ones," she said, pointing to the oldest, most yellowed articles, "these are from nineteen ninety ... almost twenty years ago. Such a long time ago."

"Yes, almost ... in August ... it will be twenty years," Ismail responded, stumbling over his words. There were so many things he could have said to her, a jumble of words that were getting caught in his throat. *It's so long ago, but it never goes away. Never.*

"But still like yesterday, yes?" She leaned toward him, took his hand and squeezed lightly.

"Like today," he said, looking down at their hands, olive skin wrapped around brown. He couldn't recall anyone ever holding his hand so gently.

"It's hard to remember, isn't it? To be in the past with ghosts." She looked off into the distance, like she'd done before, and then, not finding what she'd been seeking, she faced Ismail again.

"Yes, it's very hard. The hardest thing ..." He couldn't find the words to finish his thought.

"You know, last year, more than that now, almost a year and a half," she said, haltingly, and then stopped, her eyes moistening again. "My husband ... he passed away. I found him on the kitchen floor, just like I found you. And then soon after ... my mother ..." Another tear escaped, following the trail left by the previous one. He watched more tears stream down her face. Her sadness pulled him from the grip of his own sorrow.

"I'm so sorry," he said, watching her eyelashes darken as they grew wetter. He passed her a clean handkerchief, watched her dab her eyes, wipe her nose.

"I am a widow, and before that I lost my father, and then after, my mother. I've been mourning a long while now. I've been all in black for a long while," she said, gesturing to her clothing. Ismail studied her cotton dress, glanced quickly at her lean arms, the rise of her chest. He couldn't help himself and took a quick look at her shapely legs in their dark panty-hose. Then, he looked at her wavy hair, its shade somewhere between auburn and scarlet, hair that was not meant to be overlooked. He turned over her hand and admired her polished nails. The hue of ripe lychees, just a little chipped at the ends.

"But not all in black. Not quite," he said, smiling weakly, gesturing to the bursts of crimson in her hair and nails.

"No," she said smiling shyly, "I suppose I have been growing tired of it. Being a bit of a rebel. I don't like being a widow. I suppose I want to be finished with it. "

"Yes, I understand," Ismail whispered, and he meant it. She squeezed his hand again, and her touch sent a tingle up into the cool caverns of his chest. He reached out for her with his other arm and she leaned in, completing the embrace. They remained there a moment, holding the other stiffly. Then, she exhaled, and she pressed her palms into his back. He felt her head rest on his shoulder and his ear reach down to feel her soft hair. He allowed the pads of his fingertips to gingerly caress her ribs. Then, all too soon, her body released his.

"Well, I should get home," she said, looking down at her shoes. He followed her eyes down her legs to her leather boots. A warm blush crept up his face.

"Yes, well, let me see you to the door, then," he said, avoiding her eyes.

"Are you sure you are fine now? Not feeling light-headed anymore?"

"I am, thanks. And you?"

"Yes. Thanks for the talk." Her fingers rose up to his forearm in reassurance and he was grateful to be touched again.

"Well, thanks for coming to check up on me. And for picking me up off the floor," he grinned shyly.

"That's what neighhours are for, right?" she said, returning the smile. And with that, she said goodbye. Ismail stood on his porch, watching her cross Lochrie Street. Her house was brightly lit and he guessed her family was home, waiting for her. She paused as she opened the front door, puffing up her chest as she took in a deep breath. Ismail felt the cool evening air on his skin, breezing through his damp clothing.

He returned to the kitchen, and surveyed the mess of papers on the table. He gathered them all together, straightening their edges until they formed a tidy pile. Then, he placed them back into the manila folder and was about to take them upstairs to the cabinet. But then he stopped. As he held the weight of those articles in his hands, he realized how much he hated them. He'd kept the folder all those years, filling it with miserable stories as though it was his obligation, his duty, a penance. But they didn't even hold the truth about the children who had died, and certainly didn't capture Zubi's life with any kind of grace. He couldn't stand the folder any longer.

He turned back to the kitchen, and carried the file to the garbage can. He planted his foot on the pedal-lever, and the lid yawned open. He stared down into the darkness of its bottom, hesitating, gripping the papers. Then, slowly, they slipped through his fingers in a steady stream. They landed at the bottom of the bin with a whoosh, and he let go of the pedal. The lid clattered down upon them.

28

A GOOD FRIDAY

Ismail didn't see Celia for a few days after that night at his place. Although he *knew* she'd been at his house, he questioned if he remembered the interaction correctly. Did they really share an embrace? As the days passed, paranoid thoughts wormed through his mind: Could she be having a delayed reaction? Was she avoiding him now?

Meanwhile, the evening bore out changes Ismail couldn't deny. Something inside him had shifted, lightened just a little. When he took out the garbage a few days later, he remembered what was weighing down the bag, recalled the articles he'd relinquished that night. He had no urge to salvage them and was glad when the garbage truck drove away.

Still, when something long held is released — even a hardship — a void remains, nameless, shapeless, aching to be filled. Ismail didn't yet have anything to replace his file folder of suffering.

—

The Easter weekend approached, and he declined an invitation to stay over at his brother's family, opting instead to join them just for Sunday dinner. What the suburbs had to offer were too paltry after all he'd been through that week; he needed something fresh and new in his midst.

On Friday, he chose a restaurant in Little Italy for an early supper, a place he'd been meaning to try for years. He started with a glass of shiraz from a winery near Chatham. He scanned the menu, discovering that he didn't know what risotto was and for that reason, and that reason only, he chose the fourth item down the menu's list: Seafood with Porcini Mushrooms, Fennel and Onion, and Red Wine Risotto. He ate slowly, allowing the waiter to fill his water glass three times.

He paid the bill and tried to decide what to do next; it was still early. Despite his best intentions, he found himself dropping into the Merry Pint on his way home. The place was empty, the usual crowd likely corralled indoors by loved ones for obligatory family gatherings. He'd heard the regulars speak of holidays with a sort of dread he'd associate with visits to the dentist or tax auditor. Still, Ismail envied his bar buddies their spouses, children, their peopled lives.

He left after one drink. A few blocks away from the bar, police had blocked off a side street, and a small crowd was forming. He rubbernecked with the rest, expecting an accident or emergency of some kind. Instead, off in the distance, a procession sluggishly approached. He stood amongst the others and waited.

— ❀ —

As Celia shuffled along, she felt the melting wax drip onto her bare hand. She adjusted the candle's crude wind-breaker, an upside-down Dixie cup, but still the wax slid down, coating her fingers like a warm, waxy glove. The walk was nearly over, and as they neared the church, the procession grew fuller as onlookers joined in for the final quarter mile. Their bodies crowded the street, hemming her in, neat lines of the faithful melding into one solemn wave along Dundas Street.

Beside her was a man carrying a child on his shoulders. The little girl scanned the crowd, taking in this not-so-festive parade with wide eyes. Celia noticed that there were few young people amongst the group; mostly older folks participated these days. What would this procession look like in a decade or two, when the elders passed on? Would the little girl bring her own daughter, and carry her on her shoulders?

Even though Celia wasn't very religious, and attended church irregularly, she found the annual ritual comforting; she liked being one of the faithful millions around the world participating in the same ceremony on the very same day. In previous years, her mother and Lydia accompanied her on the walk and it dismayed her that Lydia had refused this year, saying that the wooden Jesus, carried high above the crowd, made Marco cry. It was a far too macabre a display for a child, she said. That's the word Lydia used. *Macabre*.

The child riding on her father's shoulders was now a few feet ahead of Celia, and when she looked to her left, she saw Sylvia Silva, one of the grandmothers she talked to in the schoolyard where she went to gather Marco. Sylvia was over a decade older than Celia, and a widow for over eight years already. Celia vaguely recalled Sylvia's husband, a tall insurance broker who died of prostate cancer a couple of years after Celia's father. Sylvia walked stiffly, with a stoop, and looked much older than her sixty years. Celia had seen it many times before, this accelerated aging among widows.

Celia veered slightly to her left to draw nearer to Sylvia. Tears streamed down Sylvia's wrinkled face, making it glisten in the candlelight. She walked as though in a stupor, her gaze faraway. *This speaks to us, this walk of sorrow. This speaks to us.* Celia averted her eyes, not wanting to be too infected by Sylvia's grief.

But grief is contagious, and despite Celia's efforts, she found her own eyes leaking tears, warming her face like the dripping wax on her hand. As the heaviness passed through her, she walked and cried for what was lost in her own life. At Gladstone Avenue, she mourned her mother. Nearing Dufferin, she longed for her husband. As the procession passed Sheridan, she wept for her lost house. By the time they were at Brock, Celia began to feel guilty for mourning her own small life instead of *Senhôr Bom Jesus*, but there was no use in trying to stop it. Celia felt Sylvia's arm linking in hers.

Through her tears, she spotted Ismail across the street, watching the crowd pass. She hoped he didn't find the procession strange; so many non-Portuguese people gawked and pointed, as though they were exotic animals on parade. But Ismail didn't seem to be watching in that way. Rather, there was a look of solemnity on his face, the corners of his mouth turned down, his arms hanging limp by his sides. *Just like us.* She watched him a while longer, straining to see if he noticed her, too. He'd been on her mind since that night at his place three days earlier, but they hadn't bumped into one another since then. Perhaps he was embarrassed, and avoiding her? She trained her steady stare on him and waited for him to look her way.

Finally, their eyes met and they exchanged brief smiles. Sylvia noticed the shift in Celia's mood, and followed her gaze to find out what had caused it. Somewhere ahead of them, a band started up and people sang a hymn. Celia and Sylvia hummed along.

— ❋ —

Two days later, at six-thirty sharp, Ismail rang the doorbell at Nabil and Nabila's place. Technically, he could have just walked in — they hardly ever locked the door, believing that their neighbourhood, a forest of custom-built homes, was perfectly safe. He waited on their porch, shivering. There was the thumping of youthful footsteps and then Asghar opened the door.

"Hey, Ismail *Kakaji*," the young man said, grinning. Ismail shook his hand and clapped him on his back.

"Look at you! You've grown a beard ... no, that's not a beard. What's that called?" Ismail asked, inspecting the space between Asghar's bottom lip and chin, where a tuft of hair had recently sprung up. He'd seen this style of facial hair on young men around his office, and on the host of his favourite home makeover show.

"It's called a soul patch, *Kakaji*. Much easier to maintain than a goatee or beard ... and way cooler," he said, caressing his novelty inch of fur.

"Very nice ... er, very cool. Yes." While Ismail hung his coat in the hallway closet, Nabila came out to greet him.

"Ismail. Don't encourage him. I wish he'd just get rid of that thing. Doesn't it look like he missed a spot when he shaved this morning? I should creep up on him while he's sleeping and just shave it off," she said, brushing Ismail's cheek with a light kiss. Asghar rolled his eyes. "Really, it would just take one stroke of the razor!" She mimed the deed, brandishing an imaginary blade at her son's chin.

"You just try it, Mom, and see if you don't need a wig the next morning!"

"You see how my youngest child speaks to me?" she asked, in mock dismay. Ismail couldn't help but laugh at their banter.

"Yes, well, I think you'd both be wise to keep the razors locked up around here," he counselled them.

"Yes, and our bedroom doors, too, Ismail. Come, sit in the living room. Nabil should be down in a minute," she instructed. Ismail did as he was told and found Asghar's older brother, Altaf, already there, dipping a samosa in tamarind chutney.

"*Kakaji*, nice to see you," he said, putting the samosa down and extending an oily hand.

"So, I hear that things are going well for you these days. School is good?"

"Yes, so far so good. The residency is much easier that I was told it would be," he said with an air that was neither boastful nor self-important. Altaf had always been successful in his pursuits, including those self-chosen or chosen for him. It was just the way he was. He and his brother polarized one another effortlessly.

"My son is going to be a surgeon!" Nabila chimed from the kitchen, her voice singsonging maternal pride.

"Very good, very good, congratulations. And Asghar, school going all right for you, too?"

"It's fine. I like my courses way better now. Remember I told you I decided to change my major?"

Ismail nodded.

"Well, I did it and Dad flipped," said Asghar. "But that's okay, I'll survive. He's pretty distracted with arranging Altaf's marriage, anyhow."

"Oh yes, your father told me that you've met a girl," Ismail replied, turning back to Altaf.

"We've gone on a few dates. She's very nice, and planning to go to med school. But," he said, glowering at his brother, "it is not an arranged marriage."

"Could have fooled me. *Kakaji*, her whole family came over for dinner to do the introduction. It was like a scene right out of *Bride and Prejudice*."

Ismail laughed at the reference. They'd all watched the movie on DVD the last time Ismail was over, and Asghar, not a fan of Bollywood-style films, tossed popcorn at the TV screen each time a song and dance interlude began.

"Stop exaggerating, Asghar," Nabila called from the kitchen.

"Yeah, it was just our two families having dinner together. Hardly even an introduction," Altaf said, resolutely, "and anyway it's a good way to meet a nice girl. Why not depend on our parents' network for one of the most important decisions I'm going to make in my life?"

"Whatever," Asghar scoffed, dismissing his brother. "Speaking of introductions," he leaned in closer and said conspiratorially, "you should know that Mum and Dad have invited over a lady. She's divorced. They haven't said so, but I'm pretty sure it's a hook-up."

"A hook-up?" Ismail looked at him blankly. "What for?"

"A hook-up for you!" he said, pointing at Ismail. Asghar giggled in high-pitched bursts that irritated his uncle's ears.

"A hook-up for me?" Ismail asked, incredulous. Altaf joined in his brother's laughter. Nabil and Nabila hadn't tried matchmaking Ismail since the mid-nineties, after those first two abortive attempts at re-entering the dating scene.

"What's everyone laughing about?" Nabil asked, finally making his appearance. "Hello, Ismail," he said, reaching a hand out to his brother. "Hey, boys, stop eating all the samosas. Mom put those out because we are having a guest."

"Nabil, please take off your Bluetooth. It's not sociable," Nabila said, coming into the sitting room. "Yes, what's the joke?"

"Er ... who is this 'guest' who is coming over?" Ismail asked them warily.

"She's an old friend —"

"Really, an acquaintance," Nabila said, correcting her husband.

"Yes, well, someone we've known for a long time. She's a nurse. A divorceé —"

"It was terrible — her husband, a Canadian man, was having an affair. But listen, this is the worst part," she said, her voice hushing dramatically. "He was having an affair with *her* best friend! Can you believe it? Such a scandal! I guess the moral of the story is that's what happens when you marry outside of the community, right?" She looked to Nabil, who nodded in agreement.

"Aw, come on Mom. Don't be so narrow-minded! The moral of the story could very well be 'never trust your best friend,'" Altaf interjected with logic.

"I'm not! I'm just stating the facts. They split about three years ago. She's a very nice lady. You'll like her," Nabila said.

"Yes, but Nabila —" Ismail stammered. He made eye contact with Asghar, who watched the exchange with amusement.

"We thought the two of you might like to meet one another. You know, you are both divorced, without kids and around the same age. Actually she is a few years younger, in her late forties, wouldn't you say, Nabil?" Ismail raised his eyebrows at his brother and sister-in-law.

"Don't look at us like that! It's just a little introduction over dinner. Don't you want to meet a nice woman, settle down?" Nabil asked. Before Ismail could answer, the doorbell rang.

"That must be Shakila now," Nabila said, going to answer the door.

"Like a lamb to the slaughter," Asghar muttered and Altaf snickered.

"Just be quiet and behave yourself," Nabil admonished Asghar. Then, looking at Altaf, too, he said, "You both behave yourselves."

"What did I do?" Altaf protested.

Ismail's nervousness stole his appetite and so he couldn't enjoy the mutton *biryani, kofta* curry, and *kachumbar* Nabila had prepared, a meal he'd been looking forward to all day. Shakila, in contrast, seemed not at all uncomfortable with the obvious matchmaking. He observed her fill her plate and take seconds, habits he quite enjoyed in a woman. She made good conversation, laughed easily and was pretty, with straight, shoulder-length hair that nicely framed her round face. Ismail judged her makeup to be a little on the heavy side, however, her eye shadow a tad too dark and her cheeks over-rouged. He tried not to over-focus on it, but Shakila's eyes reminded him of a Mary Pinter he'd slept with years ago, her eyelashes leaving behind a streak of black on his white pillowcase.

His own appearance made him self-conscious; if he'd known he was being set up, he might have dressed a little more formally, exchanging chinos for dress pants and a button-down shirt in a good poly-cotton blend for the casual pullover he was wearing that evening. Not that he looked shabby — he always took a minute to iron his clothes and look presentable before going out. Rehana found his grooming and his preference for a well-pressed shirt to be on the fussy side, perhaps because she wasn't used to a man doing his own ironing. Ismail had learned the skill in college, when, for the first time in his life, he was forced to launder his own clothes. He even came to enjoy the experience: the smell of starch-scented steam, the smoothing of fabric and the ability to solve simple, wrinkly problems with the press of metal.

Nabila and Nabil directed the dinner conversation like a pair of conductors leading a small, mostly compliant orchestra. They asked Ismail and Shakila questions that were likely to produce entertaining stories, or display their guests' most agreeable attributes. Even the boys were welcomed into the performance to flaunt their talents and demonstrate what a harmonious family the Boxwalas made.

Ismail learned that Shakila was a public health nurse, working mostly with seniors. ("You're both civil servants!" Nabila exclaimed, her voice like a cymbal's clatter.) She had lived in Canada for over fifteen years, arriving in her thirties. She liked to knit, do Sudoku, and had recently learned to cross-country ski. Nabil and Nabila prodded him: *Ismail, tell Shakila about your renovations! Or my brother was involved in updating the bridge over the Don Valley, right Ismail?* Ismail tried his best, dutifully describing his hardwood floors, and the skylight he'd installed. He modestly explained that he was among a large committee that deliberated on the installation of suicide barriers for the Bloor Street Viaduct. Shakila seemed suitably

impressed with his talents. This gave him confidence to
go out on a limb and announce his attendance in James
Busbridge's writing course.

"Really, *Kakaji*, I didn't know you liked to write," Asghar
remarked while taking a third helping of *biryani*.

"I haven't done much of it since I was about your age. I
sort of gave it up when I got busy with college, and then
after awhile, I lost the habit."

"So what made you go to a class now?" Shakila inquired.
Ismail thought her tone was nurselike, as though she were
conducting an assessment.

"Well," Ismail said, feeling cagey, "a friend of mine took
a similar class and encouraged me to try it as a new hobby.
So I did."

"It's good to try new things, especially at our age," Shakila
said, nodding over a forkful of *kofta* curry.

"So that's where you met that girl," Nabila murmured,
her head resting on her folded hands, her elbows on the
table. Nabil frowned at her and she raised her eyebrows at
him. Ismail pushed a lonely onion slice around on his plate.

"What girl?" Asghar and Altaf asked in unison, sensing
an off note in their parents' orchestration.

"Er ... a family friend. Ismail met one of our friend's
daughters in the class. You don't know her. So, Shakila, your
brother's children must be school-age now?" Nabil asked,
decisively steering the conversation away from his brother
and diverting the boys, who had, by then, already lost
interest in the conversation. Ismail bristled with irritation.
Nabila picked up a spoon and was poised to put more rice
on his plate, but he pulled it away and out of reach.

"Yes, tell us about your nieces," Nabila said, seeking to
restore harmony.

Shakila told them a funny story about how her youngest niece swallowed one of her teddy bear's plastic eyeballs and how she discovered it later, while changing her diaper. The tale made everyone laugh and Nabila jumped in with a similarly embarrassing account about when Asghar was a child.

Ismail felt a sudden urge to share an anecdote about when Zubi ate Altaf's Play Doh. She seemed to think it was candy, and only realized it wasn't after she swallowed. He and Rehana fretted, rushed her to the hospital, only to be told that the substance wasn't toxic and she'd be fine. Of course, he remained quiet, listening to the others' stories. Nabila slopped more *kofta* on his plate while he wasn't looking.

When they'd finished dinner, the group moved to the living room. Nabila released the boys, and Asghar and Altaf said their goodbyes, relieved to be excused from the dull company. Nabila served cake and tea, and the chatter turned toward politics at the local mosque, which Nabil, Nabila, and Shakila attended irregularly. Ismail smiled and nodded through this conversation, aware that it wouldn't look good if he were to admit he wasn't a member. By this point in the evening, he found himself participating fully in Nabil and Nabila's scheming, behaving like a proper, eligible bachelor.

After the dessert dishes and teacups were cleared away, Shakila gracefully thanked her hosts, shook Ismail's hand, and took her leave. Nabila walked her out to the driveway and Nabil checked his cellphone for messages. Ismail carried the dessert plates to the kitchen, and began rinsing them. In a few minutes, Nabila joined him.

"So, Ismail, what do you think? She's a very nice person. I could tell you liked her," Nabila said, while he helped load

the dishwasher. Both Nabil and Nabila had a habit of asking
a question and then offering their response before receiving
an answer.

"You want her number? I think you should call her. Maybe
follow up in a day or two. Don't call tonight, or even tomorrow. But don't wait too long to call, either," Nabil advised
from across the kitchen, working a toothpick through his
lower front teeth.

"I don't know. She does seem nice, but you know how
these things have worked out in the past. I'm not sure I want
a repeat of what happened with Maimoona, or what was
that other one's name? Ameena?"

"Ameera. Ameera Millwala. She was a gossip, wasn't she?
We shouldn't have bothered with her. And you know, she's
still unmarried," Nabila said smugly, shutting the dishwasher and turning it on.

"Not surprising, really. She's very negative," Nabil mumbled, guiding the toothpick to his back molars.

"But that was a long time back, Ismail. Remember? The
boys were still very young at the time and you'd only been
divorced a few years. The gossip is old news now," she pronounced, transferring the remaining *kofta* into a plastic
container for him to take home. He considered her words.
Yes, time had passed, and things were different for him. But
what about the community? He thought about Fatima's parents, Hassan and Shelina. He almost offered their example
in rebuttal, but decided against it, not wanting to reopen
the discussion with Nabil.

"I agree with Nabila. And Shakila is different. She has class,"
Nabil proclaimed, tossing his toothpick into the garbage bin.

"Yes, she is a mature, down-to-earth person. And ... I
think she likes you," Nabila said, grinning at Ismail.

"You think so? Did she say something about me when you were outside?" The creamy *kofta* churned in the pit of his stomach.

"Well, she did say she had a good time and would like to do it again," Nabila said, smiling coyly.

"But that doesn't mean she likes *me*. And anyway, once she picks up the phone to tell one of her friends about meeting me, you know it will all be over before it starts."

"Not necessarily. Nabila is right. Time has passed," Nabil said, picking up a pen. "Nabila, where is Shakila's number?"

"In my cell. Just scroll through my address book for me?" She said, spraying an anti-bacterial solution over the countertop and wiping it down with a cloth.

"Her last name is Baker?"

"No, she went back to her maiden name, Cutlerywala."

"Here it is 'Shakila Cutlerywala.'" He wrote the number down on a piece of paper and handed it to Ismail. He took the scrap and shoved it deep into his pocket.

The pleasantness of the evening left Ismail warming to the idea of a proper date with an intelligent woman. Before leaving their place, Nabila made him promise he would call Shakila, and in that moment it seemed like a good idea to him. But as he drove home along the highway, his doubts resurfaced.

By the time he reached Lochrie, there weren't any parking spots, so he circled the block twice before he found one. At each pass, he found himself slowing to look into Celia's lit window. He ambled up his walk, hesitating on his porch. Before he went in, he glanced over his shoulder at Celia's closed door.

29

SHOW DON'T TELL

ALTHOUGH AMBIVALENT ABOUT ENCOUNTERING Fatima again, Ismail did go to the next writing class. She left a message after he hung up on her and his call display indicated that she'd phoned twice more over the week. When he saw her enter the classroom, tardy as usual, he was filled with dread. At the same time, he hoped she'd choose her usual seat, next to his. He was unsure what to do with all the push-pull she elicited in him.

He watched her lug her bulging backpack all the way around the room. She landed heavily in the chair beside his, unzipped her coat and pulled a notebook from her bag without glancing his way. Ismail pretended to listen to James's lecture while discreetly sneaking looks at her, regarding her heavy bag and its weighty reality. Her skin seemed pale, her posture slack with fatigue. Eventually, she turned to him and whispered, "I called you a few times."

"Yes. I've been busy," he replied curtly, his gaze on James, who was detailing the differences between exposition and description. *Show, don't tell,* Ismail scribbled into his notebook.

"Have you been ... okay?" He turned towards her and saw that her eyes were wide, her brows furrowed. He relaxed his jaw, allowed his shoulders to fall away from his ears.

"Um, yes, I'm all right. Sorry I didn't call you back. Let's talk later. James is speaking." She moved away, sighing loudly, slumping down in her chair. Ismail hardly heard James for the rest of the class. Instead, he was distracted by Fatima's breathing, the click-click-click of her pen, and the squeak of her chair as she fidgeted in her seat. After James finished, three students were called up to read their writing. Ismail forced himself to concentrate on them, and pushed Fatima's noisy presence to the background.

At the break, Fatima leaned over, brushing soft fingers against his forearm. "Want to come out with me while I smoke?" Ismail nodded and silently followed her out the door. Worry pooled acidic in his stomach; he was aware that everything had changed between he and Fatima since the last time they'd spoken at the university, the night she told him her troubles. In just two weeks, he'd met her friends, partied the night away with them, permitted she and Sonia to stay in his home, met her parents. And now, she knew something about his life, too. He buttoned his jacket, protection from her and the cold.

Ismail watched a large snowflake land, its intricate pattern vanishing into the outer layer of his coat. They stepped into a little alcove to stay dry. The gothic-style lampposts gave off only a half-hearted glow, and as they stood together, just a few inches apart, he was once again reminded of the strange intimacy between them.

Fatima struck a match, casting an orange blush over her chin and lips. "I've gotta quit — I can't really afford it anymore," she said, lighting her cigarette and waving away the smoke, and perhaps also her words. He nodded in agreement, but didn't say anything. He didn't know how to speak to her, so he stared out at the falling snow.

She inhaled deeply, and reflexively, so did he. They exhaled in tandem, Ismail letting go of clouds of vapour much like her puffs of smoke.

"So, are you okay?" she asked again, taking another drag of her cigarette.

"Yes," he replied, too quickly, "I don't like this weather though." He fidgeted with his gloves, stretching the soft leather over his fingers. "It's still so cold."

"I mean about the article," she said, impatient. She took two short drags on her cigarette. "About your daughter, Ismail. The article I found on the Internet. I worried about you after you hung up on me." He contemplated Fatima's frowning expression. He found it strange that a girl with so many troubles of her own would show such concern for his.

"Yes. I'm fine ... I didn't mean to worry you. It was difficult for me, at first, to read that article. It came as a surprise — I hadn't seen it before. But ... now I am better." Ismail remembered how Celia had found him on his kitchen floor, and stayed there until he'd recovered. He recalled her soft hands, their embrace, and her small smile on Good Friday.

"Well, I'm glad. I didn't really know what to think, you know? It was a shock to read the article, but —"

"— You probably think I am a terrible person. Most people do after they hear about what happened," Ismail said, interrupting her, wanting to finish her sentence before she could.

"That's not what I meant. I mean, it was really shocking to read. But, I mostly felt bad for you. All this time I've been so focused on myself, and never really stopped to think about what your life might be like. You know, the problems *you* might have. And then I thought about how she and I would have been about the same age." A waft of cigarette smoke blew into his face and stung his eyes.

"She would have been only a year older than you."

"I'm really sorry, Ismail," she said, her voice barely more than a whisper, and his shoulders tensed once again. Although criticisms were hard to hear, sympathy was somehow even more difficult; hatred could elicit his anger, at least, but kindness only left him sad.

"It must have been really hard to ... lose your baby." She exhaled, and allowed her cigarette to fall to the ground. Ismail watched as she squashed it with her boot, the nicotine staining the snow a yellow-brown. *Ochre*, he thought, *is that what ochre looks like? No, that's closer to mustard.* He knew she was still speaking, but couldn't be sure how many of her words he missed.

"That's gotta be the worst thing a parent can ever experience. To lose a child like that ..."

"Hmmm," he murmured, and watched the snow fall.

"... of course, my own parents are of a different breed. They don't seem to mind losing me. They were only too quick to throw me away," she muttered, jamming her fingers into her pockets. She paused and he collected his thoughts, relieved that she was no longer talking about him.

"Yes, well ... they're making a terrible mistake. They are losing a lot. I can tell you that ... that their lives won't be as full without you in it," he said quietly, watching Fatima's face soften, her chin tremble. He realized sympathy was having the same impact on her, so he changed his approach. "But, don't worry, Fatima. Your situation might not be permanent. They could still come around. After some time you could work all this out with them."

"Yeah, I guess. Though it doesn't feel like that. You know, I called them this past week, hoping that they'd have calmed down a little. My father picked up even though I called when I thought he'd be out. I wanted to speak to my mom, but he ... hung up on me," she sniffed, and Ismail looked down at her and saw that her face was streaked with tears. He passed her a handkerchief, the gesture reminding him of Celia, in his kitchen, the previous week. Fatima accepted it, dried her face, her eyeliner rubbing off onto the white cotton. He gazed out into the wintry night, the abandoned soccer field and at the glow of lights at the intersection, considering the neglectfulness of parents and the vulnerability of children.

The snow was falling more heavily then, obscuring the night. Fatima and Ismail stood there, side by side in the gloom of the alcove, and anyone passing by might have thought they resembled confidants, friends, or perhaps father and daughter.

"You will be all right, Fatima, whatever happens with them. You will manage." He patted her shoulder awkwardly, feeling her thin frame through her coat. Protectiveness welled up inside him. "You will manage," he repeated. And then he said these words inside his head: *We will manage.*

She nodded and they returned to the classroom.

Two more students were called upon to read their work aloud during the second half of class. He still hadn't written anything much himself, and feared he might not be able to squeak by undetected through to the following week, the eighth and final class.

An hour later, as he was rushing to put away his notebook, he saw James approach. "Oh good, you're still here Ismail, I've noticed that you haven't signed up to share your writing with the class. I think you might have been away when we did the sign-up during the second week of class."

"Yes, I was away," Ismail agreed, sheepishly. He knew the sheet had been passed around on week two, but hadn't exactly been proactive in signing up. "But listen, James, do I really have do it? I've been enjoying the class, but I'm not a very good writer myself."

"It wouldn't be fair to the others. Remember the class guidelines we set up early on? Everyone has to share something." Ismail nodded and James continued, "There's still a spot available next week, our last class. Why don't you share something short? And remember, it doesn't have to be great, it just has to be an attempt." Ismail regarded James's earnest expression.

"Really, next week is the last class already?" Ismail asked, trying to look innocent.

"So you'll bring something for next week, then?"

"Yes." Ismail agreed. James smiled and returned to the front of the classroom.

"Thought you'd get away with not having to write anything in a writing class, didn't you?" Fatima said, smirking.

"I suppose. I really don't want to get up in front of everyone ..."

"It's not as terrible as you think it will be. A little nerve-wracking, but that's all," she advised.

"I wish I'd written something weeks ago. I don't have a clue what to write about now."

"Everyone always says to start with something you know."

"I'll bore everyone to tears."

"I wouldn't be so sure of that. I think there is a lot about you that's interesting," she said, regarding him with her arms crossed over her chest.

"Hmmph," he muttered, putting on his jacket.

"Ismail? Listen ... here's something I've been meaning to give you. I wrote it in class a few weeks ago — do you remember when we had to do a sketch of a character's deepest desires? You know, that week when the furnace overheated?" He nodded and recognized the folded square of paper she held tightly in her hand.

"This is what I wrote. I reworked it this past week," she said shyly. "You can have it, but look at it later. Not now. Okay?" She held the paper out to him, and he reached for it, understanding it was a gift being offered. He watched her pack up her bag, heft it onto her back, and hurry from the room. He slipped her writing into his breast pocket.

While he waited for his car to warm up, he unfolded Fatima's page:

> *His deepest desire is covered over by an ancient scar, thick now with years of layered, intricate webbing, evidence of something hidden. The scar sits over his sternum, the years-old skin reaching out a few centimetres in all directions like a spider's web, and then, suddenly coming to a full stop. The whole mess of it lies hidden beneath a navy blue or black or grey bureaucratic jacket, then a buttoned to-the-neck dress*

shirt. A stylish tie — perhaps with thin stripes, or a swirly pattern, maybe one he carefully chose during a Boxing Day sale — cinches his collar, further preventing anyone from glimpsing his injury. But then, it was hot today, and he had to unbutton, didn't he?

I imagine that sometimes, when he is alone, maybe after stepping out of the shower, his skin still damp, he glances at himself in the steamy bathroom mirror, and spies the pink smudge on his chest. It's a vulnerable, shiny patch that refuses to blend in, refuses to be invisible. He might rub the spot, sensing its bumpy ridges, its waxy edges, wanting to smooth it down with his thumb. The scar may grow warm under his touch, friction bringing to life something usually ignored, something he'd rather forget. Eventually, the mirror will de-fog and his reflection will come into perfect focus and he'll look away. He will try to forget the wound. Again.

But trying to forget keeps him from what he wants most. His deepest desire, the one he doesn't even know he has, the one he has made himself stop wanting for far too long now, lies beneath that scar, way under the tender skin, and just below whatever hurt that caused it in the first place. What he longs for most is to be able to love again.

Ismail read the passage all the way through, and then read it once more. He folded the sheet back into its quarters, the memory of its creases still fresh. He placed it in the glove compartment, on top of a *Perly's* guide and beside a tiny yellow barrette. He looked into the rearview mirror at the empty back seat, and then drove home.

— ❈ —

At Celia's, the house was quiet, except for the murmuring of the television upstairs in her daughter's room. These days, Antonio and Lydia had taken to watching their favourite evening programs — like *Law and Order* and *CSI* — in their bedroom after Marco was in bed. Maybe they could do without Celia sitting with them, complaining about all the violence on television, suggesting they switch to her shows — *So You Think You Can Dance?* or *Canadian Idol.* Now, those were good programs to watch before going to sleep.

Perhaps Antonio and Lydia just wanted some privacy and Celia couldn't find fault with that. It had been a year and a half since Celia had moved into Lochrie Street, and rarely had they been alone, just the two of them. Celia hardly ever went out at night and most evenings, after Marco's bedtime, Antonio and Celia bookended Lydia on the chesterfield, the three of them with their eyes locked on the television.

Celia heard laughter now from upstairs. Lately, Lydia had been making some vague comments about trying for another baby, so maybe they weren't even *watching* the television, Celia mused. She agreed that Marco needed a brother or sister, someone to play with, someone with whom to grow old.

After a time, both the television and the laughter went quiet. She listened to the stillness of the house, welcoming it. She'd lived with the noise of others all her life, going from her parents' home, to José's, and now to Lydia's. What would be next? Ping-ponging between her older brother in Vancouver and her son in Montreal when Lydia got tired of her? She always imagined that living alone would be a terribly lonely existence. Now, she questioned if that was true.

She sat by the living-room window, gazing out into the night. A dog-walker passed, a slight woman being dragged along the sidewalk by a beefy German shepherd. Then two teenaged boys rushed by, a snowball fight in progress. They ran in fits and starts, stopping to form more snowballs and then launching them with laughter and threats they didn't mean. Later, a pick-up truck full of old appliances drove past, looking for treasures on recycling night. The street went silent again for a few minutes. She was about to head to bed when another vehicle approached, its headlights illuminating the dark sidewalk. She looked more closely and recognized Ismail's car, passing slowly. She checked her watch.

She searched the night sky. So many stars out. She put her coat over her shoulders, and went outside in her felted house slippers. The nights were still cold, and wind nipped at her heels, but she stood on the porch and waited.

— ❄ —

That late in the evening, Ismail couldn't find a parking spot in front of his house. He drove around the block and finally found space one street north. He locked the car and walked south to Lochrie. When he turned the corner, he saw Celia on her porch, gazing skyward. He approached her house.

"A very clear night. Lots of stars," she called out.

"Oh yes," he said awkwardly, and tilted his head up to see, "there are."

"Look, there's Orion," she said, taking a step toward him, off her porch, and onto the path that led to the sidewalk.

"It is bright tonight. Orion is more clear than usual."

"Yes. I love a starry night," she said, walking a few more steps closer to him, her eyes fixed on his. He looked away, her gaze too intense.

"And look over there." He pointed. "What's that one over there called? The one shaped like a 'W'?"

"Cassiopeia," she said. A couple more paces, and she was right in front of him.

"That's right. I always forget the name of it." His gaze dropped from the stars above down to the flowers in her eyes.

And that's when she rose onto her toes and kissed him.

— ❀ —

His lips were smoother that she expected a man's to be, but never mind, they were warm. She imagined herself a ballerina, balancing perfectly on the tips of her toes, her face tilted to meet his. It was just a short kiss, a peck, really, his lips suspending her in the air for just a moment. Heat tickled her head, rushed down her spine, and brought life to cold feet. The kiss thawed the frozen night.

She opened her eyes, saw raised eyebrows stretching his face long. But then he smiled. And so did she.

Celia wasn't sure what to do next. Everything that had come before — the wandering onto the porch, the astronomy, the reaching up for him — all seemed simple, automatic, as though she were a marionette being directed by someone else's hand. And then suddenly, the strings were cut, and she was dropped back to the ground. So, she said good night, uncertain but giddy. He looked back at her, wide-eyed. She turned away, skipped up her walk, and shut the door the behind her.

Oh! It had been a long time since she'd kissed a man. And it had been ages since her very first kiss with José, the act that started a whirlwind courtship she never thought to stop. They'd met at a dance, were necking that same evening, and even more the next night. Celia followed the heat of her youthful passion and the urgings of a boy hopped up on hormones.

This thing that was happening with Ismail was different. She didn't know what to call it. *Not passion, exactly, but nice.*

— ❋ —

Ismail ambled up the steps to his porch, managed to slip the key into the lock and absent-mindedly dropped his coat onto the foyer floor. All of him was numb, except for his tingling lips, lips that no longer felt attached to his face. He replayed the moments before her kiss over and over in his mind: the scent of her fruity shampoo lingering in her red hair, her pink, bare feet in her bedroom slippers, the way she had said "Cassiopeia."

Cassiopeia, Cassiopeia, Cassiopeia, Cassiopeia, Cassiopeia, Cassiopeia.

He sat on the living-room couch, then stood up, walked into the kitchen, and then back to the living room. He peeked out the window at her lit-up house, then sat down again. He turned off the lights, climbed the stairs, and looked out from his bedroom window, nervous energy prickling through him, a light cool sweat under his armpits. This perspiration was different from the liquid heat of his anxiety. Celia's kiss had caused him to be cool and damp and light in his limbs.

He had an urge to talk to someone, to chatter like a teenager with a cellphone on public transit. He'd start with the minutiae of his day and end with the grand finale of being kissed by a woman he barely knew. Names of confidants ran through his mind: Nabil? No, he would just tell him to smarten up and call Shakila. Ismail knew that Fatima would love to hear his news, but they weren't exactly peers. He also wasn't sure what to say about the writing she'd given him.

He dialed Daphne's number, let it ring twice and hung up, still angry with her for dropping him at the beginning of the class; he didn't want to pollute his good feelings. Then, James's voice came to him. He went into the spare room, turned on his computer, and watched the black screen chug to life. What was happening inside his mind felt too urgent and quick for his aging computer, which was still warming up. Instead, he scrambled to find a piece of paper and a pen. In messy handwriting, out came the flurry of words:

The widow kissed me! This woman who has been a regular presence in my life, appeared like magic and then disappeared once again. I haven't allowed her dowdy, polyester camouflage to fool me, oh no. I've perhaps always known there was someone different lurking underneath, a woman who is direct, to the point. No beating around the bush. No room for my clumsy hesitations. I suppose she wanted a kiss and so she kissed me. Simple.

Was it fate or something more mundane like proximity, the fact that we are neighbours, and if we left our drapes wide open, we could see right into one another's lives? But there was romance, too, from that lady in bedroom slippers. She spoke of pinpricks of light shining through the dark night sky. Never before have the constellations been so interesting or beautiful to me. And then, in one quick movement, that

*starry night became a mere backdrop to the firecrackers that
exploded inside of me when she kissed me.*

*She kissed me. It was short, yes, just enough to leave me
questioning if it happened. It was the kind of kiss that happens in the best and worst Bollywood films. The sort of kiss
that at once satiates a longing never before acknowledged
while leaving behind a desire that simmers long after.*

*Then, she pulled away, took hold of my hands, and left me
there with the clear night sky, in a fit of delirium, the empty
street my only company. I almost believed it to be mere fantasy until I came inside, glimpsed myself in the hallway mirror and saw the evidence: a ruby red smudge on the corner of
my mouth. I'll never wipe it away.*

30

NO UNNECESSARY WORDS

THE NEXT MORNING, ISMAIL awoke to the telephone's ring. It was 8:00 a.m., and he'd already slept through a full hour of the radio broadcasting *Metro Morning*. He reached for the phone on his nightstand.

"Hi, Ismail." Although she'd quit smoking a couple of years ago, she still had that husky, unmistakable, nicotine-tinged voice.

"Daphne?" Ismail sat up in bed, rubbed his face awake, switched off the radio.

"Hi. I saw from the call display that you phoned last night. You didn't leave a message, which isn't like you, so I wondered if everything was all right ..." Ismail remembered that Daphne preferred to screen her calls. Very likely, he'd been screened out the night before. Still, she was calling back, and he supposed that was good of her.

"Yes, things are fine ... I just called to say hello. It was nothing important. I didn't mean to concern you."

"Okay ... well, that's good. We should get together some time. Catch up."

"Sure, that would be nice, Daphne. I'm available tomorrow, or Thursday or Friday this week," he said, hoping he didn't sound too eager.

"Um, I'll have to check my schedule ... I'll email you and we can set it up."

"Oh ... sounds good," he replied, sensing she wouldn't. Perhaps it was better that she didn't agree to meet him, only to cancel later.

"Okay."

"All right."

"Yeah, good."

"Well, thanks for calling, Daphne. I'm running a little late this morning, so I'd better go. Bye." Before Daphne could say goodbye, he pressed the "end" button on the phone's keypad, and let her go.

Later that day, after two reminders (an email from Nabil's BlackBerry and a text message from Nabila), Ismail succumbed to their pressure to telephone Shakila. *And what harm could there be in one dinner with the woman?* he thought. Luckily, she wasn't home when he phoned, and then she returned his call when he was out, so the whole awkward business of arranging the date was completed by voice mail. Ismail wasn't sure what kind of cuisines she ate, other than Indian food, so he suggested meeting on Friday at Siddhartha, one of the few Little India restaurants which he knew had tablecloths and a clean washroom in the basement. It was common ground, halfway between each of their west-end and east-end homes.

—

Two days later, Ismail dressed and set off for the restaurant. He arrived fifteen minutes early and considered ordering a beer to calm his nerves. While he waited for the server to come and take his order, he calculated that it had been almost two weeks since he had last allowed himself to drink to the point of intoxication, right after the debacle at Fatima's parents' house. He re-committed to avoiding further involvement in Fatima's complicated family situation and ordered a Kingfisher.

He finished the beer while waiting for Shakila. He checked his watch, saw that she was already ten minutes late, and entertained worries of being stood up. He was about to order another beer when Shakila finally entered the restaurant, almost fifteen minutes late.

"Ismail, sorry I'm a few minutes late. The traffic was really terrible. An accident blocked traffic all the way up Coxwell." Ismail stood and they shook hands. His palms were already damp, and so he kept the handshake brief so she wouldn't notice. He watched her carefully drape her red parka around her chair before she sat down. As she unravelled her silk scarf, perfume wafted his way.

"Your perfume is very nice." It was the only thing he could think to say.

"I hope it's not too overpowering? I didn't put too much on?" she asked, her hands tightening around her scarf.

"No, no, very nice. Noticeable, but not overpowering in the least. Just the right amount," Ismail fibbed.

"You know I can't stand it when women overdo it. Sometimes you walk into a room and waah! It's like you can't even breathe!" she exclaimed, her fingers floating up to her mouth.

"Yes, men can also be the culprits with their aftershave," he added, wanting to seem balanced about the issue. "At work, we have a policy against wearing any cologne or perfume. Too many people are allergic these days."

"Yes, we do, too. So I don't wear perfume to work," she said and he wondered how long they could discuss scents before the line of conversation would exhaust itself. The waiter arrived to take her drink order and scooped up Ismail's empty Kingfisher bottle.

"I'll have a mango *lassi*," she said, her eyes following the empty bottle up to the waiter's tray.

"Another Kingfisher for you, sir?"

"Yes," Ismail said, and then noticed Shakila's terse smile. "Uh, wait, I'll have a mango *lassi*, too," he said, observing Shakila's shoulders relax. He supposed that Shakila didn't approve of drinking or perhaps abided by religious prohibitions against alcohol.

Just like at their previous meeting, Shakila proved to be a pleasant companion. She told interesting stories, had articulate opinions about current affairs (Barack Obama's presidency, Fidel's ailing health, the City budget), and was an attentive listener to his stories (students in his writing class, the state of the City's bridges). Ismail learned that she liked Chinese and Italian food. She neither drank nor smoked and attended the mosque on special holidays.

As they stood side by side at the buffet, they briefly brushed up against each other and he liked the padded feel of her hips where they met his thigh. Before they sat down, she passed him a fork and knife, and he made a corny joke about her surname ("A true culterywala, then, hehe"), and she laughed and he blushed. Ismail willed himself to be calm, and hoped he wasn't perspiring too much. After dinner, they ambled around Little India, bought chocolate *burfi*, and looked at saris in shop windows. When he walked her to her red Saturn, she hugged him goodbye and kissed him on the cheek.

"There is a good Chinese restaurant not too far from here that you might like, in the east-end Chinatown," he ventured, as he pretended to inspect the hood of her car, "I've been there once with my friend Daphne. Um, it's called Beijing House. Would you like to go there with me ... maybe on Monday night?" Ismail hoped he wasn't being too forward, suggesting another date in just three days, but he didn't want to wait a week. Although he couldn't explain the urgency, he felt that if the relationship with Shakila was going to work out, he needed to know as soon as possible. He would have suggested the weekend, but she'd already told him she was going to be busy looking after her niece and nephew.

"That would be nice. I'm free after six," she said, and walked around to the driver's side. "Let's call each other tomorrow or Sunday so I can get the address."

Ismail smiled broadly, nodding like a simpleton. It has been much too long since he'd been on a real date with a lady and he was thrilled to have a phone call and a second date to look forward to.

As he leisurely drove west along Danforth Avenue, he evaluated the dinner, concluding that it had been a success. *Perhaps I'm not such a washout with the ladies.* Just a few days earlier, Celia had kissed him out of the blue, and now Shakila had agreed to see him again. *Two ladies in four days!* After so many years of loneliness, he felt his luck might be changing. His self-satisfied grin accompanied him, all the way past Pape.

When Ismail approached Broadview Avenue, his thoughts turned to Fatima, that house with the falling-down door and untidy yard. He considered her situation and this dampened his elation. He weighed her parents' faulty reactions to her gayness against his own liberal beliefs and wondered: what if Zubi had turned out to be a gay rebel? Would he bluster like Hassan or pressure like Shelina? He wanted to believe that he'd be a different sort of father, one who would listen, negotiate. Surely he wouldn't threaten to abandon his child if she didn't conform to his values? But he wasn't so sure.

Ismail crossed the Don Valley, driving over the bridge with its complex netting that was supposed to stop the city's most desperate and alone from jumping. He contemplated Fatima's written gift to him, and the way she'd glanced something within him he'd barely recognized himself. When the traffic light changed from amber to red at the next intersection, Ismail found himself unbuttoning his jacket and top shirt buttons to finger the web of tight skin crisscrossing his sternum. He felt for the injury, long ago suffered and never forgotten. *Perhaps the girl is right.*

He passed the ROM, then Christie Pits, and turned south on Ossington Avenue. The roads were clear and he got home quickly. For the first time in a very long time, Ismail Boxwala felt like a lucky man.

— ❋ —

Earlier that evening, Celia gazed through the dirty glass of her bedroom-den window, spying on Ismail's house. It looked abandoned, with all of its lamps extinguished and the day's post lingering in the mailbox. The neighbouring houses contrasted his, surrounding it in a carnival of light and sound. On the left, a party was in progress, laughter and music leaking out with each arrival. On the right, silhouettes moved behind gauzy curtains while a television flickered blue, an electronic hearth.

Celia couldn't help but ponder the dark house's occupant. Until a short time ago, Ismail's presence had been predictable; she could tell that he spent many of his after-work hours and weekends at home, and probably alone. The recent change in his schedule troubled her. Could it be those girls keeping him out late again? She hoped that if he was spending time with them it was with the one with the baggy pants and family problems, and not with the girl in the short red dress who'd stumbled out of his house before her. Since that morning, she'd been mulling over that red dress: *What sort of grown man goes out with girls so young?*

She contemplated all the places a man could go on a Friday night. Perhaps Ismail was at a café or bar — José certainly liked to spend evenings at the Delta doing whatever it was that men did there all night long. He'd roll into bed with the stench of beer and cigarettes on his skin and she'd scootch over to avoid being pawed by a drunkard. José went to other places, too, places she knew nothing about until after his death, where he played cards until dawn. She never asked what kind of cards he played there, didn't know what to ask. Maybe Ismail was mixed up in the same kinds of things, Celia wagered. *Men. They're all the same. Only interested in girls, and drinking and getting into trouble.* And then the criticism turned inwards: *Ya! So pretty dumb to kiss him, then, eh?* She took a deep breath to slow her thoughts. *But maybe he's different?*

At the house to Ismail's right, the television switched off, startling her from her thoughts. She watched the party house a while longer, and then turned away from her window. She picked up one of Lydia's home decor magazines. Lydia had perused it earlier, bending back pages she wanted Celia to look at, articles about finished basements. She told Celia she wanted her opinion about what colour to paint the downstairs walls and although no one was saying it directly, Celia understood that they were preparing to move her into a subterranean mother-in-law suite very soon. Antonio had already started hanging drywall and she'd overheard him say that one of his buddies was going to come next week to install plumbing.

The magazine had all sorts of tips about how to make underground rooms cheery-looking. Apparently pale yellows were the best shades for dark, dingy spaces and pot lights a fine substitute for sunshine. She put aside the magazine and paced her bedroom-den restlessly, the four walls too close. She went out into the living room, hoping for the company of others, but remembered that everyone had already gone to their rooms. She heard faint murmurs of conversation and laughter upstairs, her daughter and son-in-law entertaining themselves on a Friday night.

She switched on the television to drown out their happy noises. Eighty-three stations clicked past her, and still she found nothing good on at 10:07 p.m. Eventually, she paused at the Shopping Channel, and watched the hosts marvel about a mop that used steam instead of soap to clean floors. They demonstrated how the mop's heating action could skate through grease and evaporate grime; a proposition she found reassuring. A one-eight-hundred number danced across the screen.

The number flirted with her, urging her to dial, and when she finally did, she was connected to a salesman with a deep voice. She kept him on the line for a few minutes, asking inane questions, and offering him false hope for a sale to meet his quota. At one point during the conversation, she thought she heard an extension phone being picked up and then discreetly hung up again, her daughter policing her illicit, late-night shopping.

When she'd run out of things to ask Mr. Deep Voice, and attempted to say goodbye, she thought she detected a whiny rise in his lovely baritone. He appealed to her with special offers of extra pads and deeper discounts that would only be valid for the next fifteen minutes. She hesitated, appreciating the desperation she heard in his voice. Or maybe it was his humanity; a real person reaching out to her on a lonely night. Nonetheless, she turned down his entreaties and felt guilty for leading him on like that.

She glanced back at the television. One of the hosts seemed to be working herself up into a sales frenzy, when the other yelled, "Gosh Jeannie, I can't believe it! We've sold one thousand mops this hour! The Wonder Mop did it again!" They cheered for their mop and Celia sighed and turned off the TV, a small clench of regret in her belly.

When she looked out the living room window again, the streetscape had altered. Things had quieted somewhat at the party place, the music safely contained within its walls. Next door, Ismail's front rooms were now lit. He'd come home at last.

Celia looked long at Ismail's closed drapes and remembered the starry night a few days back. Her lips blushed with the memory of his warm mouth on hers and that brought the rest of her into a flush, too. The downy hair

on her arms and the back of her neck stood up in anticipation of something more. Her stomach did flip-flops, and
her knees felt like buckling, even though she was sitting
on the couch.

Her wanting made her feel ridiculous. What was she
doing? Why kiss a strange man, and then run back into the
house? He probably thought she was crazy. *A little widow
gone batty in her loneliness. Was this kissing thing a symp-
tom of the agonias, too — one that no one ever mentioned?*

And what could she really want from him, anyway?
His company? She certainly didn't want another husband,
another man to look after. No, she was finished with that. So
why think about him so much? She continued her internal
interrogation for a few moments, her questions and answers
snarling like a knotted ball of yarn. And then, a moment
of clarity, an aha! that unravelled the tangle. *Yes, that's
what I want.* She nodded to no one. *Another kiss. That's all.
Nothing less, nothing more.*

What would Ismail think about an unplanned visit at
10:42? She shrugged, decided not to care too much, for she
knew analysis would only lead to hesitation and inaction.
She slipped on her burgundy boots, crossed Lochrie Street
and before she could raise her arm to ring the doorbell, he
was there, waiting, opening his door wide to her.

There was no conversation, no small talk, no unnecessary
words. There was just an embrace, and one long kiss.

A kiss that made heat travel up and down and through
her body, like a joyful hot flash.

A kiss that made lightning burst beneath tired eyelids,
and thunder rumble through her limbs.

A kiss that erased past and future, making nothing else but itself exist.

That was the sort of kiss it was.

— ❀ —

Ismail heard her soft footfalls on his wooden porch and went to meet her at the door. Perhaps he should have questioned her presence, but he didn't. And he wasn't surprised when she leaned into him, held his face, and pressed her lips onto his. She was like a hurricane, drawing him to its eye, and he yielded to its force. They travelled to a place where they could be completely alone, quiet and still, protected from the storm whirling around them.

When she released him, he gasped for air.

— ❀ —

It wasn't until Celia finally pulled away, that she smelled it. A woman's perfume, faint and faraway and unfamiliar. But there it was, nonetheless, a light spray on the speckled skin of his neck.

That was when she realized that she did want something more.

The thought made her afraid and so she turned away from him. She forced herself off his porch, down his steps and onto the sidewalk. She was crossing Lochrie when his voice stopped her. A human voice, filling the silent night.

— ❀ —

"Wait," Ismail called out, and she paused in the middle of the empty street. She kept her back turned to him and he feared the slightest misstep would start her walking again. "Come back, Celia." Still, she didn't move.

"You can't just come to the door and kiss me like that and then go away again. Come back," he pleaded. And Ismail was telling the truth. He didn't think he could bear for her to leave him right then. He'd never been kissed like that. Not by Daphne, or any of the Mary Pinters, and not even by Rehana. He couldn't let her go away and leave him standing on the other side of her closed door. He couldn't. She still faced away from him, but he could tell that her arms were crossed over her bosom.

"I mean, this is the second time now. Don't you think that we should have a chat? Have a regular interaction? Maybe go out on a date or something at least?" Ismail's words felt too mundane for the magic that had just happened between them, but those ordinary words were all he had.

A car approached, its headlights brightening the black tar. There wasn't enough room to drive around her. She came up onto the sidewalk, faced Ismail. He didn't dare step closer, lest she change her mind.

"Please, come in and talk about it," he begged. She stared down at the ground silently.

A couple stepped out next door, lighting up cigarettes, a blast of loud music following them out onto the porch. They looked down at Celia, and then across the short railing at Ismail, and back at her again. They lingered, witnessing the standoff over puffs of cigarette smoke.

"Please, Celia, why don't you come in for a minute? Just one minute?" One of the smokers coughed, drawing attention to himself and Celia looked his way. Perhaps the audience made her self-conscious, and so she relented. Ismail held the screen door open, and she went inside.

— ❀ —

She was back in his foyer, the door closing behind her. He beckoned her farther inside and so she took off her boots, placing them carefully on the mat by the door. She suddenly felt like a stranger to this man. He was all awkwardness, too, with his wringing of hands and offers of tea. They both seemed to need the formality and so she accepted, and waited in the living room for him to return with a tray of cups and biscuits. She examined the domesticity of the scene and blurted, "I'm not looking for another husband, you know."

"All right," he said, holding out a cup for her. She didn't take it, but he kept his hand outstretched, anyway.

"I mean it. I had one husband all my life. I can't have another now. Besides, it's just not done. A widow is not supposed to remarry. We're expected to marry just once in our lives." She held up her index finger at him and didn't know why she was telling him all this.

"I'm sure I'd make a terrible husband, anyway. I've already been married once before, too. It didn't turn out so well." His self-deprecation made her smile. She reached for the cup and he sat down next to her.

"Why, do you play cards?" It seemed to her like an important thing to ask.

"Cards?" he asked, with raised eyebrows.

"Gambling. Do you gamble?"

"No."

"Do you drink?"

"Sometimes ... but I just meant —" He struggled to regain control of the conversation. "I have been on my own a long time. I wouldn't know how to be a husband again." She nodded. His answer didn't surprise her.

"Good, because ... I won't take care of you," she said resolutely. "I've done enough of that in my life, too."

"Okay," he said, and blew on his tea.

"I mean it. I like you but I can tell you ... you've got some problems. And I'm not going to get involved in them." There was a long pause while they sipped the orange pekoe.

— ❋ —

Her bluntness should have been intimidating to Ismail, but it wasn't. Rather, he was glad to be talking, finally speaking about the strange chemistry that wafted like the sweetest incense between them. Even so, the evening had a kind of surreal feeling to it. He hadn't counted on coming home from his date with Shakila to find Celia on his doorstep. To be kissed again. Not like that.

"So Celia, what do you want, then? What are we doing here?" That wasn't really what he meant to say. If he'd been more suave, he might have said that her kiss left him breathless, that he'd been waiting his entire life for a kiss like that. Celia searched his eyes and then placed her cup upon the table. Ismail did the same.

"How am I supposed to know?" she said with a shrug and a smile. Then she drew closer to him, leaning in, her lips reaching for his.

— ❋ —

This time, kissing Ismail sent Celia into a spin. She closed her eyes, and submitted to it. It was like riding the Tilt-a-Whirl with José at the Canadian National Exhibition. They used to go every year, buying tickets for a ride that would make her insides flutter and her head dizzy. Safe, but just a little dangerous, too.

She opened her eyes, looked straight ahead at Ismail's damp forehead and closed eyelids, at the bliss in his face. She leaned in closer, felt his grip tighten around her waist. She allowed her hands to roam, up and down his back, settling on his neck. She kissed him again and fragments of his question — *what ... are ... we ... doing ... here?* — grew wings and fluttered about them, transposing into nonsensical, dancing word fragments: *ting ... wha ... do ... we ... are ...* Meanwhile, their bodies drew into one another, forming an unspoken, wordless, pact.

— ❋ —

They remained on the couch for most of the night, necking the way Ismail imagined teenagers did in cars at lookout points. They never took off their clothes, kept their hands chastely above the waist, and barely spoke. One kiss breathed into another. When they finally broke their embrace, the sky had lightened and sleep had passed them by. Celia left Ismail with the rising of the sun.

31

PRIVACY

AFTER CELIA LEFT, ISMAIL fell into bed. When the telephone rang a few hours later, he opened his eyes to see that his clock radio was blinking 10:12. He hoped it was Celia calling and so he picked up on the third ring.

"Ismail, it's me, Shakila," she said cheerily.

"Oh. Hello ... hi. It's nice to hear from you." Ismail coughed, trying to clear the sleep from his voice. Overheating in his bed, he pushed the covers off.

"Did I wake you? You sound like you just got up."

"No, no. Well, yes actually. I had a late night," he mumbled, and then guessed this sounded bad. After all, he'd just been out with *her* last night. "Uh, I ended up going to bed late. I ... watched a movie."

"Oh yes? Which one?" Her tone was simply curious, but Ismail started to sweat as though in an interrogation. Lying never came easily to him.

"Um, well, just something I caught on TV. Some made-for-TV thing. Not very good," he said, hoping he sounded convincing. He fanned himself with the covers. A sudden guilt washed over him, but its source felt murky. Was it that he was lying to Shakila? Two-timing her? Turning Celia into a bad movie? He decided he was likely guilty of it all.

"Well, I just thought I'd call and confirm the place for Monday. Beijing House, did you say?"

"Oh yes, yes. Beijing House. Yes. It's on Gerrard, just a few doors east of Broadview ... on the south side."

"Six-thirty good for you?"

"Perfect," he said, wiping his brow with his bed sheet. They said their goodbyes and he flopped down onto the mattress.

— ✳ —

Celia didn't go to bed at all. Her mind and body buzzed with an energy she hadn't experienced in a long time, and she didn't want to waste it by sleeping. She cooked up a feast of eggs, sausages, and corn muffins and waited for the family to stir. Marco stumbled down first, and greeted her with a sleepy hug. Celia held him tightly and breathed in the smell of discount brand shampoo. She sat him at the table and spooned scrambled eggs onto his plate. He told her that he'd dreamed of dinosaurs the night before, a topic that was his main interest during the daytime. Nearly all his pajamas, sheets, toys, and books had Tyrannosaurus rex or Brontosaurus motifs on them and now it seemed that his subconscious was being overpopulated by these creatures, too.

Lydia and Antonio arrived half an hour later, making appreciative noises over her breakfast preparations. When they sat down at the table, their cordial behaviour told Celia they were readying themselves to make an announcement.

Lydia was especially polite and Antonio only picked at his sausages, even though they were his favourite kind. Marco was sent off to watch cartoons.

"*Mãe*, there's something we wanted to talk to you about," Lydia said carefully, while Antonio made geometric patterns in his scrambled eggs.

"Yes?" Celia waited.

"Well, here's the thing. You know Antonio has been working on the basement, right?" Celia nodded. "Well, we sort of mentioned this idea before, but ... we'd like to do it soon. Well, we'd like to convert your room back into a den, and make you a nice suite downstairs. You'd have your own bathroom, and more privacy — we wouldn't even go down there, except to do laundry, and Antonio is going to build a wall so that the washer and dryer are in a separate area from your room and —" Lydia said, without taking a breath.

"I understand," said Celia, cutting in. "That will be fine."

"You don't mind?" asked Antonio. "We don't want you to feel, well, pushed aside, by this change. It's just good to have ... more space ... for us all. My cousin recently built a suite for his mother-in-law and they say they all get along better." His words sounded rehearsed to Celia.

"Not that we aren't getting along," Lydia clarified. "It's been good having you here. Really." Lydia looked at Antonio, who nodded and murmured his agreement.

"And it's good for Marco to have you here. And you know we are trying for another baby, and it will be great to have you around to help out," Lydia continued.

"I don't mind," Celia lied, knowing that her honesty wouldn't do much good, anyway. "No, you kids have been great. Very generous," she said, perhaps a little tersely, her jaw tightening shut. Her true feelings skated across the bony ridges of her palate, bumped against her teeth, and bounced silently on her tongue: *Ungrateful children! Putting me in the basement!* She knew she was probably being unfair, but all the same, she didn't like being assessed by how *helpful* she could be to her daughter. *What's next? Moving me to the shed out back?*

"Good, well, I should have it all ready within a couple of weeks," Antonio said, standing up from the table. Celia looked at his plate, the grease from the cooled sausages congealing yellow. She watched him leave the room without bothering to clear his plate, a habit she'd corrected out of her own son at a young age. *Who did he think was going to pick up after him?* She eyed Lydia disapprovingly, as though it were her fault. When he was out of earshot, Lydia pulled her chair closer.

"I'm glad you are okay with this, *Mãe*. I think this will be better for all of us."

"Yes, it's fine," Celia repeated, helping herself to another corn muffin. She spread a generous layer of butter over it.

"It's good to see that your appetite is back these days. You seem much better lately. More content," Lydia said, speculatively.

"Yes, I do feel better these days," she said, stuffing the muffin in her mouth. Her tongue pushed into the velvety butter, felt the coarseness of the cornmeal. The sensation reminded her of Ismail's tongue and kisses that started at midnight and continued until sunrise. Celia felt her daughters' eyes on her. "Mmmm, these muffins turned out good," she said, helping herself to another.

"So, what were you doing last night? I heard you talking to some man on the phone and then you went out. I stayed up until midnight waiting and then I guess I fell asleep."

"Oh, I just went out for a breath of fresh air. And the man was a salesman at a shopping channel. I nearly got sucked in to buying a new mop they were selling." Celia rolled her eyes in mock dismay. Then, regarding her daughter's suspicious expression, she added, "You know, the mop that uses steam instead of detergent?"

"Yeah, I've seen those."

"They seem good. I thought I'd buy us one. Very sanitary."

"Yeah, but *Mãe*, how late were you out?"

"Not that long," she said, studying the plate of muffins.

"You're still wearing the same clothes as yesterday like you never went to bed or something. And your bed looks like you didn't sleep in it."

"Don't be ridiculous. I wear black every day. Of course they look like the same clothes I wore yesterday," she bristled. She rose from the table, and retreated to her bedroom-den. She bounced on her bed a little, rumpled the covers.

— ✳ —

An hour later, Celia brought up three cardboard boxes and two green garbage bags from the basement. She dumped them out and fanned their contents across her bed. There was a fuchsia blouse, strappy pumps, and a midnight-blue pleated skirt. She fingered her blood-red handbag, her favourite green dress pants, and a lavender angora sweater.

Her things were loud, probably too flashy for a widow. She knew she was supposed to start small and slow, with a brooch or scarf, in subtle shades to interrupt the black of mourning. Gradual brightening that would barely be noticed, in mere whispers of colour. A switch to mud brown or dark blue first. Then chocolate and navy so no one would talk.

The slowness would kill her.

She surveyed her clothes, stroking cashmere and leather, admiring checks, stripes, and florals. She became reacquainted with dresses and scarves and pantsuits, old friends for whom she hadn't realized she'd been longing.

She stripped out of her black skirt, dark hose, and sweater and found an ivory silk robe at the bottom of a cardboard box. It had been an anniversary gift from José, back when he still liked to look at her naked body in daylight. She cinched the belt tight around her waist and inspected herself in her dresser mirror. Her skin was luminous against the ivory of the robe, her figure trim, and her legs still shapely. Wrapped in silk, she didn't look all of her almost fifty-one years. No, that's not right, she reconsidered. She felt the way a woman of her age ought to feel, the way she might have felt, had her life not fallen away from under her.

She took a very long shower, draining the house's small hot-water tank. She luxuriated in the steam, shaved her legs for the first time in more than a year and scrubbed the rough under her feet. When she returned to her bedroom-den, she climbed into her bed naked, not bothering to move the clothes and bags and shoes she had laid there earlier. Like a multicoloured patchwork blanket, her bright outfits kept her warm, and she fell into the deepest of sleeps.

32

BRUISE

ISMAIL WANTED TO SEE Celia again, but the unconventional nature of their encounters left him uncertain how to proceed. He didn't even have her phone number, and since she'd intimated that she hadn't mentioned their new friendship to her daughter, he cautiously kept his distance, waiting for her to part her bedroom drapes or emerge from the front door.

He found excuses to go outdoors frequently over the weekend, lingering a long while on his porch when getting the newspaper, dawdling in the garden, pretending to inspect the new buds, all the while conspicuously watching her curtained window. He felt like a loiterer on his own property. Her son-in-law appeared a couple of times, carrying lumber and tools into the house. Once, when he left the door ajar to unload something from his car, Ismail peered into the foyer, but didn't see any sign of her.

As more time passed, her continued absence riddled him with self-doubt. Had he done something to turn her off?

Was there a reason she was avoiding him? Ismail reviewed each of his words and deeds, but found nothing faulty in them. This should have reassured him, but rather, it left him feeling further adrift and unsure; at least if he could have found a social blunder of some kind, he might figure out how to rectify the problem.

Ismail busied himself the best he could, cleaning his home, changing the bed sheets, and stocking his fridge, in anticipation of her arrival. By Sunday afternoon, he couldn't keep hold of his anxiety any longer and headed to the Merry Pint. But there was no relief to be found there; the carousing and joking of the regulars didn't offer sufficient distraction and the advances of the Mary Pinters only repulsed him. He kept to himself and felt further alienated by the revelry around him. Not knowing where else to go, he stayed and ordered another beer.

— ❈ —

Meanwhile, Celia slept, and it was only after eighteen hours of comalike slumber that she awoke to the sound of hammering in the basement. The morning before — her conversation with Lydia, her long shower, and her reunion with her old clothes — felt like a distant memory, and so when at first she awoke from her bed with her blouses, skirts, and purses piled on top of her, she was disoriented. Outside, the sun shone. Across the street, a newspaper sat on Ismail's porch. She put this all together and calculated that she had slept clear through Saturday, and it was already Sunday morning.

She propped herself up in bed, and found herself naked, her dressing gown a silk pond on the floor beside the bed. Never before had she slept without clothing, and this novel intimacy of cotton sheets on her skin made her think of Ismail. She laid back again and enjoyed the flood of sensations: his lips pressing against her mouth, cheeks and neck, his hands encircling her waist, squeezing her shoulders and back, and once or twice, straying toward her rump.

She hugged herself, closed her eyes, and her hands tingled. The pads of her fingers recalled the feel of his lean arms, the small of his back, the wiry hair around his temples. She balled her hands into a fist to hold on to the bawdy feeling as long as she could.

She looked out her window again and saw that the newspaper was no longer on his porch, and supposed that she'd just missed glancing him. *Strange.* She'd grown accustomed to sensing his appearances even before they happened. A pang of disappointment welled in her chest and she reassured herself that he was near, just across the road. But she would wait to see him again. There were other things she needed to attend to first.

She rose from her bed, upsetting a skirt and two blouses, all of which slid to the floor. She covered herself with her silk robe and surveyed the jumble of clothing. Brown sandals lying in her way invited her to step inside them. Across the room, a naked hanger swung gently on the armoire's rod, as though nodding in agreement. Then, a dark green blouse beckoned to her from the pile on her bed. Ever so slowly, she smoothed it out with her hands, placed it carefully on the hanger, adjusted its shoulders, fastened each shell button, and then placed it on the rod. A second blouse greeted her when she returned to the bed. She looked at it for a long time, then shook out the wrinkles, found a hanger, and arranged it beside the first. She repeated the ritual with every blouse, dress, skirt, and pair of pants, as she methodically arranged them in her armoire. Hours passed.

Trancelike, she turned to her shoes. She looked for their twins and stepped into each, her bare soles absorbing the body memory of other times: high heels that pinched her toes during her daughter's wedding, sandals that let in sand during a trip with José to Toronto Island many summers ago, the comfortable brown pumps good for taking Marco to the park when he was still a toddler. Finally, when she'd sampled each pair, she displayed them, two by two, on the armoire's floor.

Her dozen handbags came next. She had always been a thrifty woman, only buying a new purse every two years and making sure to maintain their good condition. She caressed each, sniffing their smooth leather. Some held souvenirs from the past: dozens of coins; a favourite pen she'd thought she'd lost; and a brochure for the Seniors' Program at St. Christopher House. She had meant to enrol her mother over a year and half ago, hoping recreational activities might stimulate her appetite. She left the brochure on the dresser, and counted up almost eight dollars in change. Then, on her tip-toes, she positioned the bags in a neat row on the highest shelf of the armoire.

Lydia passed by her room a few times during the day, a silent witness to the transformation. She didn't comment on her mother's long sleep, or the clothing brought up out of the basement. Celia noticed her quiet presence a few times that day, but, not wanting to be disturbed, carried on with her work as though she hadn't.

When everything was put away, the bed and floor finally clear, Celia looked out her window at the clouded-over sky. Down the block, she saw Ismail's retreating back as hurried across the street; her second miss of the day. For just a fleeting moment, she questioned where he was going, and pondered the perfume she'd smelled on his collar two days earlier.

She turned back to her bedroom, for there was still much work to be done. Her mourning clothes hung at one end of the armoire, dowdy and neglected, having been pushed aside as she added the new outfits. With the same ceremony and care she took to unpack and hang the rest of her clothing, she took down each black skirt, housedress, and dark sweater from their hangers. They were neatly folded and placed into bags and boxes to be given away. She kept just one dark outfit for occasions she hoped wouldn't come too soon or often. When the task was finally complete, the day turning to dusk, Lydia entered the bedroom-den, bringing with her two glasses of wine. Celia, thirsty from her day's work, was pleased to accept the drink.

— ❋ —

On Monday morning, Nabila called Ismail at work to inquire about his first date with Shakila. He had a mild hangover and couldn't muster much enthusiasm despite her giddy queries. He guessed she was fresh off the phone with Shakila, because there wasn't a hint of surprise in her voice when he mentioned their plans for a second date that evening.

"Oh great, where are you going?" Nabila asked.

He drummed his fingers on his desk, knowing she likely knew the answer to that question, too. He craved the opportunity to speak to his sister-in-law honestly, the way people did over coffee after AA. If only he could confide in Nabila about Celia, and ask her whether he should cancel on Shakila.

"Sorry, what did you say?

"The restaurant? Which one are you taking her to?"

"Oh, right. Beijing House. Look, Nabila, I've got to go. I have a meeting in a few minutes," he fibbed.

Ismail troubled over his situation, his thoughts travelling in concentric loops:

I really like Celia.

After Friday night, I can assume Celia likes me, too.

But Celia hasn't contacted me for some reason, so I don't know.

Shakila seems to like me. I like her enough, too. I like Celia more.

Should I keep seeing Shakila? Hedge my bets?

There may be something dishonest and disingenuous about this.

I hope no one finds out about my two-timing, especially Celia.

I really like Celia ...

He arrived at the restaurant a few minutes early, and this time Shakila was already there, waiting for him. They shared orders of chicken corn soup, vegetable fried rice, sizzling beef, and once again made easy conversation. Shakila showed him how to properly use chopsticks, holding her hands over his, guiding his clumsy fingers. Despite her charms, his guilt and indecision were like a four-foot backyard fence rising between them; it permitted friendly conversations while keeping her effectively on her side of the grass.

Not surprisingly, Ismail was less attracted to her than before, fixating on her heavy mauve eye-shadow and clumpy eyelashes. Her purplish-pink lip-liner, a shade darker than her lipstick, was also was a distraction. His addled brain superimposed Celia upon Shakila, teasing him with visions of her perfect mouth and dark, flowered eyes.

The waiter brought the bill and Shakila insisted they go Dutch. Ismail appreciated that; he thought women sometimes talked an equality line while expecting men to pay for everything. He'd bought many free drinks at the Merry Pint without ever receiving reciprocation.

They both had work the next day, and so the date ended early. While Ismail was glad for this, he needed more time to figure out his next steps. Should he ask Shakila out again, or break things off? When she suggested they get together again on Friday night at her place, Ismail shrugged and smiled; a feeble agreement at best. He scribbled down the driving instructions, all the while wishing he could be honest with her. But what would he have said? His thoughts hadn't developed beyond the repetitive mental loops he'd been travelling all day.

IreallylikeCeliaWhatshouldIdo?

Shakila kissed him on the cheek and hugged him for a long time before getting into her car. Ismail held her stiffly, feeling her cheek against his neck, inhaling her strong perfume. He watched the traffic whiz by on Gerrard and wished to be part of that moving mass, travelling westward and away.

Back on Lochrie Street, Ismail found himself standing in front of Celia's house. Guided by a gravitational pull more powerful than his shyness or fear combined, he didn't hesitate. His feet carried him up her walk in decisive strides. His knuckles gave three self assured raps — *bang, bang, bang* — against the cold wood, preferring the directness of knocks over the subtlety of a bell.

— ✳ —

Celia's internal alarm system was functional again and so she sensed when Ismail's car pulled up to the curb. She looked at her watch and saw that it was almost nine o'clock, much later than usual for him on a Monday night. *Tuesday he comes home late, but not on Mondays.* She heard his knock and rushed to the front foyer, but Lydia reached there first.

"Hello, Lydia. How are you?" he asked formally. "Is your mother home?" Lydia nodded and looked quizzically at Celia, who had just squeezed herself into the narrow entranceway. Lydia retreated to the living room, far enough away to give them the illusion of privacy.

"Hello," Celia said, shyly.

"Hello," then lowering his voice to a whisper, "was it all right for me to come here? I didn't have your number to call you and I wanted to see you."

"Yes, it's ... fine," she said, looking over her shoulder at Lydia, who sat on the couch, pretending to read a magazine.

"You look nice. Different," he said.

"Thanks," she replied, glad that he'd noticed. She was wearing a cherry red, low-cut blouse with a long, navy blue skirt. Silver earrings with red stones dangled from her ears. A touch of lipstick, a hint of mascara.

"You said you were getting tired of the black, and look at you. You aren't wearing it anymore."

"I'm still getting used to it," she said, her face made crimson by his compliment. She hadn't been out all day, and, except for her family, he was the first to see her transition.

His gaze was steady and she felt her blush travel past her cheeks, down her neck, and across her chest. Celia saw him watching its slow progression, only looking away when the heat reached her cleavage. The warmth continued southbound, over her stomach, and came to rest someplace just above her thighs.

She pushed him closer to the door, out of Lydia's line of vision, and reached up to kiss his cheek, landing on the same spot where Shakila's lips had been less than an hour before. She spied the purplish imprint she knew another woman had left behind. She sniffed the air and smelled a familiar perfume.

"Who wears such strong perfume and purple lipstick?" Jealousy raised the volume of her voice, surprising her.

"Sorry? What do you mean?" Ismail asked, backing away from her enough to glance himself in the mirrored closet doors. "Oh," he moaned, and wiped the lipstick into his cheek until it resembled a small bruise.

"You've been seeing a woman these last few days ... and seeing me, too," Celia brought her voice down to a stern whisper.

Just then, Lydia came into the foyer, and tugged her away. Celia wished Ismail hadn't been there to see them erupt into an argument, hear their voices bounce off the living room walls.

"*Mãe!* You've done all *this*," she said, gesturing at her mother's clothing, "for *him*? You came out of mourning for my father and grandmother for *that man*?" She crossed her arms tightly across her chest.

"Lower your voice!" Celia said, her own rising to a yell. "No! I did it for myself. Weren't you the one who told me I should stop wearing black?"

"How you can disrespect my father's memory like this? All this time you've been carrying on with him!"

The accusations stung Celia, leaving her speechless. She noticed Ismail peer around the foyer wall, and then retreat behind it once again, like a child hiding from arguing parents. Lydia paced, her silent rage threatening to engulf Celia. She struggled to push it away, turning her back to Lydia, and that's when she saw him, *José*. He sat on the sofa, the cushions sagging beneath him. He fluffed a pillow and placed it behind his back. He slowly shook his head, and Celia stared at him to make sense of it. Lydia continued to pace, oblivious. Then José stood, his right arm waving elegantly, his wrist flicking gently open. He mouthed the word, *Go.* He pointed towards Ismail with his eyebrows. *It's okay. Celia, go! Go!* And then he disappeared.

Although the gesture was a small one, Celia knew it was grand.

She watched the spot where her dead husband had sat, a part of her knowing that he'd never been there, another part of her waiting to see if he'd reappear. The couch cushions remained unbothered. She turned and went back to the foyer, where Ismail waited and fretted.

— ❊ —

Ismail was wishing he'd looked in his rearview mirror before visiting Celia. He should have known the lipstick smear was there; Shakila had reapplied a thick layer of it after dinner and when she kissed him goodbye, he'd felt something pasty on his skin.

When Celia finally returned to the foyer, his eyes brimmed with unspoken apologies.

"Will you come over? To my place? I need to explain all of this properly to you. It's not what you think." He continued to rub at his cheek, and sweat beaded his brow. Others may have read his perspiration as confirmation of guilt, but Celia seemed to know otherwise. She took his hand and led him out the door, and they crossed over the half-dozen metres of asphalt that separated their homes, hands entwined, in full view of anyone who might be watching. Curtains in surrounding houses swished and swayed and repositioned themselves.

33

ISMAIL AND CELIA

THEY RETURNED TO THE same couch where they'd spent the previous Friday night, taking familiar positions, only this time Celia sat a few inches farther away from him, her body holding itself straighter and taller than before. Ismail inhaled a big breath, coming clean in one long sentence, his words unravelling his story and his panic. He explained about his brother's matchmaking right before their first kiss, described the two dinner dates, and confessed that she had been all he could think about for days.

Telling her everything was easier than he'd imagined. Perhaps it was Celia's forthright questioning ("So, you want me or you want her?"). Maybe it was that they'd maintained few pretenses in their strangely developing relationship. After all, she'd seen him collapsed on the floor, crying over newspaper clippings. She'd kissed him in the street without warning. They'd both spied on one another for months.

While they talked, he watched her anger wash down and

out of her, dissolving her cold stare, relaxing her jaw, and softening her shoulders. She let it happen, for she wasn't interested in staying mad. But still, she held on to a smidgeon of caution, for there was still something important she needed him to do.

"And what about her?" she asked.

He checked his watch. It was a few minutes before ten o'clock and he felt as though a deadline was about to pass. He excused himself, took the telephone into the kitchen and scrolled through the phone's call display to find Shakila's number. While his heart thudded heavily in his chest, he made his second confession of the day.

"It's been lovely meeting you ... but I'm afraid that I just don't see us together in a long-term way ... I'm sorry ... if I led you on."

"I suppose I'm not surprised. I wasn't sure if there was, you know, that spark thing, between us." Ismail thought she sounded disappointed.

"You're a very nice person — I'm sure the right person is out there. It's just ... not me," he reassured.

"You, too. Well, no hard feelings."

"Yes ... and thanks. Well ..."

"Good night," she said.

"Good night." What had seemed so very complex and to Ismail just a few hours before had turned out to be a rather simple undertaking. He hung up the phone, and returned to the living room.

"So I called Shakila and broke it off," he said to Celia, wringing his hands.

"Yes, I heard. How did it go?"

"Just fine. Not as awkward as I imagined." He sat down beside her. "I should have done it earlier, though."

"I've never been in that situation. Breaking up with someone."

"Me, neither. I've always been on the receiving end of these things." They both looked into their laps. Finally, she broke the silence.

"I have to tell you, I have no idea how to do this," she blurted. "The last time I dated anyone it was over thirty years ago. José was my first and only boyfriend. I was just out of high school when we married. I think you are much more experienced at this than me."

"I wouldn't be so sure. I haven't had a truly serious relationship since my ex-wife Rehana. And that was a long time ago." Although she knew he wasn't exactly lying, she could tell this wasn't the whole truth.

"But you've been out with women?"

"Yes, a few," he said, looking off into space, and she wondered who he was thinking about just then. She waited for him to continue, unsure of how much she really wanted to know.

"Yes," he said, crossing his left leg over his right, his eyes meeting hers and then darting away again. They waited for the silence to pass. And then he said, "But you know, dating experience doesn't mean much. I don't have any special wisdom. I'm probably pretty terrible at it, and to tell you the truth, I feel very clumsy." Celia looked at Ismail's graceful hands, admiring his short, neatly trimmed fingernails.

"But you — you're not clumsy at all," he continued. "You have been the one to take all the initiative. This," he said, gesturing to the space between them, "wouldn't have ever happened if it hadn't been for your ..." he paused, appearing suddenly stumped.

"... my what?"

"I don't know. Your initiative ... your gumption. Your ... magic."

"Ah yes," she laughed, "my magic. Wouldn't that be something if I had magical powers ... I would have my old house back. I could have saved my husband. Maybe my mother, too. I wouldn't be living in my daughter's house."

A look of sadness cast over Celia's face then, her pink cheeks growing pale. He wasn't sure how to interpret her expression. Did she really want her old life back? Did she want José back, too? He wouldn't have blamed her if she did; if he could have gone back to the morning before Zubi's death, he would have flown there in a heartbeat. Every day, he wished for Zubi to be alive again, for his mistake to reverse itself. And on some days, he even wanted Rehana, too. He fantasized about how things might be in this second-chance reality. By then, Zubi would be in university, perhaps still at home, or insisting on moving out on her own. Rehana and he might have entered a new stage of life together, satisfied that they'd raised their daughter well and planning their retirement in ten years.

He found it funny that he could think all this while in Celia's company, while wanting her so much; he could inhabit a middle space of yearning for what could have been with Zubi and Rehana, while anticipating what might be with Celia. Perhaps, he considered, watching her glazed-over expression, Celia was soaking in the waters of her own past and present lives, too.

"You're right," she said, breaking the silence that had grown between them. "I have been forward, haven't I?" A broad smile overtook face. "So," she continued, "I will continue being forward, then."

"Good!" He laughed, giddy all of a sudden.

"Shall we go steady?" Her face turned earnest. "Is that what people still call it?" Ismail wasn't sure if people still said that, but he nodded anyway.

"So we'll go steady, then," she said.

— 34 —

STEADY

CELIA AND ISMAIL LAY on their sides, face to face, regarding the other shyly from this new perspective. They were tentative at first, glad for the darkness of his bedroom, each relying on inadequate past experience to guide them. Their kisses began feathery and light and soon became deeper, hungrier. Their uncertain bodies became easy and they took turns removing their clothes as though in an egalitarian round of strip poker; first his shirt, followed by her blouse, and so on until their clothing lay in a heap on the floor. Ismail smiled when he saw the orange bra that had once revealed itself to him from Celia's fluttering clothesline. Their bare skin pressed together, made heat, their limbs wrapping around the other until they resembled a tight knot.

They spent the night talking and laughing and making love, sometimes all three at the same time. The combination was new to Ismail, for whom sex had always been a fairly serious project, his performance of great concern for him. Celia, too, found it to be a novel experience. It wasn't that José hadn't been gentle or considerate, at times. It was just that it had been a long, long time since sex had been a romantic affair; in his last few years, it had turned into a furtive, late-night activity, his breath boozy and his movements ungainly.

Around 3:00 a.m., Ismail marvelled at how his middle-aged body was still functioning and Celia took that as an invitation to climb on top of him. They fell asleep sometime around dawn, his head on her shoulder.

Ismail called in sick the next morning, and Celia phoned her daughter to say she wouldn't be back in time to take Marco to school. Her answers were curt monosyllables and he assumed she was being questioned for her absence. He poured her coffee and took out eggs and a frying pan to make omelettes.

"So how was that, talking to your daughter?"

"Hah! Can't you guess?" she said, with a laugh and then a grimace.

"It sounded, er ... tense."

"Can you make mine sunny-side up?" she asked, thinking that it had been forever since anyone had cooked her breakfast.

"Of course." Ismail turned on the burner, watched it glow red, and then put a pat of butter in the pan. "So, are you all right?" He hadn't yet learned how to read Celia's expressions.

"She asked me if I was here. I said 'yes.' She asked if I spent the night. I said 'yes.' Then she asked, 'in his bed, *Mãe*?' and I said 'yes.' Then she started lecturing me about being careful with strange men, and being a vulnerable widow, and calling when I'm not going to be coming home, et cetera, et cetera. She even tried to guilt-trip me, telling me that Marco was upset when he came down to my room and saw that I wasn't there! I hung up on her," she said with an exaggerated shrug.

"Oh," he said, and waited.

"You know, the conversation reminded me of when Lydia was twenty, and she'd stayed out all night with a boyfriend for the first time. I was so mad," she said with a sigh. "I never told José because I knew he'd be crazy mad. I have to admit, I probably asked her the same questions. I gave her the same lecture." She sat down at the table.

"Of course you'd have to react like that when she was young. But you're her mother ... she shouldn't be lecturing you. You're not a twenty-year-old," he said, taking her hand. She squeezed his.

"You make me feel like a twenty-year-old ... in a good way," she said, looking up at Ismail and batting her eyelashes at him. "Not that fifty is all that old. My hairdresser told me it's the new thirty."

"That's funny. Although I wouldn't want to be thirty again. But yes," he agreed, standing taller, "you make me feel young, too. Imagine, I barely slept, and I feel wonderful!" He turned and cracked eggs into the pan with a flourish. "I suppose it will catch up with me later today, though."

"It's all the good brain chemicals that get released. What are they called again?"

"Endorphins." They'd talked about this during the night when he told her about being in AA. She'd been particularly interested in one of the anecdotes he'd recounted about a member who'd quit drinking and became a sex addict, chasing the high in a new way.

"Right. Endorphins. They feel good ... all the more reason for my daughter to just be happy for me, yes? She's been bugging me to get out more, to stop moping around. And here I am doing something that makes me happy. Can you believe she asked me if I used protection?" she whispered. "I'd never be so forward with her!" Ismail poked at the sizzling eggs.

"Well, I guess she ought to be concerned for you. She doesn't know me at all. For all she knows, I could be a pervert, or ... worse." Ismail was about to say "a psycho killer" to be funny, but the word caught in his throat. He busied himself at the stove.

"That's why I lectured *her* when she was young. Because she didn't have any sense back then. But this is different. I'm fifty. If I don't know things by now, a lecture won't do me any good."

"I have a feeling I'll get a lecture from my older brother when he finds out that I broke things off with Shakila," he said with a smirk, feeling as though nothing could hurt him in that moment. "And when I tell him that I am seeing my beautiful neighbour, I'll receive an epic lecture, one of the magnitude usually reserved for his youngest son."

"Hmmm. I hope not," she said, frowning. He'd told her about Asghar and his relationship with his father the previous night.

"You know, Asghar will be glad that I'm taking over his role for a while. The poor boy can have a break while his uncle catches fire," he joked, and this made her smile. He popped four slices of bread into the toaster, feeling charming again.

Ismail served the eggs onto her plate, perfect, sunny yolks facing up. After a quick breakfast, they returned to bed for another couple of hours, Ismail pretending to chase Celia up the stairs. Later, at noon, he walked her to the door so that she could pick up Marco from school. They stood in the foyer and made plans to meet for dinner after Lydia came home from work.

"Oh, but wait," she said, pausing at the door. "Don't you have something you do on Tuesday nights?" A look of alarm spread across Ismail's face and Celia blushed, rushing to explain, "I'm sorry, I seem so nosy. I used to spend a lot of miserable afternoons and evenings just staring out the window. I know half the neighbourhood's routines by now."

"No, it's not that. It's just that I forgot that it was Tuesday already! It's the last writing class tonight and I'm supposed to present my homework to the class."

"That's the class where you met the young woman who's having trouble with her parents?"

"Yes, Fatima." He was surprised she'd remembered this detail. He told her he guessed the girl was fine because he hadn't heard from her in a while. Celia paused, considering her next question.

"And that other girl, the one with the short red dress who left early that same morning, who was she?"

"Oh no ... you saw her, too?" He stammered out details about Fatima's birthday, misplaced keys, and the spare bedroom. Once again, interpreting his nervousness as truthfulness, Celia was satisfied with his answer. She stepped out onto the porch, kissed him goodbye, and they promised to meet later. The air was cool, with just a hint of spring's warmth riding the breeze.

— ❀ —

Celia was glad to arrive to an empty house. She reached for her long, burgundy coat with the fluffy faux-fur collar, and pulled on her matching boots. As she walked the two blocks to Marco's school, she noticed a subtle transformation within her body. There was an almost imperceptible stiffness in her walk, and a faint feeling of being turned inside out, her privates somehow exposed to the wind while under several layers of clothing. She paused on the street, hugged her thighs together to hold on tight to the sensation.

A young postman approached. She'd seen him walking his route many times before and had said hello once or twice. He'd always been businesslike with her, passing her the mail and hurrying off again with his brisk postman walk. But that day, he glanced up from his parcels and looked long at her, his eyes scanning her up and down. His mouth curled upwards into a grin and she smiled back, feeling a warmth spread up her spine. *Hello to you, too!* she cooed in her mind.

By the time she approached the schoolyard, a small group of mothers and grandmothers had already congregated by the doors, waiting for their children to spill out. She approached the semi-circle of widows, sensed the sudden hush in their conversations. She nodded to them and took her place beside Sylvia Silva.

"*Bom dia,*" she called out to the widows.

"*Bom dia,*" came the chorus. Celia felt several pairs of eyes size her up. She looked away, allowing them a moment to take her changes in. Not for the first time, she felt different from these women. Yes, they spoke the same language, belonged to the same church, but unlike many of them, she'd grown up in this country, played Canadian games in a schoolyard very much like the one in which she stood. Her mind tripped over a question that had been brewing there for some time: shouldn't she be allowed to stand with these ladies, but choose her own way too? Be included and also a little different?

She felt a pang of longing for her friends from the old neighbourhood, women she'd once believed she had to lose in order to inhabit her new life. Perhaps it was time to meet up with Adriana or Joana. But would it be the same? Over a year and a half had passed, and she was not the same old Celia. Would they have her back?

There was a whisper and a click of a tongue. When she turned back to meet the women's gazes, Sylvia had taken a step closer to her. She leaned over and said, "Such a pretty coat you're wearing." And then, in a louder voice, she said, "You look good, Celia. Really good." Sylvia threaded her arm through Celia's and together they waited for the junior kindergarten class to be released.

— ✳ —

After Celia left, Ismail did chores: he washed dishes, swept the barely dusty floor, made the bed. He took a shower, discarding the sliver of soap he'd been using for days and lathered up with a brand-new bar. He dressed. And then he wandered the house restlessly. The elation of new love accompanied him, but also along for the ride was a familiar discomfort; something was missing. He paced the living room, climbed the stairs. His chest was tight and his back slick with sweat. He pulled his shirt-tail from his trousers and billowed it out to cool himself. He undid a couple of buttons and rubbed the skin there, soothing the bumpy scar over his sternum. It prickled and itched with each stroke.

The sensation drew him outside to his car, to search the glove compartment for the sheets Fatima had given him the previous week. Standing in the street, he reread her words: *The scar may grow warm under his touch, friction bringing to life something usually ignored, something he'd rather forget.* He stood there while cars pulled in out of parking spots, delivery trucks passed and cats lazed on sidewalks. Eventually, he went back inside, sorted through the papers scattered over his desk and finally found his notes about Celia's first kiss. Turning on the computer, he transcribed the nearly unreadable handwriting onto the computer screen, and not wanting to tarry, he printed them out, making them paper and ink, material and real. He resolved to read them in class that night. Fatima's pages, and his new writing, would be like a call and response to one another.

— ❋ —

Celia fed Marco his lunch. He seemed to have forgotten that she wasn't home that morning, and any distress Lydia noticed in him had long dissolved. She wasn't surprised. He chatted with her about all the day's preschool news (he played trucks, the teacher scolded a boy for kicking a girl, he ate his snack). Celia sat close, running her fingers through his hair, nostalgic for the days when Lydia was that small, their mutual adoration simple, their roles clear. She kissed Marco's cheek and her mind travelled to Ismail. She contemplated him as a father, almost two decades ago, imagined him feeding his daughter her lunch on a sunny afternoon. Her eyes welled up, unable to imagine her own children's deaths coming before her own.

Marco babbled on awhile longer, and then, realizing his *vovó's* mind was elsewhere, he jumped up out of his chair. After a moment, Celia followed him, and saw he was already distracted by his after-lunch television show. She left him to change her clothing and ready herself for her daughter's return. She would fix Lydia's favourite meal to ease their reunion that evening. She took out the chicken to defrost, chopped an onion, a tomato, a clove of garlic. She headed down to the basement for wine for cooking and drinking.

Over the weekend, Antonio and his friends had started framing and dry-walling. She wandered through the outline of new rooms, her slippers leaving behind evidence of her trail in the dust. At the far end of the basement was an area that housed the furnace, washer, and dryer. Beside it was a roughed out washroom. Finally, she came to the pantry. She pushed aside cans of tomato sauce, a large bag of rice, and stacks of toilet tissue. She fingered a nine-dollar merlot, but then saw a twelve-dollar bottle, a favourite of José's. She guessed Lydia had picked it up before his death to serve when they'd last come for dinner. Celia rubbed the dust off the bottle with the edge of her apron, imagining a genie José springing forth from it. She waited, but the bottle yielded nothing. She studied its label, admiring the seaside scene that harkened back hometown memories for José and made him sigh each time he looked at it. She would use only a little for the recipe, and then put the rest aside to go with dinner.

She walked to an open space at the far end of the basement, the place she guessed was designated to be her bedroom. She stood at its centre, imagining her bed and dresser shoved up against the outside walls. Perhaps there would be room enough for a chair, too. A small, dirty window brought in a shaft of light, illuminating the cement floor. She stood in that weak sunshine for a moment, considering which houseplants might be able to survive such inadequate conditions, but couldn't think of a single one. She gazed out the window and caught a glimpse of Lochrie's asphalt surface, her mind travelling along its width to Ismail's house. Oh yes, she thought, perhaps a nice fern, or maybe even a dracaena.

— 35 —

ENDINGS

ISMAIL ARRIVED AT THE empty classroom much too early. After a few minutes of nervous clock-watching, James finally bounded into the room, and he gradually relaxed as the rest of the students drifted in one by one. As usual, Fatima arrived last, rushing in with smoke on her breath. He noticed that she wasn't lugging her heavy backpack, and thought this was probably a good sign.

"How are you, Fatima?" he whispered.

"Not bad," she said tiredly. "So, tonight's the last class. I'll be glad to have this evening free. I've got term papers piling up."

"Yes and ... it's my night to read something. I suppose it will be good to have that out of the way." Ismail told her that the pages she gave him the week earlier had, in part, inspired his own writing.

"Oh yeah. I'd almost forgotten I gave that to you. So ... what did you think?"

"I think ... that you are quite perceptive."

"So you liked it?"

"I wouldn't say I liked it. Not at first. But it was true."

"Huh," she mumbled, looking thoughtful.

James concluded his final lecture, appropriately on the topic of story endings. Then, he asked Ismail, the last person left to read, to share his work. Ismail wiped his damp palms against his trousers, and carried his pages up to the front. He breathed in for one count and exhaled for two.

"So, er ... my piece is still sort of in rough form. I've been procrastinating the entire eight weeks, because I've been terribly nervous about doing this. So," he cleared his throat and continued, "here it is. Please be generous with me." His admission raised a few laughs, and this calmed him some-what. He took a deep breath and started:

The widow kissed me!

Ismail read slowly, wanting his words to be heard and understood, especially by Fatima.

Was it fate or something more mundane like proximity, the fact that we are neighbours, and if we left our drapes wide open, we could see right into one another's lives?

With each pause, he looked up from his page and met Fatima's eyes.

The sort of kiss that at once satiates a longing never before acknowledged while leaving behind a desire that sim-mers long ...

Fatima's expression shifted from neutral, to wide-eyed, and then, a broad grin spread across her narrow face.

I'll never wipe it away.

Ismail wasn't sure what the others thought of his piece; he doubted it had any literary merit. Fatima led the

applause, and didn't stop clapping until after he returned
to his seat.

"Bravo," she whispered, as he sat down beside her.

Ismail followed Fatima outside for the break, still euphoric
from his reading. A few of the other students had offered him
positive feedback, and he felt proud for having faced his fears.

"Congratulations," she smiled while lighting up, forcing
her cigarette to the side of her mouth. "So, is it fact or fiction? Did the widow really kiss you, or was that just a big
ol' fantasy?"

"Wouldn't you like to know," Ismail teased.

"I would!"

"Well, it is."

"Omigod! No way! So, what else happened? Was there
more?"

"Well, a gentleman never kisses and tells, but yes. We
are ... dating." He was enjoying the banter, glad to be sharing the good news with someone, finally.

"Wow, Ismail, that's great!"

"And how are things with you? Any change in your situation?"

"Nope," she said, blowing out smoke. Ismail looked more
closely at her and saw that her black and blue hair was more
unkempt that usual. The whites of her eyes verged on pink
and there were puffy bags under them. "Talked with my
mother. She is a little more sympathetic, but not budging
about me moving back. She's brainwashed by my dad. She
refuses to give me any money."

"You look like you haven't been sleeping. Have you found
a place yet?"

"Not yet. Most people want first *and* last," she com-plained. "And I don't quite have it. Almost, though."

"So still with friends, then?"

"Yeah. It's fine. I'll be fine. Don't worry," she reassured, her tired-looking eyes contradicting her positive-sounding words. "I created this mess, right? Couch-surfing isn't so bad."

"Have you ... been eating enough?" She didn't seem well to him, her already slim face looking drawn.

"Yeah, yeah. Really, you don't have to worry about me," she said, looking down at her boots. He followed her gaze to a small, salt-stained hole in the boot's stitching, where a bit of red sock peeked through.

He opened his wallet and pulled out eighty-five dollars, all the cash he had. He held the money out to her. "I know it isn't much, but ..." She looked at the bills, but didn't take them. "Really, take it, Fatima. I don't want you to go hungry. Or if you don't need if for that, hold on to it for rent." He reached for her hand, opened her closed fist, and placed the money into her palm.

"Thanks." Her fingers closed around the bills and she furtively stuffed them into her coat pocket. "That's nice of you. I'll pay you back when I can," she mumbled. She took a last drag of her cigarette, and then stubbed it out.

Class ended early that night, and the students dispersed slowly, some gathering around James Busbridge at the front of the room, like acolytes hesitant to leave their guru. Others milled by the door, exchanging email addresses. Ismail, too, was unsure about how to say farewell to the familiar strangers around him. He turned to Fatima and reached out a damp hand to her, remembering that this was how they greeted one another eight weeks earlier. She shook his hand and they vowed to stay in touch, but he wasn't sure they would. He gave her his home phone number, and encouraged her to call if she needed his help. She'd barely looked him in the eye since break-time, the eighty-five dollars like an unmentionable shame between them. Ismail let her leave the room first, and followed at an appropriate distance, watching her slightly hunched form cross the campus.

As he drove along College Street, he revved the engine, navigating the downtown streets as fast as he could. It was the end of March, a warmer night than usual, and everyone seemed to be out on the sidewalks, basking in the above-zero temperatures. His passage was slowed twice at pedestrian crosswalks, where he stared down old men with canes and young mothers with strollers, willing them to hurry up. His irritation lifted when he turned onto Lochrie. He was almost home, almost home to Celia.

FRESH SHEETS

ISMAIL RANG OVER TO Celia, but he needn't have. She'd seen his car pull in, and already had on her coat and shoes when he called.

"Did everything go all right with Lydia when you got home?" he queried.

"I got the silent treatment. I even made her favourite meal, but she refused to eat it," she said with a heavy sigh.

"I'm sorry about that, Celia."

"You don't have anything to be sorry about, and neither do I," she said with a vehemence that surprised him. "Anyway, this will pass. I think she is just in shock. Besides, I don't want to talk about her. I've had enough stress in my life. I'm coming over now!" She laughed, but Ismail couldn't tell if it was truly a happy laugh. He hung up, knowing he would only have to count to twenty, and she'd be at his door. Then, the phone rang again. He assumed it was her calling back.

"Yes, my dear?" he answered, trying to sound suave.

"Hello?" There was a pause, and a sob.

"Fatima?"

"Yeah." She sounded like she was trying to catch her breath.

"What's wrong? What's happened? Are you all right?" She started to cry again, in short hiccupping bursts. Meanwhile, the bell rang, and Ismail opened the door for Celia.

"Noooo," she managed to say. He beckoned for Celia to come in and gestured that he was talking to someone on the phone. Celia smiled, took off her pumps. She wore an orange sweater the colour of her hair. A plunging neckline. Ismail forced his attention back to Fatima.

"Tell me what's going on. What happened?"

"Look, can I ... come over? I don't know what else to do, really," she whined.

"Okay, okay, don't worry. Fatima, can you just hold on a second?" He held the phone against his chest, worry for Fatima and desire for Celia yanking him in opposite directions. He apprised Celia of the call.

"Is it serious, do you think?" she asked, and Ismail nodded. "Of course, of course, tell the girl to come over," she said. She leaned in to give him a quick peck, but he held on too long and she had to push him away and remind him that Fatima was on the phone.

"Alright, Fatima, come over ..."

"Are you sure?" she sniffed.

"Yes, yes, it's fine," he said.

Ismail filled Celia in on Fatima's troubles, and while they waited for her to arrive, they considered what could have caused her latest distress. Had she spoken to her parents? Did one of her friends renege on their offer to house her?

Ismail suspected it was something more grave, but pushed away the thought, happy to be distracted by Celia.

She kissed his cheek a second time and he pulled her in again, pressing her up against the kitchen counter, his body hungry for her after their half-day's separation. He groped her soft waist, felt her pelvic bone push into his. Her hands reached up and under his shirt, grabbing at his back.

"Lift me up onto the counter," she whispered, blushing at her own words. Ismail was in the process of negotiating the manoeuvre when the doorbell rang for the second time that evening. He reluctantly drew away from Celia, tucked in his shirt, and Celia patted down her rumpled hair.

He opened the door to a red-eyed Fatima and introduced her to Celia.

"Nice to meet you," Fatima said listlessly. Celia frowned and stepped forward to help Fatima take off her backpack. They all moved to the living room, and with little prompting, Fatima recounted what had happened to her.

"Well I was staying with Monica, this girl I was dating. You remember her — the girl who I danced with at my party?" Ismail looked at Fatima blankly. She persevered, "She's short, Indo-Caribbean? I think you danced with her, too."

"Oh yes. Monica." Ismail vaguely remembered her. She was one of Fatima's posse assigned to ensure his good time that night.

Fatima continued on. In the midst of a heated argument, Monica demanded that she leave, and feeling insulted, Fatima left in a hurry, before she had a chance to find other accommodations. Ismail cast a sideways glance at Celia, trying to gage her response to the dramatic story.

"I don't know what her problem was. Everything was going fine, and then one day, she kicked me out," Fatima blustered. Ismail observed Celia listening attentively, her eyes wide, nodding at each detail.

"That's terrible," Celia cooed. Fatima nodded and sniffed, and Celia put her arm around the girl's shoulders. Ismail felt a pang of jealousy at their instant intimacy.

"Yes, just terrible," he mumbled, joining in.

Fatima took a deep breath and told them that after leaving Monica's, she ran into the boy who had sexually harassed her at her party.

"He apologized, and he seemed really sincere. He told me he didn't even remember doing it because he was drunk, but other people told him off the next day. He said he'd heard I was still looking for a place and offered his couch as a way to make up for his stupid behaviour at my party." She explained that she didn't have any alternatives, and although she sensed it might be a bad idea, she agreed. She hoped he was a nicer guy while sober.

"And besides, his place is right across from U of T, which made life way easier for me. That was yesterday. And it had been fine. He made me dinner, I slept on his couch, and he said I could stay until the end of the week." Ismail held his breath, able to predict the story's end.

"When I got back to his apartment after the writing class, he was weird. In a strange mood. I think he was high or something. He cornered me and demanded that I sleep with him if I was going to stay over."

"What?" Ismail gasped, alarmed. "What did he do to you?"

"In the end, nothing much, I guess. But it really freaked me out. He pushed and shoved me, and it was really scary, and I felt trapped. But then I remembered this thing from a Wen-Do class I took last term. I yelled and karate-chopped him on his collar bone," she said, her hand slicing at the air. "I think I may have broke it."

"Oh my!" Celia gasped. Ismail rubbed his temples.

"I grabbed my backpack and got out of there. Then it hit me what close a call it had been and it freaked me out ... I phoned Ashton and Sonia, but neither picked up." She paused, staring down at her feet. "Then I called you," she said, looking up at Ismail, her eyes welling up again. "I was stupid to trust him. But ... I didn't have anywhere else, and so it was like I didn't have a choice." Celia patted Fatima's back. Ismail stood up to contain the anger buzzing behind his eyes. He paced the living room, and thought about doing terrible, violent things to the guy. He'd karate-chop other bones, leave him with two black eyes, kick him in the groin. Fatima's breathing calmed while his pulse quickened.

"Ismail, you should sit down," Celia advised.

"My friends are great, but I know I've pretty much worn out my welcome everywhere. It's going to be awhile before I can save up enough for first and last and I'm really tired —" she sniffed and continued, "— of staying on people's couches for a day or two and then moving on." Ismail stopped pacing and braced himself for the request he knew was coming next. Yes, he wanted to help the girl, but just how much? He glanced Celia's way, but couldn't read her expression.

"So, then I started thinking ... you offered to help me, and I know this is a lot to ask," she said, her voice cracking, "It is a lot to ask, but ... could I stay here, in your extra room just until I find a place? I could pay you some rent, or do something in exchange, like cook or clean if you want. Just for a couple of weeks, or a month, until I have enough to find my own place?"

Ismail's pulse raced and his body overheated. *Fatima? Living in my house?* It didn't seem an ideal time to have a houseguest with he and Celia only just getting to know one another. How could it work to have Fatima stay over? These thoughts looped around his mind, gathering momentum with each round. Then, he felt Celia's cool palm on his knee and he looked up to meet her gaze. She gave an almost imperceptible nod and a slight smile. His calm returned.

"Yes," he said sighing. "You can stay here. Until you can find a place you can afford." Fatima's face crinkled up as she squeezed her eyelids shut. She opened them again and a few tears slid down her cheeks.

"Thanks, Ismail. That is really cool of you." She reached into her pocket. "Here, take this back. Maybe this can be for the first week," she said, dropping the bills he'd given to her earlier onto the coffee table.

"Listen, why don't I get your room ready now, so you can get some rest? Tomorrow, after work, we can talk some more. We'll finalize those kinds of details later," he replied, suddenly exhausted. He left the money on the table.

— ❄ —

Until then, Celia had been clear on the fact that she liked Ismail. Her first impression of him a year and half earlier was that he was a decent sort of man. More recently, her body bellowed its attraction for him. The idea of having a boyfriend, a new companion who looked at her with fresh and wanting eyes, was growing on her.

But it wasn't until she watched Ismail haul Fatima's backpack up the stairs, and witnessed him smooth fresh sheets on the pull-out bed in his office, and offer the girl a clean pair of his pajamas, that Celia realized that she could love him.

—

When they got into bed later that night, he stared at the ceiling and whispered to her, "I don't know how this is going to go, Celia. This girl, she is in so much difficulty — I just can't say no to her, but it's not going to be easy to have her staying here." She felt him cross his arms over his chest under the covers, the sheets pulling away from her and tenting around him.

"I think the two of you are going to get along just fine," she assured him. She kissed his forehead, smoothing out the deep-set lines settling there. She curled into his stiff body, her back to his side, inviting him to turn toward her and encircle her with tense arms. It took a few minutes, but his muscles grew supple, his knees bent, and his toes reached for hers. As they lay silently beneath the sheets, she felt him slowly transform into her young lover once again. She pulled back just far enough to look over her shoulder at his face, and saw a twinkle in his eye.

— 37 —

HOUSEGUEST

IT WAS THE BEGINNING of May, and spring was finally asserting itself. Gardens were full of ripe garden shoots and early flowering bulbs, offering the promise of summer's growth. Even with the cool nights, people lingered on their porches, chatting and watching passersby until late. Curtains opened to welcome the sunshine. The neighbourhood felt alive again.

Fatima had been living in Ismail's house for just over a month, still having trouble finding a place of her own, despite all her searching. She gave him regular reports, sharing anecdotes about dingy basements, cockroach-infested bachelors, and earnest interviews at collectively run vegan households. Her updates were entertaining, but also delivered with a hint of apology — Ismail knew she worried about staying beyond his limit, as she'd done with her friends — and he tried to reassure her otherwise.

The truth was that Ismail didn't really mind her living there; she wasn't as troublesome as he'd first guessed. In particular, their agreement — that she cooked three times a week in exchange for rent — was working out very nicely for him. When he swung open the front door on her cooking nights, the aromas from the kitchen reminded him of the early, happy years of his marriage to Rehana when he hadn't yet seen the inside of a Patak's curry jar, and silence and resentments hadn't yet invaded their home. In those days, he and Rehana maintained a comfortable after-work routine: they recounted workday stories during supper, and then she washed the dishes while he dried. After Zubi was born, they still conversed and ate together, but their focus turned to their baby. Each new expression, movement, or gurgle was an endless source of delight, concern, or evening's distraction.

After the tragedy, their dinners became less frequent as they found ways to avoid facing one other across the kitchen table. Rehana warmed leftovers, telling Ismail she wasn't hungry. She'd occupy herself with the laundry or close herself up in the bedroom, doing some sort of exercise routine. He'd take a plate to the living room, bend over the coffee table, and watch game shows and sitcoms until bedtime. Sometimes he'd find her spooning cold food straight out of the Tupperware while she stood over the sink, late at night.

Fatima was an unexpectedly skilled cook, coached by her mother when she was a pre-teen, as well as being good company. Ismail shouldn't have been surprised by the latter; in hindsight, this quality was one of the main reasons he'd continued attending James's writing class. He'd never met anyone quite like her and, most of time, looked forward to chatting with her during breaktime. Their relationship back then was still unnamed, and mostly unacknowledged, at least by him.

Their supper conversations were lively, often stimulating debates about current affairs. Since Daphne, Ismail hadn't engaged with anyone in this way. One night, Fatima announced that she was self-labelling as a post-colonial, anti-capitalist feminist, and her explanation and definition of this identity lasted the entire duration of a *daal*, rice, and *raita* dinner. She seemed to enjoy educating him about "queer theory" (as she called it), and he was a receptive audience, tending to ask dozens of questions about this topic which was so strange and confusing to him.

"What do you mean gender is fluid? You're either a man or a woman," he insisted.

"Oh come on Ismail, we've been though this before. There are dozens of gradations within each of those categories which make them meaningless. I mean, I'm not much of a girly girl. And well ... you're not exactly a macho man."

"What do you mean by that? Okay, so I don't like hockey and I like to iron but —"

"Exactly," she'd say with a smirk.

Ismail always believed himself to be liberal in his political viewpoints, but Fatima's influence left him feeling a tad more informed, and less stodgy than before. He liked to think he expanded Fatima's thinking, too, most notably when she discussed her parents. Yes, he listened and sympathized, but he also inserted a few grey ideas into her black-and-white thinking, advising her to keep an open mind regarding her family, and to give them time to cool off. He believed the scandal would be a temporary blemish on the

complexion of her life, with perhaps a few members of the
community enjoying the gossip for years. But he also knew
that another family's disgraces would eventually replace
hers. When he felt up to it, he sometimes shared examples
from his own life, after Zubi's death. These stories, repack-
aged as a way to offer her comfort and perspective, helped
him, too.

Of course, there were a few wrinkles in their domestic
life. Fatima was not the tidiest of roommates, and Ismail
was often made irritable by her detritus: books and pens
left on the dining-room table, sweaters draped over kitchen
chairs and an assortment of feminine products straying all
over the bathroom counter. He purchased a wicker basket
that he used for the daily task of de-cluttering and most
nights, walked a circuit of his house with the basket in the
crook of his arm, picking up after her. Celia teased him,
telling him he reminded her of an illustration of Little Red
Riding Hood from one of Marco's fairy tale books.

Despite her lack of neatness, Fatima maintained a certain courtesy with Ismail that he appreciated. She allowed
him to shower first in the mornings so that he wouldn't be
late for work. She discreetly went upstairs to her room or out
for a walk while Celia visited. Fatima even asked permission
when, twice that month, she and Ashton held some sort of
political meeting in the basement. Fatima unrolled a rem-
nant carpet and arranged some of the furniture Ismail had
stored down there — a couch with food stains, the kitchen
table bought in the eighties, and some folding chairs — and
despite the exposed drywall taping and poor lighting, she
and her friends made themselves comfortable. On those
nights, Celia and Ismail watched as half a dozen scruffy-
looking young people filed past them on their way down to

the basement, murmuring hellos and leaving a pile of sneakers and steel-toed boots by the front door.

"What are they discussing down there?" Celia wanted to know.

"I can't tell. Fatima said they are an unofficial university queer collective." After a month of dinners with Fatima, he no longer cringed when anyone, including himself, said the word *queer*. "They weren't allowed space at school for some reason. Something about a 'fascist response to their radical politics'," he said, rolling his eyes.

He could tell Celia was still curious, because she used a tray full of cookies and juice as an excuse to go down and listen for a minute or two. Unlike him, she didn't seem to need any kind of sensitivity training to be comfortable with Fatima and her non-conformist friends. To her, they were youngsters who needed refreshments.

Ismail experienced that month like a vacation from his life. He didn't step foot into the Merry Pint once and didn't miss it. Instead, he courted Celia, who visited most evenings, sometimes joining Ismail and Fatima for dinner. More often, she drifted over later, stayed the night, and crossed back in the mornings, quietly descending Lydia's stairs to her basement room. On a couple of Sunday mornings, Ismail insisted that she sleep in with him, bullying her with kisses and cuddles until she gave in. "All right, Mr. Ismail," she'd call him when he was bossing her. "Then you'll have to sneak me back into the basement." They lolled in bed, devising foolish and elaborate plans to distract Lydia while Celia crept inside. Sometimes it involved dressing Ismail as a salesman, or prank telephone calls that would draw Lydia away from the side door. In the end, Celia needed none of this, walking straight-backed across the street, in through the front door, and yelling out a "hello" to whoever might have been downstairs when she arrived.

On those mornings when she stayed late with him, Ismail cooked breakfast, sunny-side eggs for Fatima and Celia. They broke their yolks together, resembling a kind of prefab family, a mix and match collection of woman, man, and child, assembled by their strange circumstances. At times Ismail believed that their peculiar combination was superior to that of blood family; without the burden of shared histories, they managed to fit together fairly happily.

Pressure from their families arrived from all sides that month. Nabil and Nabila called with expressions of "concern" for Ismail, strongly suggesting that he reconsider dating Shakila and cautioning him of the perils of cross-cultural relationships (*"Just look what happened to Shakila!"* Nabila admonished.) They also insisted that he evict the "trouble-girl," an argument in which Ismail refused to engage.

Fatima's parents were also phoning (and Ismail puzzled over which person in their three degrees of separation had given them his home phone number). First, there was a message from Hassan that contained oblique accusations of Ismail's inappropriate and lecherous behaviour. Listening to his comments left Ismail red in the face, balancing on a beam of shame and outrage. Fatima, however, seemed to take it all in stride.

"It seems he doesn't get the whole queer thing, after all," she quipped, as she deleted the message. Fatima mimicked his gruff voice, "Vaat sort of man does these things for a young girl?" It sounded to Ismail that she was growing insensitive to her father's insults. However, she was more vulnerable to her mother's tactics. Shelina called, sobbing and pleading into the answering machine for her daughter to change her ways and come home. Ismail stood by, watching Fatima sob and fold herself into the couch, unsure how to comfort her. He passed her a clean, white, handkerchief and patted her arm. He pressed the Delete button on the machine.

Another day, he picked up the phone, forgetting to check the display first, and heard Shelina's voice, raspy with indignation, filling the air.

"How dare you interfere with my family?" she charged.

"Would you rather she slept on a park bench?" he countered, knowing he was doing nothing to diffuse the situation by being overdramatic. He continued, "This is the best thing for Fatima. You should be grateful I'm helping."

"How would you know what is best for my daughter? Your opinions are not valid here. You were no kind of father!" She shouted into his ear, "Look what happened to your daughter!"

"What?" he gasped, his mind filling with white noise. He didn't know how long it lasted — perhaps it was just a fraction of a second, or many of his racing heartbeats. Eventually, Celia walked into the room, and her presence cleared his staticky mind. "You may be right. I may be incapable of being a father. But I am more than capable of being a friend to Fatima." Celia took the phone from his shaking hand, and hung it up for him. It would be a long time before Shelina and Ismail would be able to have a civil conversation.

— ❀ —

Across the street Celia had no more support than he. Lydia vacillated between lobbing criticisms and offering warnings, which resulted in frequent spats between mother and daughter. After she was moved down to the basement, Celia didn't make much of an effort to get along with Lydia, her bristly resentment getting in the way of making peace. Except for helping out with Marco, she avoided the family much of the time. She took a new volunteer job working with Portuguese seniors at St. Christopher House, which got her out of the house and occupied many of her afternoons and evenings. Then at night, she often visited Ismail, not bothering to say goodbye or tell anyone where she was going. She returned home in the morning, removed the previous day's clothing and showered away her indiscretions. She and Lydia could almost pretend she'd been in her basement bedroom all night long.

Despite all of their detractors, Celia and Ismail rode the high of their all-consuming relationship, basking in one other's attentions like newlyweds honeymooning in the Poconos.

Each had already experienced love, imperfect marriages, and solitude. They were too old to waste their time with hesitations and others' judgments.

A NEW YEAR

ON MAY SECOND, HER birthday, Celia awoke early, alertness prickling through her body. After over a year and a half of mourning, she was still getting used to waking up and wanting to open her eyes to the day. She untucked herself from Ismail's sheets, and crept quietly out of his house while he slept. She crossed the street and heard Lydia and Marco busy in the kitchen, their voices light and excited. Celia went down to her room, stripped out of her clothes, and wrapped herself in her ivory dressing gown. Sensing that she should wait there, she hopped into bed and arranged the covers around her. Lydia and Marco soon came downstairs, making a production of bringing her breakfast in bed. She exclaimed at everything her grandson pointed out on the tray: *Oh my, these eggs are perfect! Did you butter this toast yourself? Such delicious coffee — the best I've ever tasted!*

Celia met her daughter's eyes. In her expression was a softness she hadn't seen for some time. Lydia smiled, bit her lip, and Celia recognized the apology waiting to be said. She nodded to her daughter; it was enough.

Marco climbed up into bed with Celia and presented a large box with a red bow. Inside was an angora sweater, a birthday gift, but also a peace offering in a pinkish-purple hue, a bright, loud colour.

— ❋ —

Ismail fussed all day. He vacuumed the house, fluffed pillows, disinfected the bathroom. He spent half an hour choosing the striped shirt and dress pants he'd wear that evening. Then he visited three different neighbourhood bakeries, looking for the right cake. He backtracked to the first one and bought a vanilla cake with chocolate icing.

He had two gifts ready for Celia and was immensely pleased with himself for selecting them. The first was a silk scarf with turquoise and magenta swirls he'd seen Celia eyeing in a shop window on Dundas a week earlier. She hadn't said anything to him, but had paused long in front of the mannequin which wore a long black evening gown, the scarf the accessory around its plastic neck. He was sure she wasn't interested in the dress.

The second gift was a freshly cut key to the house, a symbol of their progressing relationship. She came over so often, even had a drawer where she kept a nightie, and so it felt fitting that she should have a key, too. He was certain she'd love both presents.

Fatima scoured websites for Portuguese chicken recipes and was making *Frango no Pucara*, a supposedly popular Azorean dish, as a birthday gift. She'd consulted Ismail to make sure Celia would like it, but neither of them knew anything about Portuguese cuisine.

"Can you get some of those little round potatoes to go with it?" Ismail had eaten them at a local restaurant once and figured they were Portuguese.

— ❊ —

Celia sensed that something was up. She'd always been a woman perceptive to the cues around her, and these skills had grown more finely tuned over the previous year; an unexpected gift of the *agonias*. So, before she went to Ismail's (for what he said was going to be pizza and a movie) she put on a skirt and her birthday sweater. She walked into a house decorated with balloons and streamers, and the dining-room table set formally with candles, linen napkins, and too much cutlery. Fatima excitedly brought out the meal, and Celia looked into the serving dish and pretended to recognize the recipe.

Later, Ismail and Fatima brought out a cake and sang "Happy Birthday" to her in Portuguese, reading words from pages they'd downloaded from the Internet. It was the first time she'd ever heard Ismail sing in his off-key voice, and the dissonant sounds made her laugh. There were six candles for her, five in a row and one underneath to resemble fifty-one. The ritual was one she hadn't experienced in a long time; in her house, they'd long ago relegated candle-blowing to children's birthdays. But while she listened to Fatima and Ismail sing out-of-tune, mispronouncing the *muitas felicidades*, she did feel young, like a girl looking forward to a life ahead full of both promise and uncertainty. When last had she felt this way? Was it when she married, birthed her two children? She couldn't pinpoint it. The song ended. Not knowing what to wish for, she blew out all her candles with an open mind for whatever might come.

Ismail slyly placed two boxes before Celia, one large and the other tiny.

"Open the bigger one first," he instructed excitedly. She tore the pretty wrapping paper and unsealed the box to find the scarf she'd noticed in the Marla's Ladies' Wear window last week. She fingered the rich fabric.

"Ismail, you are so attentive. Look at this!" She wrapped the scarf around her neck, felt the silk against her skin.

"It's looks good on you," Fatima said, nodding.

"Not too flashy for me?"

"No, it's perfect for you," Fatima confirmed, "And look, it goes with your sweater." Ismail smiled broadly and Celia reached over to kiss him. She also kissed Fatima's cheek for good measure, and thanked her again for the dinner.

"One more." Ismail pushed the small box toward Celia. She paused before she unwrapped it, letting its lightness rest in her palm. Although she didn't know what mystery the box held, she knew enough to be nervous.

— ❈ —

Ismail watched Celia lift the shiny key from the box. She frowned, holding it up and away from her, as though it was something unsavoury. The silver caught the light and shone in her eyes. He exchanged glances with Fatima, and rushed to explain.

"I just thought, since you and I are spending so much time together, that perhaps you'd like your own key. You know ... to come and go as you like," he said, his voice cracking a little.

"Oh! I thought that this meant something else ... so ... I was a little caught off guard."

"Sorry?" he asked, confused.

"Oh, you thought he was asking you to move in," Fatima said, interpreting for Ismail. He looked long at Fatima, and then finally understood her words.

"Well, er ... we've never talked about it, but that would be nice, too," he fumbled.

"I think I should leave you two alone for this conversation," Fatima said, already standing. Ismail looked up helplessly at her.

"No, no," Celia said, reaching over to touch Fatima's forearm and pull her back down. "Stay. We haven't cut the cake yet. Ismail, I think it's too early for me to move in. And ... I love the thought behind it. Maybe we can talk about your invitation later. Maybe in a few months?" she said with a tense smile.

"Oh, yes, yes. That's what I really meant. I didn't mean to make you uncomfortable ... or pressure you to move in," he stammered. He reached for his handkerchief and dabbed his forehead. Fatima watched with raised eyebrows.

"It's all right, Ismail. It's very nice. Really. I love having it. I just misunderstood. First, though ..." Celia paused, her face losing its worry lines. He watched her as she eyed Fatima, and then him, and then Fatima again. Ismail rubbed his palms, itching with perspiration, against his trousers. She smiled, "First, don't you think it's time to ask Fatima to move in? You know, more long-term?" He'd repeatedly told Celia how much he enjoyed Fatima's presence, but only mentioned the idea of her staying recently, and in passing. He flushed and stared at Celia. He was still getting used to her being constantly one step ahead of him.

Ismail and Fatima exchanged brief, nervous looks. Fatima looked away first and twisted her napkin in her hands while Ismail played with his dessert fork. He put the fork down and idly scratched the scar stretching across his sternum.

A long pause balanced in the air while Ismail considered his words. He wanted them to come out right.

— ✺ —

Celia watched Ismail struggle, worrying that she had prompted a conversation that needed more time to develop, but to her, the earlier talk about the key seemed like fertile ground for it. She knew it was a seed in Ismail's mind, a seed growing roots each day. But was it ready to sprout? She wasn't sure.

His long fingers reached through the space between his shirt's buttons, his fingernails reaching for the place she recognized as his vulnerability. He'd told her the story it, of the wound only partially healed. She'd asked him if she could have a look at it, and he'd succumbed, a dark look passing over his eyes while he laid flat on his back and she propped herself up on her elbow and hovered over him. He flinched a little when she ran her calloused thumb over its waxy rise and then she felt his muscles relax as she continued to stroke the scar. When he closed his eyes, she ran her lips over it.

He abruptly drew his hand away from his chest and, it seemed to her, willed himself to continue speaking. The seed had germinated.

— ✺ —

"Yes, this *is* something I've been thinking about." Ismail turned to Fatima and she finally looked up to meet his gaze. "Well, you see, it's just that I *like* having you here. The house is rather big for just me. And you're a good cook! Like tonight, this dinner you made for Celia. Just wonderful!" he blathered, realizing he was losing his train of thought. He paused to find it again, and explained that the arrangement might be a solution to her financial problems.

"You know, to take the pressure off you looking for a while ... you could stay until the school year starts, or even after, until the end of the school year if you wanted and then we can see ... and then you can decide what to do next." He didn't hear her over his own rambling, but saw that she mouthed the word "okay."

"Yes?"

She nodded, her eyelashes darkening with her tears. She batted them away. "Um, that would be really cool. Really nice of you. I mean, just for a while. Maybe until the end of summer or something?" she said, dabbing her eyes with her napkin.

"Or until your parents support you again, or you win the lottery," Ismail quipped, wanting her to stop crying.

"The latter might come first," Fatima said, dourly.

Celia beamed and leaned over and hugged her. Then, for the first time since he'd known Fatima, Ismail did, too. He held her in a stiff embrace until she stopped crying.

"Maybe she should move out of the office, though, so that she can really spread out," Celia whispered in his ear. He knew what she was intimating. It was time to open the door to Zubi's room, clear it out, strip the wallpaper, and make space for Fatima. It was time to give Zubi's room away.

— 39 —

DUST

EARLY THE NEXT MORNING, while Celia and Fatima slept, Ismail opened the nursery's door. Sunshine streamed through the southeast-facing window, catching floating dust motes in their rays. Ismail once read that dust particles are mostly composed of skin cells, and that each person sloughs off an entire layer every day or two, abandoning millions and millions of microscopic flakes into the air. Humans regenerate and renew, abandoning pieces of themselves in the process.

He ran his fingertip over the wooden dresser, the way children do on dirty cars. He spelled out his baby's full name — Z-U-B-E-I-D-A — across its surface, his finger becoming coated with grey dust. He looked at each of her three photographs, taken at various ages, lingering on the one of her at sixteen months old. She sat on his lap, his hands holding each of hers, while they smiled for the camera.

He cleaned off the photos with both hands and then rubbed his right against his left, both hands warming with the friction. He imagined Zubi's skin meeting his one final time. One last touch.

But he knew that there was more than Zubeida there in that dusty room. Years ago, Rehana and he shed their skins, too, leaving behind previous versions of themselves. He always believed that Rehana had discarded their life together more easily than he ever could, shrugging it off like an old coat, and leaving it behind on the floor as she exited the house.

He stroked the top of the dresser with open hands, cleaning the dust away, revealing the dark wood beneath. He smeared the grime deep into his palms, over his knuckles, bathing his hands in it. Perhaps he wanted their skin — Rehana's and his — to meet one last time, too.

Ismail wasn't certain how long he stood in the nursery. By the time he left, Celia and Fatima were already in the kitchen, their voices fluttering up through the floorboards. He went to the bathroom and held his hands under the tap, watching the water trickle off his fingers in dark grey streams. He went back to the nursery, glanced at it once more. Then, he heaved opened the window that hadn't been unlatched in almost two decades, letting in the warm spring breeze.

— ❁ —

Downstairs, Celia sat at the table while Fatima fiddled with the coffee maker. It was an ancient-looking thing, rarely used by Ismail, and it often malfunctioned. Fatima frowned, tapped the On button a few times, cursed under her breath, and finally, dark brown liquid began to flow. "Hah!" Fatima said, relishing her victory over the machine. Not for the first time, Celia thought Fatima looked at ease working in Ismail's kitchen. She watched her dig through the cupboards and fridge, looking for ingredients to make pancakes.

"Yup, I'm going to have to make a trip to No Frills. What kind of man doesn't have maple syrup in his house?" Fatima grumbled, and Celia smiled at the insult.

"But first I need some coffee," Fatima declared, and poured them each a cup. It was good; only a few grounds had slipped past the filter that morning. Celia sipped her coffee and thought: *Yes, she is a good girl.* It was a confirmation, of sorts, a kind of answer to a question she'd been mulling over in her mind for some time.

Celia hadn't expected to react so squeamishly when she saw the two kissing girls. Nothing about Fatima had bothered her before, so why then? And it was something she wasn't even supposed to have seen, really.

She'd been in Ismail's living room, waiting for him to finish a phone call with his brother. She listened as he stammered, then agreed, then made counter-arguments, caught up in defending himself against Nabil's judgments. She opened the drapes to look outside and studied her daughter's house across the street. The lights in her old bedroom-den were on, and she guessed that Antonio was up late, perhaps doing the hardware store's books. Upstairs, the rooms were dark except for the flickering light of the television in the master bedroom. The living-room drapes were parted slightly and she thought she could see a figure of a woman in silhouette behind them. She stared at the figure a while longer, imagining a woman dressed in black, a shadowy mirror image of herself, gazing back at her. What did she see? What did her mourning-self think of this new version, this Celia with red hair, flashy clothes, and a middle-aged Indian boyfriend?

As she continued to look out on to the street, something moved in her peripheral vision. She leaned further out. That was when saw them, Fatima and her friend Sonia Gandhi — that was Ismail's pet name for Sonia — slanting into one another on the porch. Fatima's long fingers cupped Sonia's face, her head bent in a long, ardent kiss. Sonia gripped Fatima's forearms, her chin tipping to meet Fatima's mouth. Hands moved across shoulders and backs, and flew beneath blouses. Celia backed up from the window, her face hot. She crossed her arms over her chest and listened for Ismail's telephone voice in the other room, heard his first attempt to say goodbye, and his explanation to his brother that Celia would be waiting for him.

She scanned the street and hoped no one else was watching the kiss (which was still in progress). She knew some of the neighbours were already talking about her, enjoying the gossip of her relationship with Ismail. What would they say about two girls kissing on her boyfriend's porch? She parted the curtains slightly and looked for the shadow behind the drapes at Lydia's place. It still hadn't moved. She looked more closely, saw the pointed edging of foliage; a new potted plant on the windowsill.

Celia heard the door open and the girls bounced their way up the stairs to Fatima's room. Ismail joined her a moment later, complaining about Nabil and Nabila's interference. They stepped out for a late night walk.

"I saw Fatima and Sonia kissing on the porch earlier. Are they dating now?" Celia asked.

"Fatima and Sonia? Sonia Gandhi?" Ismail looked shocked. Celia smiled and nodded.

"I thought they were just friends. Well ... I guess that's good for them. Sonia Gandhi seems like a very nice girl."

"She does," Celia admitted.

"You know, she gets all *A*'s and has a tuition scholarship? And she has a part-time job. Very responsible," said Ismail.

"That's good."

"She even gets along with her parents, from what I can tell. She'll be a good influence on Fatima."

"You sound just like a parent yourself. Like a father evaluating an eligible bachelor. Only in this case it's a bachelorette," Celia teased.

"Hmmm," he said, frowning. She realized she'd put him in a contemplative mood when all she'd intended was to be funny. It happened often between them, this moody misapprehension of her jokes, and she guessed it would take time before they'd truly understand one another well. There were other things she found strange about him; the bottles of Patak's curries lined up in his cupboard, the way he guzzled back non-alcoholic beer when he seemed under stress, his love affair with the newspaper on Saturday mornings. She supposed he could compile his own list of the things he found incomprehensible about her, too. They walked on in silence, the image of the girls returning to Celia's mind.

Fatima held a pen in her hand and seemed to be waiting for Celia to say something.

"Sorry, what?" Celia asked.

"I'm going to get maple syrup and pancake mix from the grocery store. You want me to pick up anything else?"

"Oh. No, thanks. I don't need anything." Celia watched

as Fatima walked down the hallway, put on her shoes and grabbed her keys.

"You okay?" Fatima called out from the foyer, pausing. "You don't look yourself." Celia rose from the table and met her in the hallway. She pinched Fatima's cheeks with both hands. They offered up little flesh between her fingers.

"Such a good girl, you are. A very good girl. I'm just fine." Fatima looked self-conscious, and perhaps a little pleased. Celia let her go and Fatima turned the doorknob and then glanced back at Celia over her shoulder, her eyes still curious.

— 40 —

NEW ROOM

ISMAIL KNEW THAT IT was best not to take short-cuts. He and Fatima removed everything from Zubi's old room, until its four walls echoed their voices. Empty, it appeared so much smaller than when the old furniture occupied it. They turned their attention to the wallpaper, but its glue was steadfast, and so it needed to be soaked overnight. The next day, it grudgingly yielded, scraping off into yellowed, curled-up teddy bear piles. Pocked blue walls were exposed, a souvenir from a previous resident's time.

When Ismail and Rehana first moved in, the walls were robin's egg blue and he thought they could be left as they were, but Rehana was adamant that they use neutral colours. She was funny about that; although she refused to learn their baby's sex in advance, she had a strong feeling it would be a girl. Still, she wouldn't let Ismail paint the walls pink, just in case the baby was a boy. She chose wallpaper — what she judged to be a whimsical pattern of prancing bears. Ismail never thought the bears looked quite right; they wore top hats and their tiny T-shirts only reached partway down their stomachs, their fuzzy potbellies and bottoms indecently bared. In the end, he painted the trims wintergreen to match their T-shirts, which only drew attention to, and emphasized, their nakedness.

Fatima chose sunset-orange paint, three coats to completely conceal the blue, and the room glowed sunshine, even at dusk. She told Ismail that her bedroom walls in Mississauga were grey, a compromise between the charcoal she had originally wanted and the lilac her mother suggested. She preferred darkness during her adolescence, wanted a feeling of a cave. But, now she was over that, she said. Ismail told her he would have let her paint her walls black, or purple, or lime green, if that's what she'd wanted, and she smiled at the sentiment.

The ceiling required some discussion, however. Fatima fancied the puffy white clouds Ismail had stenciled on years ago, and wanted to keep them. Ismail disagreed, the one and only time he would exercise his veto power. Those clouds had been drawn for Zubi, a gift for her alone while he was an expectant father, overwhelmed with the responsibilities he'd soon be shouldering. Rehana took charge of purchasing all her clothing, toys, the latest gadgets, but the ceiling was something special he could create for his child, something peaceful for her to gaze at when she awoke alone in the mornings. Sometimes, Zubi used to point up at her bedroom-sky and Rehana or Ismail would enunciate "cloud" or "sky." She'd attempt to repeat them, her mouth contorting itself into something that sounded like "cowed" or "sigh." She tried and tried, but the words were much too difficult for a toddler to say.

Ismail rolled "Midnight Blue" latex on the ceiling. While the paint dried, Fatima searched for online constellation diagrams. He held the ladder and directed her while she pasted glow-in-the-dark stars to the ceiling. When night fell, they turned out the lights and stared up at the Big Dipper. Later she'd stick up more stars, forming Cassiopeia and Orion, too. She told him that she liked having the whole sky to herself. He hoped it gave her something peaceful to look at when she woke up alone in the middle of the night.

He donated the baby furniture, still in good condition, to Value Village. It was evening, just past closing time, so he left them by the cargo bay doors. Perhaps a young father would browse through the furniture section the next day, looking for a bargain, and claim the set. Would the new owner wonder about the donors, imagining a child grown up and graduating to a new twin bed? Would there be any essence of Zubi left behind on the mattress, a partial fingerprint on the side rails? Before he drove off, he took one last look at the crib. It was unlike him to do so, but he uttered a short prayer for the next child who would sleep within it. *Please, let the little one be safe.*

Fatima and Ismail hauled in the heavy hide-a-bed from his office, which Fatima had been sleeping on for weeks already. Her youthful spine didn't seem to mind its lumpy contours and she insisted that he not buy her a new bed. Ismail thought it was because she'd been reading Marx and was against over-consumption of any kind. But really, it was because she was convinced that she could talk her mother into letting her have her things from her bedroom at home. Perhaps Fatima didn't intend it this way, for she was just as stubborn as her parents, but the furniture negotiations served to put her in ongoing contact with her mother. Ismail encouraged it, for tense and difficult communication seemed better to him than none at all.

And Shelina seemed to be softening. The phone calls were gradually losing their shrill and accusatory (from both sides) tones and no one was hanging up in tears anymore. Ismail and Celia overheard some of the conversations and hoped Shelina was growing to accept her daughter's choices, and would influence Hassan to do the same. Celia told Ismail to prepare himself for the day when Fatima might choose to return home to Mississauga, but he shrugged off the idea.

After a couple of weeks of back and forth, Shelina conceded. Fatima and Ashton rented a van and nervously set off for the suburbs. They returned within two hours, a silver Audi following closely behind. Shelina was in the driver's seat, a determined look on her face, while Hassan slumped sulkily beside her. Through the spotty windshield, Ismail spied them glaring at one another. He speculated that Hassan usually drove the car, and that Shelina was the one to initiate the trip into the city, with Hassan only getting into the passenger seat at the very last minute. Ismail amused himself imagining the terse argument they must have just concluded before pulling up.

Shelina broke the impasse, opened her car door, and strode out to meet Ismail. She was cordial, but didn't look him in the eye for long, the sour words from their last phone interaction still curdling between them. Stiff and business-like, she turned her attention to helping the kids unlatch the van doors. Her husband remained in the car, perhaps still deliberating about whether or not to join in. When he finally got out, Ismail extended a handshake, but Hassan side-stepped it while Ismail's white shirt sleeve flapped in the breeze like a peace flag.

"We thought we'd come and see our daughter's room. Make sure everything is all right," Hassan said brusquely, his tone imperious. Ismail held his tongue. Shelina inspected the exterior of the house and pronounced it to be "cute," which Ismail interpreted to mean "small." He muttered a barely audible thank-you to Shelina's unflattering praise and turned to help Ashton empty the jam-packed van. Fatima, sensing the tension, took her parents inside for a tour.

— ✳ —

Celia heard the noise on the street and, seeing that the U-Haul had returned, went out to join the men. Ismail tromped around the interior of the truck, the metal carriage reverberating with each bothered footfall. Celia had learned that when Ismail was stressed, he tended toward organization and a measured sort of bossiness. Right then he was instructing Ashton about the order in which they should unload the truck. Ashton stood by, eyebrows raised, but more or less compliant.

She reached up as he passed down the dozen garbage bags Ismail had identified as the first to go. They were Fatima's clothes, and as Celia hauled them, she was reminded of her own move to Lochrie Street and the wardrobe she'd bundled haphazardly into plastic. She hadn't much time to pack her things back then, and had been advised to "liquidate her assets" and pay off the debts as soon as possible. That was only five weeks after José's passing, and two after her mother's death, and the creditors were like jackals closing in on the scent of death and rot. Worries were phantoms that kept her up each night.

—

Fatima burst out onto the porch, a forced cheeriness raising the pitch of her voice. Her father emerged after her, following just a step behind. Celia saw it immediately: Fatima was her father's daughter. Her dark eyes, heavy brows, sharp cheekbones — all his. Even their gaits were the same; shoulders and hips revealing a stiffness that was habit for her, but joint pain for him. As they descended the steps together, they were like a pair of marionettes animated by the same hand. Shelina trailed a few paces behind. With her round face, light brown eyes and limber movements, she was their reluctant third wheel.

There was a brief standoff as the Khans surveyed Celia, sniffing out a stranger in their midst. Fatima nervously introduced Celia as Ismail's neighbour, her eyes widening and brows waggling for Celia's benefit. Celia patted Fatima's arm to let her know she wasn't bothered; she knew Fatima was all too familiar with the nuances of her parent's prejudices. Perhaps she didn't want them to suspect that her protector-landlord had a girlfriend, and a Portuguese one at that. Fatima needed her folks to think Ismail was not so different from them.

Celia supposed she was doing the same thing by not telling Sylvia Silva too much about Fatima. She and Sonia Gandhi were now an item, and half the neighbourhood had seen them holding hands on the street. She kept her mouth zippered shut when people asked questions, aware that she wanted to protect the occupants at 82 Lochrie from scrutiny, or at least further scrutiny — a few neighbours still remembered Ismail's past, if only vaguely. Even more, she wanted to avoid being judged by association, and she hated that about herself. She loved Ismail for all his flawed history and adored

Fatima, too. She even thought the girls made a good couple.

So why did she dodge the truth to avoid the critiques of small-minded people? Or maybe she was the one being small-minded by unfairly judging her neighbours. She'd long suspected that Sylvia's niece had a female companion, and it was rumoured that the riding's favoured local politician was gay, too. Would Fatima and Sonia Gandhi really arouse that much neighbourhood scorn?

She was so involved in all her own meandering contemplations that she didn't notice that the Khans had already lost interest in her. She looked up to see that Hassan was making a big production of trying to carry a chest of drawers up the porch steps all by himself. Luckily, Ashton had followed Hassan up the stairs, anticipating the accident waiting to happen.

— ❋ —

Ismail, not caring if Hassan fell on his backside, only watched as he bobbed and swayed under the dresser's weight. No, he would let him fall. But Ashton stepped forward, steadying Hassan on the fifth step, and he and the dresser made it safely upstairs.

After, there was some discussion about how to take the rest of the bulky pieces inside and eventually, after some crabbiness from Hassan and eye-rolls from Fatima, everyone agreed to Ismail's suggestion that they form an assembly line from the van to Fatima's room, with stops at the curb, front hallway, and stairs. He assigned Shelina and Hassan the middle spots, and Ismail stood at the van, so that he wouldn't have to be too near them. He drafted the order on the side of a cardboard box:

Ismail
Celia
Shelina
Hassan
Ashton
Fatima

They worked efficiently, passing bags and boxes and a desk into the house. Ashton and Ismail carried up the mattress, while Shelina and Fatima took in the box spring. Hassan put the frame together. There was even some laughter as they teased Fatima about the quantity of her possessions. Ashton quoted Veblen, something about conspicuous consumption and Fatima not-so-playfully swatted his arm. But in the end, when it was all done, Ismail thought Fatima grinned like a little girl.

— ❊ —

With Shelina and Hassan's departure, Celia felt a collective sigh of relief wafting through the house like a warm summer's breeze. Ismail put his arm around her, the first PDA, or Public Display of Affection, as Fatima liked to call it, all afternoon. Celia sank into Ismail's shoulder, her face turning into his armpit, smelling his musky sweat. The four of them needed a break, and Ismail offered everyone some of his non-alcoholic beer. Ashton, curious about what it tasted like (unlike Celia and Fatima, who already knew) accepted one. He headed home after a few grimace-inducing swigs.

Celia watched as he and Fatima hugged for a long time at the door, Ashton's muscular arms roping around her. She thought their bodies seemed familiar and intimate in the way that only ex-lovers-turned-friends could be. She'd seen Lydia like this with two ex-boyfriends with whom she still kept in contact, touches easy, bodies remembering. She pondered if José were to come back, would it be like this between them? She knew every scar, each tired muscle, the gurgling sounds his stomach made. How would they greet one another again if they were no longer together? It was an absurd notion — José still alive and as an ex-husband — but sometimes her mind jumbled things in this way.

Half an hour after Ashton left, Sonia arrived, having just finished her shift at the coffee shop. The girls left Ismail and Celia alone in the living room, and giggling and pop music took over the upstairs.

"So what do you think of the parents?" Ismail whispered, even though it would have been impossible for the girls to overhear them.

"I think they will come around. I think it is already happening."

"Yeah, I can see it in Shelina. She was almost nice, or trying to be. But that Hassan. What a *gandu*! A real ass!"

She agreed with him but not as heartily; she knew families could repair themselves the way she and Lydia were trying to do. Hassan and Shelina were sewing seams, where once there was a tear. *Messy and crooked stitches for sure, but still ...*

"I can tell they're making an effort," she insisted. He shrugged.

They sat on the couch, their tired bodies leaning into one another, their limbs warming. Celia closed her eyes, felt heat between them, the boundary between where her skin and his began almost imperceptible.

But their minds were busy travelling in two separate directions. Ismail guiltily hoped Fatima wouldn't reconcile with her parents too soon, for he wanted her to stay. He liked the way she took up space in the house and mistakenly believed that she was responsible for the bad memories visiting less often.

Celia's mind was on the house across the street. The rift between she and Lydia was healing, each of them offering needle and thread and fingers to the effort. They had almost been getting along well since her birthday. Now she wondered, would that all change? Would their edges fray again when she told her daughter that she was moving out on her own?

— 41 —

THAT MAN

ISMAIL WAS NOT ALTOGETHER unsympathetic to Celia's plans. He knew she had always lived with other people, first her parents, then her late husband, her mother again, and last with her daughter, all the while playing the roles of dutiful daughter, wife, mother. Of course she wanted to be on her own and he tried to be supportive, at least outwardly. Privately, he couldn't help but maintain the fantasy that after a period of time she'd have her fill of independent living, and get it out of her system. She'd realize that it would be duller than she imagined, and lonelier, too. Then, she would want to come live with him. He envisioned them waking up together each morning, sharing meals, being together like a real couple.

He had to admit that his version of their future included marriage (just a small civil ceremony, nothing fancy), and growing old together. He couldn't really explain his matrimonial longings. He'd done it once before, quite badly, and he'd come to accept and even appreciate his unmarried status, which was made less bleak now that he was dating and had a roommate. Still, he wished for Celia to marry him one day. And there would be the added benefit of increased acceptance from their families. They, too, would see them as a real couple and stop criticizing the union.

Ismail confessed his hopes to Fatima one night over dinner, and with a mouthful of the chicken tetrazinni she'd prepared, she pronounced, "Fat chance." She told him that widows get smart about marriage after their husbands die and aren't likely to make the same mistakes twice. "No offence," she added.

Ismail only half-listened to her while she prattled on about patriarchy and its yoke-hold on women. She was missing the point; it wasn't that he wanted Celia to be his wife. He longed to be her husband, the good husband, the one who wouldn't keep secrets from her, die prematurely, and leave her homeless. He wanted to be loyal to keep her safe. Yes, he wanted to be that man.

— ❋ —

A small apartment was all Celia felt she needed. A galley kitchen that accommodated just one cook. A bathroom no one else would mess. A tiny, unshareable bedroom. A living room not well disposed to entertaining. A place of her own.

The desire had been developing within her, over the winter when she couldn't articulate it, and through the springtime when she wasn't sure she should. Perhaps it began just before the move from her bedroom-den to the basement. It wasn't that the basement turned out to be so terrible, for her subterranean room did provide her more peace and quiet than the room on the main floor. And having her own bathroom was convenient. No, it wasn't the space that was the problem. The issue was that that she could be so easily moved, that it was someone else's decision where she slept at night. For years, she'd falsely believed she was in charge of this — after all, she considered the house on Shannon to be hers. But then it got taken away and she was moved, and then moved once more. She wouldn't allow this to happen to her ever again.

Ismail raised the topic of her living with him again in July, two months after her birthday. He was much more direct and confident about the proposal his second try, providing her with cogent arguments about its benefits. He'd even listed them on a neatly typed piece of City of Toronto letterhead (which he assured her was scrap and not an improper use of tax dollars): more time together; less sneaking around; reduced costs for them both; co-habitating couples live longer (she scoffed at this one and corrected it to say "co-habilitating men live longer").

She turned the paper over to see if there was a list of drawbacks, but the other side was blank. She thought this funny; Ismail tended to be painstakingly thorough.

She did like spending time at his house, enjoyed completing the family that he and Fatima were forming. But something told her it was not quite right for her, a tingly buzzing in her head that said *No, not yet. Not now.* There was something else she needed to do even if she had no idea what it was. All she knew for sure was that she required a home of her own.

And so, she got a herself a job. Her volunteer work at St. Christopher House morphed into a part-time position in their adult day program when Linda, the animator, went on maternity leave. For seventeen dollars an hour, five hours each day, four days a week, she dreamt up recreational activities to occupy the Portuguese seniors. Celia never knew she had so many crafts and games and theme parties stored up in her mind from her years of parenting and babysitting. She took the seniors on mall walks, ran contests to improve their English, and cooked *arroz doce* with them.

One lady, an eighty-year-old with dementia and a spine like a comma, became her favourite client. Maria's husband dropped her off, settling her down in a well-worn corner chair, the same one each day. In the mornings he had the countenance of someone resigned and irritable, but when he returned at two-thirty, he was a different man altogether — more patient with his wife, even jovial, the lines around his eyes less deeply set. Celia was curious about what he did during his respite hours, but never asked. Meanwhile, Maria participated in every activity she could do from her seat and became the de facto knitting instructor. She produced half a dozen knitted scarves a week, even with her failing mental faculties and arthritic hands.

When Celia received her first paycheck, its dot-matrixed print peeking through the plastic window of the envelope, her eyes grew wet. It was her money, money she'd earned and didn't have to share with anyone. She delighted in the notion that she could be frugal or a spendthrift. She unsealed the envelope, ran her finger down the columns of deductions and pension contributions, and tore along the neat perforation. Then, she made her calculations. With the small survivor's pension from the government and this new income, she realized she had enough.

Sylvia Silva knew an elderly lady three streets over whose son had duplexed the house when he left for the suburbs. In exchange for checking in on her once a day, she got reduced rent. They called it a junior one-bedroom, a euphemism for *tiny*. Just what she wanted. She showed it to Ismail first.

"Well it shows promise. A little paint would help." She could tell he was containing his urge to dissuade her from moving out on her own. He looked down at his shoes, sighing, exhausted by the effort. Then, he rallied again, "And it's still in the neighbourhood, close enough to your job and Lydia and me ... so that's nice."

"Don't worry, I'll still spend time with you," she said, squeezing his hand, and he held it tight. They looped through the apartment again, and this time he gave his full attention to the tour. He opened and closed cupboards, checked that faucets worked, peered into the hall closet.

"I'll install some shelving for you, to make the most of your storage space. And I'll paint it for you, anything you need." They crowded into the bathroom's small space. She leaned into him with a long kiss, his tailbone pressed up against the vanity.

All of her things fit into the same-size van that Fatima used for her move, a detail she dwelled on when, finally alone, she wandered the four hundred square feet of her apartment. She realized then that she missed her things from Shannon Street, all the bric-a-brac she'd gathered and collected over the years to make a home, most of which had been sold or sent to Goodwill. Only her bare necessities, her bedroom furniture and clothing, went with her to Lochrie Street.

Lydia, Ismail, Antonio, and Fatima arrived to help her, and that move-in day was the first time they'd all congregated in one space. Perhaps it was the discomfort of the encounter, but they discussed her need for more furniture as though she wasn't there.

"What about the table in the basement, Ismail?" Fatima asked.

"Yes, I was thinking the same thing. It needs sanding and refinishing, though."

"My brother just replaced his couch, but I don't think they've gotten rid of the old one yet. I can ask him," Antonio offered.

"Good idea," Lydia agreed.

"I don't need a kitchen table. I have a galley kitchen!" Celia blurted. "And look, this is a junior one-bedroom. There really isn't a living room, just a wide hallway! I don't want to fill it up with things that will just be in my way!" She shook as she said all this, her anger seeping out of her in tiny tremors.

"But *Mãe*, you need furniture. Where are you going to sit?" Lydia countered, gesturing to the empty space. Arguing with her mother had become a reflex.

"Yes, Celia. Your place is very empty right now," Ismail reasoned.

"Celia's right. She should unpack and then decide what *she* wants," Fatima said, backing toward the door. Celia thought it curious that the girl who knew her for the shortest amount of time often listened to her best.

"Well, you just let us know if you change your mind, and I'll call my brother," Antonio said, following Fatima to the door.

"Want me to stay and help unpack, *Mãe*?"

"There isn't much to do. I'll be fine." They said their goodbyes, and left, but Ismail kept one foot in the door.

"I can stay and help, you know. I have time today." She would have preferred him to leave, anxious to have her apartment to herself. But she knew that her time alone was coming and sensed the need behind his offer. She could wait a little longer.

"Yeah, sure, why not?" she said, and he rushed to open boxes.

— 42 —

MOVEMENT

ISMAIL SAW DAPHNE AGAIN, one month later. He was on Queen Street, out for a stroll during his thirty-minute lunch hour, and there she was, across the street, standing outside the Eaton Centre. She wore a bright green sundress, much like the one she wore to the bar the day she wooed him into taking the writing class. She hadn't yet spied him, and he debated about whether to call out to her. As he approached the crosswalk, she looked up, and she waved him over.

It wasn't as Ismail expected it might be. It was the sort of conversation one might have at a class reunion with someone once very familiar. You might reminisce about the grouchy Tenth Standard teacher, or recall the funny story about when Dilip Mukherjee kissed Shanu Gupta and was sent to the office for discipline. With this person, there may be a sense of shared experience, and perhaps a deep fondness, but after a few good laughs, and the hot veg and non-veg buffet, it would be quite alright to say good night, and perhaps to not meet again for another ten years.

And so it was with Ismail and Daphne. When they embraced, he felt her bony spine through the thin fabric of her dress, and smelled the lavender in her hair. They updated one another about their achievements and successes: she and her girlfriend planned to marry that winter and one of her poems would soon be published in a local literary magazine. Ismail told her about dating Celia, finishing James's creative writing class and meeting a new friend there. After the news, there was a brief, awkward pause. She said it had been nice to run into him again and he agreed that it had. And then, amidst the lunchtime shopping crowd, they parted company, pleased to have seen an old friend, but not yearning to meet again soon.

— ❋ —

The autumn brought more change. Shelina and Hassan still wanted Fatima to come home and "straighten out," but they didn't harp on this each and every time they spoke. She visited them over the summer, secretly gathering information for the story she'd tried to write in James Busbridge's class. These interviews opened up conversations the Khans had needed to have for a long time.

Her parents reinstated limited financial support, agreeing to pay for Fatima's tuition and books. After she deposited their money, she switched her major to English and Creative Writing, realizing that writing wasn't going to be just a hobby for her. She didn't tell her parents about her academic program change until mid-September, when they couldn't rescind their tuition payment. She'd expected renewed conflict, but surprisingly, they only kicked up a relatively minor fuss, perhaps wearied from the spring's tensions. However, there were phone calls in which they lectured and scolded her for making a decision that wouldn't "pay the rent." In an ironic turn of events, Shelina even tried to enlist Ismail's help in counselling her daughter toward a more practical vocation.

"She seems to listen to you. I don't approve of it, but it's the reality," Shelina admitted. And then, she added, "I hope it wasn't you who influenced her in this silly decision."

He did have a talk with Fatima about her studies, and listened to her in a way probably impossible for a worried parent. She showed him the completed short story inspired by her parents, and he thought it was good. Only it wasn't what he expected at all, a recounting of their immigrant experiences, or a tale of identity and angst. Rather it was about a set of fictional parents afraid to tell their teenage son that they were divorcing. In the story, they avoided the truth and the son discovered it through a family friend and felt betrayed.

"Do you think that was the crux of the matter for your parents? Not that you're gay, but that they found out the way they did?"

"Well, the queer part wasn't easy. And they're still weird about that. But yeah. I think it was a betrayal for them not to know me. The betrayal of me growing up and having my own secrets, my own life."

"You've got to get it published," he said excitedly. She shrugged.

"What about your story?" She took the pages from him, and folded them. Ismail knew she wasn't one to allow a compliment to linger long before turning the focus elsewhere. "Remember? You were going to write about your daughter? Do you still want to write about that?"

It was a topic they hadn't discussed since that day after she'd Googled him and discovered his past, and his reaction was different now. His breath didn't escape before he could catch it, his pores didn't flood open in fear and he didn't have an urge to rush out to the Merry Pint. Instead, he noticed a familiar melancholy waft through the room and settle on his shoulders. He lifted them, tested their strength, and let them drop again, realizing they were strong enough to hold what was landing there.

"Perhaps I'll write it one day. But it doesn't feel pressing," he said.

— ❋ —

It was the second anniversary of José's passing. Earlier that day, Celia had been to Lydia's house. The late autumn day was brisk, but the sun was bright, so they took Marco out for a walk to the park. They spoke about work, the new car Lydia and Antonio had purchased, and their holiday plans. While Marco ran in concentric circles around the jungle gym, the women stood quietly, the silences between them still awkward.

"You know *Mãe* ..." Lydia ventured, "I think Ismail is OK. I think he's nice."

"You do?"

"I think it was just the timing of things that got me so upset. I thought you were ending your mourning just to be with him and forgetting all about ..." she sniffed, not able to finish her sentence.

"You know I won't ever stop mourning, I won't ever forget." Celia felt her own eyes moisten as her daughter began to cry. "But listen, it's good. Life is ... it's good. Sometimes, I even feel happy. I have whole days now when I don't feel sad," she said, squeezing Lydia's hand.

"I know, I know. I don't know why I'm so emotional," she said wiping her eyes, "I've been like this for days now." Celia put her arm around her daughter's waist, sensing the answer.

"Are you late?"

"Late?"

"Late with your *menstruação*?" Celia clarified.

"How'd you know? It's just been two weeks, so we weren't going to say anything until a couple more weeks passed." This made more tears leak from Lydia's eyes.

Celia laughed, and held her weeping daughter.

Later at home, she stood in her galley kitchen and undid the tape on a white bakery box. Inside was a slice of lemon meringue pie, her mother's favourite, and beside it, a piece of chocolate cream cake. She lifted both onto a single plate, and inserted a candle into each.

She lit a match, her hand trembling, and looked around her quiet apartment, searching the corners for ghostly company. There was none, and she didn't mind. The wicks became flame.

She closed her eyes, and made a wish.

— ❀ —

That October, Fatima brought home a Polaroid camera she found at a yard sale. Wanting to test it out, she made everyone pose for her, in various groupings.

"I've got lots of film, come on you guys!" she instructed. "Wait, first the two of you," she said, pointing to Ashton and Sonia. Then she waved in Celia and Ismail.

While Ismail crowded in with the others, he tried to cal-
culate how many photos she'd have to take if she shot every
possible combination. He mentally listed:

> Ismail and Celia
> Ismail and Fatima
> Fatima and Sonia Gandhi
> Sonia Gandhi and Ashton ...

And then, side-tracked by the commotion, he gave up
his calculations.

At the end of the photo shoot, he took a picture of
Fatima and Celia. Fatima pulled out the snapshot, blew on
it, the image gradually forming, filling the white space. She
pressed the photo into his palm with a shy smile. He took it
to work, and tacked it up on his cubicle wall.

His worries about Celia moving out on her own turned out
to be unfounded. She seemed happier, and they continued
seeing one another as often as before. Sonia Gandhi, too,
was a constant visitor at 82 Lochrie, as the girls continued to
date that autumn.

Ismail reflected on how, just a year earlier, his house
had been an empty shell. Now, it overflowed with noise and
women. They filled the silence with their voices, crowded
the bathroom counter with feminine beauty products, ate
all the food in his fridge.

Sometimes, the old memories were there too, extra
guests in an already full house. He'd shut his eyes and follow their whispers, hear their sad regrets, visiting with Zubi
and Rehana and remembering times he'd rather forget. Like

quicksand, the memories would pull him deep into his past, his body sinking, his head about to go under. Then, from down the hall, he'd hear an odd ringtone and be distracted by a young woman talking too loudly on her cellphone. He'd eavesdrop on her chatter, vicariously entering the world of a twenty-year-old. He'd barely understand most of what she'd be talking about, but nevertheless, her voice would rescue him from the mud.

When he'd open his eyes again, he might see before him a woman with flowers in her eyes. They'd walk outside, hands entwined, noticing drapes fluttering, or lying still. They might survey the little houses and shops of Little Portugal, taking in the overgrown autumn gardens, the stately churches whose bells called out each and every Sunday, without fail. They'd stroll past three generations of women and girls walking home together with their groceries. They'd greet house-proud older men, hoses in hand, washing their front walks.

Just like the changes they'd witnessed from within 82 Lochrie, Ismail and Celia would know that everything outside and around them was in motion, too. With each moment, something was changing, stretching, growing. Lives were beginning, and others were ending. The movement might be minute, perhaps imperceptible to the naked eye, but certainly, definitely, real.

GLOSSARY

Agonias	A culturally specific condition (experienced by some Azorean immigrants) that includes emotional, spiritual, and physical symptoms.
Arroz doce	Portuguese rice pudding.
Badam halwa	A South Asian dessert made of almonds and clarified butter.
Bhai	Brother. Often used to show respect for an older brother.
Biryani	A South Asian dish made with rice, meat, vegetables, and spices.
Bom dia	Good day.
Burfi	A South Asian sweet made with condensed milk, sugar, and other ingredients.
Chalo	Come on! Let's go!
Daal	Curried lentils.

Desi	South Asian.
Dupatta	A South Asian scarf, often worn over the head or around the shoulders.
Frango no púcara	A Portuguese chicken dish made with vegetables, ham, wine, port, and spices.
Gandu	An Indian curse word to describe someone who is idiotic.
Hijabi	A woman who wears a *hijab*, a traditional Muslim head covering.
Kachumbar	South Asian salad made with onions, tomatoes, cucumber, and chilies.
Kakaji	Father's brother. The *ji* connotes respect.
Kameez	A South Asian long tunic-type shirt.
Kofta	South Asian dish with meatballs or vegetarian balls.
Lassi	A South Asian yogourt-based drink.
Leitão assado	A Portuguese roast suckling pig dish.
Maasi	An auntie, and sometimes specifically a mother's sister. Also spelled *Massi*.
Mãe	Mother.
Masjid	Mosque.
Menstrução	Menstruation.
Muitas felicidades	Best wishes.
Pai	Father.

Pastéis de nata	Plural from of *pastel de nata*, a Portuguese egg tart pastry.
Raita	A salad made with yogourt and cucumbers.
Shalvaar	Loose, pajama-like trousers.
Shrikhand	A creamy South Asian dessert made with yogurt, sugar, nuts, and spices.
Sabão	Soap.
Vovó	Grandma.

ACKNOWLEDGEMENTS

THERE WERE MANY PEOPLE who helped me to develop this story.

Thanks to all those who read early versions and offered valuable feedback: Nuzhat Abbas, Saira Zubeiri, Teenah Edan, Emily Kingvisser, Sobia Ahmed, Susan Nosov, Rob Ferreira, Anjula Gogia, and Shauna Singh Baldwin.

For insights on matters botanical, municipal, and anatomical, I thank Hershel Russell, Mike Mulqueen, and Fariya Doctor.

For help with Portuguese-Canadian references, I thank Rob Ferreira, Marcelo Caetano, Clarinda Brandão, and Katia Gouveia. Dr. Susan James's work on *agonias* provided inspiration for Celia's emotional experiences.

Coleman Barks's translation of Jelaluddin Rumi's poem, "The Guest House," was often on my mind when I wrote the passages relating to Ismail's memories.

This novel is a work of fiction, and not about any particular case of what's often referred to as "Hot Car Death." My heart goes out to those who have suffered this experience.

I'd like to acknowledge the support I received from the Toronto Arts Council and the Ontario Arts Council, who provided funding which bought me more writing time.

Thanks to Beverley Slopen, my dedicated agent.

To all the fabulous staff at Dundurn, a big thank you for all your hard work. Special thanks to literary midwives Shannon Whibbs and Margaret Bryant.

I am grateful to all my family and friends who encourage and love me. There are too many of you to mention here.

As always, an immense debt of gratitude to my partner, Judith Nicholson.

OF RELATED INTEREST

Something Remains
Hassan Ghedi Santur
978-1-554884-650
$21.99

Andrew Christiansen, a war photographer turned cabdriver, is having a bad year. His mother has just died; his father, on the verge of a nervous breakdown, gets arrested; and he's married to a woman he doesn't love. To make matters worse, Sarah, the gifted actress from his past, storms back into his life, bringing with her a hurricane of changes and the possibility of happiness. Keeping Andrew sane is his beloved camera through which he captures the many Torontonians who ride in his taxi. Also there is his friendship with Zakhariye, a Somali-born magazine editor grieving the death of a son. *Something Remains* probes the various ways humans grieve when the lives they build for themselves fall apart.

Valley of Fire
Steven Manners
978-1-554884-063
$21.99

John Munin is a rational man, a gifted Montreal psychiatrist who believes that the soul and psyche are interesting only in dissection. Even relationships are ripe for analysis. Munin plans to present a case at a major medical conference in Nevada. But something has happened to the probing psychiatrist recently, and in the aftermath, his orderly world crumbles in the crucible of the desert. Set against the bizarre backdrop of Las Vegas where fate can change unalterably with the turn of a card, Munin is forced to question all of the truths he has held dear. Do events happen due to careful planning or is life just a game of chance? If God played dice with the universe, would he win?

Available at your favourite bookseller.

DUNDURN PRESS
w w w . d u n d u r n . c o m

What did you think of this book?
Visit *www.dundurn.com*
for reviews, videos, updates, and more!